THE PORTRAIT

MAYA RUSHING WALKER

This is a work of fiction. Names, characters, places, and incidents either are the product of the author's imagination or are used fictitiously. Any resemblance to actual persons, living or dead, events, or locales is entirely coincidental.

First paperback edition December 2018

First large print edition May 2019

First hardcover edition May 2019

Published by Apollo Grannus Books LLC, www.apollogrannus.com

Cover design by Streetlight Graphics, www.streetlightgraphics.com

ISBN 978-1-7325158-0-2 (paperback)

ISBN 978-1-7325158-1-9 (ebook)

ISBN 978-1-7325158-3-3 (large print)

ISBN 978-1-7325158-4-0 (hardcover)

www.mayarushingwalker.net

To my family:

Phillip
Sophia
Isaac
Grace
Allegra

'It isn't what we say or think that defines us, but what we do.'

— SENSE AND SENSIBILITY

PROLOGUE

*G**ibraltar, November 1799*
  "There are those who feel that your neck isn't worth saving."

"Yes, sir."

The admiral waited politely, but no explanations or excuses followed the terse reply. He nodded approvingly. Hated excuses. It wasn't gentleman-like, as it were. "But I have taken responsibility. And I want you to go home."

He squinted as the dark shadow in front of him raised its head. The light reflected from the turquoise Mediterranean beyond was so powerful that the admiral could not make out the expression on the shadow's face.

"Home, sir?"

The admiral paused. An odd response, he thought. "Home, young man, home. Back to your people. Take some time. Do some shooting, break in a new horse – whatever it is that you do. In any case, the whole mess will blow over if you are not around to remind everyone of what happened. Perhaps a year, or a little longer."

There was a silence. Somewhat nettled, the admiral said,

"Given the circumstances, it could have been a great deal worse."

He toyed with the miniature ship on his desk – carved out of wood, it was a replica of his own first command, the HMS *Worthy*. God love her, she was still afloat, somewhere in the West Indies.

He jerked his mind out of its wandering reverie to deal with the subject at hand. Avebury. Damn it all, he'd stuck his neck out for the man. But he liked him. He had that certain something: a grittiness that bespoke a man who had risen through the ranks with an edge of gentlemanly refinement. He didn't know too much about the lad's people, save that his entry into the navy had been helped along by a well-placed distant cousin. But he was an impressive commander, well-liked, and ran a ruthlessly ordered fighting ship. Not to mention all that prize money—

He cleared his throat to try again. "Avebury, you're a fantastic sailor. A real leader of men. One of my best. I wouldn't go this far for just anyone, you know."

"Yes, sir."

"I don't want to lose you. But my influence will only go so far. Go home. You're a rich man. Enjoy the society. Take a bride. Do the things that normal men do."

"Normal men, sir?" He said it in such a quiet voice that the admiral had to lean forward to hear him.

"I say! It's not meant as an insult, boy," the admiral said impatiently. "Merely a figure of speech." He leant back in his chair and nodded dismissal.

For a moment, Avebury didn't move. But then he slowly backed away from the huge desk and took his leave.

The admiral sighed deeply and shook his head. The sooner Avebury was out of the Mediterranean and out of active duty, the better. Bright lad, a born sailor, but this latest fracas had almost been too much – and it still might return to haunt him. Better he went back to England, where his standing would surely protect him from … well, from whatever might happen.

CHAPTER 1

*B*ath, May 1800

"Let us move you closer."

"Thank you, I am quite all right."

"Stop being so accommodating, Catherine. It is easily done. Perhaps if we call for a footman and your chair—"

"I am perfectly fine, Melinda."

"Well, you never say a thing, when I am sure you would rather—"

Catherine put a gloved hand on her friend's arm. "I am rather thirsty, I suppose."

"Let me procure a glass of lemonade!" Melinda exclaimed. Having found a way to be of use, she hurried away. Two fat matrons and a young man with a keen glint in his eye bore down upon her as soon as she reached the refreshment table.

Catherine leant back on the pillows of the window seat and adjusted her shawl. Thank goodness Melinda was so easily distractible: her constant flutter and anxiety were enough to give anyone the headache. It was true that their spot was some distance away from the stage where the musicians were now tuning their instruments, but Catherine enjoyed the view of the milling crowd, the swish and swirl of silken gowns, the young men in pursuit of blushing girls guarded by dour chaperones. She had long been accustomed to the notion that she would never be one of those pretty hopefuls, and the covert glances cast in her direction did not bother her. She was a fixture on the Bath scene – the occasional pitying look invariably came from a newcomer. Her acquaintances certainly knew better than to direct any such sympathy her way.

Melinda was blushing at the overtures of the young man. He offered his arm. She smiled and barely dipped her head in Catherine's direction. The young man turned slightly and caught Catherine's eye. The usual expression of polite sympathy crossed his face and Catherine smiled automatically. It was a frozen smile, but it was the most she felt inclined to offer the curious. The man turned around again. When Catherine managed to catch Melinda's eye, she frowned to indicate that Melinda should stay where she was. Melinda gave her a grateful wave of acknowledgement.

Catherine leant back again in her seat. It gave her some small pleasure to consider how annoyed Melinda's stepmama would be if she knew that the very proper Lady Catherine Claverton was encouraging the attentions of some young man of unknown background. Melinda's stepmama was a notoriously difficult person, prone to palpitations, who made it virtually impossible for Melinda to show herself in society – she would not accompany her stepdaughter herself and considered almost no one else appropriate. But she was willing to very grudgingly acknowledge that Lady Claverton's company was unexceptionable.

Catherine accepted the role with good grace. At twenty-four, she was really far too young to be anyone's chaperone, but no one had ever regarded her as a girl. And she did not mind being passed over by the gentlemen. Melinda needed her. It was a pleasure to be needed.

She adjusted the skirts of her gown. One could at least wear pretty clothes, she reflected, even if one could not be a beauty. She turned slightly in her seat, running a critical eye over the crowd. The room was filling. Most of the faces were familiar. Stuffy old Bath, with its outmoded social rules – it was bound to be a dull evening.

Loud laughter beckoned, and she glanced in the direction of the door. Ah, unfamiliar faces. She peered at them from behind the lacy shade of the window-seat curtains. Two pretty girls, not likely to be much past their coming out. Two men in naval uniform. One leant over, whispered conspiratorially to the girls. They tittered loudly. The other officer hung back, looking some-what uncomfortable. He scanned the room, as if he expected to find someone he knew there.

"Look, John. Seats." One of the girls tapped the arm of the officer at her side with her fan and headed off into the crowd, pulling her friend behind her.

"Fanny, wait!" the officer called in alarm. He looked back at his colleague, who was still surveying the gathering.

"You go ahead," the other officer said.

"Silly chit," his friend muttered, taking off after the two girls at a rapid clip.

Catherine, safely ensconced in her lacy refuge, watched as the man pushed his way through the crowd, murmuring his excuses, to where the girls had spied a group of empty chairs. However, there were only three. The man turned around and lifted his hands apologetically.

"Quite all right," muttered their abandoned companion. "Quite all right." He didn't seem the least bit put out. In fact, he seemed relieved. He heaved a sigh and edged along the perimeter of the room until he was so close to Catherine's seat that she thought he would smack into her knees. She held her breath, but he stopped just inches away from the curtains and stood fiddling with his hat. He had thick, curly brown hair that was almost unkempt in appearance and refused to stay put at the back and around his face. His features seemed almost to have been carved in rock: they were stern, and his nose was strong, chiselled. Surprisingly for a sailor, his skin was smooth – barely weather-beaten at all, only tanned to gold.

Catherine stole a look at his boots. They were scuffed at the toes. She could see that they were well-maintained: lovingly cared for but heavily used. A man of action, she concluded. The compulsive neatness of his uniform seemed to reinforce the character suggested by the boots. It was not a new suit of clothes by any means, but it had an air of shiny readiness. Was this what was expected of a naval officer, she wondered. Had he ever flogged a man, or used the cat-o'-nine-tails? Catherine shivered, and cast another look at his face.

No, she decided. He was grave, but not cruel. His eyes were lovely – changeable, grey and green and blue at the same time, like storm clouds on a spring day. His mouth was soft. He could smile, she thought, if he wanted to. It was a finely cut mouth, in fact …

She flushed and looked away. Her voyeurism was getting the better of her. One of the reasons she liked to sit on the fringes of society was that it gave her licence to eavesdrop, to stare, to imagine. Thinking her private thoughts, thoughts that no one in the world would imagine someone such as she might have, made her happy. She always had the better of everyone in society: they could not conceal what they really were and they did not know that Lady Catherine Claverton was watching. But yet she should be careful, lest she give herself away.

Her father, she reflected, had intended her to spend her entire life sitting in her room. He would be so furious if he could see her now. She suppressed a smirk.

The officer muttered an oath. Three very large, very loud matrons sporting garishly dyed plumes had taken up positions squarely in front of him. They chatted loudly and fluttered their fans; not supposing anyone to be watching, one of them surreptitiously pulled at the seat of her gown, which was cut much too tight to flatter.

Catherine choked back a loud snort. The officer looked around. His questioning gaze landed on her, half-hidden in the window seat. A little embarrassed, Catherine smiled at him. He bowed slightly.

"They really aren't very good," she said in a whisper.

He raised an eyebrow, then nodded toward the musicians. "They aren't?" He seemed rather nonplussed by the statement.

Catherine shook her head. "Not very. You aren't missing much. By not being able to see, I mean." The concert suddenly began with the violinist leaping energetically into a divertimento that required far more skill than he possessed. Gamely, he staggered on.

A rueful grin crossed the officer's lips as he inched a little closer to Catherine's seat. "Are you musical?"

"A little," Catherine confessed. "But it would make no difference. I heard them play last Thursday."

"Ah." The officer looked back in the direction of the musicians, but his view was still thoroughly obscured by the three fat matrons with their bobbing feathers.

"Is this sort of crush usual?" Irritation edged his voice.

Catherine blinked. "Crush? Do you regard this as a crush?" It had never occurred to her that a boring Bath musicale might be a crush. In London, assemblies and parties in the best homes were often crushes but not this.

A flush stained the officer's cheeks. "I beg your pardon. I seem to be demonstrating my ignorance of society," he said stiffly.

"Not at all," Catherine said hastily. "I imagine that you have been at sea for a considerable time. Have you a long shore leave?"

The officer did not reply at once. When he turned, those

stormy eyes caught her gaze. He was a beautiful man, if such a word could be applied to one in naval uniform. The clouds in his eyes stood in sharp contrast to his dark hair and tanned skin. A spring shower, Catherine thought with bewilderment. A spring shower, passing through the meadow at Albrook Hall. Green and blue and swirling grey mist. Words, whatever they might have been, died at her lips, and she felt the warmth ebb away from her extremities.

For an icy moment, they looked at each other while the musicians sawed away energetically in the background. Most people did not dare look her full in the face.

"I have indeed been away from these shores for a very long time," the officer said finally. "I am not aware of the ... the niceties of social discourse."

"Do not let it trouble you, sir," Catherine said quickly. Her mouth was dry; she searched for a way to ease the tension. "I do not know your name."

"My name is Avebury. Captain, Royal Navy."

Catherine saw something flicker in his eyes. She searched her memory, but came up blank. She didn't know any Aveburys. She held out her hand. "Catherine Claverton."

He bowed slightly, barely touching her gloved hand. "And you live in Bath? Miss – is it Miss? – Claverton?"

"Er ... yes." Catherine hesitated. She was not being quite accurate, but she felt uneasy about correcting him. "And you?"

"How did you know?" He said the words in a low voice, so softly that for a brief second Catherine wasn't sure she had heard him at all.

"Know?"

"That I've just returned – that I've been gone from England for so long."

She wanted to look away, but the intensity of those changeable eyes held hers pitilessly. Here was a man who expected to have his questions answered. "I-I ... your boots," she concluded feebly. "And your uniform. You look like someone who is … accustomed to a demanding life."

His gaze softened. He looked at her, his eyes sweeping over the pink gown, the silk shawl, the fine blonde hair dressed in a modest style that put her on the edge of matronhood.

She looked back at him, her heart ceasing its fitful pitter-patter. Why, he was neither stern nor severe, after all – he was merely ill at ease, shy.

"I give myself away, it seems." A hesitant smile seemed to touch his lips, then fade away.

"Do not be concerned by it," Catherine said apologetically. "It is I who am at fault – I sit here behind the curtains, spying. It is inexcusable, and I beg your pardon."

"Are you alone at this concert, Miss Claverton?"

The piece had ended. Well-bred applause echoed politely through the room and, from a distance, a voice called for Avebury to hurry over and occupy an available seat.

He glanced in his friend's direction. "Forgive me," he said. "My friend calls me."

"Of course." Catherine held out her hand. "You must join your companions."

"He has brought his sister to the concert as a treat, you see. He would not forgive me if I left him for the evening with only her and her friend for company." He smiled ruefully.

Boldly, she leant forward to grasp his hand. "I hope we meet again, Captain Avebury. Bath is a quiet town, but we do our best. Perhaps you will honour us with your presence at the assemblies?"

"I am not much for dancing, I'm afraid," Avebury said. He bowed.

Catherine watched as he moved off into the crowd, eventually easing himself into a seat guarded for him by the blushing girls, who seemed very much in awe of him. As the music struck up again, she smoothed her dress over her legs, feeling her useless limb, twisted and bent, through the lush pink fabric. Her eyes tingled. She tasted salt tears in the back of her throat, and was immediately ashamed. She had not cried in a very long time. Why now? "Neither am I, Captain Avebury," she said softly. "Neither am I."

For a moment she felt bitterly sorry for herself. The missed opportunities. The cruel looks, whispers, comments. The discomfort of servants when they had to wait on her. The sheer force of will that made it possible for her to have any kind of life outside the walls of her home – it exhausted her.

But here I am, she reminded herself. *I am here. And I am in control. I will not let myself fade out of sight because of a single withered leg. I will not. I will not let Papa hide me away – not now, and certainly not after he is dead.*

She was jolted from her musings by Melinda's hand on her elbow.

"Dearest," Melinda said in a low voice. "We will need to leave, and do so as quietly as possible. If I send for a footman, there will be a disruption. Do you suppose you could lean on me just until we are outside the door? Papa has sent the coach for us."

"Leave? Why—"

Melinda wasted no words. "Your father, Catherine. You must go to him immediately."

Catherine drew back. She saw Melinda's concerned expression, and felt her own face stiffen. "Is he dying?" She said the words with such coolness that even Melinda was shocked.

"Catherine, you must go to him."

"Is he dying?"

"He is near the end."

"Then I will go. But if he is not dying, I will turn around and head home. I have no need to see him more than once." She rose, placing as much of her weight as she could on the arm Melinda proffered. "Let us get this over with."

As she limped heavily out of the room, she cast one last,

regretful look over in the direction of Captain Avebury and his friends. She was sorry to have misled him into thinking that she was Miss Claverton, and not Lady Catherine Claverton. She wished she could have stayed to explain herself.

But Bath was a small town. They would meet again.

CHAPTER 2

*W*hen Jocelyn managed to turn around, it was to find she had gone. The golden-haired vision in pink hidden in the window seat had disappeared, as if she had been a spectre, a phantom from his imagination and his deepest dreams.

His heart sank.

She did not know him – no one knew him. But, after a few minutes of observation, she had guessed more about him than anyone normally discovered. And perhaps she had guessed still more – he wanted to know what her beautiful eyes had seen. Perhaps she was a ghost indeed. Or perhaps a fortune-teller, like the Oracle at Delphi.

Jocelyn tried not to grimace at the tittering of the two girls next to him. It was beginning to grate, the constant giggling. He neither liked nor disliked Lieutenant Forster, who had latched onto him as soon as he had stepped ashore and was anxiously awaiting to hear whether he would finally receive his first command. When Forster explained he had promised to accompany his younger sister to Bath, Jocelyn thought it seemed as good a place as any to sit and think about his fate.

He had thought he would go to London, where he could keep an ear on the news from the Admiralty and pick up any rumours that he was being sought. He almost laughed bitterly but caught himself just in time. The soprano began to inexpertly negotiate a trill and the girls giggled again. Sooner or later, someone would come in search of Jocelyn Avebury. And then the ugly truth would emerge.

But he held a half-hearted belief that he could hide, that he could outrun his pursuers. He wasn't trying too hard to evade them. He hadn't changed his appearance or rid himself of the uniform. The uniform – ah, that was the one source of any pride he had ever possessed. He had offered up his life time and again for the sake of His Majesty's uniform. And not once had God seen fit to accept the sacrifice. He had been returned, sent back over and over again, to the life that he had been given.

For a price, he could leave his London agent and hire one who was more adept at avoiding the law. Then no one would be able to track his movements through watching how he disposed of the vast amounts of prize money he had acquired over the years. But he'd spent barely a penny of it. Money, it seemed to him, was a largely useless commodity: it would never buy honour, or bravery, or truth. And, if you were on the run, it followed you and made it possible for the law to find you. So he had considered handing his business affairs over to a shady lawyer in Portsmouth. He had also considered fleeing to the West Indies, or to the Americas. But it all seemed pointless. The good admiral had tried to do him a favour, but it was only a matter of time before the truth became known. And, had the admiral known the truth, he would not have wanted to stick his neck out for Jocelyn.

Applause was breaking out. He stretched his legs and hoped that the concert had reached its end.

"... splendid," Forster was saying something. He nudged Jocelyn in the ribs and winked.

"Is it over?" Jocelyn asked.

"Lord, I hope so." For a moment, they sat, surveying the crowd. The musicians made no move to pack up their instruments, but began tuning and polishing again. Forster groaned.

"John, we are so thirsty. Would you fetch us some lemonade?" Miss Fanny Forster addressed her brother, then leant over to catch Jocelyn's eye. "Are you enjoying yourself, Captain Avebury?"

"Very much," he replied. "I'll go with you, Forster." He caught the look of disappointment that flashed over Miss Forster's face, but extracted himself from the chair with relief. The chairs were too small – or his legs were too long. He followed Lieutenant Forster to the refreshment table.

"Bath always has these insipid entertainments," Forster muttered under his breath. "But it's the only place that m'father would allow Fanny to come to without Mother." He cast a disgusted look about the room. "It's no wonder."

Jocelyn took a quick look at the high-necked, modestly cut garments on the ladies around him. His mind turned to the vision in pink. Miss Claverton's gown had been cut quite low, he realised. The exquisite lines set off a porcelain complexion and a long, lovely throat adorned with pearls.

Those blue eyes.

He sipped at his lemonade idly.

"… deathbed."

"How positively dreadful."

"But you know they haven't spoken in years."

"Yes. He was …" The voice behind him dropped, and he only heard a faint mutter that sounded like "crueller beyond imagining."

Jocelyn tried to move out of the way. The two conversants elbowed forward appreciatively. Then his ear caught the word "Claverton." He paused.

"Certainly she will be quite wealthy. But the title will die with the earl. There were, apparently, sons from the earl's first marriage, but none of them live. Lady Catherine is his daughter by his second wife and they had no other children. It was a disappointment: he needed sons."

"Pity. No wonder he hated her so much. If only she had been a boy! Such an ancient title, reverting to the Crown."

There was an unkind snort. "I imagine Lady Catherine won't suffer."

"Oh, no! But to have one's father despise one – it isn't to be wished for. Even with all the money in the world."

Jocelyn had heard enough. He pushed through the crowd, away from the table. Lieutenant Forster was chatting with an attractive, dark-haired young woman whose scowling mama stood by protectively. Naval men were not in favour here, apparently.

So Lady Catherine Claverton. Daughter of an earl.

And – like himself – alone in the world.

CHAPTER 3

*C*atherine rapped on the roof of the carriage. The lurching eased, then stopped.

"My lady?"

"Do not push the horses so," Catherine said sharply. "I will not have them ruined."

"Yes, my lady." The door shut. Catherine could feel the wide-eyed gaze of her maid upon her. Never mind. Perhaps others felt differently when rushing to the side of a father on his deathbed. She, however, preferred the company of her horses, and she controlled her stables with an iron fist. No horses would give themselves up for the sake of the Earl of Delamare. She leant back in the comfortable darkness.

The maid nodded off again. Clara was a country girl without the finesse society considered necessary in one who was lady's maid to the daughter of an earl. But she was stout and honest, and did not flinch when her mistress needed to be lifted or required other assistance in the bath or in her dressing room. No, there were no dignified London dressers for Catherine – the ministrations of her rustic helpers would do very well. She usually travelled with her companion, the London-bred Miss

Lydia Barrow. But for this particular task, she preferred the company of as dumb and innocuous a servant as she could find.

She, Catherine Claverton, was in control. She might be a cripple, but she would not be dominated. Not by her father, not by her servants, not by society ... Catherine ticked her potential masters off on her fingers. She smiled briefly. There was a confrontation ahead of her, to be sure. She did not relish the thought of it, but avoidance was only a temporary solution. It would have to take place.

She hoped her father was already dead and she would be spared the unpleasantness of actually speaking to him. The discussion would still have to happen, but his man of business would be a less unpleasant substitute.

These were not well-bred thoughts. Catherine chided herself as another grim smile curled her lip. But that Delamare's daughter thought them was his own fault. He had banished his only child to a solitary life on a distant estate – but he had given her a tremendous gift by doing so.

Freedom.

She answered to no one.

Another girl would, perhaps, have sorrowed at the open disdain of her father. Another girl would, perhaps, have been afraid for her position – after all, the earldom was reverting to the Crown. Another girl might have feared for her safety: with no husband and no father to protect her, hungry men lurking behind every corner would reach sticky fingers for her gold.

At least she had no fear that any man would have designs on her virtue. She smiled into the darkness. "I fear nothing," she said aloud. Startled at the sound of her voice, she glanced at the maid who slept on. She would have to watch herself. The next few days would be filled with tension. She could not break. She would not allow it.

· · ·

CATHERINE DOZED OFF AND ON BUT, EVEN AS SHE DRIFTED, SHE WAS aware of the pace of the horses. She calculated they would arrive at Albrook early in the afternoon, although they could have made the journey in much less time had it not been for her concern about the horses. But she knew this concern was somewhat artificial; her true concern was for herself. With the change in her circumstances, how would she keep the control she had of her world?

However, when she finally caught sight of the grand Tudor façade, her heart constricted in spite of her determination to master herself. Albrook – the prison of her childhood. She hated every stone in its foundations, every blade of grass in its sweeping expanse of lawn. As a child, she had plotted its destruction, wishing for strength, for an army. But, as a cripple and as a girl, her means were limited, her friends few.

Stern faces greeted the carriage as it drew up: the housekeeper, the butler, the usual gathering of upper servants. Clara got out first and, once on the ground, she turned and extended her arms for Catherine. Two footmen started to move forward, but Clara stopped them with a sharp word. Her mistress descended, leaning on her for support.

No one spoke.

A gentle spring breeze ruffled through the wisps of hair that slipped over Catherine's ears and about the sides of her face. Ah, springtime at Albrook. How well she remembered the damp fecund smell of the earth, the sheep droppings, the rotting leaves of last year's summer.

"My lady," the butler began. "We are—"

"Take me to my father," Catherine interrupted. She spoke as loudly as she could manage, and her words seemed to ricochet off the sandstone of the portico. She saw the butler pause, glancing at the housekeeper as he did so. Catherine addressed her next.

"Is he awake?"

"No, my lady," the housekeeper said.

"Is the doctor here?"

"He has just left, my lady. He will return this evening, and wishes to wait on you at that time."

"Very well." Clara had sent the footman for a chair, which she made comfortable with a cushion and a shawl before helping her mistress into it. There was a chilly silence. Catherine leant back. She looked from one stony face to the next. These people, she thought, have never bothered to treat me with even the formal courtesy my title deserves. *When the earl is dead, you will all lose your livelihoods. And I won't be a bit sorry.*

She almost smiled. But, instead, she nodded at the footmen and they gently lifted the seat and carried her inside.

In truth, she could have walked in on her own two feet having learnt over the years how to overcome the ugly, lumbering limp that the Albrook servants surely recalled from her childhood. She could walk tolerably well now, compared to those sad days. But she preferred to enter the doors of this prison in such estate as she could arrange, the better to remind her jailers that she was not the shy young girl whom they had treated as a weak-minded invalid.

She was carried into the library, which surprised her, but she recalled that it was the one room where the fire was kept stoked at all times, even in the spring and through much of the summer. Certainly no such effort had ever been expended on the nursery where she had spent most of her long lonely hours. The footmen lowered her chair, and Clara set about assisting her with her hat and shawl, while bidding the footmen to await Lady Catherine's pleasure outside the door – she would wish to be taken to her father shortly.

A tall man with a long thin face hurried into the room. He held out his hands, and Catherine reached forward eagerly to grasp them. Beaseley had aged tremendously since she had seen him last, the skin on his hands grown more papery and wrinkled and his grey hair thinning and showing more of his scalp than she remembered. In spite of herself, she felt her heart moved by his devotion to the family. Beaseley had made the difference between a life of privation and shame and the independent existence she currently enjoyed. It could not have been easy, walking the line between the rage of his employer and the suffering of a child.

"Lady Catherine! I beg your pardon, for I have only just arrived. I hope you are in good health?"

"I am, thank you, Mr Beaseley. Pray, tell me what news?"

Beaseley shook his head. "I am sorry to say that the news is not good." He paced restlessly as two young maids brought in the tea tray. Clara dismissed them and set about pouring the tea.

"Clara," Catherine said, "you may leave us. Do not wander far. I will need you shortly."

The door shut behind her. For a moment, the only sounds were the crackling fire and the baa-ing of distant sheep. Catherine looked around the room. It had not changed at all. Soon, she would leave this room, leave this house, never to see it again, and it would be a burden lifted from her heart. There would be no necessary public demonstration of respect, no dutiful acknowledgement of her family. The Clavertons of Albrook would simply cease to exist. Yes, she herself was a Claverton, but – and here her lips twisted in an expression of disgust – she would do her best to rid herself of the association as effectively as they had rid themselves of her.

If she could change her name, she would.

Albrook could fade into the history books, as far as she was concerned. She could imagine weeds taking over the elaborate formal gardens, rust stains under leaking windows, and the chapel – with its generations of dead Clavertons buried under the floor – abandoned and silent. She could imagine paying a visit, preferably under gloomy grey skies, just to see this place die. It was unfortunate that she would not live long enough to see the buildings tumble down onto their foundations.

She shook herself a little. It was a strange daydream, but one she had enjoyed off and on for years.

"I trust that you have just come from London, Mr Beaseley?"

Beaseley was staring out of a corner window, absently stroking his flyaway hair. He turned, startled. "I beg your pardon, Lady Catherine?"

Catherine laughed. "Come, Mr Beaseley. What occupies you so? We have known of my father's illness for these past four years. I am sure nothing you could tell me would shock me! Is there some new trouble in his business affairs?"

Beaseley shook his head. "No, my lady. That is … that is … it is … as you know, there are no heirs to the earldom. The title will revert to the Crown. And you, of course, are the last Claverton. Most of the family assets will come to you. Certain properties belonging to your late mother will also come to you, as well as monies that …" His voice trailed off.

"I'm not interested in Albrook," she replied. "Close it up, do with it as you wish. I will stay at Wansdyke."

Beaseley bowed.

Catherine sipped her tea. Beaseley was a kind man. She had known him all her life. He had eased the transition to living with her governess at her mother's country property near Bath all those years ago. He had made sure she was never short of funds, and had left her to handle the matters of her household on her own, with no interference from Albrook. Were he a different sort of steward, he could have made her life quite difficult and unpleasant. He might have refused to speak with her directly, or have required that she appoint a manager of her own. But he had known her mother, and he also knew how to handle the earl. But Beaseley was not all-powerful.

He could not make the earl love his daughter.

Catherine pushed the thought away. She said lightly. "So, I

will be quite rich. How lovely." Beaseley looked at her blankly, then realised that she was joking.

"I do not anticipate any problems, my lady," he said. He hesitated and seemed about to say more, but Catherine decided that she was bored with the topic.

"That is good to hear." She yawned. "I am quite tired. I wonder if I might go up and see my father?"

"He has been unconscious for several days. The doctor does not believe that he will recover."

"Well, good." Beaseley did not flinch at her candour. Catherine put down her cup. "You may send for Clara."

CHAPTER 4

*T*he footmen carried the chair as far as the earl's rooms. When they had set her down, she rose and made her way to the heavy doors. She knocked. Warren, her father's ancient valet, opened the door almost immediately. Stooped and grim, he moved aside without a word.

For a moment, she stood silently in the doorway. Her father lay in the great curtained bed, the room still as death. Thick curtains covered the windows, and the smell of sickness was heavy and fetid in the air. In spite of herself, she felt a thin edge of nervousness in her stomach. Her father had always awed her. Even as she hated him, she could not deny that he was the image of a Crusader lord, afraid of no one. She could not remember ever entering his bedchamber as a child. The very notion would have terrified her.

"Leave me with my father, if you please," she said over her shoulder. She heard the faint rustling of Clara's gown and the soft click of the door. Then the silence became so heavy that her ears hurt and her gorge rose. She was being suffocated, crushed in velvet layers of sickness and silence.

Slowly, she moved forward. Without either Clara or a crutch

to hold on to, she still hobbled slightly on her twisted leg. The rhythm was familiar to her ears. It was the sound of being alone.

A chair had been placed beside the bed. She grasped its finely carved back gratefully and paused, a little out of breath. *I must do this,* she thought. She raised her eyes, and stared at the wasted frame of the terror of her youth. She looked until her eyes watered and tears gathered. She blinked.

"I am here, Papa." She whispered the words. They fell dully into the silence, the velvet counterpane muffling the edges of her voice. She tore her gaze away and looked around the room. There was nothing comfortable about it – it was made for the sleep of earls.

A harsh sound escaped the earl's throat. She looked quickly back at him and bent a little, trying to see his face. The eyes were closed.

"I see that, as usual, my presence does not interest you," she said, feeling a little bolder now. She waited. No response. Carefully, she eased herself into the chair. "I came all the way to see you, Papa. Will you not speak to me?" Catherine watched the light, rapid rise and fall of the bedclothes heaped over his chest. A tic quivered the corner of his mouth. She suddenly wondered whether he could hear her – perhaps, although he could not rouse himself from this state of sickness, he might be able to hear and understand. A luxury, this! To be able to speak to him without fear of recrimination, without fear of a roar of temper, without fear of an argument.

She hesitated, still watching the frail form. She had rehearsed so many times the words she would say to him if she were able. If society could be relied upon not to condemn a girl for hating her father, if there was any hope at all of him listening to her – even for a moment – without losing his temper, if it might ever occur to him that it was too cruel to blame a child for the loss of an earldom, if … and if and if. But somehow the words did not come flying off her tongue with the ease she had anticipated.

"I disappointed you, Papa," she said. "But it was not my fault." She considered this notion. No, it was not her fault. She would have been born a boy if she could. She was an excellent rider, and guns did not frighten her. She was skilled at cards. She enjoyed her books. In fact – and here she almost laughed – she displayed a woeful lack of proficiency in most of the womanly arts. She would have been a much more successful boy.

She painfully lumbered across the room to the windows, pushed aside one of the heavy velvet curtains and peered through the dusty glass. The view of the park surrounding Albrook Hall must have pleased him, she thought. She remembered staring at the same view from the dirty window of her nursery, hour after hour, day after day, rain and shine. The view was engraved, etched in her brain. She was startled by the realisation that it must be etched in her father's brain as well.

How very strange. Was it possible to have images permanently seared in one's being? And, if so, why was this one so powerful? She was yet a child when she left Albrook. This place was not her home.

"Perhaps we have more in common than I had supposed," she said to the window. She nodded at the view. "Look at the wood, the rowing boats on the lake – I could tell you the colour of every boat and where the missing oars might be. I could tell you which horses have been exercised, when and by whom. I could tell you that the dairymaid's child belongs not to her husband, but to the stableboy's friend who now sleeps with the bay mare because his wife will not take him back. But these are things that you know, I assume. Are there any besides us? It is unlikely." She touched the glass with her fingers. "I know I am not a boy. But my blood runs thick here, too."

She turned, the light from the window streaking harshly across her father's motionless form. "There is no one else. Just you and I. Clavertons, both of us. I am crippled in body but you are crippled in spirit." She let the drapery fall, and once again the room became a dusky, silent cave. "We might have been a comfort to one another." She said this accusingly. Then mused, "Now your body too has failed you. But I – I am free. Freer than you could possibly have imagined. An irony, is it not?" Slowly, she approached the dying man again, dragging her bad leg. She placed her hands on the bed and leant in for a good look at this person who had had no use for his own flesh and blood, who had told her governess – loudly and within earshot – that he wanted to hear nothing of the cripple.

"Maybe you enjoyed your noose," she said. "Maybe you enjoyed being a prisoner of your own name. I do not. I am grateful that you freed me."

Her mother had not been the earl's first Countess. She had married him after his first wife, and all their children, had died. It was his last effort to save the family. Catherine was their only child, and the earl had flown into a rage when, on the day she was born, he received the news that his only living child was a girl and a cripple. When his second wife died, the earl sent Catherine away and became a recluse. But he and she were the only two Clavertons left on the face of the earth.

Catherine stared down at the wizened shrunken features of the man who had once frightened her so desperately. Despite her bold words, she knew deep inside that she was lying. She was a Claverton, and she would run from this fact for the rest of her life. This place was part of her, and she of it, try as she might to rid herself of its clutches.

Despair clutched her heart.

"God help me," she whispered. "God help me! My only fear is that I am your daughter and I will share your fate. I do not want to die alone."

CHAPTER 5

For four days, the earl dangled between life and death. The London physicians who attended him shook their heads gravely and predicted he would not wake again. On the fifth day, Catherine decided that she had had enough.

"I cannot stay here forever," she said to Beaseley. "He may linger for weeks."

Beaseley inclined his head. "Yes, my lady."

"I will return to Bath. I leave the management of this house in your hands, of course."

"Yes, my lady."

"And, should there be any news, ensure I am notified at once."

"Yes, my lady."

Catherine looked at him. He was polishing and re-polishing his spectacles with his handkerchief, his mouth grim. "Why, whatever is the matter?"

Beaseley jumped guiltily. "Nothing, my lady."

"Then why do you fidget?" Catherine frowned. She returned her cup to the tea tray. "You have been uneasy with me since my arrival. I know the circumstances are grave, but—"

"I beg your pardon, my lady." Beaseley had been pacing up

and down in front of the windows, but he now slowly circled the room before coming to stand before her for a moment. He then seated himself in a chair next to her own.

"I have hesitated to mention this matter," he began. "But, after much thought, I have decided that the time has come for you to be aware of … certain facts."

"Facts?" Catherine drew back a little. "What facts?"

Beaseley looked down at the floor. He sighed, then seemed to come to a decision. "This is very difficult for me, my lady. I would ask your indulgence if I struggle to explain."

Catherine blinked. She had noticed Beaseley's nervous silence but had attributed it to the general tension in the great house, the coming and going of the London doctors and the misery of the staff. They had certainly been confiding in Beaseley, begging him for assistance as they went about their dreary tasks, waiting for the earl to die. She herself had not given him much thought at all, save her usual acknowledgement of his perpetually awkward position. "Certainly. You must speak freely," she said.

Beaseley rose again. Hands in pockets, he went to the fireplace, where he stared absently into the flames. "By telling you all, I am breaking my word to the late countess."

"My mother?"

"Yes, my lady. Before she died, she asked me to come to her in great secrecy. No one, not even the earl, knew."

"For what purpose?" Catherine watched as Beaseley turned and walked to the windows opposite. A damp spring day, with the mists rolling in over the pond, provided a dreary vista for his detached gaze.

"To discuss the settlement of her own estate."

"I know," Catherine said slowly, "that she was orphaned quite young and raised by a … an uncle, was it? Or a cousin? I never met any of them."

"A great-uncle. When he died, there was no one else. You would not have met any of her people. Your mother was under the care of her mother's best friend. But she was quite a bit older than the countess, and died before you were born."

"But you have not told me anything that I do not know. When I left Albrook, it was to go to Mama's house. And the Bath residence is – was – also Mama's." Catherine's brow wrinkled. "Is there not also something else? A farm? I don't quite remember. I have a vague memory of Nurse telling me about Mama's people. But Papa ... well, you know how he dismissed everyone – all those who knew Mama and would have remembered her to me." She tried to keep her tone light, but it was a memory of which she did not often speak. Not only had the earl seen fit to send her away, but he had also removed any who connected her to her mother. He had not only disowned her as a Claverton but had also permanently separated her from the other side of her family.

"The house at Wansdyke-on-Avon is not your mother's ancestral home." Beaseley's voice was flat, definite.

"I beg your pardon! It most certainly is," Catherine began hotly. She stopped, then spoke more slowly. "At least ... at least, I always believed it to be so." She shifted her gaze from Beaseley to the far window. In the distance, she saw a young boy walking one of the mares; it was Willow, the old bay. She remembered her as an excitable young horse; it was amazing how calm she had become in her old age. "But there was no one to tell me any stories of Mama's family. When I arrived at Wansdyke, all the staff were new. My governess had never known Mama. And the villagers had never seen her. I assumed that such a grand house could only have once been the seat of her family."

"That is not very far from the truth: your grandfather's family did own Wansdyke. And the house is yours, as it was always meant to be. It was never placed in the earl's possession. It was the cause of some disagreement when the marriage contract was drawn up, but it was out of your mother's hands because ... well, you will see why. At any rate, it duly passed from your mother to you on her death."

"I don't understand. What are you trying to tell me?"

Beaseley turned from the window. "What I am about to say is very important. It is also confusing, so please listen carefully."

Catherine nodded, but with growing trepidation. "You are beginning to make me nervous."

"I apologise, my lady. There is nothing bad in what I am about to reveal, save for my own part in the business. You see, I swore an oath to your mother that I would not reveal the particulars of her estate until either you were of an age to handle them or the earl was dead." He paused. "I agonised for many long months about whether to tell you before the earl died. I was waiting for you to reach your twenty-fifth birthday, but it seems the earl will leave us before that date."

"But why? Why should it make any difference at all?" Catherine shook her head. "I'm afraid I don't see why—"

"Forgive me, Lady Catherine. But I don't know when I may see you next. And this is better explained in person than by letter. When the earl is dead, there will be difficult decisions to make about his estate and the properties, and they will consume my attention. I don't want your needs to be neglected."

"All right. That is fair. Tell me, then – what did my mother charge you with?"

"Your mother, Lady Catherine, was the Countess Delamare through her marriage to your father. But she was also the Countess St Clair, a title she held in her own right from her mother, the previous Countess St Clair."

"But I have never heard of such a thing!" Catherine protested, a little alarmed. "Are you absolutely sure?"

"Most certainly. In fact, all of the staff here at Albrook knew her as the Countess St Clair before she married your father." He paused. "After you were born, however ..." His voice faltered, but his gaze held steady. "... after you were born, the staff were forbidden to mention your name, and certainly never to speak of you as the heiress to the St Clair title. In fact, he allowed people to assume that your mother had ceded it to him on their marriage. Nevertheless, you have been the Countess St Clair since your mother's death."

Catherine jerked back in her seat. Her voice trembled. "Who-who is responsible for keeping this from me?" she managed to choke out.

"Primarily, your mother," Beaseley said. "She feared what would happen if it became known while you were still a child that you were both extravagantly wealthy and held your own title. She did not want evil people to manipulate you for their own gain. And she hoped that your father would come to love you as his own flesh and blood, without the constant reminder—"

"—that my mother had borne an heiress for her own line and left his bankrupt! Oh, how she misjudged him!" she cried. "My poor mother! She thought that her actions would protect me, but she underestimated the power of my father's resentment!"

"And secondarily, of course, your father. As I said, he would not permit the name to be mentioned in this house, the servants could not address you as countess and, when he sent you to Wansdyke, he dismissed the old servants. No one knew your mother or could tell you anything about her."

Catherine felt numbly in her pocket for a handkerchief. She wiped her eyes, but they filled again. She was unaccustomed to having her armour pierced. Venturing into the hotbed of gossip that was Bath after years spent alone at Wansdyke had taught her how to maintain her calm. It had not been easy to insinuate herself into society; it would have been far easier to remain in seclusion as her father had intended. Those difficult first excursions into the public eye – when she had been stared at, whispered about, and occasionally laughed at – had led her to believe she could endure anything.

But now she discovered she was not quite at that point. There was, apparently, some feeling in her yet.

"Shall I send for Clara, my lady?" Beaseley was looking concerned. She shook her head.

"No." She choked a little on the word, but raised her head. "No. I ... there are things I need to know, questions ..."

"Of course, my lady." He bowed. For a moment, the silence hung thick between them.

Catherine spoke. Her voice rasped. "This is in writing?"

"Yes. That was the source of the disagreement when the marriage contract was drawn up. Your mother insisted that the St Clair properties were to be held in trust for future heirs to the title. They never entered your father's hands. The documents are in my possession. Your mother passed them to me and required my oath of secrecy." He looked deeply upset. "I am sorry that I felt I could not honour her request to the end. With your father so ill – and unsure as I am when I might see you next – it seemed impossible."

Catherine shook her head. She was still confused. "My mother, and her mother before her – Countess St Clair. Does the title only pass through the female line?"

"No, my lady. It is an earldom."

"An earldom!" For a moment, she couldn't speak. Beaseley filled the silence for her.

"It is a very old title, much older than your father's. It was originally meant to pass to heirs general – the heir might be male or female, at the pleasure of the Crown. But your grandmother was the only living heir of the last earl, and your mother was her only heir, so both became countess without challenge. Should you have a son, he would become the next Earl St Clair."

A son! The thought had never entered Catherine's mind. She had a fleeting image of a plump golden-haired child, laughing and toddling. A son who would become the next Earl St Clair. She shuddered and chided herself. It was a ridiculous, far-fetched thought.

She looked at Beaseley blankly.

"You have a castle in Wales," he continued. "It is more or less in ruins, although there is a manor house on the site as well. It has not been lived in for a very long time, although it is the seat of the St Clairs – with the line passing through several females, maintaining even that has been a difficult task. The women married into other families," Beaseley said apologetically. "And they ... well, they made only token acknowledgement of the needs of the St Clair estates. But if ... if there were a male heir, the family could thrive and grow once more."

Catherine stared. This hardly seemed possible. A male heir? A St Clair earl?

She suddenly understood. This was why her father was so deeply angry. This was why he wanted her hidden away in Bath. Because, were she to one day bear a son, the St Clair dynasty would live to see another century but the Clavertons would be gone.

"Why did my father not become involved? I was a mere child when my mother died; ten years old. Did he not want more control over the disposition of her estate? He could perhaps have taken my mother's wealth into his own hands. Did he not see fit to somehow derail my mother's wishes?" Catherine tried to calm her racing heart. She brought up the image of her father, lying unconscious in his bed. He had been a powerful man once, even if he was now a broken shell of a human being. Why hadn't he tried harder to steal her mother's legacy?

"He told me that I was to keep aside anything that was to go directly to you. He wished to avoid touching anything that she had owned. So it is intact, every last guinea. And it will all come to you." Beaseley gave a great sigh, as if with those words he had finally discharged the last bit of tension from his body. "He can be a difficult man. But he is not dishonest. The properties and assets that you will receive from him are also considerable. He has made no effort to deprive you of the Claverton inheritance either." He watched Catherine anxiously.

"I am not interested in Papa's affairs," Catherine said coldly. "I suppose I ought to feel some attachment to Albrook, to the beautiful things that my family has owned for three hundred years and more. But I do not."

"I am very sorry, my lady." Beaseley shook his head. "I have always tried my best to do my duty to your father. But it was very hard when the countess died. Very hard. To see you sent away—"

"Thank you," Catherine said, cutting him off. "I don't know how I would have gone on without your assistance. I know that you were the one who made it possible for me to live so well at Wansdyke. I can only assume my father intended me to remain in seclusion. He would be sadly disappointed were he to learn the truth. Had he ever done so, I have no doubt you would have somehow rescued me from his displeasure."

"You are very good, my lady."

Catherine rose slowly from her chair, placing her weight on the writing table next to her. Carefully, she limped over to the windows, leaning against the heavy dark furniture in her path. Beaseley watched her, his brow creased with concern.

"Mr Beaseley. You broke your word to my mother in order to tell me that I am, and have been all along, the Countess St Clair." Catherine paused to catch her breath. The words seemed strange on her lips, but she savoured the sound of them. She raised her eyes to his and put one hand gently on his arm. "I know how difficult this decision was for you. And I thank you." She looked out of the window. The bay mare was gone, but the ubiquitous sheep were still there, waddling about stupidly in the grass. She lifted her chin.

She was a Claverton of Albrook, it was true. But she now had an opportunity to do the one thing that her father had never wanted her to do. Should she?

"If you please, Mr Beaseley, I would like to hear more about my mother."

CHAPTER 6

"Cursed insipid entertainments," muttered Forster. He cast a despairing look about the room.

"Think of your sister," Jocelyn said reassuringly. "She could not be here if you were not."

"I sometimes think that she would be better off at home, reading her silly novels, than giggling at these worthless entertainments." Forster looked grim. "How shall I stand it, Avebury? Another two weeks."

Jocelyn maintained a sympathetic silence. The past week had indeed been filled with boring outings like this one, a dress ball at the home of an important personage. Every doting mama seemed to bear down on a man in uniform the minute he appeared. Forster had counted on at least a pleasant flirtation or two while in Bath, but so far he had not had much luck or attention beyond that of the occasional polite matron. He was rapidly lapsing into disgruntled whining and becoming rather a bore.

"Got to try to get the new list," he was saying to Jocelyn. "I will make it this time, surely. I've heard there are newly repaired ships out there, ships captured from under Bonaparte's nose..."

Jocelyn stopped listening. Forster's obsession with his first

35

command was also beginning to annoy him. He preferred not to think about the navy at all at this juncture. Sooner or later, they would come to find him. He did not plan to spoil what little time he had by anticipating their moves.

He moved his gaze restlessly around the room. The giggly Miss Forster was happily away through a country dance. Several of the matrons who routinely snubbed him were present, as well as the pinch-faced Miss Lovell, thirty years old and still hopeful. Weary, he considered an early departure, but was reluctant to leave Forster to deal with his flibbertigibbet of a sister and her friend alone.

Then he saw her. Tucked away on an elegant gold chaise longue next to the doors that led to the garden. Her fine blonde hair was swept up in a simple knot adorned with a single pink rose. She wore white – something shimmery and iridescent that settled lightly around her like cream – and her slender shoulders peeked temptingly from the airy confection. She was smiling, clapping her hands in time with the music.

"Pardon me," he said to Forster, who was still speculating about ships, and moved away through the crowd. He kept his eye on her, as if she would fade away in a puff of smoke if he blinked. Spying, she had called it. She was doing it again, he knew: from her vantage point in the corner of the room she was taking careful note of everyone's shoes.

He had no idea why he felt so compelled to approach her, except for some vague notion that she had seen something in his boots. She therefore knew him better than anyone else did.

"Good evening, Lady Catherine." She turned slightly. He saw the brief moment of surprise. Then an expression of pure pleasure crossed her fine features. It was a strange sensation, feeling his mere existence pleased someone so.

"I have been found out!" she exclaimed. Her voice was one of chagrin, but her eyes sparkled. She held out her hand. "Please know that I meant to find you and to apologise sooner. I have had some family business to attend to, and was obliged to leave Bath for a while. But I knew we would meet again."

"Apologise?" He went around to the other side of her chair and stood beside the doors, where he could hear her better over the happy rhythms of the country dance.

"Yes, apologise," she said sincerely. Her smile softened, became grave. "I did not mean to disguise my identity. But it looks as if I have been found out in any case."

"There aren't many Catherine Clavertons in Bath," he said, smiling.

She laughed. "I expect not! And how long do you plan to be in Bath, Captain Avebury?"

"I'm not sure," he replied. "Several weeks, at least."

"Well, good. I will make it up to you." The country dance was ending. He saw Miss Forster searching the room for him.

Something made him turn and say to Catherine, "May I have the honour?" For a fleeting second, he imagined himself whirling her pale, sparkling beauty about the room, melting her coolness with his heat. But the silence that followed told him it was ridiculous. He never danced, anyway.

He felt his face flush. Then he saw her expression. Her lip was trembling, and she appeared to be controlling herself only with considerable effort. Her face had gone white.

"Good God. Have I said – or done – aught wrong, Lady Catherine? Are you all right?" He looked around desperately, seeking help. Surely she was not attending the ball alone?

"No," she whispered. She reached out and grasped his hand tightly. "No, please do not call anyone. I just … I only …" In quick confusion, she ducked her head. When she raised her face, however, her eyes were shining. She seemed … happy! But why?

"I beg your pardon, Captain Avebury." The music started up again, and in spite of himself, he moved closer to her so that he could hear her speak. Her grip on his hand tightened.

"I beg your pardon," she said again. "But I do not dance."

"But-but I have upset you."

"No, no. Not at all. My mind was … elsewhere. Please do forgive me. As I said earlier, I was away from Bath because of family – my father. He is quite ill and not expected to live."

Jocelyn remembered the overheard conversation. "I am so sorry. How foolish of me." He felt like an idiot. Being at sea had eroded his sensibilities and his knowledge of social graces. Of course she would not dance at such a sad time. But then, why was she there at all? At a ball where she could not dance? Confusion threatened again and he felt his head swim. She still had his hand in her firm grasp, the glorious light was still in her eyes. She did not look like a woman anticipating a sad event.

"I thought, Captain Avebury, that you did not dance?" She tilted her head to see him, a mischievous smile teasing her lips.

"I-I … I do not dance, usually. But—"

Lady Catherine threw her head back and laughed. He could see the rows of her teeth, as white as the double strand of pearls wound about her long throat. Everything about her was white, white, white, like the brightest light. Her laugh was musical and sweet. "I will stop teasing you, Captain Avebury. Are you here with your friends?"

Jocelyn glanced uneasily about the room in spite of himself. She answered the question for him. "You must be. You would not be here alone. Do you ride?"

He looked back at her. He suddenly realised that, for once, he liked not hiding.

"Not very well," he said.

"Really? Because you've been at sea for so long?"

"Yes." They looked at each other silently. The hint of a teasing smile ebbed slowly away from her lips, leaving something sober, something soft, in her look. He looked down at her hand, still warm and firm on his. He could feel a pulse. Whose it was, he couldn't be sure. Had they perhaps exchanged pulses?

"Might I persuade you to call on me here in Bath? Or is that dreadfully forward of me? I'm at Mansion Place. It's very close. Are you at the White Hart?"

Slowly, he shook his head. The White Hart – no, he avoided fashionable inns like the plague. He thought he ought to pull his hand away. It would not do for all the matrons who disapproved of him so to begin to talk. It would not do for Lady Catherine at all.

Lady Catherine was leaning forward. Automatically, he bent to hear her. "Please come," she whispered. "We'll ride out to Wansdyke."

Wansdyke? He had no idea what she was talking about. But he found himself nodding. As if in relief, she suddenly released his hand. She smiled.

"Good, then. I will expect you." It was a dismissal. He stepped back, a little perturbed. Then he saw her companion, a pretty young woman, dark-haired and dark-eyed, returning from the dance floor. A besotted-looking gentleman was at her side.

"Melinda, meet my friend, Captain Avebury. He has just returned from the glorious sea, have you not, Captain Avebury? This is Miss Melinda Carlyle." Melinda blushed and curtsied. Her escort, Mr Kingsley, begged the honour of escorting the ladies to supper, but Lady Catherine shook her head.

"We are to leave early this evening, Mr Kingsley. We are very sorry." Melinda looked disappointed, but she obligingly made her own apologies to Mr Kingsley, who drifted away into the crowd.

Jocelyn stood, unsure as to whether he should stay or leave.

"Captain Avebury."

He turned back to Lady Catherine. There was something determined, yet hopeful, in the set of her jaw. He stared at her mouth. Her lower lip was full and as pink as the rose she wore in her hair, her upper lip perfectly chiselled, the little indentation firm and delicious-looking. Alarmed at the involuntary workings of his mind, he coughed and nearly choked.

"Yes, my lady?"

"Would you mind seeing to our carriage for us? We travel alone tonight, and so—" He knew he did not mistake Melinda's quick gasp of alarm and Lady Catherine's swift pressure on her friend's arm. He bowed.

"Certainly," he said in a frosty tone. As he walked toward the door, he heard Melinda's agitated whisper, "But we hardly know him!"

He kept his spine rigid. Lady Catherine was mocking him. That was it. He did not know what kind of game she was playing, but she was no innocent girl. The more he considered it, the angrier he got. With a few curt words, he ordered their carriage. He contemplated leaving. It was all so ridiculous. For a few minutes, he had imagined that Lady Catherine Claverton wanted to know him. That she somehow already did know him. But, of course, she was just flirting. A beautiful woman like Lady Catherine, with title and fortune …

Jocelyn frowned. He could hear the sounds of the carriage as the driver brought it around to the front entrance. No one else was leaving so early, before supper, so the entrance was relatively deserted.

Something was odd, not quite right. She was a young woman, in Bath society, with face and fortune to recommend her as well as a noble name. And yet he had not seen anyone soliciting her hand for a dance or even striking up a conversation with her.

As he began to chew on this new and strange realisation, he heard a muffled thud and scrape. He turned quickly. Lady Catherine was approaching, leaning heavily on Melinda's arm. Jocelyn stood blinking, confused for a moment. And then he understood.

Lady Catherine walked with a limp. It was not a bad limp – or perhaps it was. It was hard to tell because of the skirts, and because Melinda bore her weight. He watched as they made their way through the double doors, the attendant footmen preserving their blithe and impassive expressions. On closer inspection, the limp appeared to be slight, but he knew with the instinct of a soldier that it would be much more painful, much uglier than it appeared. Lady Catherine had learnt to disguise it, and Melinda was accustomed to the lurching predictability of it. Between them, they created a smooth shuffle-scrape-step that made it look no more than a slightly twisted ankle.

He tore his fascinated gaze away. His eyes met hers. He knew with unerring instinct that if he offered any assistance, she would never speak to him again.

She looked away, but her cheeks were pale. *What are you trying to tell me, Lady Catherine?* he wondered.

The carriage was waiting. Jocelyn bowed politely as the two women crossed his path. Catherine stepped up into the carriage first, leaning heavily on Melinda's arm. She pulled herself up neatly and settled herself in. She was plainly very accustomed to doing so. She kept one hand on the door, and looked over at Jocelyn.

"Good night," she said softly. "I shall count on seeing you. Mansion Place. Do not forget."

"Good night, my lady," Jocelyn replied. He watched as the carriage rolled down the drive.

CHAPTER 7

*S*o Lady Catherine was a cripple. He considered the notion dispassionately. On the one hand, it was a terrible shame. She was a beautiful young woman, certainly the most stunning woman at the ball. But now it was no wonder that she was not surrounded by a coterie of male admirers. She was rich and beautiful – but not quite marriage material.

On the other hand, it was ridiculous. What exactly did those men who ignored her expect from a woman? A pretty face and some maidenly accomplishments, no doubt. Lady Catherine could probably paint watercolours and play the pianoforte tolerably well. Perhaps she could sing. She had a title and a fortune. What did they want that she could not provide? An heir, perhaps?

The thought interested him. He turned it over in his mind. He had seen many injured soldiers and sailors, soldiers and humble citizens of far-flung countries – limping delivery boys and maimed street beggars. He knew well enough that the single word concealed a thousand injuries, all of them individual and each painful in its own way. He'd had crippled sailors under his command. They worked as hard as the next man. They did as much as they could, and then some.

But a crippled female – how might her abilities as a wife and mother be changed? How would lameness affect her role in society? Perhaps the eligible young men of Bath did not believe that Lady Catherine was capable of bearing an heir.

But perhaps Lady Catherine was uninterested in finding out whether this was the case.

Jocelyn lolled about the entrance, reluctant to return to the stultifying ballroom. Spring had arrived with warm breezes and the scent of flowers and young women in airy, gauzy gowns. He hadn't realised how much he had missed the spring. Aboard ship – in the Mediterranean, or the Indian Ocean, or the West Indies – spring was no more than another wave of hot air. The birds changed, true. But it had not struck him that he longed for the smells of a wet and fecund English spring, the odour of damp earth and moss. Cold stone foundations. A cottage on a moor. Bluebells under the trees.

He did not hear the person approach.

"Bath is a poor hiding place." The voice spoke directly in his ear and was attended by a tobacco-smoke smell.

Jocelyn stiffened. He turned around slowly. The man was a little taller than he, golden-haired, bronze-skinned, with an easy carriage. And, from the points of his shirt-collar to the fine leather of his boots, obviously aristocratic.

"One would be a fool to hide in Bath," Jocelyn replied. He had never seen this man before. Was this his time of reckoning, he wondered. But he had supposed that the messenger would be someone from the Admiralty. Not a finely dressed man in his thirties.

"Such a small town," the man continued. He examined his cheroot with indifference, then tossed it into the gutter. He looked at Jocelyn. "But in Dover, Brighton – or even London – one might be able to get lost in a crowd."

"If one were hiding," Jocelyn said curtly.

"Ah." The man nodded. Jocelyn glanced at him, his resentment rising. Not at being found – he had not been taking particular care to disguise his movements – but at who had done so. If the messenger had been intended to humiliate him, he had been perfectly chosen. Although it did seem odd that they would send such a person.

"You knew my brother," the golden-haired man said abruptly. He peered at his fingers intently, then reached into a pocket for a handkerchief. He wiped his fingers with distaste.

"Your brother?" Jocelyn asked blankly.

"Tobacco. Stains everything brown." The man frowned and peered more closely at his fingers. He slanted a glance up at Jocelyn, who was frowning in confusion.

"Jonathan Waters."

Jocelyn shook his head. "I'm sorry. I don't recall—"

"You saved his life. During a knife fight. It was, I believe, in an alleyway. In Bombay."

Jocelyn's brow cleared. "Was that your brother? Oh! Only I thought he said ..." That had been the fateful day, the fateful occasion. He would never forget it.

The man nodded, staring absently at the distant shrubbery. "He should have been dismissed from the service."

"But wait! His name wasn't Waters. It was ... Rowland, Rowles ... something or other." Jocelyn drew his brows together, trying to remember. "He was lieutenant on the *Majestic*."

"Yes." The man nodded. He turned to Jocelyn. "That's right. His name is Jonathan Waters, but he's Viscount Roland. One of those strange family inheritances. He prefers to be addressed as such." He shrugged lightly, but his dark blue eyes were not laughing. "After you returned him to the *Majestic*, the ship's surgeon managed to keep him alive. Barely. He's missing a finger, of course."

"I'm glad to hear that he survived," Jocelyn said. "It was a brutal fight. We left port immediately and I never heard of his fate."

"Actually, Captain Avebury, it was a miracle that you survived."

Jocelyn flushed. "Not at all."

"Oh? I take it that the natives simply ... ran away when you appeared? There were apparently some nasty knife wounds. Quite a feat, to calmly return to your ship when you are covered in blood."

Jocelyn did not reply.

Suddenly, the man laughed. "Come, come, Captain Avebury. I meant to thank you. But, gentleman that you are, of course you don't wish to be identified as a hero."

"I'm not a hero."

"But you did not have to go in search of my brother when he went off like that. Especially when I am sure you knew what he was about."

Jocelyn looked sharply at him. The man's face was smoothly impassive. "I dislike not knowing your name," he said abruptly.

"I beg your pardon. My name is Barrington. Jonathan is my younger half-brother."

"How did you know where to find me?"

"It's not difficult to find someone who isn't hiding." A small smile curled Barrington's lip.

Jocelyn nodded. "Exactly so," he said, keeping his voice bland. "I wish you and your brother well. Where is he, by the by?"

"Aboard the *Surrey*." An uncomfortable pause. "He avoids alleyways. My mother and I would like to thank you for rescuing him. I am well aware that you took a grave risk in doing so."

"'twas nothing." Jocelyn turned to leave. A hand on his arm stopped him.

"They would have strung him up without so much as a Christian funeral. He certainly deserved to be punished – but no one, not even Jonathan, deserved to die at the hands of savages." Barrington paused. "We owe you a debt that will be difficult to discharge. You were under no obligation to search for him in the first place and, when you found him, you could have chosen to leave him where he was."

"No one would have done such a thing," Jocelyn said. "I simply followed my conscience."

"Would that all of our fine officers possessed such a conscience." A flash of anger flickered on Barrington's face then disappeared. He spoke softly. "We know what you risked to save him, what bravery was required. We know you did not tell your officers where you were headed, lest they prevent you going. And that you alone could speak the native tongue well enough to gain entrance into that den of thieves. We merely wish to thank you."

Jocelyn nodded curtly. He wanted to leave, to get away from this all-knowing stranger. He turned on his heel. As he strode away, he heard Barrington say softly, "I know all about it, Captain Avebury."

He kept walking.

"The Admiralty will come for you," Barrington said, a little more loudly. "But you are not without friends."

At this, Jocelyn stopped. He turned. "Friends?" he said bitterly. "I have no friends."

Barrington walked over to face him. "What I say is true. When the time comes, you will see who your friends are."

Jocelyn shook his head and turned to walk away. As he put out his hand to pull open the door, Barrington called after him.

"I have your best interests at heart."

He tugged open the doors and returned to the ball.

He had asked her to dance.

"Really, Catherine," Melinda complained. "Speaking to naval men whom we don't even know."

With her eyes closed, leaning into a darkened corner of the

swaying carriage, Catherine could almost imagine herself dancing. She would rest one hand lightly on the arm of her partner and trip gaily down the line of dancers. She would not miss a single step.

"We know nothing about his family, his property. Nothing. Why on earth are you so intent on befriending him?" Melinda's voice rose sharply.

Catherine opened her eyes. "Because he seemed interesting."

Disapproving silence.

Catherine sighed. "You do not have to worry about me, Melinda."

"I do worry about you."

"You need not. I can take care of myself."

Melinda did not reply. The sound of the coachman murmuring to the horses melded with their steady clip-clop. It was not very late, but the streets were empty. *A pathetic substitute for London*, Catherine thought.

She reached out for Melinda's hand. "I am sorry if I alarm you. I will try to be more prudent."

"I'm only thinking of you, dearest."

Catherine squeezed her hand. "I know. Are they saying dreadful things about me?"

"Not within my hearing. But I would imagine that the world is puzzled, wondering why you are attending balls at this time."

Catherine shrugged lightly.

"Although, of course, now you have a title of your own, everything will change."

"Will it?"

"Certainly," Melinda said in a surprised tone. "You are the Countess St Clair. You will be able to do anything you please."

"Yes," said Catherine dryly. "Anything at all." For a bitter moment, she reflected on her life. I have done everything that I please, she thought. I did it long before any title came my way. I did it in spite of my name, the loss of the Delamare title, and the aching load of my family. I did it alone, no thanks to anyone. What more can a title do for me?

She remembered Beaseley's words: "Should you have a son, he would become the next Earl St Clair."

The truth was, she wanted a son.

She bit her lip until she tasted blood. She knew it was impossible. Impossible.

But to head her own family, to bear an heir! To become the reason for the flourishing of the St Clairs, after a lifetime of knowing that the reversion of the ancient Delamare title to the Crown was her fault.

She wanted it desperately.

She wanted the St Clair line to blossom once again, to spread, to exert power and influence. All she needed to do was bear a son.

A son would marry and produce more St Clair children. A son would be the centre of a St Clair family home, fill it with the happy voices of people who loved each other. A son would mean there would be no dilution of the title. Instead of daughters to marry into families where they would be silenced, where the St Clair story would be secondary to those of their husbands, the St Clairs needed sons to ensure that their voice would be heard forever.

If she did not marry and produce children, the St Clair line would be gone forever: her mother's sacrifice – as well as her own – would have been for naught.

She would do it. But how?

CHAPTER 8

*L*ydia Barrow provided Catherine with the excuse that enabled her to live alone. She was not a relation; in fact, no one really knew where she had come from. On the very day Catherine bade her governess goodbye, Lydia had arrived, carrying one small valise.

Catherine was aware that the staff gossiped about her companion's origins. Lydia spoke well, but a little too carefully. She was a little too proud in front of the staff, a little too brusque in her requests. The staff knew when someone was hiding her discomfort.

But Catherine did not care. Lydia's presence made it possible for her to live at Wansdyke without brother or father or husband.

Mutual friends had introduced them in town. Lydia was the daughter of a lady of quality, the result of a scandalous affair with a duke. Although London-bred, she did not move in the circles that mattered and her parentage was a closely guarded secret. Lydia's need of a genteel position in a household that would not pry into her secret matched Catherine's need for a tight-lipped companion.

She was not a true companion in that she did not care for

walking in the shrubbery or riding in the fields. At Wansdyke, Catherine did those things alone. At Mansion Place, Lydia sorted through the invitations and managed Catherine's callers, but Melinda usually accompanied Catherine into the world. Lydia did not care for society.

~

IT LOOKED LIKE RAIN. GREY, DAMP, COLD. THE FIRES WERE LIT. The maid brought in a fresh pot of tea. Catherine leant against the window, gazing down on the cobblestoned street, watching as pedestrians hurried to and fro. Lydia sat sewing quietly in a corner.

"I want to go back to Wansdyke," Catherine said without turning around.

Lydia continued sewing.

"They will want me at Albrook any day now. I would rather not receive condolences here in Mansion Place."

A fat raindrop spattered onto the glass. Umbrellas appeared. The flower seller ducked into an entrance.

"I would rather be riding."

Still no answer. Still more raindrops splashed.

Catherine turned away. She glanced at Lydia. "Have you managed to procure anything black?" she asked listlessly.

Lydia looked up. "It is already packed."

"I am tempted not to wear mourning at all," Catherine muttered. She limped over to a chair. Just as she had eased herself into it, there was a rap at the door. Lydia put down her sewing.

"My lady." It was a maid. "Sir Lyle Barrington." She curtsied and held open the door.

"Sir Lyle," Catherine murmured. She began to rise, but Sir Lyle held up his hand.

"Please do not disturb yourself."

Lydia gathered up her sewing. She dropped a silent curtsey and stole from the room.

"Am I so disliked?" Sir Lyle came to kiss Catherine's hand.

Catherine laughed grimly. "Lydia hates everyone. How are you, sir?"

"Very well, thank you. Is that tea? I will help myself."

"Let me ring for refreshment."

"Absolutely not. I am merely cold and damp, and would like something hot immediately. Atrocious weather."

"It is no longer hot, or fresh," said Catherine and rang the bell. "So you did not come here to see me in particular? Were you merely on your way to someplace else, and thought to warm yourself here?"

"In a manner of speaking, yes. It would be nice to … er … warm myself," Sir Lyle muttered. He shot Catherine a smile and poured himself some tea.

"You are impertinent," Catherine returned, but her cheeks were hot.

"And you, my lady, should have pretended ignorance of my double entendre."

"Must I be stupid on top of everything else? Is it not enough that I cannot walk or run?"

Sir Lyle raised his cup. "You walk very well. And I imagine that you can run quite well too – will you give me the opportunity to watch you? At Wansdyke, perhaps?"

Catherine laughed. "You are dreadful, Sir Lyle. No, I cannot and do not run. So you will have to forego that pleasure. But where have you been? You are tanned, even more so than usual."

Sir Lyle lifted an unconscious hand to rub his jaw. "Am I? I can keep no secrets from you, Lady Catherine."

"You keep many secrets," Catherine retorted. "I wish you would share them with me."

Sir Lyle bowed slightly. "Certainly. I have been to the continent and beyond. Greece. India. Shall I tell more?"

"Yes, absolutely! How very exciting." A maid brought fresh tea. Catherine motioned to her to remove Sir Lyle's cup. "You shall have hot, since you are chilled."

"Yes, ma'am," Sir Lyle murmured. He smiled wickedly.

Catherine frowned at him over the maid's head. Once the girl had gone, she begged him to describe his journey.

"Really, it was only occasionally exciting. More often it was tedious." Sir Lyle shrugged. "I have some shipping interests here and there. Ran myself ragged checking up on the vessels. Making sure Bonaparte is not disturbing our trade."

"Not exactly a man of leisure, are you, Sir Lyle?"

"Never, Lady Catherine. Except when I am with you, of course."

"Now, now." Catherine dimpled. "That is enough for one morning."

Sir Lyle laughed. His lips parted in a wide white grin. Catherine could not help but admire the way that his darkened skin set off the gold of his hair, the intensity of his eyes.

"I beg your pardon, Lady Catherine. I have overstepped the boundaries of friendship."

"Do not be a bore," she returned. "I merely wish to keep the conversation … appropriate. Are you in Bath for long?"

"For a little while. I have some business to attend to."

"You are always attending to business! What a very busy person you are!"

Sir Lyle shrugged lightly. "That is the fate of a man whose fortune is invested in trade," he said. "I should feel flattered that you will even speak to me."

"Nonsense!"

"I meant to inquire after your father. How is the earl?"

"Not well. I am sorry to say that we are awaiting the end."

"I am sorry. This must be a difficult time."

Catherine shrugged. "It has been expected for some time. You have been away – you could not have known."

"I hope you know I am happy to be of any assistance."

"Thank you." She inclined her head. There was a moment of silence.

"Lady Catherine."

She looked up. She had been brooding over the thought of having to wear black. It was not a good colour for her. Sir Lyle put a chair next to her own and sat down. He leant forward.

"You are distracted this morning."

"I am sorry. The last few weeks have been rather difficult."

"We have known each other for a long time."

"We have."

Sir Lyle chuckled. "Bath's favourite outsiders."

Catherine smiled weakly. "Yes. Although I have never understood why you are unaccepted. My leg makes me so. And my refusal to follow the rules."

"It is my interests in trade. Stodgy Bath matrons dislike it immensely."

"Well, that has not prevented them from setting their daughters at you," Catherine returned.

"Unfortunately. All of them cross-eyed or worse."

Catherine giggled. "Surely they are not that bad!"

"Every bit that bad." Sir Lyle looked away. He seemed to compose himself, then reached out for Catherine's hand.

Surprised, she allowed him to take it. "Why, whatever is wrong?"

"Nothing at all. Lady Catherine, I am here to ask for your indulgence."

"My indulgence?" Catherine wrinkled her brow in a puzzled frown. Then she tried to laugh. "For your bad manners?"

She liked Sir Lyle. She did not know precisely what he traded and where but had maintained an on-off friendship with him for years. He treated her almost as if she were a young widow, not an unmarried woman. Perhaps that was a consequence of her refusal to conform to society's expectations. She almost liked it.

She certainly appreciated that he thought her smart and independent. But his intensity did occasionally unnerve her.

"I suppose my manners are quite bad," Sir Lyle admitted. He held Catherine's hand firmly in his own. "I should be approaching your father but, being that he is ill—"

"Come, Sir Lyle," Catherine said with impatience. "You have never hesitated to speak frankly with me."

"I would like to see you … often. Do you take my meaning?"

Catherine opened her mouth to speak. Sir Lyle's grasp on her hand tightened. Her heart began to race, and she stammered, "I-I do not know."

"Surely you understand what I wish for us. If your father were not so ill, I would ask him for permission to address you."

Catherine pulled her hand away. She laughed nervously. "This is absurd, Sir Lyle. We have known each other for years. I never suspected such interest on your part."

"You were a schoolroom miss when I saw you last."

"I was not. Well, perhaps I was."

"I am much older than you are, my dear. It would have been – shall we say – inappropriate for me to pursue you when you were a child."

Catherine pouted. "Thank you very much for saying so. I am grateful that you did not wish to corrupt my innocence."

"Do not change the subject, Catherine. May I call you Catherine?" He did not wait for an answer. "I am in England for a little while. I would like to see you. May I? Perhaps we will find that we should suit. I expect we shall."

But I am afraid of you, Catherine thought. *I do not know you, and you do not know me. Years of friendship aside, we are strangers. And if you find out … if you find out what I really am, you will utterly destroy me.* She swallowed.

But if she married, she could have a son.

Wait! Could that be the reason for Sir Lyle's offer? Did he know of the title?

"Sir Lyle," she said carefully. "Is there any reason for your sudden interest?"

For a moment she thought he would laugh. But he said gravely, "Does it seem so sudden, after all our years of friendship?"

"You have never thought of me in this way before."

Sir Lyle pretended to be hurt. "Did you not know? You have held my heart in your hands all along."

"Oh, come! We have known each other for years, it is true. But many of those years were spent with you on the opposite side of the globe, tending to those ships of yours. And not a letter or word from you until you found yourself wandering past Mansion Place again."

"Did that disappoint you?" His lips twitched.

Catherine made a sound of frustration. "You know perfectly well what I mean."

Sir Lyle rose. He went over to the far window and peered outside. "The first wave of visitors is arriving."

Catherine half rose from her seat. "What?"

Sir Lyle turned. "Two fops and a gossip-monger. I expect they are here to quiz you on your new title."

"Oh, no!"

"And one or both … gentlemen will probably ask for your hand."

"I must get Lydia," Catherine exclaimed. "She will turn them away." She pulled herself up.

Sir Lyle went over to help her. He took her arm. "Wait. Catherine, you cannot stop them. The word is all over Bath."

Catherine turned to look directly into his face. "And you? Is that why you are here? You of all people do not need my money."

"Your title would be of immense assistance to me," Sir Lyle said bluntly. "It would open doors that are currently closed to me."

Catherine turned away. "I do not know what to do," she muttered. She shook her head.

"Our son, Catherine. Our son would be the next earl. You would be the matriarch of a dynasty."

Something caught in her throat. She shook her head mutely again. "I do not know," she whispered.

"I will stop tormenting you." Sir Lyle released her arm. With his fingertips, he turned her head gently until she looked at him. "You know I am very fond of you."

Catherine tried to smile. "And I of you. I cannot think right now. I must – I must go to Wansdyke."

"You cannot avoid the curious forever," Sir Lyle warned.

"I will handle them," Catherine said.

"I am sure you will." Sir Lyle removed his hand. "I will see you at Wansdyke, then. If you will allow me."

"I would not turn you away, Sir Lyle."

"That is all I ask."

He bowed and left.

She could not decide. She had thought she would have time, time to think carefully about her course of action.

Marry Sir Lyle? Yes, he had a reputation as a rogue, and he was in trade, but he was still a gentleman. Even her father would not have objected to such an alliance. She could be the mother of the next earl within a twelvemonth.

Why, then, did she feel so uncertain?

CHAPTER 9

The note was short. The child who handed it to Jocelyn was rosy cheeked, well scrubbed. A happy, healthy boy of eight or so, lurking hopefully about the inn as his parents cleaned and cooked and attended to their guests. Jocelyn obliged him with a generous tip, remembering the skin-and-bones children in the streets of Bombay.

How happy you are, he thought, watching the boy scamper down the stairs with his prize clutched tightly in one hand. *How happy I was – once.* But his world had come to a crashing halt around him before he was even that old. He envied the boy's simple life of hard work and hard play. There was something very clean, very honest, about a child's life.

Your name is on the list. They will discuss your case within the week. Do nothing, go nowhere.

No signature.

Its meaning was both clear and obscure. He knew what the list was and what case the note referred to. At last, they were to decide what was to be done with him. And, depending on who was present at the meeting, his exemplary record would speak for itself, or the truth about his past would come out and there would be a court martial. Perhaps worse.

Do nothing, go nowhere. Was that meant to be helpful counsel, or a warning that he should not flee?

He wondered who had sent the note. Barrington had said something about friends. But he dismissed the thought. He had no friends in high places – or anywhere else, for that matter. If there was a way to gain favour with the Admiralty, he would take it. He wanted nothing more than to get back to sea. He would do anything, anything at all. But he had no friends in high places.

Forster was visiting friends nearby; his tiresome sister and her friend were with him. Although the afternoon was advancing, the sun was still high in the sky – a sign of the impending summer. Lovely weather for a countryside walk. That settled it. Jocelyn picked up his hat and walked out, leaving the note and all of its implications behind him.

The Kingsmith Arms lay on the edge of town. It was a respectable country establishment without the air of fashionable address the more popular Bath inns commanded. Jocelyn declined the groom's offer of a ride into town on the cart. Instead, he walked behind the inn, jumped over a stile, crossed a stream by a rickety bridge, and headed across a muddy field scattered with dandelions. Startled rabbits scampered away as he strode easily through squishy mounds of wet green grass, his feet locating the smoothly tramped path with the instinct of one born and bred in the country. He breathed deeply of the ripe scent, thrust his hands in his pockets and slowed his pace slightly. He came to a fence and hesitated. He did not know where he was heading or whether he would be able to find his way back, but he decided to follow the track the cows had trodden up the slight hill that rose some distance behind the inn. Although the slope appeared gentle, some sections of the path were still steep enough to cause Jocelyn's boots to slip and his pace to falter. Breathing hard, he climbed on. He turned as his way flattened out and he neared the top of the hill, eager for a view of the little farms dotting the countryside and the not-too-distant golden stone of Bath. Afternoon sunlight placed a yellow halo over all; his heart considerably lightened, he turned to resume his climb.

Once at the top, he saw the parties responsible for creating his path grazing peacefully in a wide green field. He felt a trifle disappointed. Was this all that lay beyond? He had hoped his walk would show him something more interesting than field upon field of munching cows and yellow dandelions. If he wanted a different view, his only choice was to follow the stream at the foot of the hill until it disappeared into a distant copse.

The stream was a pathetic thing compared to the wide Avon, but sparkling clean and obviously spring-fed. It had cut deeply into the moist earth and it seemed that any woods that remained in this part of the country rose up about it – perhaps because the steep banks made it too hard for animals to reach the water and the wet ground surrounding it made the approach difficult.

Jocelyn stopped to drink, and was pleased to discover that the water was ice-cold and delicious. He strode on, pausing only to pick up a handful of dense clay from the bank. No good for crops, he noted. Then he laughed. It was a wonder that he could remember anything at all about agriculture given his rural child-hood up north was long past and that, ever since he turned thir-teen, he had spent all his time either on board a ship or trying to get onto one.

The trees grew denser, and the stream widened until, Jocelyn realised, he could no longer step across it or splash through it with ease. He wondered whether the view above the high bank on the other side was still one of boring cows and grass, and decided that it was not worth negotiating the claggy mud to find out.

"I have missed England," he said aloud. The words fell flat in the damp of the wood. It was a spectacular change from the salty air of the deck, where even the laziest sailors sprang to duty at the mere sound of his voice.

"England!" he boomed, wondering if volume would make a difference to the resonance of his voice. He felt as if his throat had been invaded by a miasma of dense fog. How very odd. Sea air was damp; life aboard ship was damp. Why, then, did England feel so wet? So ripe? So earthy? Perhaps that was it. No man could survive at sea without support from land. But, in England, a man could till an acre and Mother Earth would make him king. *As long as he has an acre*, Jocelyn reflected. He laughed out loud, pleased at the thought. He had plenty of money. Perhaps he should just set himself up as a gentleman farmer somewhere. Not around Bath, certainly, but somewhere. Down in Cornwall, or up north near the Lakes.

If they are going to get me anyway, he thought, *perhaps it would be as well to make them knock at a door of my own.*

He imagined the scene: the starchy correctness of the butler, the polite curiosity of the housekeeper, as the men from the Admiralty came to take the master away.

It was possible that he would be allowed to return to duty, without a devastating court martial. Here, alone in the little wood, he could acknowledge that. His admiral in Gibraltar liked him. Respected him a great deal, in fact. Thought he was destined for greatness.

What rubbish!

There were some who liked Avebury – and a few who hated him.

Jocelyn knew a great deal about the hatred of men. He had seen it work its violence in so many places, in so many ways. Strange, when he was not a man of violence himself. Rage and anger confused him on a fundamental level – he was not prone to either feeling. Had all emotion been stamped out of him on that cold November day when his father had been executed? He had been a lad of seven. His eyes had not actually seen the death blow. But his soul had absorbed the energy of the howling mob.

He knew how deep feelings of rage ran, but also how soon they were spent. While he would never understand it himself, he was not a coward, and he would not run. He had no particular reason to save himself.

Voices. He ceased his contemplation of the stream, looked up and slowed his pace. He cocked his head, listening. A raindrop splashed on his cheek. He hadn't noticed the drizzle, the merest shadow of a cloud obscuring the bright sun, shaded as he had been by the trees and sheltered under his hat and the thick fabric of his uniform.

No, not voices. One voice. A lady. Singing. Humming, perhaps. But in the rain? The song came from beyond the high bank on the other side of the stream. A milkmaid? No, for once he could not hear any cows in the field beyond, thank goodness! And it was definitely a female voice, not a boy's. So it could not be a farm hand.

Jocelyn came to a stop and looked down at the water. He was curious, but the stream was too wide to cross without soaking at least his boots and probably his clothes, too. The bank was too steep and muddy for him to climb up without getting filthy. He shrugged and was about to walk on when, from the corner of his eye, he saw the plume of a feather waving above the top of the bank. He turned his head. At first, all he could see was the feather, but it danced and shook until the hat to which it was attached also came into view. And then, very slowly, a face. It belonged to Lady Catherine Claverton.

CHAPTER 10

"Captain Avebury!" The words barely emerged from her lips. Little loose strands of blonde hair surrounded her face. Her hat was damp. She seemed nonplussed, startled as she peered at him over the top of the bank.

It was certainly a great deal easier to address her here than in the cloying surroundings of a Bath ballroom. "Good afternoon, Lady Catherine!" he called up to her. "Are you also taking a walk?"

"A crawl might be a more apt description," Catherine replied, the hint of a smile in her eyes. "My horse isn't fond of this mud, and refused to jump any of our usual fences. So I've been walking – but now I can see why he refused to allow me to ride him today." She made a face and held up her hands. The palms of her gloves were caked with brown mud, utterly incongruous against the fine kidskin.

"Good God," Jocelyn burst out. "Did you fall?"

The hint of a smile vanished. Jocelyn realised too late that, while he had not been thinking of her limp when he spoke, she must be accustomed to people treating her like an invalid. Now he wondered how she managed to ride as easily as she implied.

"No," she said carefully. "But this bank is rather steep. I was hoping to stand at the very top, but the climb is quite beyond me, I'm afraid."

"Then it will gratify you to learn that I was thinking of making the same climb, but from this side," Jocelyn said, smiling. "It is indeed rather steep. Perhaps too steep for me, too."

A proper smile finally appeared on Catherine's face. "You exaggerate, sir," she teased.

"I do not, indeed. Let me demonstrate." Hardly knowing what he intended to do, Jocelyn plunged into the stream and promptly sank up to his thighs in cold water. Gasping, he pushed forward, his boots slipping over smooth grey stones, creating ripples that scared silvery little fish, making them zip away in great big schools. He could feel the liquid seep up toward his crotch and, in a burst of energy, fought his way to the slippery bank beyond.

Catherine's pale face looked down at him from the top of the bank. "You have convinced me," she called, pleading. "Do not go any further."

Without replying, Jocelyn began to scramble up the side of the bank, grabbing tufts of wet grass to help his hand-over-hand ascent. He did it automatically, it was just like climbing the rigging of a ship, he thought. Except the rigging of a ship wasn't usually wet and green and slimy. Not on his ship, at least. Just as he stretched for the top of the bank, his boot slipped and he went sliding back whence he came, the front of his uniform soaking up the mud as he went.

With a cry of dismay, Catherine moved instinctively to catch at his hands, but his descent was completed before she could grab at him. "Do not come up," she pleaded. "You will make yourself ill – you are soaking wet!"

Jocelyn dug the toes of his boots into the side of the bank, and began to slowly pull himself up again, this time jamming his elbows into the mud. Grunt, grunt, heave, heave. For a peculiar reason he could not have described, his heart was lighter, his spirit at ease. The harder he worked, the better he felt. What was this strange sensation? Perhaps it was the same concentration as that which kept him happy at sea. But he had never experienced this calm mental energy on land – there, he was awkward, silent, nervous.

He was at the top and staring into Catherine's unhappy face. "There, you see?" he said, breathing hard. "Here we are, each stuck on our own side, but both covered in mud." He smiled at her.

Something about their face-to-face encounter struck Catherine, and she burst into peals of laughter. "Oh, you absurd creature!" she gasped. Suddenly, she teetered and began to slip slowly back down her side of the bank. She grasped wildly at the ground, nearly falling over backwards in an effort not to fall and cover her riding dress with grass stains and mud. Jocelyn grabbed her hands then, having steadied her, let go, pulling a wry face at the new layer of mud on her gloves.

"Don't slide back without taking me with you," he said, trying to lighten the moment. In the wide fields behind Catherine, a brown horse nibbled peacefully at the grass. And, on a hillside further in the distance, Jocelyn could see the outlines of a grand house surrounded by shrubbery and a carefully cultivated park.

"Come with me, then," Catherine said, still panting from her near accident. She coughed. Jocelyn looked back down at her. Her face was very close to his. He could suddenly feel every wet inch of his clothes clinging to his skin. Involuntarily, he shivered.

"See, you are cold," she chided. "You must come home with me, to Wansdyke."

"Wansdyke? Is that Wansdyke over there?"

"Yes. I only stay at Mansion Place when I must. Wansdyke is my home." She paused, then said, "You never visited me at Mansion Place."

Jocelyn examined his muddy palms, then studied Catherine's side of the bank. There was a sudden steep drop to a small ledge which allowed her to stand precariously and look over to the stream, but the slope flattened out quickly behind her. Grimacing, he dug his nails into the earth and pulled himself up using only his chest muscles and biceps. He winced as he brought his legs over. What a disgrace! At sea, he climbed like this every day. He could feel the strain in his chest, a burning ache that ought not to be there. This was the wretched result of mooning about in Bath, brooding about God knew what ridiculous, uncontrollable—

"Are you all right?" Catherine put a hand on his arm and gently turned him to face her. Seeing her horrified expression, Jocelyn examined his previously pristine uniform. It seemed beyond rescue.

He looked up at her. The rain had stopped, and the wilted feather on her hat drooped by her ear. She was wearing a perfectly ordinary navy-blue habit with no trim or decoration. It was damp but relatively clean. However, she had pushed back wisps of her hair with muddy gloves, leaving streaks of dirt along her temples. He was suddenly filled with admiration for this woman who had taken her horse out into the mud and who, when the animal had refused to go any further, had insisted on struggling by herself to see a view. And who didn't seem to mind a bit of mud in her hair.

"You've got mud in your hair," he said cheerfully.

"Is that all?" Lady Catherine said, pressing her lips together. "I'm sure I must look a fright."

"For a lady on a ride, not bad at all." Jocelyn cast another rueful look at his clothes. "I apologise for my ... er ... dishevelled state. I enjoyed the climb, however. I am grateful to you for your suggestion."

That was too much for Lady Catherine. At first, only giggles escaped, but then she laughed harder and harder until the tears ran down her cheeks. Jocelyn hung back, surprised to be the source of so much merriment.

"You are so … so original," she gasped. "Tell me, Captain Avebury, do you do this often? Scramble up muddy riverbanks? Or did you climb this one just to show me that I should not be upset that I hadn't attempted it myself?"

She was too smart. She knew a backhanded attempt at sympathy when she saw it. For a moment, Jocelyn regretted his clumsy attempt at gallantry. "Would you accept the argument that I wanted to see what was on the other side?" he offered sheepishly.

"Never," Lady Catherine retorted. "I am not an idiot."

"Obviously not," Jocelyn agreed. He smiled at her, but she pretended to pout.

"You do not strike me as a man who wants to look at cows."

"Will you perhaps accept the notion that I am a man who enjoys a climb?"

Lady Catherine pursed her lips. Then she dimpled. "Why, of course. You are a sailor, are you not? But those clothes! You are freezing, I can see that. Come, lend me your arm. Help me to my horse."

"Where is your groom?" Jocelyn asked in a tone of mock severity. "Surely you are not riding alone?" He offered his arm and she leant in close, placing her boots firmly into the mud as she bore down on her good leg.

"I prefer not to go out with my groom," Lady Catherine said darkly. "He thinks I ought not to ride at all. He is a complete fool."

"Your maid, then?"

"Miss Barrow usually comes with me. She rides tolerably well. But today she has the toothache. It is just as well. She is city-bred, you know. She would loathe this mud."

"And who is Miss Barrow?" They squished through the mud together for a moment before Lady Catherine answered.

"She lives with me – for countenance." Lady Catherine slanted a mischievous glance up at him. "I couldn't possibly live alone, of course. Not even on my own estate. What would people say?"

"Why do I suspect that you don't care in the least?" They were approaching the brown horse, who ignored them studiously while it munched. It moved two steps away.

"You are right, Captain Avebury." Lady Catherine stopped. She turned to face him. "I don't care, in particular. But there are limits to what even the daughter of an earl can do or say in society. There are always limits, are there not? To everything?"

Jocelyn chewed on that thought. He looked off in the distance at the fuzzy outline of Wansdyke. Were there limits even for the titled, the lawmakers, the favoured few? He knew his own limits, limits that had been placed on him at birth. And Lady Catherine's leg was a limit, of sorts. But it was not a limit that he considered terribly important, in the grand scheme of things. A lame sailor could still do quite a bit.

"You disagree?" Lady Catherine was gazing at him intently.

Jocelyn shook his head. "No, not at all. But I have spent a life at sea. These limits imposed by society – they seem unimportant compared to some others." He released Lady Catherine's arm and walked over to the horse. "Shall I help you up?"

Lady Catherine made her way toward him. He watched her step carefully through the mud, knowing that he needed to let her walk on her own two feet. She rested a hand firmly on his arm. "Only if you come home with me," she said. "You are soaked and it is my fault because I teased you. I am very sorry for that."

"You should not be." Jocelyn cupped his hands, and she placed her right foot on them. He heaved her up into the saddle. She grasped the reins and turned to him.

"Are you going to come?"

Jocelyn hesitated. He really had no desire to re-enter the world of Bath society. He was happy to chat amiably with the admirable Lady Catherine outside, in a green field, while they were both covered in mud. He did not want to awkwardly navigate the furniture of her drawing room, trying not to spread that mud around her home. He did not want hostile looks from her staff. He did not want to meet Lydia Barrow and her toothache.

"Perhaps another time," he said. That nervous feeling in his stomach was starting up again.

"Oh, don't be so infuriating!" Lady Catherine said. "I know that I will not see you again; you didn't come to see me in town, not even when the whole world was coming to Mansion Place."

"The whole world? Indeed?"

Lady Catherine bit her lip and turned away. Her voice was a bit muffled as she replied. "Yes. The entire world has been on my doorstep for the past week and more. So I came back to Wansdyke because, after a while, I wanted them all to go away." She looked down at Jocelyn. "They all seem to know of my title and properties – a name and estate of which, until recently, I had no knowledge."

"And these are beyond those from your father?"

Lady Catherine laughed bitterly. "Oh, Captain Avebury. Perhaps this is why I like you so much. You really know nothing about me, do you?"

"I don't know much about anything at all, it seems," Jocelyn said.

"Do not take offence, I beg you, Captain Avebury. I am only too used to being tolerated merely because of my father." Lady Catherine shifted in the saddle, causing the horse to glare balefully up at her. She patted its neck. "Lazy beast," she muttered.

"At least you know that is not the case with me," Jocelyn said mildly. "And I do not take offence. I am very ignorant of the things you landlubbers hold in esteem." He backed away a little, preparing to take his leave.

Lady Catherine tightened the reins. "I hope you will visit me," she said softly. She spoke gently to the horse and walked him closer to where Jocelyn stood.

Jocelyn shaded his eyes. The setting sun, bright behind,

silhouetted her erect and secure in her seat. It was hard to imagine that this woman could not make it across a room without limping. It was hard to imagine anyone cared about her difficulty.

"In all honesty, I will probably not," he admitted. "I do not seem to fit in genteel circles."

"Surely you do not plan to leave?" Lady Catherine seemed dismayed.

Jocelyn thought of the note. Go nowhere. Do nothing. "No," he said shortly. "I have no plans."

"I hope you will feel free, then, to walk in the grounds of Wansdyke."

Jocelyn laughed. It seemed ludicrous. "I am afraid your groundsmen will take me for a poacher. Or perhaps the ghost of some long-lost sailor relation."

Lady Catherine was, apparently, no longer in the mood for jokes. She turned the horse round with a nimble twist of the reins. Then she seemed to think better of it. "Captain Avebury," she called over her shoulder. The horse, which had been walking in the direction of Wansdyke, stopped obediently at the sound of her voice. Jocelyn tilted his head and squinted into the setting sun.

"Are you very rich? That is to say, were you very lucky while you were at sea?"

Jocelyn considered. He looked at the stone shape of Wansdyke, at the sculpted grounds surrounding it, at the spotted cows in the distance. He thought about the humble cottages of his childhood neighbours. He thought of the grand Bath drawing rooms in which he had recently spent his time.

"Why do you ask, Lady Catherine?"

She answered quickly. "I beg your pardon for my impertinence. But – I think you are too happy to be poor."

"Am I?"

"Yes. If you were poor, you would be looking for ways to be rich. But instead you are walking in the mud."

"Perhaps I belong in the mud."

"No one who knows you could think such a thing."

Jocelyn smiled. He turned his back and began to trudge toward the stream and its trees.

"Captain Avebury!" A desperate note tinged her voice.

He turned around, but continued walking – backwards. He shaded his eyes again.

"Were you? Lucky, I mean?"

"If you only knew how absurd that question is, Lady Catherine, you would not ask it!" He could not help it; laughter bubbled up in him. Lucky? Jocelyn Avebury? He tossed his head back and chortled. The deep-throated burst of merriment continued until his aching chest started to protest. He turned to walk back toward the bank. Then, before he knew it, Lady Catherine and her horse were almost on top of him. Startled, he turned, flailing, not sure in which direction to head. Lady Catherine brought the animal around at a quick trot and stopped squarely in front of him.

"I dislike it when my questions go unanswered," she said. Her voice was calm, but she was angry. She had asked him a sincere question, and he had laughed at her.

"You need not scare a seaman so," Jocelyn said, gasping. "I thought I told you that I am not very good with horses."

"Meet me here tomorrow. Please?"

She looked both shy and defiant: there was a mulish cast to her mouth but a pink flush on her cheeks. Wind, exertion? An awareness of the impropriety of her request?

"Lady Catherine, I—"

"I am lame, you see," she burst out suddenly. "Perhaps you think that you alone are uncomfortable in the very proper circumstances of Bath society. But I was not brought up to participate in society at all. My father locked me away as best he could. So that I would not embarrass him. And because he hated me for not being a boy." She paused to take a breath, her chest heaving. "So I speak my mind. Perhaps I am too free. I beg your pardon if I offend. But you do not make an issue of my deformity. And I think you can tell me about the world. I want to learn. I want to think of other places – to be elsewhere in my mind."

She leant down, inched closer to him, grasped his shoulder with one hand. She tended, Jocelyn realised, to rely on touch to keep attention. It was the result of being unable to walk after people. Despite the muddy kid glove, he sensed the warmth in the pressure of her fingers.

"Surely," he said slowly, "surely you know that we should not meet in such circumstances. People—"

"Oh, bother people!" She sat upright again, twisted the reins viciously in her hands.

"Lady Catherine," he said, "I am but a sailor in His Majesty's Navy. I have no wish to disgrace you."

"I can handle myself," she said. There was a proud glint in her eye. "You can handle yourself when you are on your ship, I assume. Well, this is my ship." She gestured around them, toward Wansdyke. "I can handle my destiny. If you can handle yours."

Jocelyn bowed his head. "I cannot but admire your words, Lady Catherine."

"Will you be here? In the afternoon?"

"I would be most happy to attend you. Suppose it rains?"

"Do you think a little rain would stop me?"

Jocelyn shook his head, smiling. "No, I do not." He watched as she spoke to the horse, which began an amiable trot toward Wansdyke. "Lady Catherine!" He saw her half turn, slow the horse down. "I was very, very lucky at sea!"

He saw a huge smile cross her face, and her acknowledging wave. Cheerful, he turned back to his path, but he shivered and thrust his hands into his pockets anticipating the muddy scrambles that would take him back to the inn.

To go nowhere. Do nothing.

Had the warning come from Barrington?

It must have. But why? What did Barrington have to do with his hearing?

He didn't want to think about it. He preferred to think about the pink-and-white Lady Catherine. He was not worried about becoming attached to her. He could not see himself developing a serious attachment to any lady. It would simply not be fair.

But he did crave the freedom of spirit he had felt when he stood muddied head to toe in the brown earth of England. Perhaps it would be good for his spirits to spend time in the company of someone who laughed at him so easily.

Then, when the summons came, he could bravely head off to his fate.

CHAPTER 11

*C*atherine checked the angle of her hat in the mirror. "I do not suppose you would like to come along,"

"Not today," Lydia Barrow said. She examined the stitches in her embroidery, then pulled the needle through once more before biting off a thread. "You have spoilt two riding habits. It is very damp."

"Not for long. It will be summer soon."

"Does Captain Avebury not mind the damp?"

Catherine laughed. "Not at all. Yesterday he proved that he could pull a fish out of the stream with his bare hands. I believe he must be country-bred."

Lydia looked up at that. "Do you not know?"

Catherine paused. Then she picked up her gloves and turned around. "No," she admitted. "He tells me what it is like to be commanding a ship in a violent storm, and what it smells like in Bombay. I've heard all about the Chinamen and Malays who work on the ships, and their strange ways. And about the many wives of the Muslims. But not very much about the man." She began to pull on her gloves.

Lydia bent over her needlework again. "I could find out. If you would like."

Catherine pulled the fingers of her gloves taut. Lydia had made her offer in the barest murmur; she could pretend not to hear without appearing to be too rude. She knew that Lydia would make use of connections she would rather not know too much about. On the other hand, to know more about Captain Avebury ... It was extremely tempting. And it was always better to know.

"Yes," she said slowly. "Do that for me. Jocelyn Avebury. Royal Navy. He would have gone to sea as a child, I suppose. Quite young."

Lydia nodded and kept sewing. "There is that message, also. You really ought to respond."

"Do not remind me of that," Catherine said sharply. "The impertinence of that man! I refuse to speak to him. His demands are unreasonable."

"He still has the portrait."

"I will get it from him." Her voice was shaking; she swallowed. Her throat burned. She had been a fool – oh, she had been a fool indeed.

Lydia looked up, then stuck her needle into the cloth and rose. "That will be difficult."

"Everyone has a weakness. I'll find LaFrance's. Money, women, power – everyone has his Achilles heel. He will be sorry for trifling with me." Catherine took Lydia's arm and hobbled into the hallway. A footman held the door open as they emerged into the sunlight.

"I will see about the captain," Lydia said in a low voice. Catherine nodded. The groom held the gentle brown horse for her at the bottom of the steps. Lydia stopped her before she began her descent. "But do consider that message."

Catherine grimaced. "I will go to London myself to deal with LaFrance, if necessary. He will not defy me."

Lydia shrugged. She handed Catherine off into the hands of the groom and stepped back. With a brief nod, Catherine mounted, took the horse round and headed for the fields.

Captain Avebury was chasing sheep. Catherine slowed her mount to a walk, then stopped. Her eyes followed him as he ran round and round in circles; the sheep baa-ed, panicked. Still, he ran, hatless, his curly brown hair ruffling in the breeze. He looked as carefree as a boy. How old was Captain Avebury? Thirty? Somewhat more? Sometimes, she wondered if he was right in his mind. Yet he was possibly the most stable, the most collected person that she had ever known. She fancied that sea captains had to be solid and calm if they were to control a ship full of men out on the open sea. But here was this one, chasing sheep with the exuberance of a young boy.

Perhaps he had gone to sea as a lad and never had the chance to experience the carefree joys of a child in a field of sheep. Catherine shifted herself in the saddle and smiled wryly. Well, neither had she.

He saw her and slowed his run to a trot. He waved, coming toward her.

"You are chasing sheep, Captain Avebury?" She pretended to be shocked.

"Certainly. A great deal of fun. You can join me."

"You are dreadful," Catherine laughed. "You know very well that I cannot."

"Not on that big brute. Come, I'll help you."

"How ridiculous, Captain Avebury. Chasing sheep! Wherever did you come up with that idea?"

She turned and slid nimbly down from the saddle, whereupon the horse promptly bent its head to chomp on a juicy tuft of greenery. She placed her hands on one strong arm and leant comfortably against him in a position that they had worked out by mutual, silent agreement. He was easier to walk with than Melinda; he did not walk as slowly as she did, and he seemed far more solid and sure-footed. Leaning against Captain Avebury was like leaning against a comfortable old tree.

"Look, there's a crotchety old ram there. Perhaps if we chase him, he'll turn and chase us back." There was a glint of mischief in the blue-grey eyes, but Avebury picked up his pace. He was apparently not joking.

"Captain Avebury!" Catherine squeaked. "I do not want to be chased by a ram!"

She hobbled along, half-laughing, half-protesting. Almost by instinct, she slipped her hand into his, and he ran ahead, pulling her behind. To her surprise, she could run – she could run! It was more of a thumpity-thump gallop, to be sure. But it was passably smooth, and she could run! Like an excited child, she cried, "Look at me, Captain Avebury! Look at me!" Her hat flew off, but she had no interest in retrieving it. Thrilled, she let go of his hand and ran headway into a stupid-looking group of young sheep, causing them to scatter, making loud noises of annoyance.

Avebury slowed and turned, watching her thump across the field gleefully. "Careful!" he called, but too late.

She was going too fast to stop herself, and when the ground fell away slightly beneath her feet, she tumbled. Flailing, she went down hard, headfirst into the grass. For one humiliating moment, she lay there, tasting grass and grit in her mouth. The baa-ing of sheep grew louder and louder, until she sensed them gathered in a semi-circle about her.

Avebury was kneeling next to her, not in the least bit panicked, as Melinda would have been. "Lady Catherine, are you hurt?" It was his grave sea-captain voice, Catherine decided, the one he used to establish authority over a situation.

She smiled into the turf, then rolled over onto her back. She squinted into the bright sky, felt the damp of the grass seeping into her clothes, into her hair. She stretched out her arms, then held her gloved hands in front of her face. Grass stains on the pair, now.

"Oh, Captain Avebury," she said, closing her eyes. "That was splendid. It has been years and years since I have made the effort to run like that. I felt like the wind." The smile faded a bit, and she added softly, "I used to try to run when I was a very small girl. But my father saw me from a window, and then Nurse told me I had to stop, because he found it disgusting to watch." Her voice trailed off, the image of the green lawns of Albrook fresh in her mind.

"You know," Avebury began in a conversational tone.

Catherine opened her eyes. She shaded her brow with a hand.

"I would not lie on the grass. The sheep, you know." He sounded apologetic. With an appalled cry, Catherine started, trying to scramble to her feet.

"Oh, good gracious!" she exclaimed, wobbling as she tried to pull her bad leg out from under her. Avebury pulled her up with a strong hand. Frantically, she beat at her habit and tried to do the same with her hair, which only caused it to tumble down her back in a messy tangle. She looked about wildly, then saw Avebury's expression.

"Oh, you dreadful creature!" she cried. "You are teasing me!"

"It was far too tempting," Avebury admitted, avoiding Catherine's infuriated lunge toward him. "Was that blow meant for me? I will come and take my medicine, ma'am."

Meekly, he came forward.

Catherine pretended to swat his arm. "This is the proof I needed. You are a country-bred boy. I am right, am I not?"

"I'm afraid so, ma'am. A city boy would not have thought twice about lying on the grass in a field where sheep are grazing." His voice was grave, but she could see the laughter threatening in his eyes.

"Where are you from? The north?"

"I was born in the north. Yorkshire."

"You do not sound like you are from the north at all. Is your family from there?"

She was trying to put her hair back to rights, and failing miserably. It was useful not to be able to meet his eyes right at this moment. She detected a strained note in his voice.

"They were once. But we moved to London when I was just a little boy."

"I see." Catherine gave up trying to make herself tidy. "My hair will just have to do as it is. Where has my hat gone?" She pulled out a handkerchief and wiped grimly at her chin.

"Let me fetch it for you." Avebury strode across the field to retrieve the hat. He was so tall, so sturdy, so confident. But he was uncomfortable talking about his family. He had to be of good background, Catherine decided. The Navy wouldn't have advanced him otherwise, surely? Even if he had risen up through the ranks, beginning as a lowly ship's boy, they would have expected him to know how to behave in polite company.

A family in trade, perhaps? That was not such a disgrace. Sir Lyle had shipping and trading interests. There were worse places in which to invest one's money.

And I have the countenance to overcome any number of bad connections, she thought comfortably. *No one would dare speak ill of my husband.*

CHAPTER 12

*S*he started as she realised what she was thinking. Dumbly, she took the hat Avebury proffered. She stared blankly at her handkerchief, now adorned with mud and grass, all of it wiped from her chin and neck.

"Lady Catherine? Are you well?"

"Why – yes," she stammered. "Quite all right. Just … daydreaming." She put on her hat. "There. We can pretend my hair isn't a mess. Is there mud on my face still?"

Avebury bent to brush away something from close to one ear. "All gone."

"Thank you," Catherine said, her voice faint. She was disconcerted. This was all very strange. She was unaccustomed to feeling self-conscious in front of him. Even though she leant against him, grabbed his hand for support, let him help her up to and down from her mount – he was so casual, almost brotherly. She had never felt even slightly vulnerable. He did not frighten her the way that Sir Lyle did.

But would he marry her? Was he in the least bit interested?

She tried to glance at him from under her lashes, like a young girl at a ball, intent on flirting. She felt ridiculous, so she tilted her head to see him better. Avebury was looking at her, a slightly puzzled frown on his face. Then he looked away, across the fields, toward Wansdyke.

"Why do you live at Wansdyke?" he asked.

"Why? What do you mean?"

"Is it your father's property? Will you have to leave it when he is gone?"

It was the first time he had asked about her father, and his first acknowledgement of her father's condition. She hesitated before replying; she wanted to be honest, but she had never had to explain herself before. Everyone in Bath knew the story. Everyone in Bath pitied her, even while they envied and disliked her. No one had ever asked about her family in such a dispassionate way.

"It was my mother's property," she began. "It passed directly to her from her father. The Mansion Place apartment as well – she took the waters often when she was ill, before she died. I don't remember anything about it, of course. I was very, very small. I came to live at Wansdyke with my governess when I was ten. My father did not want to see me, you see."

"Does your father not have anything to say about how you live here?"

Catherine cast him an amused smile. "No. Even if he had, I would ignore him. Papa's only concern is that I keep up appearances – but he never could bring himself to care enough to come down to Wansdyke to scold me. He has always sent me a great deal of money – which, of course, I spent before asking for more – so I deal with his agent, most of the time." She laughed. "It upsets him that I choose to go out in society. He thinks it a disgrace that a deformed child like myself should have ball gowns made and attend functions as if I had had a proper coming out."

"It seems that you have a limited use for those niceties, Lady Catherine. Or am I mistaken?" Avebury turned his eyes away from the view of Wansdyke and back to her. She thought she glimpsed a faint tinge of envy; perhaps it was a trick of light. "Is the approval of the ton important to you at all?"

"Not very," Catherine began, but she stopped seeing something shadowy, something painful, flit across Avebury's face. "What is it?"

"I beg your pardon?"

"Something – you just thought of something."

"Not at all." He turned, hands in his pockets. "Will it rain, do you think?"

Bewildered, Catherine looked about. Little white clouds, puffy and light, were visible in the distance, but this was as clear a day as one could hope for at this time of year. She watched Avebury's retreating back as he headed in a leisurely fashion toward the sheep, kicking clods of earth out of the way as he went.

Something was wrong. She could feel it. What could it be? "Captain Avebury!" She hobbled along.

He turned around and waited for her to catch up.

"Have I said something wrong?" she asked, panting. She reached out to lean against his arm.

"Not at all, Lady Catherine." He smiled, but his eyes were blank.

"Does it bother you that we meet this way? Would you rather not? Do you think me dreadfully fast? Do I disgust you?"

That forced a laugh out of him. He shook his head. "So many questions!"

"I speak my mind," Catherine said. "Isn't that better than lying behind polite words?"

She saw the exact moment when his face froze. Her own voice echoed in her head. *Isn't that better than lying behind polite words?*

Avebury looked away. "You do not disgust me, Lady Catherine."

"Wait, Captain Avebury, please," Catherine begged. She pulled at his arm until he stopped beside her. Still, he avoided her eyes. He examined his boots, bent to flick off a blade of grass. "You are upset, Captain Avebury. Are we not friends? Will you not tell me what is on your mind?"

"Many things, Lady Catherine. Many complicated things that I cannot possibly explain in an afternoon." Avebury looked up from his boots. "But you are kind to be concerned."

"I am more than concerned!" Catherine protested. "I am—" She stopped herself. She was ... was what?

"I am your friend," she ended weakly.

"As I am yours." Avebury smiled down at her. "Come, let us walk before all this glorious sunshine is gone. And before your very dour Miss Barrow decides to come in search of you."

"Unlikely!" Catherine laughed, following along. She knew him better than to press too far.

"We need a picnic," Avebury said. "And a blanket for the grass."

"Next time. But it will be your responsibility. I can hardly carry a hamper when I ride. And I cannot convince Lydia to walk with me."

"Does she not scold you for riding out alone to meet an officer?"

"Not at all. It is scarcely a clandestine meeting when I do not hesitate to invite her to join us. I would like to introduce you to her. Why will you not come back with me to Wansdyke?"

Avebury shrugged. "I am very ill at ease in grand surroundings. I prefer to view Wansdyke from a distance."

"Well, one day you must come. It is a great deal less grand inside."

Avebury did not reply. Catherine glanced up at his profile. He was becoming very dear to her – but did he feel the same about her? She had gathered that his voyages had been extremely profitable so he had no reason to marry for money. Social status and prestige seemed not to matter to him. Could she convince him that a life with her might be ... interesting?

And he could return to sea, of course. He would be recalled to duty at some point, anyway. Perhaps she could go along. And she could surely find someone in the Admiralty who would see fit to make him an admiral. He could certainly take her along if he were an admiral. And if not – why, she could make do with an occasional visit. She had never expected to be married at all; she could continue to live alone while he was at sea, she imagined.

She knew why marrying her was advantageous to Sir Lyle; she could make it advantageous for Avebury, instead. No matter who her husband, her marriage would be one of convenience, after all. Both parties should have what they wanted. And, as long as she had an heir – as long as she could bear the next Earl St Clair, she would be happy.

She felt herself blushing a little at the thought.

But most of all, her heart sang, *I would be free, free of the limitations placed on unmarried ladies, and free to do anything, go anywhere, be anything I choose. I would have beaten Papa at his own sad game. I would not be a prisoner of this cursed leg. I would not be a prisoner of my sex. I would have the family and tradition that the Clavertons denied me. And I would be living proof that Papa was wrong. He would not love me. But I will have someone who will love me – my son. And I will love him, every inch of him, and never, never leave him!*

She hadn't needed that portrait after all. And now, she deeply regretted having it made. When she got her hands on it, she would burn it.

She would wait for Lydia to tell her what she could discover about the captain. Perhaps there would be a clue to his secret unhappiness.

"Captain Avebury," she said shyly. He looked inquiringly at her. She took a deep breath. "Tell me about … about India. What do the natives wear? And can you really smell the spices in the breeze?"

For a moment, a little wrinkle between his brows suggested incomprehension. Then his face – indeed, his whole body –

relaxed. Catherine felt him draw her closer, his pace slow, as peace suffused him.

"India …" he began. "Well, their most remarkable spice is the clove. And you can really smell it around the warehouses, if they are packing the cases and the wind is right …."

CHAPTER 13

"Sir Lyle is here to see you, Lady Catherine." Her butler's words stopped her in the hall. "He is waiting in the drawing room."

"Where is Miss Barrow?" she asked, continuing to strip off her grass-stained gloves.

"She has gone out, my lady."

Catherine almost groaned. This was highly inconvenient. "Send him my compliments, if you please, and tell him I regret—"

"I thought I heard your voice." The door leading from the drawing room opened, and Sir Lyle emerged into the hall. He dismissed the butler with a nod.

"Good afternoon, Sir Lyle," Catherine said. "I have just come back from a ride. Would you mind waiting a little longer, while I change?"

"That must have been some ride," Sir Lyle said, looking amused. "Did you fall?"

Catherine glanced down at the stains on her clothes. "No," she said coldly. "But it was very muddy. I beg your pardon, I really must change. I will have tea sent in directly."

Sir Lyle bowed slightly, and retreated.

~

WHEN CATHERINE RETURNED, SHE FOUND SIR LYLE ENGROSSED IN a volume of poetry that she had left open on a table next to her usual chair. He sprang up as she entered, and came to offer his arm. After she had settled into her chair, he stepped back, but remained standing.

Catherine opened her mouth to ask him what brought him out to Wansdyke, but she stopped herself just in time. She said instead, "It is good to see you, Sir Lyle. I thought you would visit me sooner."

"You disappeared from Mansion Place quite abruptly. But I can quite see why. It is indeed beautiful here."

Catherine inclined her head. "At this time of year, it is hard to be elsewhere," she admitted.

"I would certainly not want to be elsewhere."

Her eyes flashed to his. He was watching her, his expression bland. She looked away.

"It is inconvenient that Miss Barrow is not here at the moment," she said, ignoring his comment. "I'm afraid I cannot ask you to stay for long without her presence. I don't receive many visitors here, and I did not expect—"

To her surprise, he burst out laughing. It was a warm, pleasant sound.

"Now, now, my dear Lady Catherine! You cannot expect me to believe that you care for such things. You live as you please, do as you please, think as you please – do you not?"

"Why, whatever do you mean?" Catherine felt her cheeks growing warm. "I do not normally entertain gentlemen without Miss Barrow present."

"Forgive me," Sir Lyle said. "I did not mean to embarrass you. But you are not one for maidenly blushes, I hope?"

"That would depend," Catherine said, feeling her temper rise. "Are you here to provoke me? I fear I am as sensitive as any

86

female, and my feelings are as easily wounded. At what do you think I would not blush?"

"Please accept my apologies, Lady Catherine." Sir Lyle made his way over to her. She looked up at him. He was very tall, perhaps even as tall as Captain Avebury. But how different he was in looks – so very blond, rugged: handsome in a very masculine sense. "I am boorish, insensitive." He knelt beside her and took her hand. "I am here because I want to be with you."

Catherine felt her pulse quicken. She inclined her head mutely.

"I admire you very much, Lady Catherine. You are a woman of great beauty and sensibility."

"And lame, Sir Lyle. Do not forget lame." Her voice was bitter.

"Not important," he said smoothly. "Why should that matter? How has it affected our friendship?" He kissed her hand, a long, lingering kiss. Gently, he turned her hand over, and pressed his lips into her palm.

"You … you do not really want to marry me," Catherine said. She cleared her throat. His lips were nibbling softly at the fleshy part of her palm, at the base of her thumb.

"Really?" he murmured. His lips travelled to her wrist.

"You just want the title," she continued. She closed her eyes, tried to concentrate. He was stroking the inside of her elbow. "For business reasons. Even I have some pride, Sir Lyle. Why should I marry someone who only wants me for my—"

Sir Lyle lifted his head. "Fie, Catherine," he said gently. "Do you really think that only your title matters to me?" She opened her eyes.

His face was very close. A bead of sweat trickled down the back of her neck. But she did not allow her gaze to waver.

He sat back slightly. "You are afraid of me."

"What?" Catherine tried to laugh. "That is ridiculous."

"Have you … heard something?"

"About you? Nothing."

"Nothing?" He cocked his head. "Can that be so?"

"It is indeed. Why should I have heard anything?"

"There are those who despise me."

"That is true of all men."

"Ah. You are very wise." His face softened. He looked away, toward the French doors leading out to the gardens. "We are alike, you know. You and I. We are both passionate souls."

"You have been reading novels, Sir Lyle." Catherine tried to laugh.

"I read that in your poetry book. I thought that you would like it." He smiled at her. "You are tempted. Admit that much. Give me hope."

"Tempted? By you?"

"By love."

"What of love?" Catherine objected. "Who is speaking of love?"

His grip suddenly tightened. He leant closer. She stiffened. "You forget yourself, sir," she said hoarsely, before he kissed her.

The closeness, the cloying heaviness of it – she could feel every inch of herself through the warm pressure on her lips. She wondered fleetingly if she smelled of grass and mud and sheep. Sir Lyle smelled of tea and something she did not recognise, something heavy and heady and strong, like horses or ale.

He was gentle, but she could feel the power behind the gentleness. She realised dimly that she was indeed afraid. She knew nothing of him, really. Dared she marry him merely to have what she wanted? Would someone like Sir Lyle allow her to live the way she wanted? Would he seek to control her, as her father had?

She thought of Captain Avebury, amiably chasing sheep. Saw an image of him on the deck of his ship, drenched and shouting orders. He, too, was a man. Would he be any better?

Sir Lyle was whispering against her lips. "I can promise you happiness," he murmured. "I will honour you for a lifetime."

She could marry Sir Lyle – and take the risk that he would try to own her.

Would Avebury marry her? Assuming that he would was, in itself, a risk. What if he had no interest in marrying a crippled countess?

But she was not afraid of Avebury. She was sure that she knew him, sure he was gentle and decent and would not try to own her.

Catherine drew back. She pulled her hands free and smoothed her hair with shaking hands. "I have said I will consider your offer," she said, trying to sound calm.

Sir Lyle rose, then leant forward and dropped a kiss on her forehead. "It is all I ask," he said, his voice bland and pleasant. "May I call again?"

"Certainly," Catherine replied.

Sir Lyle bowed. "Good afternoon, Lady Catherine."

"Good afternoon."

She listened to the tapping sound of his heels on the marble hallway. They faded, followed by the sound of a door shutting.

She breathed a sigh of relief. Her hands were shaky.

It seemed dangerous to play with Sir Lyle. But if his affections were not engaged – if he was interested only in her title …

Captain Avebury had never made the smallest advance toward her. Could she persuade him to marry a crippled countess and give her an heir?

CHAPTER 14

Sir Lyle visited almost daily. Catherine would return from her walk with Captain Avebury to find him reading through her poetry books and waiting for her. He never asked about her rides; she did not offer any information.

Catherine thought the two men so different to each other she was sure they would not get along. Sir Lyle was confident, yet cynical. Captain Avebury was sweet and without pretension. But the shadows lurking in the captain's eyes made her suspect that Sir Lyle's brand of cynicism would not appeal to him. She looked forward to her outings with Captain Avebury; they made her feel like a girl returning to a childhood she had never had. She trusted him implicitly. He taught her about a world she had never thought she would see. He made her laugh and had absolutely no interest in either her family or her twisted leg. Sir Lyle, however …

"We must stop," Catherine said, gasping, struggling to sit upright. Despite the early summer sun, the stone bench in the shade of the shrubbery was cold. In the distance, sheep bleated, the shears of pruning gardeners clip-clipped.

"I beg your pardon, Lady Catherine." Sir Lyle sprang up from the seat. He walked a few feet away, adjusting his cravat as he went, and feigned great interest in the puffy white cloud of sheep, down in the faraway fields.

Catherine rearranged her lace fichu. "I am sorry," she said into the awkward silence.

"You should not be," Sir Lyle replied. He stretched, then glanced at her over his shoulder. He grinned. "This is what comes of my eagerness to please."

Catherine said nothing. She twisted her hands in her lap.

Sir Lyle turned back to his view. "I know that your father's condition makes it impossible for you to consider my offer properly at the current time. But I wish ... I wish—"

"Say no more," Catherine begged. She put a hand on her chest, grasping the fichu tightly, as if to prevent further incursions.

"If you only knew the depth of my affections, Lady Catherine." Sir Lyle returned to the bench, knelt in the grass before her. He took the hand that lay limply in her lap and kissed it fervently.

Catherine tried to laugh. "You would not like me so much if you really knew me, Sir Lyle. I can be stubborn, wilful, hot-tempered—"

"All of those are fine qualities for a lady of quality, Lady Catherine," Sir Lyle murmured against her palm. She felt her heart begin to race. Her hold on the fichu went limp.

"Oh, Sir Lyle. It is very complicated. I like you very well. But—"

"Is it because of your father, Catherine? Is it because he is ill?" Sir Lyle put her hand down gently in her lap and reached for the other. He disengaged it gently from the fichu. "You are a lady who knows her own mind. Surely you feel comfortable making such a decision on your own?"

She was tempted to lie. It would be a convenient thing, a lie. She could say that she feared the judgement of society, that she feared the ugly rumours that might start if she were known to have made such a decision for herself.

It was absurd, of course. Sir Lyle was no fool.

"Is this all that I am good for, Catherine?" Sir Lyle leant forward. Catherine closed her eyes. "You would have me make love to you, but you would not marry me? How have I failed you?"

"You have not failed me," Catherine whispered. *I am in love with a ship's captain, but I do not know if he loves me. I am in love with a ship's captain, but I do not know if he possesses enough consequence to be the father of an earl. I have had a scandalous portrait painted, and you will kill me, and the artist, if it ever comes to light. God forbid that ever comes to pass!*

"Then you are afraid of me." Sir Lyle traced a finger over her lips. Catherine opened her eyes. He was watching her intently.

"Yes," she said. "Yes, I am afraid indeed."

"Afraid of what?"

She thought of the portrait. But what she said was, "That you will own me."

Sir Lyle looked incredulous for a moment. Then he laughed and raised himself to sit beside her on the bench. "Own you, Lady Catherine?"

Catherine looked away. She disliked his mocking tone.

"You are perhaps the most independent female I have ever met. I can scarcely imagine how I would contrive to 'own' you, Lady Catherine."

She said nothing. A little breeze that ruffled wisps of escaped hair along her temples brought with it the smell of hot grass. It was different, that smell of clean fresh hay. Different to the fecund smell of wet earth that had persisted throughout spring. Ah, summer ….

I don't wish to be owned. The words had ambled idly through her brain but hardened some corner of her heart nonetheless.

She would take her chances with love. Her position was good

enough to withstand the gossip that would come should Avebury have no status. Perhaps his people were farmers or tradesmen. No matter. Sir Lyle probably had more consequence, and would certainly be a less questionable choice as father for her child, but she wanted Avebury. She wanted him to father her son. For a while she had thought Sir Lyle's suit would win out, but now she knew this could never be.

She turned to the unsuspecting peer, who sat with her hand still limp in his lap. "Sir Lyle," she said, her voice suddenly grown hoarse. "I am sorry. I don't wish to marry you."

He was silent for a long time. Then he raised his head. "Is there no hope?"

"I am sorry."

Again the silence. The clip-clip noises had ceased; possibly the gardeners were having their tea.

"You will think me dreadfully impertinent," Catherine ventured. "But I wish to keep you as ... as a friend. We have known each other for such a long time."

"A friend, Lady Catherine?" Sir Lyle grinned. "What sort of friend would I make?"

Catherine attempted to pull her hand from his grasp, but he suddenly tightened his grip. She tried to sound firm but the result was an awkward stammer. "A-a g-good friend."

"A good friend?" He shook his head. "You are too beautiful, too desirable, Lady Catherine. It will be hard to be friends."

"Sir Lyle," Catherine breathed. "Please, stop." He was lifting her hand to his lips, kissing the inside of her palm and wrist, something he knew she liked. His eyes met hers.

"Have no men told you how beautiful you are, my dear Catherine?" He put her hand down. "Perhaps this will help." He leant close, tilted her chin in his hand. But when he bent to kiss her, she sensed the danger, the vast darkness just beyond the kiss. He parted her lips, tasted her mouth, demanded her compliance. When she tried to back away, he caught her against him, one hand against her back, the other running a finger along the edge of her bodice. She felt the fichu slip away behind her neck, his fingers reaching past the skin, burning a trail on the tender skin of her breast.

This is not a game, she thought wildly. *First that damned portrait, and now Sir Lyle! A man's feelings are not to be trifled with. Oh, Catherine, you are a fool!*

She wrenched herself away, gasping.

Sir Lyle sat back, breathing equally hard. They stared at each other. Then he smiled grimly. He rose. "Good friends, Lady Catherine?"

Catherine fumbled about the seat for the fichu, but it had gone. She pressed a palm to her chest, still panting, and tried to look dignified. "Good friends, Sir Lyle," she said.

He gave a courtly bow and strode away.

CHAPTER 15

I am a fool, Jocelyn thought as he stared over to Wansdyke, the great house resting peacefully in its grounds. He urged his mount on, but the blasted horse could tell that a seaman was astride and refused to listen. Jocelyn was tempted to hit it, but decided that it was probably not the thing to do. The horse was bigger and stronger, and would win an altercation. A belt around the ear would sometimes work on a drunken cook. But not on a brute like this.

He circled the horse around until it had danced and neighed to its heart's content. Then he tried to use his knees to tell it who was in charge. Grumpily, the animal loped off toward the great house.

When they were yet some distance away, the horse found something interesting to look at. It stopped, refused to budge. Jocelyn sighed and slid down to his feet. He had no interest in arguing with a horse. He was not much given to arguing in general, and particularly not with horses.

I must be in love, he thought wearily. *The things I do to please Lady Catherine!*

But, of course, he knew his thoughts were not serious. He was in perfect control of his faculties. Falling in love with Lady Catherine was simply not an option.

A groom was leading a fine-looking chestnut from behind the house. He paused to call over to Jocelyn. Jocelyn waved a casual response, tried to look as if he knew what he was doing.

"Vicious brute," he muttered. He kicked the ground under the horse's head. Amazingly, the animal began to walk calmly along. After a shocked moment, Jocelyn grabbed the reins, and guided him gently in the direction of the house.

"Need help, sir?" The groom nodded at him.

"Thank you," Jocelyn began. His voice died away as the front door opened to reveal a figure he recognised.

Barrington made his way down the steps and glanced in the direction of the groom, his eyes fastening on first the chestnut, and then on Jocelyn.

Jocelyn stiffened. Barrington nodded toward the groom. "I'll take him," he said in a low tone. The groom obliged, then took Jocelyn's grey. The horse followed docilely.

"You are here to see Lady Catherine?" Barrington made no move to mount the fine chestnut beast, who was nuzzling him with obvious affection.

Jocelyn gazed with envy as Barrington murmured something to the horse and patted its nose. Was this a talent he would never acquire?

"You seem to like my horse," Barrington said, when Jocelyn did not reply.

"Horses do not like me, I'm afraid," Jocelyn replied dryly. He made an awkward move to pat the animal, then dropped his arm. He backed away slightly, relieved to open space between them.

"Ah! Suddenly I am enlightened. You are Lady Catherine's mystery man."

"I beg your pardon?" Jocelyn was startled. Barrington's face was inscrutable, enigmatic but there was a tightening, an electric heightening of the atmosphere. The sensation of a storm about to happen, a fight about to explode between two men who despised each other. A dark alleyway, a quick knife. A howling mob. That quick switch from laughter to rage.

"Lady Catherine returns from her daily rides covered in mud and grass." Barrington cocked an amused eye at Jocelyn. "I do not think much riding takes place, however."

"What do you mean?" Jocelyn said. He did not raise his voice, but he knew that Barrington wanted to goad him. Curiously, he felt a small twinge of something in the pit of his stomach. Was this something of the violence that men felt when taunted by other men? It was an alien feeling.

"Accept my apologies. I did not mean to be … crass." Barrington stroked his horse, the motions smooth and languid. Jocelyn was not fooled. He could see the control each long movement was taking. Something had happened to shake Barrington's composure. Presumably something to do with Lady Catherine.

"If you are planning to see Lady Catherine, you will have to wait. Her friend, Miss Barrow, seemed eager to have a word with her."

Jocelyn shrugged. He turned away. The front door seemed to be miles away from where they stood, on the path to the stables. Grimacing, he started to walk. *This is the last time I try to make the trip to Wansdyke on a damned stupid horse,* he thought sourly.

"Have you heard anything yet? From the Admiralty?"

Jocelyn's pace slowed. He did not bother to turn around, but shook his head slightly. "Did you send that note to me?" He tossed the words carelessly over his shoulder.

"I was afraid you would leave town. It would be far better if you did not."

Jocelyn tramped along the carriage drive in silence. Then he heard a cackle, a throaty gurgle. He turned, pausing his steps.

Barrington stood, shaking his head, shoulders quivering with mirthful laughter.

"Are you feeling quite well?" Jocelyn asked tentatively. If Barrington were crazy—

"Marry her!" Barrington shouted. He doubled over, the force of his laughter making him lose his breath. He coughed and spat, then coughed again.

Jocelyn wondered if he ought to assist. But Barrington sensed his concern, held up a hand as he coughed and wheezed. "Marry her, dear boy," he choked out. "What a clever fellow you are! She will take care of you better than a foolish idiot like I could."

"I do not know of what you speak," Jocelyn said, his indignation rising. "Lady Catherine—"

"You, Captain Avebury, would be a fool, and an absolute fool at that, if you did not take advantage of this opportunity to save yourself." Barrington stopped hacking and wheezing. Delicately, he produced a handkerchief and wiped his mouth. He eyed Jocelyn with mild surprise. "Do you mean that you do not understand me?"

Jocelyn, to his annoyance, felt his colour rise. He looked away, feigning impatience, then down at his shoes.

"Ah. You do understand me after all," Barrington said shrewdly. He walked the horse a little closer to where Jocelyn stood. "Listen to me, Captain Avebury. Listen well. Marry Lady Catherine, and you could very well be out of trouble and at sea within the month."

Jocelyn's eyes darted to Barrington. "No," he muttered.

"Yes," Barrington nodded. "You seem to have only the dimmest understanding of what an earldom is. Her father sat in the House of Lords. He has hundreds of highly placed friends. And Lady Catherine ..." Here he paused. His eyes narrowed. Then, with a quick move, he swung onto his mount. His steed seemed energised by the load, neighing and tossing its head. Barrington controlled him swiftly with one hand.

Jocelyn glared resentfully. There was a grace, a beauty to his movements that he could never hope to attain.

"Lady Catherine will marry you, sailor." Barrington raised a hand in salute. "She has her own ... needs. Her own life to live. Allow her that, and she will marry you." He whirled the horse around and took off at a trot.

But before Jocelyn could take his eyes from the erect figure on horseback, Barrington brought his horse up sharply and turned.

"Don't fall in love with her, Captain Avebury!" he shouted. "You will be sorry!" He turned back and left at a canter.

CHAPTER 16

"*W*hat have you discovered?" In the drawing room, Catherine pressed Lydia for news.

"A distant cousin helped him into the navy. He was at sea by the time he was twelve. Midshipman, lieutenant fairly quickly. Very bright, good at his books. And well-liked. Not a bad word about him."

Catherine sat back in her seat. She didn't know what she had been so afraid of hearing about Captain Avebury. His history sounded like a perfectly ordinary success story. A hard-working young man of no particular background makes his way in the world. Yes. She'd heard of such things happening, especially in the navy.

"Family?"

Lydia frowned slightly. "That's somewhat unclear. It seems that he came from Yorkshire and moved several times to addresses in and about London. His parents appear to be dead. He spent several years with a family by the name of Bowles. Henry Bowles is an attorney at law; he is widely respected and now very old."

"Perhaps he meant to be a clerk to Mr Bowles?"

"Possibly so."

"Is he a relation?"

Lydia shook her head. "Perhaps. If so, it must be quite a distant connection, because no one knows. And it has been years since anyone has seen the captain."

"Aren't there any Avebury relations about?"

"Not one. Not one that I could locate, at any rate."

"I see." Catherine shifted slightly in her seat, trying to avoid a spot lit by the sun that penetrated the curtains. She felt naked without the lace fichu that was still lying under the stone bench out in the shrubbery. This was a London-made dress, too revealing for Bath.

"There is something not quite right," Lydia murmured, almost to herself. Catherine looked back at her.

"Indeed? In what manner?"

"I don't know. I may be wrong. Perhaps he is merely an orphan with no direct relatives."

"You feel something is wrong." Catherine tensed herself. She knew better than to mistrust Lydia's sense of the not-quite-right.

Lydia did not reply. She removed her hat, examined its slightly shabby feather. "There was an incident and there is an inquiry. There are those who say absolutely that it will do no harm to Captain Avebury's career; he has the respect of his admiral and of commanders who were once lieutenants under his supervision. He is so well-liked that it is difficult to find anyone who would speak against him."

"What kind of incident?"

"A missed communication. It is difficult to discern the situation, because much of the matter is confidential." Lydia replaced her hat. She looked at Catherine, then smiled. "You must be in love."

"I? In love?" Catherine laughed. "You know me better, Lydia."

Lydia shrugged. "Perhaps." She grew serious again. "Captain Avebury was late for a rendezvous at sea, and as a result, certain messages were not delivered. This led to the deaths of several of our spies in France. Highly placed spies, upon whom we relied for information."

"And how is Captain Avebury responsible for this missed communication?"

"This is the problem. He accepted the responsibility without comment. His lieutenant, however, accused him of wilfully remaining in port in order to accept a cargo of opium."

"Opium?"

"Not for his personal use. His lieutenant claims that Captain Avebury supplies opium to officers throughout the navy."

"Oh, that's absurd!" Catherine began to laugh.

"Captain Avebury is very rich. Wealthier than you realise."

Catherine's laughter faded. "You don't mean—"

"That is exactly what I mean."

"That is truly absurd."

Lydia raised her hands, shrugged. "I only tell you what I hear."

"What of the lieutenant?"

"Awaiting court martial. He had no sooner accused the captain when he mysteriously became involved in a brawl aboard ship. He killed a man."

"No!"

"He claims that the captain organised it to get rid of him – he will almost certainly be executed for his role in the brawl." Lydia paused. "Captain Avebury has no other enemies that I have been able to discover. He has something of a following and is so admired that even the lowliest crewmen have aught to say against him. But, unfortunately, his lieutenant hit a nerve when he accused Captain Avebury of remaining in port in order to enrich himself. Captain Avebury is well known to be a wealthy man. People whisper when money is tainted."

"And, thus, an investigation."

Lydia nodded. "Nothing may come of it. But the lieutenant has sworn to prove his case against the captain."

A knock sounded. Catherine motioned to Lydia, who went to open the door.

"Captain Avebury," the butler intoned, stepping back into the hall.

"Good afternoon," Avebury said. He looked around the room, until his eyes found Catherine. She sat nervously, clutching the neck of her bodice.

"Was this a bad hour to call?"

"Not at all," Lydia replied immediately, holding out her hand. "I am pleased to meet you. I am Miss Barrow. Forgive me, I have just been out, and need to change my dress. Excuse me, Lady Catherine." With a small smile, she left the room, shutting the door firmly behind her.

"You appear to be unwell," Avebury said to Catherine. "Should I return at another time?"

"Certainly not," Catherine said, trying to sound cheerful. "I have such a terrible time trying to convince you to visit at all that I am not going to chase you away now. Do have a seat."

"Thank you very much." Avebury sat down in a stiff-backed chair. He surveyed his surroundings once again. "A very nice room. Very nice indeed."

"Stop it," Catherine said crossly. "This is not a museum. This is my home. Do you hate it? If so, please take the opportunity to say so. Do not hold back."

"Something is wrong," Avebury said, rising once more. "I have intruded upon something. Something between you and Miss Barrow, perhaps? She is younger and more pleasant than I expected from your stories. I had imagined her with a wart on her nose, blackened teeth—"

"You odious man!" Catherine said, laughing. "Stop it at once! She may be outside, listening."

"Ah, that sort, is she? Then I direct this comment to you, Miss Barrow! The sort of despicable person who would listen in on other people's conversations—" He leapt forward, wrenched open the door. A startled maid nearly dropped a tray of tea and cakes.

"Lord, sir!" she squeaked.

"I am so sorry," Avebury said, taking the tray. "You should lie down for half an hour. Get over the fright, you know." He shut the door in her face.

Catherine clapped a hand over her mouth.

"It's too late," Avebury said. He brought the tray over and set it down. "Poor girl. She's heard you laughing at her, and now she's completely undone. She'll need a draught from the apothecary before the night is through."

"You are a positively dreadful man!" Catherine hiccoughed. She wiped her eyes with a handkerchief. "Let me pour the tea."

"On no account," Avebury said. He reached for a cup. "Sailors are quite good at this sort of thing." He looked up at her. "I will leave, if this is not a good time."

Catherine shook her head. "Please do not. No one makes me laugh the way you do, Captain Avebury."

"Then something is wrong after all."

"No, no. Nothing at all. I am tired and cross and exasperated. Nothing more than that. I am pleased you are here. What made you finally come to see me?"

Captain Avebury was stirring her tea. She reached over to poke his elbow gently. "You didn't ask about sugar."

"And that is because I put in two spoonsful. That is how many you ought to have."

"Impertinent." Catherine sniffed, but accepted the cup. "You didn't answer."

"You didn't let me. You were talking about sugar."

"Well, then? Why are you here?"

"I was invited. By the lady of the house. So I came. I am rather proud of my manners. You needn't think that a naval officer is as rough as a common sailor. We do know how to behave, you know."

Catherine smiled at him over the rim of her cup. "I do know. Never think I do not."

"Thank you." Avebury bowed slightly. He nodded toward a shelf of small porcelain jars. "Are any of those treasures things that I should know about?"

Catherine followed his glance. "Some of them. Do you like art?"

"Not in the least."

"There is a splendid vase in that corner...."

"I'm afraid not."

"Books?"

"Occasionally. But only to read. Not to admire."

Catherine pretended to heave a sigh of disapproval. "You are really a hopeless case, Captain Avebury. Is there nothing you admire?"

It must have been coincidental, the way that his eyes turned to her and lingered. For a moment, she imagined that the gentle humour in the stormy blue eyes said something – something that language could not possibly convey. Something, she realised with a knot in her stomach, she desperately wanted to hear from him.

A hot flush rose to her cheeks and she turned away. "Shame on you, Captain Avebury," she said, her voice shaking. "Do not mock me, please." To her embarrassment, she felt her eyes fill.

"Lady Catherine, I know something is wrong." Avebury put down his cup.

"Nothing is wrong," Catherine said, sniffling. "I am just very tired."

"Then I will leave at once." But, as Avebury spoke, a loud knock sounded. Lydia burst into the room.

"I beg your pardon," she said and turned to Catherine. "Lady Catherine, you are wanted at Albrook at once."

Catherine rose. "My father?"

"Yes. I will pack for you. Shall I come with you?"

"No – no, thank you, Lydia. Clara will do. Tell her to expect a stay of a fortnight. And to bring her black dress."

Lydia nodded and withdrew.

Avebury cleared his throat. "I will excuse myself to allow you to get ready for your journey."

Catherine took a deep breath. She sat back down in her chair. "Captain Avebury. Please. Wait."

Avebury bowed. "I am at your service, as I hope you know."

Catherine tried to smile, but the corners of her mouth felt stiff. "Will you sit next to me?" She patted the chair next to her. "I have something I wish to say to you."

Avebury looked at her for a long moment. She felt his gaze scrutinise her face, gauging her mood, trying to ferret out her purpose. Oh, he knew her so well, he did. All because of those ridiculous long walks when she behaved in ways outrageously at odds with the decorum she tried to maintain in public. Was that person the real Catherine Claverton, or was she merely an actress who enjoyed playing the role of a female with two good legs? Could Avebury possibly understand the reasoning of the woman who owned Wansdyke and meant to bear the next Earl St Clair?

"Please," she said again, patting the chair. Avebury came forward but, instead of sitting in the chair, remained standing.

"I promise I will visit again, if that concern is what keeps you. Don't waste another moment with me, Lady Catherine—"

"Let me speak, please, Captain Avebury," Catherine interrupted. "I've got so little time before they come to fetch me. You would oblige me very much by sitting down. I have no wish to raise my voice."

Avebury sat.

Catherine turned her head away. She needed to focus on something – anything – to keep her purpose in mind. If she looked at him, she would think of the summer breeze and the ubiquitous farm animals, and then she would be unable to concentrate on saying what was in her mind. She finally settled her gaze on a crystal fruit bowl she could see on a table beyond Avebury's left shoulder.

"I do not have the time, unfortunately, to say as much as I would like." Her voice sounded amazingly smooth to her ears, calm and cool. "But there will be a lot of time later – if need be. Right now, I need to ask you a favour. As a friend."

"Of course, Lady Catherine. Anything at all," Avebury replied. His voice was equally cool.

"Do you know about my father, Captain Avebury?"

Avebury's gaze did not falter. "A little. He is ill, and not expected to live, I collect."

"I have told you that he sent me away when I was a child."

Avebury's expression did not change. "Yes."

Catherine weighed her words carefully. "Will you understand if I say that it is very important to me that I marry before my father dies? He may regain consciousness. And if he does, I would like him to see me a married woman. Not the crippled girl he wanted to throw away."

Avebury sat, impassive.

Please do not despise me, she thought.

An eternity ticked by. She took her eyes away from the fruit bowl and looked at him. His expression was grim. Her heart sank.

"Why do you feel a need to tell me this, Lady Catherine? I could not possibly find fault with your logic."

Catherine was taken aback. Did this mean that he did understand?

"Well," she said. "Well, I—"

"You do not have to defend your actions to me. What you and Barrington decide to do is none of my—"

"I beg your pardon!" Catherine exclaimed. "What has Sir Lyle got to do with any of this?"

For an unguarded moment, she saw the bewilderment in his

eyes. Then he shifted in his chair and looked away, breaking the connection.

"I saw him outside. Barrington, I mean."

"This is not about Sir Lyle." Catherine's voice shook. An image flashed before her – the lace fichu, floating to the ground. Mud ground into its dainty trim. "This has nothing to do with him. Nothing at all. This is about me. And you."

At this, Avebury's head shot up. He blinked. A wary look replaced his prior confusion.

"Would you … would you consider marrying me, Captain Avebury?"

CHAPTER 17

*H*e had seen it in her eyes. He knew he had. That nervous flicker. She was either hiding something, or she was so complicated, had so many hidden levels, that there really was no core to her – merely onion-skin layer after onion-skin layer.

He had seen it at the mention of Barrington. How the devil was he involved? Avebury could not imagine that Barrington had hatched this scheme with Lady Catherine in order to save him and send him back to sea. It was ridiculous – and Barrington, for all his sneaky demeanour, appeared to be a gentleman, indeed, was a gentleman if he heard her correctly. It would be grossly improper for him to counsel her on marriage—

Unless, of course, she loved Barrington but, for some reason, could not marry him. But what might such a reason be?

Not my concern, he thought. *I am not in competition for Lady Catherine's hand. If he wishes to marry her, he ought to do so. He will have my blessing.*

Do not fool yourself, hissed his inner mind. *You would not spend so many hours with a woman you did not admire.*

All right, he argued back. *Very well, I do admire her. But one can admire from a distance. Love can be chaste.*

Love?

Catherine cleared her throat. Startled, he looked at her. He had forgotten she was there.

"I am deeply embarrassed," she said in a low voice. But her eyes held firm. "Forgive me for being so indelicate. But there is no time."

"Lady Catherine, I must say that I do not understand. This is so sudden." Avebury found his voice. "Will your father's people not find it odd? And, forgive me, I am just an officer of His Majesty's Navy. My sort do not typically marry the daughter of an earl."

"Or one who holds an earldom in her own right?" Catherine leant forward, her entire body tense. "I want to continue the St Clair line, Captain Avebury. Which I cannot do unless I marry. I want very much to keep my mother's legacy alive."

"You mean to say that not marrying would mean the extinction of the line? Of your mother's family?"

"Yes." Catherine lowered her gaze. "My father has hated me my entire life for causing the extinction of the Delamare earldom. He holds me directly responsible, even though I could not help being born a female. You can understand that I do not wish to be responsible for the end of another family."

"Those words are too strong, my lady."

"Ah, but they are true. They sting, but they are true." Catherine paused. "Captain Avebury, the future means a great deal to me." Then, colouring a little, she said, "I want very much to have a child. A child who would be the next earl. Then I could be content. You need not think that I would keep you in England – I would be your most ardent supporter, should you wish to continue in your naval career. I could even help you, perhaps – there are people that I could call on, people with whom I could—"

"You have heard, then? About my trouble." He interrupted her. "You know what happened in Gibraltar."

Catherine raised her gaze to his, her blue eyes wide and unintimidated. "Yes."

"You know I am in disgrace."

"I would dispute that, Captain Avebury. You are so well-liked, it is hard to find anyone who would say so."

Jocelyn gave a short, harsh laugh. "The Navy has been my whole life, Lady Catherine. It owns me. It is hard to contemplate sharing my soul with anyone else. Did you discover that in your investigations of me?"

"I beg your pardon, I have no wish to offend. You are my friend, a very dear friend. And you would never say aught about yourself. I would not have gone behind your back had you yourself told me the facts of the matter." Catherine was beginning to sound angry. "I trust you, Captain Avebury. I have no reason to believe anything is other than you tell me."

For a moment, Jocelyn stared at her. Then he turned away. He rose, went to pour another cup of tea. He stirred it distractedly, neglecting to add sugar. He put down the spoon but made no move to pick up the cup.

Was this to be merely a civil arrangement? If it were, she would break his heart. He did not know if he could bear to take her in his arms knowing she was indifferent. Yet, were he to refuse, another man would enter the picture. There would be another man to father her son. And she could offer him a great deal. Sir Lyle had told him so, and Jocelyn knew it was true.

"You know nothing about me, Lady Catherine. I might be a rogue, a dishonest knave. Perhaps your life itself would be in grave danger were you to marry me. Would you give your son a father such as I?"

Catherine rose. She leant heavily on the arm of her chair. "Captain Avebury, you are my friend. Everyone else has no use for me and, therefore, no desire to know me. A man such as you could not possibly be dishonest or evil." Her voice shook a little. "I would trust you with my life, Captain Avebury."

"Lovely words, Lady Catherine. Lovely words indeed. But what if your trust is misplaced?"

Catherine lifted her chin. "Then I will suffer the consequences."

Jocelyn shook his head. "You have an impressive degree of courage. Far more than I possess, I fear."

"Please, Captain Avebury. Do not insult me. Please." Catherine began to make her way over to where Jocelyn stood beside the tea tray but stumbled and fell heavily against a small table. Taking a monumental leap, Jocelyn managed to prevent it, and the vase that graced it, from toppling. He offered his hand to Catherine, who had grabbed hold of a chair. She looked at it, then up at Jocelyn.

"Will you not join me on my journey through life?" she asked simply. "I am alone. As are you. Perhaps together we may find something of the life that others talk about, the life girls such as I only dream of. We are friends. There is trust, liking, between us." She took his hand, held it tightly in her own.

Jocelyn felt the moist warmth of her palm against his. He looked at their hands, hers small and slender in his large, work-scarred grasp. She had no idea, he realised, of how beautiful she was, of how much a small gesture such as this could make a man's head swim. He looked at her face, so desperately trusting and hopeful. She was a fool to trust the likes of him. There were secrets that she did not know – that no one knew – would she still trust him if she knew he was not who he claimed to be? That the name she sought to take as her own was not even his? And a child? He did not feel ready to think about bringing an innocent babe into the world under a false name.

But he was alone, it was true. And the thought of a woman's body curled up to his in the dark hours of the morning made him ache with a feeling he was better able to ignore when at sea.

Sir Lyle Barrington. What was his role in all this? Why had he brought up the subject of marriage? Why had he been so sure that Lady Catherine would marry him?

"Marry Lady Catherine and you could very well be out of trouble and at sea within the month," he had said.

Back to sea! Another command! Jocelyn felt light-headed at the thought.

A knock at the door.

Catherine dropped his hand. They both turned.

There was a second knock. The door opened.

"This has just arrived, my lady." The butler proffered a tray. Jocelyn went to take the letter that lay atop it. The door shut again.

"It is marked urgent." Jocelyn held the letter out.

Catherine snatched it and ripped it open with an exclamation of annoyance. In the span of a second, he saw her face blanch.

"Lady Catherine? Are you well?" Jocelyn's eyes went from her deathly pale face to the note.

"Perfectly," she said. She crumpled the note in her hand. "I am perfectly well." She threw it against the fireplace; no fire had been lit on this sunny afternoon, but she obviously intended it to go into the grate, where it would burn the next time it was lit.

"What say you, Captain Avebury?"

Catherine turned her attention back to him. The light in her eyes was intense. He wondered what was in the note. It seemed to have encouraged the fighting urge in her.

"Kate," he said suddenly.

She looked at him blankly.

He smiled at her puzzlement. "Has no one ever called you Kate?"

"Why ... why, no." Catherine looked bewildered. "Is that odd?"

"Do you mean to say that you have been the proper Lady Catherine for your entire life? Even as a mischievous child?"

Catherine's gaze faltered. She blinked, looked down at her

hands, then at the windows on the far wall. The manicured gardens beyond seemed to interest her. Something bitter, yet sad, was reflected in her eyes.

"I have always been Catherine," she said.

Jocelyn thought of the smell of nutmeg and cloves on the sea air, the birds swirling about overhead. Oh, how he yearned to be aboard ship. To be free again, in a place where any name other than Cap'n was superfluous.

Ah, Kate, he thought with compassion. *How little you know of the ties that bind us. What you do not know of what it takes to be free. And it has nothing at all in the world to do with your legs, or your money, or your titles.*

He could almost feel the way that her mind worked. He pitied her deeply – not for her bent leg, but for the pain that the ten year-old girl within her struggled to understand. He felt such affection, warmth and understanding for that crippled girl with a face like an angel.

I am not in danger of losing my heart, he thought. *Perhaps I love her – but the sea is where I belong.*

He reached out for her hand. She looked back at him quickly.

"Kate," he said, his heart racing. "May I call you Kate?"

Her eyes were filled with tears. She nodded once, then again.

"You may be a fool to trust me, Kate."

"I know," she said hoarsely. "I know."

"You know nothing of what has brought me to this life."

"We … we all make mistakes, Captain Avebury." Catherine was having difficulty getting the words out. She lowered her eyes. "I would not presume to judge your mistakes."

Was it possible that someone on God's green earth trusted him? Or were her words merely a convenient lie? He bowed his head for a moment, then took a leap of faith: for the first time in decades, he said a prayer to a God he was not at all sure existed.

"Let us go." He saw her lift her face, an incredulous wave of relief spread over her face. He nodded toward the door. "They will wonder why you are not getting ready."

"Oh, Captain Avebury—"

"I think Avebury will do. You will raise eyebrows if you insist on addressing me with such formality." Jocelyn tucked her hand into his arm. "We are certainly very comfortable, are we not? I am sure we can fool them all."

"I feel as if you have known me all my life."

"That sounded quite nice, thank you." He kissed her hand. "You are a brave woman, Kate."

He saw a blush tinge her cheeks. Were his attempts at congenial affection making her nervous? He opened the door for her and guided her into the hall. One of the housemaids hurried over to assist. In the background, Jocelyn could hear the sounds of a carriage being prepared, the shouts of men bringing horses from the stables.

"Take me upstairs, please," Catherine said to the maid. She turned to Jocelyn, a momentary expression of uncertainty crossing her face. "Avebury, would you care to—"

"I need to speak to the stables about my horse – a rented hack who needs to be taken back to his unfortunate master. I will see you in the carriage." He kissed her hand again, feeling the maid's abashed stare. Surprisingly, he did not feel in the least nervous, instead he felt rather smug. Take that, you impudent fools!

He recalled that his hat was still in the drawing room. He went to retrieve it, absently wondering what insane urge had provoked him to do this crazy thing, and wondering in addition whether he would actually go through with it.

Then he saw the note Catherine had received, lying beside the grate in a tight, crumpled ball, exactly where it had landed. He gazed at it for a long moment before moving slowly across the room. He felt detached from his own actions, but bent to pick up the letter.

He smoothed out the single sheet.

I must see you about this matter which concerns us both.

Meet me in London as I sense I should not be seen at Wansdyke.

L.

Jocelyn crumpled the sheet again and tossed it into the fireplace.

Sir Lyle certainly worked quickly.

What was he up to?

CHAPTER 18

*T*he journey felt much longer than it actually was. The presence of Kate's maid made it impossible for them to discuss anything and, in any case, he was too amazed at his own audacity to have made terribly good conversation.

The note had to have been from Sir Lyle. Unless ... could Kate be involved with anything else that would make her react with the nervousness he had seen on her face? He doubted that she had been exposed to much beyond the narrow confines of Bath society. She complained of the restrictiveness of Bath but, in fact, she did many things that ensured her isolation. She seemed to have a fair circle of acquaintance in London, but she could hardly be described as an active member of the ton.

What would scare a strong woman like Catherine Claverton?

He considered the notion as he stared out at the gathering dusk. They were not to stop for supper until it was time to change horses, and there was a picnic basket somewhere in the carriage. He realised with mild amusement that he had nothing to wear except for the clothes on his back, but he supposed that a message could be sent to the inn asking them to send on the rest of his clothing.

What would scare Kate?

He glanced in her direction. She too was staring out at the twilight, her face perfectly calm and relaxed. She looked older than her twenty-four years. The grey light turned her blonde hair silver, and aged her countenance gracefully. How would she take to life at sea, he wondered idly.

It was a stupid thought. She was not going to sea. But he – he would be off as soon as he could manage it, and once again feel the tilting deck beneath his feet. And Kate would have Wansdyke and whatever else mattered so much to her.

He tried not to think of a child. He did not want to think of the young earl he was planning to leave behind. He knew that it would not be the same as the abandonment he had himself faced as a child. His son would have the powerful Countess St Clair on his side. What need would he have of a sea captain – a liar – as a father?

Jocelyn had heard of places like Albrook Hall. They had a view of the house from the vast grounds and driveway long before they finally arrived at the door. It could have swallowed up a thousand Wansdykes, he thought. To a man who had spent much of his youth in a tiny cabin, it seemed outrageous. To own so much was, perhaps, more a burden than a benefit.

There were only a few members of the household staff to greet them. The butler himself stepped up to open the door of the carriage. "Lady Catherine," he said, sounding weary.

Catherine ignored the butler. She nodded at her maid, who murmured something to the butler as she climbed down. Jocelyn caught the pained look on the butler's face as he nodded and backed away.

Catherine turned to Jocelyn. "Do you not let them fool you," she said tightly. "They despise me, every last one of them." She pushed herself forward on the seat and reached out to where her maid waited.

"You must allow me," Jocelyn said, reaching for her hand. She shot him a startled look, then smiled.

"I keep forgetting," she said. She let him precede her; with his feet once again on firm ground, he lifted her easily from the carriage.

"This is Captain Avebury," Catherine said loudly to the small knot of household staff. The housekeeper was there, as well as several of the maids and footmen. They were uniformly sad and exhausted-looking.

"Captain Avebury and I are betrothed. Kindly prepare a room for him in the east wing. We will be calling on my father at once." She addressed the butler. "Is he awake?"

"No, Lady Catherine."

"That is unfortunate. Where is Mr Beaseley?"

"In the library, my lady."

Catherine looked at Jocelyn. "I would like you to see Mr Beaseley as soon as possible. Are you too tired? Would you like to rest?"

Jocelyn shook his head. He was extremely tired, in fact, and the journey, hunger and disbelief at what was happening made him light-headed. But he wanted to get it over with – whatever it was.

IT WAS A STRANGE FEELING – SHE WAS ENTERING ALBROOK HALL as her own mistress at last. No matter how many years had passed, she had never quite overcome the feeling that, at Albrook, she was merely the crippled little girl whom everyone viewed with pity. Now, on Captain Avebury's – Jocelyn's – arm, she was finally her own person. How cruel, the lot of a female: passed along from one man to the next. To think that her only hope of independence was to find a man who would marry her.

She wondered what Jocelyn was thinking now, whether he was regretting his impetuous acceptance of her offer. She wondered what had finally pushed him over the edge, what part of her attempts to persuade him to marry her had made a difference.

She dismissed the butler, saying that she would announce herself to Beaseley. When he murmured his felicitations upon her engagement, she waved him away, annoyed, and clumped down the hall in the direction of the library.

Outside the library door, she paused. She turned to look up at Jocelyn. "Beaseley is my father's man of business," she said quietly. "He will want to speak with you regarding a marriage settlement and suchlike. He has my complete trust, and he can speak on my behalf as well as that of my father. I know you have no more designs on my fortune than I have on your prize money, and I have no interest in financial discussions in any case, but he will want to go through the formalities. Decide whatever you wish. Also, there is the matter of the licence —he will be able to procure one."

"Of course," Jocelyn said. "I understand perfectly. He should be encouraged to protect your interests."

"He has always done so," Catherine said, turning back to the library doors. She put her hand on the smooth polished wood. "He is the kindest man I have ever known." She opened the door.

"Beaseley," she called, trying to sound cheerful. "I am here."

"Lady Catherine!" Beaseley exclaimed, rising from behind a desk in the far corner. He came forward, holding out his hands, then paused when he saw Jocelyn.

"Mr Beaseley, I came as soon as I received your message. This is Captain Avebury, of His Majesty's Navy. We are betrothed. I brought him with me, hoping that perhaps my father might wake one last time and see me happy." She turned to Jocelyn. "This is the man who ensured that I would not be banished to a life of privation. He did everything to make sure I would continue to live in a way befitting the daughter of the Earl of Delamare."

Jocelyn bowed. "I am honoured, sir."

"No, no, it is my great delight to make your acquaintance, Captain Avebury," Beaseley said, coming forward to shake his hand. He cocked a suspicious eye toward Catherine. "Very sudden happy news, eh?"

Catherine felt her cheeks grow hot. "Your sarcasm does not flatter you, Beaseley," she retorted. "Captain Avebury is a relative newcomer to Bath. And I wished him to be acquainted with my papa."

"Of course, of course," Beaseley said, sounding contrite. "I beg your pardon."

"I want to see him immediately," Catherine continued, "but I imagine that there are things that can only be discussed between you men." She wrinkled her nose with disdain. "It pains me to say those words, but I know well it is the way of things. Avebury, will you see me to the stairs? The footmen will bring a chair for me and take me to my father's rooms."

She took Jocelyn's arm, and let him lead her out. At the foot of the stairs, she turned to him, conscious of the listening footmen. "Thank you," she murmured. "I promise all will be well."

Before she could turn away, Jocelyn bent and kissed her swiftly on the lips. She felt her eyes suddenly fill. She knew that he meant to give her strength, that he only had the kindest feelings in his heart.

"I wish I were going to accompany you," he murmured. "Take this for strength." He kissed her again. "They are watching you. Do not cry."

"I won't." Catherine blinked hard. She turned and hobbled over to the waiting chair.

~

A SMALL CROWD HAD GATHERED IN HER FATHER'S ROOMS. TWO doctors were conferring in hushed tones. Her father's aged valet sat crumpled in a seat near the window. A maid was quietly tidying the room.

Catherine hesitated at the door. No one paid her the least bit of attention. Somewhat annoyed, she stomped loudly over to where the doctors stood. They looked up equally irritated, but their faces softened when they saw her.

"Lady Catherine—" one of them began.

"Go away," Catherine interrupted. "All of you."

The two doctors looked at each other. There was a long pause.

Becoming progressively more annoyed, Catherine pointed at the door. "There it is," she said. "The door. You may leave now."

"He is at the end, Lady Catherine." This came from the old valet who gripped a wadded-up handkerchief tightly in one gnarled hand as he gestured. "He is at the end."

The doctors looked to the valet for direction and this infuriated Catherine.

How dare they! How dare they ignore me!

"What is taking you all so long!" she exclaimed. "He is my father and I want to see him alone!"

The maid was already at the door, beckoning to the valet. He stood slowly, joints creaking, and shuffled across the room. Catherine watched him with a hard-hearted coldness that she could not repress. She could see in her mind's eye, as clear as day, the imperious face of the man refusing to admit her to her father's rooms when, as a child, she had wanted to ask why he had her favourite puppy drowned.

"I am the Lady Catherine Claverton!" she had screamed, as the door was shut in her ten-year-old face. In a fit of rage she had slammed her crutch so forcefully against the door that it had splintered, shards scattering over the hard floor of the hallway.

It was shortly after that, that she had been sent to Wansdyke.

She would never forget it, never. She wanted all of these people gone, out of her life, out of any memory of her life. She wanted to begin her life anew. The games people played might be more dangerous but she was smarter now. Wiser. She would not allow anyone to get under her skin.

With the room empty, she went to see her father as he lay still beneath the bedclothes. A faint whistling noise startled her, but she realised that it was his breathing. His lips, parched and cracked, were parted. He looked very old, far older than his years. The air reeked of unwashed skin and sickness.

"Well," Catherine said softly. "Here I am." She bent a little closer. "Can you hear me, Papa? They say you are dying. Is it truly the end? Or will you remain with us a little longer?" She cocked her head a bit, trying to see him properly. She was repulsed by the smell, but she needed to have a final look at her father.

"I am getting married, Papa," she said, a little more loudly. "So you mustn't die yet. Because I have no intention of wearing black and postponing my wedding."

A prolonged groan caused her to jump back in fright. The cracked lips moved.

"Papa?" In spite of herself, she felt the old, familiar feeling of intimidation start to bubble up in her stomach. He was going to forbid the wedding; her mind screamed in panic. He was going to have one of his magnificent rages, he was going to order Captain Avebury banned from Wansdyke—

I am my own mistress. I am my own mistress.

She forced herself to think calmly. This old shell of a human being was no threat to her. Beaseley would do anything she asked. The Delamare earldom was doomed. And Captain Avebury would marry her. No one could stop the inevitable turning of the wheels, the spinning of the earth. All would happen as she had planned.

The lips moved again. Catherine reached for a piece of clean linen from the pile at the foot of the bed. She dipped it into a pitcher of water and held it to the earl's lips. She could feel an eagerness to suck, like a babe at a breast, in the slight movements of his mouth.

Something akin to pity welled up from deep inside her. This was no man. This was a child, an infant. He needed constant care. He exerted no influence. He could not harm her.

Catherine backed away from the bed. Her eyes were misting over. *I am not going to feel sorry for him*, she thought in confusion. *This man nearly ruined my happiness. He had no use for my life, a perfectly good human life.*

But I would have loved him, with all my heart.

She turned and, as fast as she could, limped out of the room.

CHAPTER 19

"What precisely will be necessary for the licence?" Jocelyn was not sure, but he thought Beaseley had been satisfied with the answers to his gentle questions about his circumstances. Jocelyn had made it clear that he had no need of any of Catherine's vast estate, and that, in any case, he hoped to be at sea again relatively soon.

Beaseley returned to the desk in the corner of the library. "I will send a message to the bishop immediately. Where is the wedding to take place?"

Jocelyn shrugged. "I have no particular preference. My own family is dead."

"I somehow suspect that Lady Catherine would wish to have it here," Beaseley murmured. His brow creased. "It is inconvenient, of course, given her father's illness."

"Her intention is to marry while he is still alive," Jocelyn said.

"Yes," said Beaseley. "Yes, I believe it must be. So we will plan on tomorrow morning."

Jocelyn said nothing. The discussion had a surreal quality to it. Marriage! In the morning! He wondered that he did not feel much emotion at the thought. All he could think of was the sea ...

"I will need documents, of course," Beaseley was saying. Jocelyn snapped out of his reverie.

"I beg your pardon? What sort of documents?"

"We are not posting banns, Captain Avebury. Do you have any papers that will confirm your identity? I can vouch for you but, forgive me, I do not know your people – I am just looking out for Lady Catherine's interests."

Jocelyn stared at him impassively for a long moment. "I have nothing of the sort with me," he said finally.

Beaseley sat back in his seat. "Indeed?"

There was another long silence. Jocelyn knew that the next move had to be his. Beaseley was suspicious, but he was merely the earl's man of business. He clearly did not want to question Lady Catherine's betrothed. On the other hand, he plainly felt a great deal of affection for Lady Catherine.

"We were not planning such a hasty wedding," Jocelyn said. "The earl's illness forced us to ... er ... declare ourselves much earlier than would have seemed appropriate, under normal circumstances."

"Indeed," Beaseley said again. His expression remained neutral.

Jocelyn rose and strolled over to a window overlooking a fresh green lawn. Thunderclouds were threatening in the distance, and the air was quite heavy and humid. He turned back to Beaseley.

"I have my naval papers amongst my belongings at the inn where I have been staying, in Bath. Perhaps they would suffice."

"I imagine they would," Beaseley replied. "Certainly the Navy would not accept a person as an officer without proper recommendation."

Jocelyn looked at him sharply. There was a little worried crease, a slight frown on his face. But there was simply nothing to say to him, no explanation that could possibly suffice.

"I would not hurt her," Jocelyn said softly. "I swear it. I am a man of honour, Mr Beaseley."

"Do you love her?"

Did he?

He wanted to shout, "No, indeed!" He wanted to think about a ship, not a woman.

But his mind conjured up the image of Kate laughing, mud-stained and happy, lying in a grassy field with the sheep inspecting her golden hair, of the Kate who was too smart and too proud to accept the idiocies that the world wanted to impose on her. His Kate was hidden behind the pretty gowns, the enigmatic smile. The ugly limp.

"I love her," he heard himself saying.

He wanted her to realise her dreams, wanted to see her happy. Wanted to see her holding her babe to her breast.

Was that love?

He wanted to hold her close in the dark hours of the night when he couldn't sleep, to caress her, to bury himself in her strength, her confidence.

Was that love?

A chair creaked. Jocelyn focused his gaze on Beaseley again. He had risen from his seat and was walking quietly over to him. He held out his hands, grasped Jocelyn's in his own.

"Listen to me, Captain Avebury. Listen well." He stopped, as if to consider his words, then gripped Jocelyn's hands even more tightly. "Lady Catherine is like a daughter to me. I have worried about the eventuality of her father's death ever since the countess died. She is alone, and a young woman of title and fortune needs the protection of a man. I do not know your present situation, Captain Avebury, or why the circumstances of your betrothal are so peculiar. But I will help you to marry her: I will do everything in my power – as long as you promise to cherish her as she deserves to be cherished."

"I promise," Jocelyn said, his hands aching in the older man's grip. "I do not want to hurt her." This was true. Could he really cherish her as she deserved? He made a silent apology: he really was not sure.

Beaseley dropped his hands and turned away.

"I can get you the licence, Captain Avebury," he said. "Only tell me when and where you were born."

"Do not take a personal risk on my behalf, Mr Beaseley," Jocelyn said. "I do have my papers from the navy."

Beaseley waved away his concern. "I have not been the earl's man of business for so many years without learning how to arrange matters."

He could tell him the truth – he had been born in a village not too far from York. They would find the record of his birth in the village church, along with those of his father and grandfather and great-grandfather before him.

But not under the name Avebury. There was no Avebury listed in that register.

It would be too confusing to be honest at this late date. And it would certainly be a strange time to first own such a lie.

So he gave Beasley the fiction that had worked when he entered the navy as a young midshipman all those years ago.

"London," he said. "I was born in London."

THEY WERE MARRIED VERY EARLY THE FOLLOWING MORNING. Beaseley was extremely efficient; he had not only managed to convince the bishop and his assistant to arrive at a very early hour in order to perform the ceremony, but also managed to procure a proper set of clothes for Jocelyn to wear. Nor had he brought up the question of Jocelyn's origins again. Jocelyn was both relieved and disturbed but, when his thoughts meandered in the direction of what might have been, he had only to close his eyes and breathe in the salty smell of the sea, to feel on his skin the burning of the bright Mediterranean sun to regain his composure.

Whatever Beaseley had done seemed to have been enough. The bishop was a surprisingly young man, middle-aged at most, who expressed his sincere sympathies for the sad state of affairs at Albrook and did not appear to think that a hasty wedding was out of order at such a time of distress. Indeed, he shook Jocelyn's hand quite warmly, and murmured his approval that someone would at last be taking care of "poor, dear Lady Catherine."

Jocelyn would have been amused if he had not been so dreadfully uncomfortable. He wanted desperately to escape the cloying atmosphere of the dark, dank parish church – it felt more like a tomb than a place for the living body of Christ. At the conclusion of the ceremony they were taken to sign the parish register, which momentarily threw him off guard. It seemed particularly sinful to allow his false name to be placed in the book of Catherine's ancestors, and he hesitated before scrawling "Jocelyn William Avebury" in the appropriate space. Catherine did not hesitate when she bent to sign her name: Catherine Maria Claverton. Her hand was neat and steady, but he saw her pause for a brief millisecond as she crossed the last "t". Poor thing, he thought compassionately. What desperate misery must have driven her to marry a man she scarcely knew in order to punish a world that neglected her so.

She was demure, avoiding his eyes. She wore a gown of whisper-thin pale-blue silk cut modestly at the throat and covered with an overdress of some kind of net. It was cold in the little stone church, and her skin looked pale and translucent. She must have brought that gown from Wansdyke, he thought. And he felt deeply sorry that she had to celebrate her wedding in such haste, wearing a gown she had barely a few minutes to select before rushing out of the door to the waiting carriage. He imagined that ladies dreamt of their wedding days, planned for them for years in advance, bought all sorts of things for them – at least, what he could recall of his limited contact with them suggested so. What a pity that he could not have done more for her before this impetuous wedding. He would have enjoyed watching her face light up as she tried on her wedding clothes. He could have bought her diamonds and silks, outrageous hats, travelling clothes for their—

Ridiculous. There would be no wedding journey. For one thing, he was stuck: stuck in England – stuck in Bath, in fact. His mind turned to the question of when he could reasonably expect the Admiralty to send for him. He had already been two months in Bath, and he had spent some time before that settling business affairs with his solicitor in London.

That note. It had warned him, said his affair was on the agenda, but there had been no further contact. Surely by now they had discussed the case? Surely by now they had taken testimonies and reviewed the incident?

They stepped out of the chapel together, he and Catherine. Man and wife. For a second, he thought of holding her hand, but dismissed the thought. This is an arrangement. A convenient arrangement. No matter what he said to Beaseley or what he felt, the facts were plain. He would give her an earl to love. She would give him his life back.

"Under the circumstances, unfortunately ..." Catherine was saying to the bishop, who hastily denied he held any hope of being invited to breakfast.

"It would indeed be unfortunate if anyone were to misconstrue my arrival at Albrook as being ... er ... inauspicious. Be assured you have my heartfelt congratulations, Captain Avebury, and I wish you very happy." With a polite bow, the bishop set off toward his waiting equipage, his assistant trotting beside him.

"Well," Beaseley said. He looked shrewdly at Jocelyn. "Well done, Captain Avebury. Many felicitations."

"Thank you very much, sir," Jocelyn replied.

"We will breakfast," Catherine said to Beaseley, "and then go to see my father."

But, as they approached the hall, they could see the butler standing out on the terrace, peering anxiously in their direction. Jocelyn felt the sudden tension in the air. He put his hand on Catherine's arm.

They could see the butler held a piece of black crepe.

"A pity," Catherine said tonelessly. "I should not have sent the bishop away."

CHAPTER 20

*C*lara had unpacked Catherine's black dresses. Which would my lady prefer to wear now? Which should she set aside for the service? Which would she like to—

"Whatever you think appropriate," Catherine interrupted. She nodded a dismissal.

The last Earl of Delamare was no more. She had always imagined she would feel as if she had sprouted wings at this moment. Instead, she felt tired and oddly dispirited. Her last connection was gone. She had no family left.

Except for him. The captain. He was her only tie to the earth now.

She was glad to have him. That he was kind she had no doubt. But there was something else – something else. Had his love of the sea compelled him to marry her, propelled her into this insane deed? Did he really believe that the Claverton connection would extract him from his trouble?

The house was quiet. There was little fuss and hubbub. They had all been preparing for this moment for so long, it seemed almost a relief to face it at last.

Beaseley wrote letter after letter for immediate dispatch to

London. "Everything is taken care of, my lady," he assured her.

"You are too efficient," Catherine said acidly. Beaseley looked up. She shifted uncomfortably in her seat. "Do not mind my sharp tongue."

Beaseley watched her for a moment. When it became apparent that she had nothing more to say, he bent over his letters again.

Catherine looked over at Jocelyn. He had spent the past few hours staring out of the front window of the library, across the rolling green lawn to where the sheep grazed in the distance. The wedding ring was heavy on her finger: it was an old piece the dowager countess had given to her mother. Catherine shuddered slightly. She hoped it wasn't bad luck to wear a Claverton ring, but she hadn't thought to bring any of her mother's own jewellery with her. Beaseley alone had remembered that a ring would be called for.

While she was certain Beaseley knew there was something very odd about the hasty wedding, she knew without a doubt that he had spoken to Avebury and satisfied himself. What had been said, she had no idea, but he would not have turned a blind eye had he thought she was making a foolish decision.

What was he thinking, her captain of the pleasant smile and unhappy storm-blue eyes? Had he merely accepted her offer as it stood, seeing a way to get out of his miserable predicament? Was there anything more? Any possibility of more?

And, she asked herself, did she care? Did she care for anything beyond the gift of an earl, a gift that her captain had all but promised to provide?

She did care. Perhaps ... perhaps it was not love. What did she, a foolish young cripple, know of love? Perhaps it was not a grand passion of the sort that was whispered about from time to time. But he did not scare her. Sir Lyle was a passionate lover – he scared her. Now she was beginning to understand that passion was less important than constancy, steadiness, trust.

Even if Avebury did not care for her with the passion of a lover, she wanted to do good for him. He did not deserve the trouble Lydia had described. Catherine was sure he had never done anything criminal in his life. She was a shrewd judge of character – years of spying from the edges of the ballrooms had made her so – and he was decent, a gentleman. Sir Lyle was fascinating, intriguing. But she was not at all sure that he was a gentleman. She prayed that Avebury's decency would never be tested against the knowledge of that stupid portrait.

Catherine turned her eyes away from the window. She needed to get to London, quickly. In his note, LaFrance had sounded desperate. He must be out of funds yet again. She knew he was still threatening to exhibit the portrait, to find a patron who would support him, his distasteful habits and the company he kept. She shuddered.

She had heard about the struggling young artist during a period of very deep depression and, on a whim, had ordered Lydia to accompany her on a visit to his studio. The visit was to lead to a world of complications. Complications far exceeding the euphoria that she had experienced for a brief period.

I have to get to London. But I am stuck here – for now.

She suddenly pushed herself up to stand. Beaseley looked up. Jocelyn turned slightly.

"I need some air. I hate just sitting and sitting. We must have been here for hours. I have not done a thing, and I feel utterly useless."

Beaseley looked exhausted and ill at ease. He pulled at one ear, then removed his spectacles and rubbed his face. He replaced his spectacles and peered at Catherine. "I would never wish to presume, my lady," he said faintly. "Certainly, if you wish to handle the arrangements—"

"Stupid man!" she cried. She rapped the back of the chair, the knuckles of her hand producing a sharp report that echoed through the library. "Of course I do not wish to do that!"

"Kate," Jocelyn said, his voice mild. Catherine looked at him, about to give him her best icy put-down, but her voice failed her. She stared at him, and to her dismay, she felt her throat lock tight and her eyes begin to smart. She sat down again and looked down at her clasped hands. The old gold of the wedding ring gleamed dully in the daylight. She shut her eyes. It was a Claverton ring – she did not want to see it.

What he does not know about me, she thought in despair. *This good man calls me "Kate" with such affection – but he does not know the level to which I will sink in order to get what I want.*

"The countess is tired," Jocelyn said to no one in particular. He rose from his seat. "I will take her to her rooms for some rest. Will you have need of her, Mr Beaseley?"

"No, Captain Avebury," Beaseley murmured. He shuffled papers on the desk.

"Will you send word when you have arranged the funeral service?"

"Yes, of course. Most certainly."

She rose listlessly, without looking in Beaseley's direction, and took Jocelyn's arm. He guided her through the library and out into the hallway. It was empty.

"Have they all deserted the sinking ship already?" he asked.

Catherine shrugged. "Perhaps. There is really no reason for them to stay. The ones who had arranged new positions have doubtless gone. And good riddance."

"You still need the servants – surely you will still need help."

"I do not care about any of it. Perhaps I will give everything away." They began their lengthy ascent with Catherine leaning on the stair rail. Jocelyn put his arm about her waist, and she discovered something else about Captain Avebury: that he was able to support her weight so efficiently that climbing the stairs with him was like flying through the air. At the first landing, she stopped and turned.

"I beg your pardon," he said immediately. "Am I doing something wrong?"

"You silly man," she said with affection. "I was going to tell you that I have never climbed a set of stairs so easily in all my life. This is far better than being carried in a chair by those foolish footmen who moan and groan and huff and puff as if I weighed twice what I do."

"Let us see if I survive handling your weight until the top," he said gravely. She chuckled.

"You are far stronger than they – working man that you are! They are lazy, every last one of them." She paused, then looked up the next flight. She said, half to herself, "I am sure I would be amazed if I saw you on your ship, at sea."

Instead of replying, Jocelyn slipped his arm about her waist once more, and they made their way up to the next landing. At the top, he hesitated, and she nodded to the left.

"My apartment is at the end of this corridor. Banishment, as it were," she added wryly.

"Did they never think of giving you ground-floor rooms to use?" Jocelyn asked in wonder.

Catherine laughed. "You are so innocent, Jocelyn." She began to limp toward her rooms. "Had I lived downstairs, I would have been seen by the world. My father ordered me hidden. So Nurse and I lived in that dark corner." She paused, and looked along the hallway. "I am sincere when I say that I do not regret leaving this house forever," she said. "I have Wansdyke. That is enough for me."

They walked in silence for a moment. Jocelyn ventured, "Have you any interest in the property in Wales? The castle that comes to you with the title from your mother?"

"Perhaps," Catherine said. They had reached her rooms. She put her hand on the door and turned to Jocelyn. "I have considered it. But I am told it is very nearly a ruin. Though it would be a fine thing to make it a real home, would it not?" She pushed the door open.

"Leave us, please," she said to Clara, who was still unwrapping items taken from the trunk. "I am extremely tired and will take a few hours of rest. I may not be down for dinner – tell Cook I will send word if I wish to have a tray." Catherine waited until Clara had left before sinking down in a chair placed in a spot of sunlight in the bay of the window.

"Come join me, sir. Do not stand there uneasy."

"I will leave you to rest," Jocelyn said. "You are tired."

"Please." Catherine passed a hand over her eyes. There was a long pause. "Please do not leave me," she said in a small voice.

Jocelyn took her other hand and knelt before her. He kissed it. "Poor Kate. What you do not need right now is a sea captain to wait on you. You need a nap."

"I know that I do." Catherine gripped his hand tightly. "But stay, just for a moment – I was always so alone in these rooms."

"Kate—" he began, but she cut him off.

"No, it is quite all right." She dropped his hand and attempted to sound cheerful. "Of course, perhaps … perhaps you would like a few moments to yourself. I am sure this is all very daunting. And we must prepare for all the annoying people who will ask rude questions. I understand if you would rather … rather …" The last words faded away uneasily.

Jocelyn frowned at her with concern.

Acting on an impulse, she reached out to smooth the lines in his forehead, to brush back the wisps of fine brown curls. "Such a beautiful boy you must have been," she murmured, running her hand lightly over the sandy planes of his cheek, down to his chin. Then, her heart suddenly quickening, she brushed her fingers over his lips.

She dropped her hand. "You should leave me," she said, her throat aching. She wanted to weep. She suddenly realised that their son might be dark-haired, not the golden child she had been seeing in her dreams. This was reality. He would be their child, not her child. One conceived not out of love but out of her selfish need. Her visions were selfish. Her wants, her actions – all selfish. It was as if no one else in the world had their own wants, their own needs. She despised herself.

"I would like to kiss you." Jocelyn inched forward a little, putting a hand on one arm of her chair. "May I?"

Catherine tried to smile. "Of course," she said easily, leaning forward. "You are very dear to me, Jocelyn Avebury." Jocelyn put his hands on either side of her face, steadying her as he reached up to press his lips on hers. For a quiet moment, they were locked together, warmth against warmth, their lips barely moist, their breaths light and quick.

She reached up to put her hands on his. Slowly, almost of their own accord, his hands slid with hers to her bare neck, to the top of her bosom, where they rested for a moment. She could feel her heartbeat race. Then he turned his hands over to grasp hers, and pulled back gently. He kissed first one hand, then the other, and looked up at her.

"I am putting you to bed, my love. And then I will leave you so that you can rest." Before Catherine could speak, he had gathered her in his arms. He rose quickly and carried her over to the canopied bed. He set her down gently, removed her slippers and tossed them into a corner.

"May I loosen your gown?"

"Oh, Jocelyn." For a moment Catherine could not speak. She swallowed hard. "You are kind to me," she whispered. Beyond what I deserve, she thought miserably. He would not be so kind if he knew of the portrait. Oh, that cursed portrait! Perhaps ... perhaps if it were to be destroyed, she would be able to start again. They would be able to start again. Until then, Jocelyn Avebury was above her reach.

He bent to kiss her. "You have a new life, Countess," he whispered. "Live it well."

CHAPTER 21

*H*e thought that perhaps she was nearly asleep when he left. It was hard to be sure. She had been so unhappy and preoccupied, it seemed unlikely she could possibly doze off. He had loosened her gown, rubbed her hands and her temples, gently removed the pins from her hair. He marvelled at the complexities of women's dress. He had never undressed a woman before, never taken down one's hair – they usually arrived in his bed already undressed. And one could not compare the girls that loitered about the port towns of the Continent to an English lady.

It was tempting to make love to her, but he could not be certain that his attentions would be welcome. And, despite his own preoccupation with escape from England, he knew it would demoralise him terribly to find her a reluctant lover.

I'm being ridiculous. She wants an earl. She needs an earl. The whole point of this farce is to give her a son. There won't be an earl unless—

He dismissed the thought from his mind and took himself down the stairs. Beaseley was still in the library.

"And how is her ladyship?"

"Resting," Jocelyn said, shutting the door behind him. "Have all the staff left?"

"No, not all, although many have." Beaseley stood up. He removed his spectacles and rubbed his face with his hands. "A black day, Captain Avebury. A black day indeed."

"Yes. I am very sorry."

"I fear Lady Catherine will need your assistance, Captain."

"Yes," Jocelyn said. He crossed the room to the desk. "I believe she is more troubled by her father's passing than she will admit."

"Yes. She is still a Claverton." Beaseley paused, then added quietly, "I have also sent word to our friends at the Admiralty."

Jocelyn said nothing. Beaseley looked him squarely in the eye. "I hope you will not leave at the first opportunity."

I doubt that my departure could come soon enough for me, Jocelyn thought, but he remained silent. His mind turned to the slight form he had left in that dim corner room. He had felt the twisted, heavy, lifeless leg as he carried her from the chair to the bed.

"We will see what result my initial questions bring." Beaseley grimaced and rubbed at his face again. He replaced his spectacles. "I have some skill in these matters. But if you would tell me more, I could be of greater assistance, Captain Avebury!"

Jocelyn kept his gaze level. "I am under investigation, sir. A missed dispatch in the Indian Ocean. My ship departed port late. It is standard procedure to investigate all such mishaps."

"And that is all?"

Jocelyn saw the doubt on his face. "That is all, sir."

"Your papers – your entry into the service? It was all ... as usual?"

Perhaps he could be rid of this burden. Rid of it now and forever. He could explain to the good man the problem of his name, his past. He could ask his help in explaining to Kate—

Explaining what, he thought dismally. Explaining that he was a fraud? That his father was executed as a traitor? That there were no Aveburys anywhere in Yorkshire because it was a name that he had invented? That even the Navy had no idea of who he really was?

"Yes, sir." His head ached. Lies had a physically painful manifestation.

"Then we will see what we can do." Beaseley sat down again. "I am sure something can be arranged."

I hope you are right, Jocelyn thought. *I hope indeed that you are right.*

~

SHE WAS STILL AWAKE WHEN JOCELYN LEFT. SHE HAD STEADIED HER breathing so that it was deep and even, hoping to persuade him that she was asleep. It appeared to have worked. He had leant over to kiss her temple, then rose softly and left the room.

She rolled onto her back. Tears seeped from her eyelids, and she gave a little gasp of relief. Finally, she was alone, she could grieve.

Grieve for her non-existent childhood. Grieve for her youthful errors. Grieve for the aching love she felt for the captain who preferred the sea to her.

She hiccoughed and rolled over again. The pillow was fresh. She buried her cheek in it. She could almost smell the liniments and potions of the old nurse who had once looked after her in these rooms.

She dozed off, drifted into a slumber that did not seem much different from wakefulness, so she was startled when she realised that she was staring through a window at a darker sky.

Something creaked.

"Are you awake?"

Slowly, she turned her head. Jocelyn sat beside the bed, a book open on the table before him. He had shed his coat, cravat and waistcoat. His shirt gaped open at the throat, as if he had yanked at it impatiently after a long day.

"Yes," she said. "Was I asleep?"

"You were."

"How odd. I thought I was awake."

Jocelyn shut his book. "Shall I send for supper?"

"Oh, no," she said feebly. She turned her head away. The thought of food revolted her, turned her stomach. She did not know the hour, but it was likely to be cold meat or pies. She shuddered involuntarily.

"You must eat." Jocelyn came round the bed to sit beside her, and she struggled to move closer to him.

"Eventually, I shall. Right now I just want to … to crawl away somewhere and hide." The words startled her and she would have bitten them back if she could. She glanced warily up at Jocelyn; there was a shadow on his face and she could not read his expression. She focused on his throat. How old was he? Sitting there in shirtsleeves and breeches, he seemed very young. The skin at his neck was smooth. In the midst of the ruffles of his shirt, she could just make out something shiny at his throat. It appeared that he wore a silver locket.

Catherine reached out to touch it. It was warm. The fabric of his shirt was very thin, and she could feel his heartbeat through it.

"Your mother, perhaps?" she guessed.

"Yes." He reached up to remove her hand. He clasped it gently in his own, but she pressed it to his chest.

"Shhh." For a moment, they sat quietly. "I can feel your heart," she said.

She saw the hesitation on his face. Why did he hesitate? Did he truly feel nothing, no temptation, no urge? Was she no more than his sister, his friend?

He was going to leave her. He was going to take the first opportunity to get a ship so he could forget her.

The thought made her grow cold inside. *How can you?* she demanded silently. *How, when I love you so?*

She knew she had to conceive an earl quickly – as quickly as she could. Before Beaseley was able to work his magic and get Avebury a ship.

Just once, she thought. *Just once, we can pretend, you and I. We can pretend that we mean something to each other. We can pretend that our child will arrive bathed in love.*

She slipped her hand inside his shirt, her slender fingers tracing the line of his collarbone. It was substantial, heavy. A man's flesh felt so different. She did not know why she had never thought of this before, but the last time – the only time – well, she had been so angry, so hollow inside, she hadn't thought to admire the male form. She had been selfish. And he – that man – he had been selfish, too.

Jocelyn was watching her. He understood. Quietly, he turned, and removed his shirt. He had a well-muscled back, a powerful chest. He was a man of action, for all his quiet ways. He moved to sit on the bed next to her, leant down to take her in his arms.

"Kate—" he began.

"Do not speak, please," she whispered.

"What, you will not let me woo you with a line from that dreadful poetry book?"

"Dreadful—?" Catherine half-turned to look at the book he had put down, but he had used the opportunity to kiss her neck, to gently press her arms above her head, the weight of his body leaning into her own.

"I do not read dreadful poetry," she murmured. He undid the last buttons on her bodice, and bent to kiss her.

"It was awful," he whispered in reply. Gently, he pulled her skirts aside. "I would like to rip through your gown. May I?"

"What?" Catherine said, beginning to laugh. But he had freed her from the gown completely and was attending to her so well that she could not remember what had made her laugh. He lifted her gently and pulled the gown down around her ankles.

"Damn!" he said suddenly. Catherine opened her eyes in alarm.

"How many layers must you ladies wear?" he complained. He was regarding her muslin shift with irritation. "How is this to be removed?"

Catherine struggled to sit up. "You seem eager to convince me that you have not spent much time with the fairer sex," she said tartly.

"And a good thing that I haven't, too," Jocelyn retorted. "I think you would box my ears if you suspected that were the case. You ladies are dangerous." He lifted the shift over her head. His expression softened.

"Kate, you are so very beautiful. Do you know that?"

"If you do not like my poetry, I have to question your taste. Oh!"

She said no more. Jocelyn was kissing her very slowly, exploring her body with a graceful ease. It was hard to tell whether he found her at all enticing. He handled her much as she suspected he would handle a fine wine or a valuable painting. He savoured her, but would not rush his pleasure, or hers.

She had never felt beautiful. Always, there was that crooked, shrunken leg. That, after all, had been the reason she had had that infernal portrait painted – it had been a sorry attempt to feel pretty.

But Jocelyn made her feel divinely beautiful, treasured and admired. He told her in detail what he thought and what he felt as he touched her and kissed her. She blushed and would have been mortified had she not been so eager for him to love her.

This, she realised with amazement, was what it meant to be beautiful – that her body pleased him. He worshipped her body with his own. For this she was grateful and more than a little relieved. And more.

There was the exquisiteness of his kisses, the gentleness of his touch. She wanted to weep with humiliation and ecstasy all at once. To think she had ever thought she understood physical love and the desires of the flesh! She knew nothing, had known nothing. How stupid she had been! She had faced the world, arrogant and worldly – while knowing nothing at all.

She was all the more humiliated knowing she was about to disappoint him in the biggest possible way. She felt the tension mounting in her, hoping that he would someday find it within his heart to forgive her deception.

Because she loved him with all of her being, flawed and broken as she was, with everything that she could ever hope to be.

She brushed the brown curls out of his eyes. Unruly, unkempt curls. How could he command a ship with curls in his eyes? "Jocelyn," she whispered.

He was lowering his head to kiss her belly, but paused. He looked up.

He looked years younger than the strained, stiff officer in uniform at the musicale so long ago. The blue-grey eyes were clear now, without any shadows. Had the shadows been caused by his trouble with the Admiralty? Had she removed them by promising he would return to the sea?

Her heart sank, and she bit her lip to prevent the tears from coming. She shook her head and tried to smile. If he was so eager to leave, she could not tell him how much she loved him.

Forgive me, she thought.

CHAPTER 22

*S*he was not a virgin.

Had he not already harboured suspicions about her, he might not have cared. Anyone this beautiful, this vivacious and bold, this positive about her destiny, would certainly have engaged the attentions of a young man or two. Despite what she claimed about her lack of appeal to the men of the ton, and the crude way in which her father had attempted to isolate her from the world, she was so determined and so intelligent that Jocelyn found it hard to believe that she had allowed herself to remain on the fringes of society for so long.

He had never imagined himself married at all. But, had he imagined it, he would not have seen himself with an aristocratic young lady with pale blonde hair and the face and body of an angel. Instead, he reflected, he might have thought of a cheerful and rosy-cheeked young village girl, perhaps a bit shy but willing to learn. Buxom and dark-haired, heavy-bottomed, perhaps.

Most definitely not a golden-haired countess.

She seemed to have absolutely no knowledge of the art of lovemaking. Indeed, she was quite innocent. He found that he enjoyed taking his time with her pleasure. Clothed, she was brave and confident and somewhat brash – just as a countess should be. Proper countess behaviour. But underneath her clothes she was shy and sad.

She explored his body with curiosity – as best as she could manage between kisses. She seemed particularly troubled by the old wounds that she found on his shoulders and back. She said nothing, but she ran her fingers over the scars again and again.

"They are nothing, Kate," he said gently.

"They must have hurt." She turned wide blue eyes on him. She brought his face down to hers, but did not kiss him. Her expression was grave. "Did they? Hurt?"

"You make me hurt, my love," Jocelyn replied, removing her hands from his face. "My heart pains me. I—"

He stopped. He had been about to tell her that he loved her.

It would not be fair, he thought. *I'm going away.*

Instead, he kissed her again. "This is all of me, Countess," he murmured. "This is what I am, wounds, scars, everything."

He was beginning to lose his concentration. He wanted her so much that he felt the edges of his mind slipping into fog. He was giddy from the feeling of the soft feminine curves under his fingertips, from the feeling of loving a golden-haired countess. He began to kiss her with renewed intensity, heard the catch in her breathing. He had been preoccupied with making this first time easier for her, less unpleasant. But he could not keep his head much longer.

She clearly did not expect his attentions – she seemed almost perplexed. This made him happy, and he pleasured her until she began to gasp. She reached down to grasp at his shoulders, and he paused momentarily. He looked up. She opened her eyes. Their gazes locked. He thought her lips quivered, trembled as if she were about to cry.

"Kate?" he said, confused.

She drew him up. "I want you, Jocelyn," she whispered.

He hesitated. There was something akin to fear on her face –

desperation, perhaps. Was she afraid? "I am sorry," he said. "I will try not to hurt you." But he had misunderstood.

For it was then he discovered that she was not a virgin.

She was not afraid of pain. Rather, she was afraid of his reaction to the truth.

He was startled at first, but soon lost all ability to think. He only knew that he wanted to be closer, closer, closer. He wrapped his arms around her, pressed his cheek to hers. He tried to say her name, but could only gasp.

For all the anticipation, the actual climax was brief. They clung together, panting.

He leant over her on his elbows, making sure not to crush her or to put pressure on her bad leg. He put his head in his hands and tried to ease his breathing.

He heard her sobbing.

"My love," he whispered. He gathered her in his arms, smoothed the damp golden hair. "My love. Dearest love."

But he was furious. Yes, he was angry. He'd been tricked, and he wanted to know by whom.

Who is it? His mind raced. *Who is her lover?*

Now he considered it, he supposed it likely she had had a lover or two; someone like the Lady Catherine Claverton might have been so bold, so daring. It should not have bothered him in the slightest, under the circumstances.

But he knew she had something to hide, so he hated that man – whoever he was.

Because he loved her.

But as he lay there, his heart sinking, he realised that he knew exactly who it was. He knew it was Sir Lyle. And he wanted to kill him. He wanted to kill him – and her too for trying to make a fool out of him.

Why hadn't she just married Sir Lyle? He had a title, status, wealth. Why would she not prefer him to a sea captain with a questionable background? Had he refused? Was he too much a man of the world to bother with marriage? Why had he told Jocelyn to marry her? What kind of insane plot had he and Catherine put together?

But it made no difference. He was in love with her, God help him. But he wanted nothing more than to give her the damned child that she wanted so badly, and then to flee, go back to the wide blue sea, the closeness of his cabin, the rocking gentleness of the ship on a hot wind from the south. To blessed solitude.

THEY MADE LOVE AGAIN. CATHERINE WAS GLAD OF THE FADING summer light. Not only was she feeling distinctly unglamorous, but she was eager to avoid Jocelyn's gaze. His face was shadowed, and she hoped her own was as well.

His lovemaking was as gentle as his spirit. When he began to kiss her anew, she prepared herself for punishment. Surely he now knew that she was no virgin. She was afraid that perhaps his manner would change.

It did. But not in the way she had feared.

He was unhappy.

She could tell that he was unhappy even as he pleasured her, and unhappy as he took his own pleasure.

Is it me? She wanted to ask, to speak, to admit her sins. But she was terrified of his response. What if he abandoned her before she could conceive?

Is it that you wish to return to sea? Is there some other unhappiness in your life?

He was a man of the world, a sailor. He surely could not be brooding over her.

She ran her fingers over his chest. He still wore the silver locket, and she smoothed its chain over his collarbone. He put his hand gently over hers, but did not speak.

She could not let anything deter her from the mission of

bearing an heir and re-establishing the St Clair line. If she told him the truth, she would be risking her future: he would, perhaps, no longer want to have anything to do with her, and then she would be doomed.

So she hoped he did not care his bride was no virgin – and said nothing.

CHAPTER 23

They were at Albrook for ten days. They were congenial, but in a different way to their times together in the fields at Wansdyke. There was that far-off misery in his eyes; the sadness that she had always seen there had gone deeper. He was pleasant, always unfailingly polite. The old stick-in-the-muds of the ton who attended the late earl's funeral seemed to approve, although some were outspokenly horrified that a Claverton had married a sailor of no particular note. Most of them, however, seemed relieved that the earl's crippled daughter was not going to be living a life of questionable propriety alone on the outskirts of Bath.

Catherine wanted nothing at all from Albrook. She wanted Beaseley to sell all that remained in the Claverton name after all disbursements had been made, but Jocelyn calmed her down and suggested that it was too soon to make such a decision. It would take quite a long time, perhaps more than a year, for Beaseley to get all the paperwork for the estate in order. He was also, at Catherine's request, exploiting every possible contact at the Admiralty to find a new command for her husband.

Some time after they returned to Wansdyke, Melinda arrived for a visit.

"I did not expect to find you deeply mourning your father, God rest his soul. But married! And enjoying your honeymoon here at Wansdyke! Catherine, what has happened?"

"I am happy, Melinda," Catherine said. "Will you not be happy for me?"

"But it is all so sudden!"

"It was not all that sudden," Catherine said, her irritation rising. "I met Avebury in the spring, when he first arrived in Bath. And we wanted to marry before mourning made it impossible."

"I cannot believe you have gone into mourning at all: I did not think you would care to," Melinda said.

"I suppose I do not," Catherine admitted. "But still, here I am in my weeds." She gestured at her dress. "Is it so odd?"

"Of course not," Melinda said reluctantly. "And the captain is very charming. I just worry about you, Catherine. You are so impulsive. First it was Sir Lyle, and then it was Captain Avebury—"

"Sir Lyle?" Catherine's voice changed. Melinda looked at her curiously.

"Yes, Sir Lyle. He is a close friend of my brother. He led me to believe that I might expect happy news this summer. But I expected quite a different announcement!"

"Yes, of course," Catherine said quickly. "Ah, Avebury, come take tea with my dearest friend." Jocelyn had just entered the drawing room.

"If I am interrupting—"

"Not at all."

"We were just talking about Sir Lyle," Melinda said. She looked shrewdly at Jocelyn. "I know him well – he is a friend of my brother."

"Indeed?" Jocelyn glanced in Catherine's direction, but she

had suddenly found several loose threads on her skirt and was not attending. "A very decent fellow, to be sure."

"Yes, certainly. He has a lot in common with you, Captain Avebury."

The comment achieved its apparent purpose. Jocelyn turned his keen blue gaze upon Melinda and waited expectantly. "His ships, I mean. I believe he is only recently returned from— Where is it from, Catherine?"

"I'm sure I do not know." Catherine rose and limped over to the open French doors leading out to the formal gardens. She stood for a moment at the door, squaring her shoulders, before she said without turning, "Jocelyn, will you fetch my shawl? I think I shall walk a while."

"Of course." Jocelyn placed the shawl about her shoulders. "Are you sure you are feeling well enough—?"

"You ridiculous man," Catherine said affectionately. She reached out to pat his cheek. "I am perfectly fine."

Melinda half rose in her seat. "Catherine! Is it possible ... are you ...?"

Catherine turned. "Oh, Melinda. It is nothing. Do not let this dear man frighten you."

"I am not frightened, not exactly, but ..." Melinda stammered. "Catherine, you are my dearest friend in the world, and ..." She sank back into her chair, her confusion embarrassing her.

"Then do not think of it. Avebury is just very solicitous of my – my general good health, are you not, dear one?" Jocelyn bowed slightly and stepped back, watching her as she descended into the garden below.

For a long moment, no one spoke. The breeze of summer was warm, and it fluttered curtains, but did very little to heat the cold stone of Wansdyke.

"Captain Avebury," Melinda said. "Is she—"

"Perhaps."

"Good God!"

Jocelyn turned to her. For a moment, his cool gaze bored into her, and she blinked. Then he looked away.

"Captain Avebury," Melinda said. She leant forward. "You must know that I wish Catherine only the best. But she is more delicate than she seems. Having a child could prove more than she can bear."

Jocelyn said nothing. He took up a position near the French doors whence he could watch Catherine as she vanished into the shrubbery, the shawl shimmering in the sunlight.

"I worry about her. She only discovered her St Clair title very recently. And since then she has been so ... different. Angry, almost. She wants to punish everyone who ever thought that she would not be able to carry on after her father's death."

Jocelyn inclined his head. He spoke softly. "Perhaps it is fitting for her to feel that way."

"But to live for revenge? That is not the way, Captain Avebury. It is not the way to happiness."

"What is the way to happiness, then?"

Melinda struggled to find words. "To live with ... dignity. With grace. Not anger."

Jocelyn surprised her by grinning. She watched as he went to pull one curtain partially over the doors, preventing the strong afternoon sun from entering and spoiling the carpets. He positioned himself against one door, his watchful eye still on Catherine, who had made her slow and halting way over to a stone bench. The exertion had apparently made her hot: she sank down onto the seat, then loosened the shawl a little so that it draped down her back.

"Tell me, Miss Carlyle. Is Sir Lyle a frequent visitor to Wansdyke?"

Melinda shrugged her slim shoulders. "He is a very old acquaintance of Catherine's. Perhaps. I don't believe he has been back in England for long. He has not been in Bath for many months, in any case. He has been away at sea."

Jocelyn did not take his eyes from Catherine's form, silhouetted in the sunlight. "He is very wealthy, I understand?"

"Oh, very. Shockingly so. I daresay he is almost as wealthy as Catherine." Melinda laughed at her own joke. "But he does not care to be tied down – he wanders hither and thither. His mother lives just outside Bath and he visits her now and again, but he is not someone who would find happiness in one place." She watched Catherine as the shawl slipped further down her back. "She ought to fix her shawl," she murmured to herself.

"When he is not in Bath, where is he?"

"Mmm? Sir Lyle, you mean? Oh, in London. I believe he is quite a notorious rake. He is not motivated by money, it seems, since he has so much. But he enjoys risk. He likes hunting, cards, his ships – things of that sort. Women." Melinda put her hand over her mouth, embarrassed at her own audacity. "I beg your pardon," she said. "I have been quite unmannerly." She rose.

"Stay, Miss Carlyle," Jocelyn protested. "I apologise for asking you such questions. I am new in Bath and merely wish to know Kate's friends better."

"You call her Kate?" Melinda was amused. "She must love you indeed, to allow you to be so familiar. I doubt very much most men would have had the courage to address her so. Even after marriage." She picked her reticule up from the table beside her. "I will join Catherine in the shrubbery. Will you come?"

"No, not at the moment," Jocelyn replied. "I will join you shortly."

He watched as Melinda descended the stairs and walked quickly across the lawn, calling to her friend. Catherine turned. For a moment, his heart leapt and seemed to stop; the pink-and-white glow of her complexion radiated happiness and good health, and he fought the urge to dash down the stairs and enfold her in his arms. Her hair had the lustre of the gold thread that Indian women used in their saris. The edges of her shawl slipped off her shoulders as she reached out to welcome her friend. For some unspeakable, unknowable reason, Jocelyn felt his throat catch. He turned away.

Never in his life had he imagined that someone so beautiful, so brave, could love him. And love him she did. He knew she did. He wished he could tell her that she had crept into his heart, that she had insinuated herself into his mind, into his life, and that he would never forget her. He wished he could tell her that some-times, at the height of passion, he wished he didn't have to leave.

But it was vital he leave such thoughts unspoken. It would never do for her to suspect that she meant as much as she did to him. Because he would leave. And when he did, it would be forever.

CHAPTER 24

*W*hen Sir Lyle arrived some weeks later to offer his congratulations, Catherine was indisposed. Her child was expected in the early spring.

She had objected to being sent to bed merely to recover from a slight dizzy spell. Lydia Barrow had overruled her, as had Jocelyn, and she pouted.

"I cannot sit here in bed until March," she grumbled. But she was delighted, and it showed. She asked Lydia to send Clara out for skeins of wool. She was hoping to knit a blanket for the nursery. Lydia obliged, although she confided to Jocelyn that Catherine had never knitted anything in her life and her sewing was frightful.

Jocelyn was both touched and terrified. The thought of his seed growing inside her filled him with a sort of confused panic. He wondered if he would be able to sail before the birth. He didn't think he could stand to actually see his child, to know that he was visiting upon the poor soul not only the sins of a father but also those of a grandfather.

Sir Lyle was waiting when Jocelyn entered the drawing room.

"I offer my congratulations, Captain Avebury!" he said in a jolly tone. "What, is the countess not receiving guests?"

"She is indisposed, unfortunately. She sends her apologies."

"Ah?" Sir Lyle leant back in his seat, a biscuit dangling from his fingertips. "Indisposed?"

"Yes." Jocelyn offered no further comment.

Sir Lyle bit into the biscuit, chewing contemplatively.

"Well done," he murmured. He glanced at Jocelyn. "I assume that I should offer you congratulations on the impending birth."

"I did not say anything to suggest it," Jocelyn returned.

"Only one thing would be serious enough to keep Catherine Claverton in bed on a sunny summer afternoon." Something in Jocelyn's expression caused him to pause, and then to say mildly, "I say, Captain Avebury. I came to extend my warmest felicitations on the occasion of your marriage. Not to quarrel with you."

He dug around in a pocket, and produced a folded sheet of paper. Jocelyn looked at it.

"What is it?" he said flatly, without making a move toward the paper.

"It's for you."

Jocelyn shrugged. "Do me the kindness of telling me what it is, Sir Lyle. I have no wish to play any games."

"And neither have I. Although I am mystified as to why you would suppose that I have such intentions."

"I'm not a fool."

Sir Lyle raised his eyebrows. "I never thought that you were." He returned the paper to his pocket. "But, since you apparently do not wish to deal with me, I will confine my comments to the following. Lieutenant Stephen Bright told the Admiralty of matters they felt compelled to investigate. But happenstance decreed he should drop dead before he could be called upon to substantiate his claims." He patted his pocket. "I was simply going to show you the transcript of his testimony."

"Bright is dead?" The words scraped uncomfortably in Jocelyn's throat. He stared at Sir Lyle's hand, still on the pocket.

"He will not trouble you further." Sir Lyle looked at him curiously. "Why, the news distresses you! Let me pour you some wine."

"No! No, thank you very much." Jocelyn sat limply. He looked up at Sir Lyle. "What happened? How did he die? Good God, he was younger than I! He could not have been ill ..."

Sir Lyle shrugged. He walked over to serve himself more tea. "A complete mystery, to be sure. But who can tell about these things."

"Where was he? In London?"

"Yes." Sir Lyle measured sugar into his cup with precision. "He had given his testimony the week before. The Admiralty told him that they would investigate his claims. And then—" Sir Lyle snapped his fingers. "Just like that."

"Good God!" Jocelyn said again.

"If I may say so, Captain Avebury, it is good fortune in the extreme. You will certainly not be held accountable for anything on the basis of the ravings of a man who is now dead."

Jocelyn shook his head. "I-I don't know. It seems—"

Sir Lyle returned to his seat. "It's a gift, Captain Avebury. Take the gift."

There was a pause in which the only sounds were the clink of Sir Lyle's spoon and the muffled report of doors opening and closing somewhere in the house. Jocelyn finally spoke.

"I don't want it, Sir Lyle. I don't know what—"

"Say no more." Sir Lyle nodded toward the door. Jocelyn bowed his head in assent.

Another silence followed.

"You can wait for your instructions. You are free now. They will surely come."

"I have been waiting. I do not know what those instructions will be."

"Oh, come now, Captain Avebury!" Sir Lyle laughed. "You have made the correct choices, and all bring you closer to one end. We both know what will happen. You will get a ship. Probably quite a nice ship. And a mission. And you will leave."

"What is your interest in me, Sir Lyle?"

"You know what it is. You saved my dim-witted half-brother."

"There is more."

"There is nothing more," Sir Lyle said firmly, rising. "Nothing more than appreciation for the behaviour of a gentleman."

"I am no gentleman, Sir Lyle."

"That, Captain Avebury, is your own demon." Sir Lyle reached for his hat. "I wish you happy. You will tell the countess, I hope, that I also offer the most heartfelt wishes for her good health and happiness. And you may rely on me to look out for her when you have gone to sea."

What? What did that mean?

Their eyes met and locked.

Sir Lyle looked away first. He turned and went to the door. "Good afternoon, Captain Avebury."

Suddenly, the scene before Jocelyn blurred, as if a foggy mist had crept into the room and descended upon him. He blinked, shook his head slightly.

It isn't my child.

He could not believe that he had never thought this before.

It isn't my child.

Appreciation for the behaviour of a gentleman? No, that was not it. Sir Lyle's favours had nothing to do with being a gentleman. If anything, it was entirely the opposite.

Jocelyn sank down into a chair, not bothering to watch Sir Lyle leave. He covered his eyes with one shaky hand. He felt as if Catherine had cut out his heart and left him to bleed.

It isn't my child. The child is Sir Lyle's.

That would explain everything. He had been ensnared in a trap. She needed a father for the child. Sir Lyle, for whatever reason, was unwilling to name himself. The hasty marriage, the inexplicable willingness of Beaseley to procure a marriage licence without really knowing with certainty that Avebury was who he said he was. Everyone was in on it. Except him.

He felt numb.

Being taken as a fool was the least of his problems. It wasn't the first time and wouldn't be the last. But his heart! He had given his heart to her. He had thought that she loved him. She seemed open, guileless, vulnerable, even as she pretended to be tough. And he loved her. He loved that spurned, neglected girl in her jewels and pretty dresses. He could make her laugh. He used to sing to her while out on their walks, make up nonsense verses to her favourite songs until she begged him to stop, covering his mouth with her hands and giggling until she was near to collapse.

He loved her vanity and quick temper – and even that she was a better rider than he. She was a natural horsewoman, so grand and fierce when she rode, that he didn't mind at all that she made him look absurd on a horse in comparison. She had told him that her father would not invest in a decent mount for her, that he had kept only carriage horses in the stables once he was too fat and feeble to ride himself. One of the grooms had taught her to ride, and she would sometimes sneak down to his family home in the village, riding in a farmer's cart, so that she could borrow a horse. She had begged for audiences with her father, hoping to persuade him not to get rid of all the horses – she wanted just one, a mare that was the right height for her to mount without difficulty or help. He ignored her requests, of course. So she had kept a horse stabled in the village – until someone reported her to the earl.

Jocelyn admired her verve and her refusal to knuckle under. He wished he had half her spirit. But spirit would not have saved her from the opprobrium of bearing Sir Lyle's child outside marriage. So, if Sir Lyle had refused marry her, she had merely done what she needed to do. He just wished she had loved him instead.

That poor unborn child, he thought. *And poor Kate. She's been a fool. She should never have trusted Lyle, that cursed, lying—*

The mist cleared as he tried to get a grip on his faculties. He could kill that bastard! God help him if he stepped back into this room. He would break his neck, feel a satisfying crunch between his fingers—

Control, he thought. *Control. It will do the babe no good to kill his father. Besides, none of this matters – I'm off to sea. I've saved Kate and her child from certain disaster. How ironic that I, of all people, should be the one to rescue a countess from disgrace, when I am the one who should be in disgrace.*

CHAPTER 25

S ummer was passing them by; it had seemed too long in coming and had arrived in such a burst of joy that its fading seemed inevitable. Catherine's rides with Jocelyn were soon no more than a memory and her sturdy constitution was overcome by nausea and the headache. The long days were shrinking; cooler nights prompted Catherine to pull the windows shut, despite Jocelyn's protests that he had no wish to shut out the symphony of autumn sounds.

"You are such a sailor," Catherine scolded. "Have you missed the sounds of the country so much? Are there no insects at sea?"

"We will have to shut ourselves in soon enough," he said. "Why start so soon?"

The argument was mild, never resolved. Catherine supposed that it showed the difference between land-dwellers and sailors, although Jocelyn would never claim as much. But Catherine was content with what he was willing to share. It was more than she had ever thought to hope for. Their lovemaking continued to be passionate and complete. He never denied her, was ever kind and considerate.

There was, however, a single fear that still lurked unbidden in the corridors of her mind. And that was that he would leave her. The arrangement, after all, had been for him to give her an heir and for her to work to give him his freedom – a ship, with Captain Avebury at the helm, destined for points unknown. At times she was sorely tempted to send a note to Beaseley in his London office begging him to sabotage Jocelyn's standing in the Navy. But that, she felt, would be like stealing away his soul.

Even now, as she watched him idly roaming the halls of Wansdyke, she knew that his heart was dying. He needed to be at sea. Far away from her, from the ties that would smother him to death.

She was a mature woman, she told herself. She knew her purpose in life. She would bear her child. She would assume her role as countess.

She would destroy the portrait.

Ah, the portrait.

LaFrance was desperate. He hung on the coattails of a few patrons in the highest circles of the ton. It was exceedingly expensive but good self-promotion. There was talk of a commission here, a sketch there. He was very good at quickly rendering images of the precious golden-haired daughters of the wealthy. These works seemed to keep him supplied with beef and brandy: some of the notes that he sent to Catherine actually stank of drink.

She hid them obsessively from Jocelyn who had taken to inspecting the post with keen interest. She assumed that he was searching for word from the Admiralty, hoping to escape Wansdyke at the first opportunity. Her heart sank every time she witnessed his eager interest in the post followed by obvious disappointment on his boyish face.

And yet, when he caught her staring at him, he never failed to offer her a kind word and a gentle embrace. Dressed, she still appeared as slim as she had ever been and, but for a vague queasiness and lack of appetite, did not feel as if she were to deliver a St Clair earl in the spring at all. She wished she could heal whatever malady was eating away at his soul.

But first, she would ensure the continuity of her line. Her line, she thought smugly. Not her father's or her grandfather's line. Her own. She had already sent word to Wales that she intended to inspect the ancestral home. It was a castle. A small castle sure enough but a castle nonetheless.

But first of all, she had to destroy that portrait. That was the first order of business.

She spoke to Lydia. After all, it was she who had introduced her to LaFrance and his useless preening and primping friends.

"You will never succeed in wresting that portrait from him," Lydia said immediately. "He thinks it is the only thing that can make his future certain. He wants a real patron, someone who will give him a peaceful establishment where he can paint what he wishes. And to get that he will need to show a collection of his best work."

"Ridiculous!" scoffed Catherine. "He would die of boredom away from society."

"But he cannot maintain his life in town forever, and he knows that."

"I need that portrait, Lydia. I need it destroyed. Could I pay him for it?"

Lydia shook her head. "Impossible. He is convinced that it is the portrait that will give him the life he feels he deserves."

Catherine felt the noose tightening about her neck. She had to get her hands on the portrait, to destroy it, to rid herself of the threat it posed to her happiness so that she could move on with her life.

Sometimes, it seemed impossible that she had ever done such an amazingly foolish thing. That she had been so young, so vulnerable to stupid fear, stupid pride.

The St Clair earldom had saved her. She marvelled when she

thought of how different her life might have been had she remained nothing but the crippled daughter of an ailing earl, a single female with no relations who might take her in. She and Lydia Barrow would have been doomed to live their lives as elderly spinsters. The thought made her shudder. At best, there might perhaps have been a respectable youngest son who would pity her and offer his hand.

"I have to get to London," she said aloud. "I must talk some sense into LaFrance."

"My lady," Lydia said quickly, "it is impossible. Absolutely not."

"Oh, really, now," Catherine said dryly. "Surely you are not about to lecture me on propriety?"

"It was very wrong of me to accompany you in the past," Lydia said. "Very wrong indeed. I wish I had not done so."

"Well, it is too late now. And I have got to stop LaFrance. Money – I am sure he will take money."

"My lady, we must think of something else. I assure you, money will not be enough for him. And you absolutely cannot go to London. In your condition—"

"Yes, yes, I know," Catherine said irritably. "I shall look enormous. Like an elephant. Well, I will have a new wardrobe. Perhaps something can be contrived that allows me to look presentable. In any case, I will not be making any social calls. I will go in disguise, if you like. For goodness' sake, Lydia, what will it take to convince you? You will have to come with me."

Lydia frowned but bent her head slightly in acquiescence. "And what about the captain?" she asked softly.

Catherine stiffened. "He mustn't know," she said. "It would be dreadful, should he find out."

"Perhaps you underestimate him, my lady. You might consider telling him the truth."

Catherine laughed, the harsh noise echoing, bouncing off the walls like brittle chips of cold sunlight. "The truth? Oh, Lydia. You are a fool!" She rose slowly, holding out her hand for Lydia's support. Very deliberately, she made her way across her bedchamber, her limp more pronounced than she was usually willing to allow.

"You are in pain, my lady?"

"A little more than usual, I'm afraid. My joints feel … somewhat uneven." Catherine sank into a large chair next to the bed. "This chair is a little better."

"My lady, I will, of course, accompany you to London. But meanwhile, LaFrance continues to send his notes."

"Write him a reply," Catherine said. "Tell him that I appreciate his predicament most sincerely, and beg his pardon for not replying sooner. I am sure he has seen the announcement of the marriage in the paper, so we need not offer explanation. Tell him that I will pay him a call very soon, and beg him to await word."

"I understand." Lydia turned to leave.

"And, Lydia—"

Lydia looked back at Catherine.

"Avebury is never to find out. Never. Is that clear?"

Lydia nodded. She left, drawing the door closed behind her.

For a long while, Catherine sat rubbing her aching limbs. Jocelyn was away on some errand. Wansdyke was very quiet.

Tell him the truth. Why, the notion of it was … what on earth could she say? "Jocelyn, my love, there is a portrait of me in the hands of a scoundrel, and he means to exhibit it. Please, would you steal it from him and burn it?"

Catherine put her face in her hands. Her shoulders shook, and she wept. She was so sorry, so very sorry that she had allowed LaFrance to paint that portrait. If Jocelyn ever saw it – worse, if all of London saw it, as LaFrance was threatening – her life would be over.

And her child – doomed.

Similarly, her marriage – doomed.

She loved Jocelyn. He loved her as she was, the crippled child living in the shell of a young woman. She did not doubt it. It would be nice if he would speak the words – but she would not press him. The words meant nothing when compared to having him.

CHAPTER 26

When the footsteps came, she was standing beside the French doors leading down to the formal garden, idly contemplating a walk. She was terribly tired, but it had always been her habit to engage in a late afternoon walk when the weather permitted, and she was loath to change her habits. She was also indulging in secret joy. The baby was yawning, stretching, and occasionally jabbing her from within his comfortable warm cave, and she wanted to be somewhere private and out-of-doors where she could enjoy the performance. She wished she knew where Jocelyn was, so that she could share her news.

She raised her head and turned slightly. The sound of two pairs of feet echoed sharply off the floor. They stopped at the door, but no one entered.

She waited, frowning. At long last, a knock sounded.

"Yes?"

The door opened. It was Beaseley. Catherine relaxed. "Mr Beaseley, how lovely to see you. I trust you are well?" She began to walk toward him, then stopped. Beaseley was not alone.

"Lady St Clair." Beaseley stepped into the room, then paused uncomfortably. He glanced at his companion. An officer. In naval dress.

"You have a friend with you?" Catherine looked from one man to the other. The Navy man was middle-aged, slightly paunchy. She could divine nothing about his rank or importance from the decorations on his uniform, but imagined from his refined appearance and the polite manner in which he bowed to her that he was no common sailor. Perhaps this was Beaseley's naval contact; perhaps there was good news. Her heart began to beat a little faster. Perhaps Jocelyn was being sent to sea. Or perhaps he was being made an admiral and would be in London indefinitely – oh, please! She hoped desperately that this was the case.

"Lady St Clair, may I introduce Admiral Wolcott?"

"How do you do, Admiral Wolcott? Please come in," Catherine said brightly. "Mr Beaseley, I have been wondering about you. It has been a while." She reached out to support herself against a cabinet. Her legs felt wobbly, and she thought vaguely of how humiliating it would be to faint in front of her guests. She looked around and spotted a chair with sturdy armrests. Slowly, she began to make her way toward it.

The door shut behind the Navy man. Everyone turned. It was Jocelyn. He looked around the small gathering, and Catherine suddenly sensed his fear. It was fear – quite unmistakable. She paused, wondering if she should say something, but all his attention was on the Navy man.

What was he hiding from her? The thought pierced the thin cloud of achy wooziness in her mind. She felt her back throb uncomfortably, and leant on a marble-topped table for support before resuming her awkward walk over to the chair. Upon reaching it, she sank down in relief and turned her attention to Jocelyn. Yes, he was hiding something. Something of consequence.

"Good afternoon, Captain Avebury." Beaseley spoke first. "This is Admiral Wolcott."

"Sir."

"Do not trouble yourself with formalities, Captain," the admiral said easily. He had a pleasant smile, Catherine observed. Jocelyn maintained a rigid stance.

"I met Admiral Wolcott in London." Beaseley looked ill at ease. "I had some business to transact at the Admiralty. It was a ... lucky coincidence that meant I was able to travel here with him."

"Yes." Jocelyn nodded curtly. He gestured toward the room. "Please make yourselves comfortable."

"Yes, of course," Beaseley said hastily. There was a brief scuffle as Beaseley rushed to arrange chairs and Catherine offered tea. She sat back again, her nervous gaze on Jocelyn. He did not look at her.

"I have some uncomfortable news for you," the admiral began.

"For me?" Catherine said. The admiral's smile softened.

"Unfortunately, my lady, this will concern you. I am here to invite your husband to accompany me back to London."

"Is this about a new command?" Catherine looked from Beaseley back to the admiral again. Beaseley was studying his shoes.

"It is not about a new command." It was Jocelyn. Startled, Catherine looked at him, but he was gazing directly at the admiral.

"It is the investigation, is it not?"

"Yes. I am very sorry, Captain Avebury."

"What will they have me up for?"

There was a heavy pause. The admiral's gaze did not flinch, however, and he said finally, "I will not hold anything back. You have been accused of murder. And dereliction of duty."

"Murder," Jocelyn repeated, the syllables thudding blandly against the upholstered furniture.

"Murder!" gasped Catherine. She half rose from her seat, but the stabbing pain in her back caused her to drop back. "Mr Beaseley, I demand to know—"

"I am sorry, my lady. Had I only had the chance to forewarn you—"

"How can this be possible?" Catherine looked at Jocelyn, but he was looking hard at the admiral, his expression unreadable. "Avebury? Have you nothing to say in your defence? They are clearly mistaken!"

"If I may interrupt, my lady," the admiral said quietly. "I am here so that he may come with me to London for the purposes of offering that defence."

"This was the best I could do, my lady," Beaseley said. "They would have sent people here to arrest him."

"Arrest him! But-but – this is absurd! This is completely ridiculous!" Catherine looked back at Jocelyn. "Avebury! Please! Tell them! Surely you must have something to say!"

For a very long moment, no one spoke. Catherine stared so hard at Jocelyn's frozen countenance that her eyes began to fill. She dashed her tears against the back of her hand.

"Avebury," she whispered.

He did not look at her. He said to the admiral, "I have but a few things to take with me."

The admiral inclined his head.

"Wait," Catherine said, rising. Her head swirled, and she clutched at the arms of the chair, the knuckles of her hands whitening as she swayed.

"The gardens, admiral, are very fine." Beaseley rose also, nodding at the admiral. They made their way across the room, through the French doors and down the steps into the formal garden murmuring the occasional pleasantry, as if Catherine and Jocelyn did not exist.

It did not seem at all possible that the admiral was here to take Jocelyn away, that he would be arrested otherwise. It had to be an absurd nightmare. Surely, surely this was a mistake of grotesque proportions.

She felt her legs give way and fell, landing on her knees.

"Good God! Are you all right?" Jocelyn was beside her in a moment.

"Yes. Yes, quite all right – I have been having trouble walking all day. I am sure it is nothing. Most likely just—oh! Oh! Jocelyn, feel him!" She pressed his hand to her belly, suddenly joyous. They waited in silence.

"He has stopped," Catherine said, disappointed.

"Are you sure it – he—"

"Very sure. It feels just like—oh!"

Jocelyn sprang back in alarm. He gazed stupidly at the palm of his hand, then ever so gently placed it against Catherine's belly again. He felt the taps grow insistent, pushing through the wall of her abdomen as if the baby were furious at his imprisonment.

Catherine laughed in delight. "Can you believe how strong he is!"

Jocelyn removed his hand. "Kate." His face was sober.

"It is a mistake, is it not? Tell me it is a mistake." She reached for his hand again, holding it in her two small ones. It was so much larger, so calloused and sturdy, the hand of a working man, not an idle gentleman. She held it to her cheek, then her lips.

Jocelyn did not reply. He closed his eyes, his brow wrinkled as if he were in pain.

"You must say it. Say it, Jocelyn. Please."

"Kate, I may not see you again."

The sound of his voice chilled her. "Good God, Jocelyn, no! This will be sorted out. I will make sure of it. We have some influence in the Admiralty – I don't know where, exactly, but when my father was alive—"

"Kate."

"Jocelyn, do not," she said, her voice breaking. "No."

"You married me without knowing very much about me,

Kate. I'm afraid that this is what happens when you want some-thing so badly you ignore all else."

"No! Jocelyn, I won't believe it!" She dropped his hand, pulled his neck down so that her lips rested against his ear. "Tell me," she whispered. "Tell me. They have misunderstood something, or perhaps there is a jealous captain somewhere who has slandered you. These things can be fixed—"

"Kate, beloved—"

"It isn't possible, Jocelyn. It cannot be possible!" Her words ended on a wail.

"Listen to me, Kate."

She opened her eyes, loosened her grip on his neck slightly. His voice was so calm that it did not seem possible he was about to be carried off to London to face the investigation of the Royal Navy. She felt a shudder go through her, then a quiet calm began to seep into her heart, deadening it with icy certainty. *I am mistress of my own fate,* she reminded herself. *I was my own mistress before I married – and I am my own mistress still. With or without Jocelyn.*

She pulled her arms away. "I am listening," she said.

"This investigation may give me the chance to clear my name. In that case, I will return, possibly within a few short weeks." Jocelyn picked up her hands, gripped them tightly. His cloudy blue eyes were intense. "If not, you are to remember that you are carrying a child. The St Clair heir. Do not do anything foolish. Do you understand me?"

"Jocelyn, I can help you. If only I could get to London, I could—"

He gave her a little shake. "You idiot! Did you not hear me? I do not want you travelling or otherwise endangering your health."

Catherine felt a prickle of irritation. "What, do you think I am such an invalid that—"

He silenced her by kissing her so deeply that her breath left

174

her and, for a moment, she felt almost naked as he ran his fingers under the curve of her chin and around the edge of her bodice. He tightened his arms around her.

"Kate, dearest," he murmured.

"Please, Jocelyn," she whispered. "Please. I am sure I can help."

Jocelyn drew back a little. He gazed at her, his fingers arranging and rearranging the wisps of golden hair that had freed themselves from their pins. "Ah, Kate," he said, his voice hollow. "You wanted an heir. Is that not enough for you?"

"No," she said, catching his hand and pressing it to her heart. "You are the only person who has seen past my leg and my fortune – who has treated me with kindness and dignity – why should it be so odd that I love you?"

Her voice cracked at the end of her sentence. Jocelyn's gaze fell and, for a brief moment, Catherine suddenly thought that now he might reveal the truth. There was something pent-up inside him, something so awful that he could not possibly live with it alone. She was certain of it.

But he said nothing. He rose, and she rose with him.

"Kate," he said. "Listen to me, my dear. I know that you are strong. I know that you are able to take care of yourself and of Wansdyke, of the child. But should you ever have need of … need of a man, promise me that you will call upon Sir Lyle for assistance."

"Sir Lyle?" Catherine gave an incredulous gasp. "But-but why?"

"He once said that if you were ever in need, he would be honoured to be of assistance." Jocelyn gave her hands a last squeeze. "Promise me."

"Promise you? Why, of course! I would promise you anything – but Sir Lyle … I don't understand why he would—" Catherine stammered.

Jocelyn leant forward and dropped a gentle kiss on her forehead. "I must see to my things." He turned and walked toward the door.

"Wait!" Catherine cried. He stopped. "You cannot go without telling me. The murder – who was killed?"

Jocelyn did not turn around. But she saw his shoulders sag.

"It matters not, dearest Kate. It could have been anyone."

And he left.

CHAPTER 27

They left without even drinking their tea. Admiral Wolcott was courteous but insistent, and Catherine was left in no doubt that her husband was now a prisoner. She tried to convince the admiral to use the new carriage with the St Clair coat of arms on the panel, but he was again politely firm; the hired coach was still at their disposal, and that would do very well for the long ride back to London. Catherine tried to press her point. She did not like the idea of Jocelyn being taken away like a criminal and conceded only when Beaseley reminded her that she might wish to have use of the carriage. She had every intention of going to London—to do whatever needed to be done to stop LaFrance, and to try to extract Jocelyn from this dreadful mistake.

Beaseley remained and apologised humbly that he had not been able to do as she had wished and improve Jocelyn's standing with the navy.

"But truly, my lady, every approach I made on his behalf was met with uncomfortable shuffling and stammering. It was indeed perplexing until I realised that Captain Avebury was under investigation."

"Was anyone willing to discuss the details of this investigation?"

"Yes." Beaseley brushed crumbs of toast off his waistcoat before taking another sip of tea. "The late earl had a friend, an old school friend, whom he had not seen for many years. Lord Richard Whitford. He attended your father's funeral and I took the opportunity to renew our acquaintance. He's actually not a naval officer, but a diplomat and a scholar. However, I suspected that he might somehow have heard of the mess, and indeed I was right. He told me everything, and said that he had seen the dispatches from Gibraltar that described the incident."

The incident. But his lieutenant had stated only that Jocelyn had missed a rendezvous because he had stayed in Bombay to procure a cargo of opium.

"But that was not murder! Whose murder?"

"Stephen Bright. The lieutenant who made the accusation against Captain Avebury. He was found dead in his room shortly after his return from Gibraltar."

"But wait." Catherine shook her head in confusion. "I do not understand. Was Lieutenant Bright not a prisoner? Was he not responsible for the death of a man in a brawl?"

"Aye, my lady. But somehow, someone entered his room and murdered him. At first it was thought that he died of natural causes, but the coroner claims that an exotic poison from the port cities of the Indian Ocean was used. Without Bright's testimony there is no case against Captain Avebury. And so Lieutenant Bright's family claims that Captain Avebury must have been responsible for the murder."

"But that's impossible!" Catherine rose from her seat. "He has not left Wansdyke since we arrived, and before that we were at Albrook, and before that in Bath. He could not have murdered anyone – not unless he hired someone to do it, and where is the evidence of that? The proof?"

"My lady," Beaseley said gently. "He is not now under arrest.

He is under investigation because he went willingly with the Admiral. And if he cooperates with the investigators there is no reason to suppose that they will not believe him. He was not anywhere near Bright's cell, and has no contact with anyone who might have been there. This is a military investigation, so some things may seem a trifle harsh to our eyes, but the truth will prevail in the end."

Catherine gripped the arms of the chair, her knuckles whitening. "That, Mr Beaseley, is where you are wrong. Truth is completely irrelevant. It always is. Only appearances matter. And if Avebury appears to be guilty, he will be treated like a criminal."

Beaseley seemed to be at a loss. He fiddled with his napkin and uneasily took another mouthful of tea. Catherine limped over to the door and opened it. She leant into the hall.

"It seems I will need use of the carriage after all," she said quietly to the attending footman, her voice calm. "Please send Lydia to wait on me."

FINDING SIR LYLE PROVED TO BE TRICKY. HE WAS NOT IN HIS BATH apartments, nor was he at any of the several entertainments that Catherine visited. The evening was darkening when she finally thought to visit Melinda's home, where a quiet card party was taking place.

"Sir Lyle? I expect Robin would know – he went riding with him yesterday. Let me ask him. But how are you, Catherine? I have not seen you in so long." Melinda stepped back and surveyed her critically. Catherine flushed. She felt bloated and very large.

"I did not think to change my dress before I left," she confessed.

"You look well," Melinda said reassuringly. "You are not ill?"

"Sometimes. Not very. Oh, Melinda, would you ask Robin? Would you ask him now?"

"Is something wrong, Catherine?" Melinda looked over her shoulder, to the corner where her stepmama held court over a table of formidable-looking matrons. She lowered her voice. "I loathe these card parties. Perhaps we can speak in private somewhere else. If we stay, they are sure to come out and subject you to rude questions about your … your health."

Catherine waved a polite goodbye as she followed Melinda out of the room – much to the obvious disappointment of the matrons, who were clearly having a good gossip about the Countess St Clair and her delicate condition. Grasping her friend's arm, she limped along the hall to a less formal sitting room.

Melinda shut the door. "I apologise for their bad manners," she said.

"You goose," Catherine said with affection. "As if I cared about such things. Those people are nothing to me."

Melinda smiled wryly. "You were always your own person, Catherine. I admire you for that. But you are also a wife, and soon to be a mother. You cannot be as carefree as before. How is the captain?"

Catherine looked down at her hands. "It is a long story. He is in London, on navy business." The lie slipped easily off her tongue. *It is for the child*, she thought. *I will not have his father shamed.*

"And why do you search for Sir Lyle?"

"I am passing along a message from Avebury." Another lie, said even more easily. Jocelyn had told her to seek assistance from Sir Lyle if she required it, and she was determined to discover why.

"He was at his farm yesterday. Robin was full of news about the horses, but I admit I was not attending." A knock sounded at the door, and a footman appeared with a tray. Melinda sent him out again with instructions to send Robin to them.

"Have some supper, Catherine. You must be famished. I cannot believe that you have been searching for Sir Lyle since teatime. Should you not be taking better care of yourself?"

Catherine allowed her attention to drift as Melinda clucked over her and set out a supper of cold meats. Catherine had no appetite, but pecked politely at what she had been offered. She glanced impatiently at the mantelpiece clock. It was quite late.

At last, the door burst open. "Well!" Melinda's brother Robin strode into the room. Tall and dark, like his sister, his good looks were emphasised by his sporty disregard for fashion. He favoured well-worn riding clothes, and his grip on Catherine's hand was firm and commanding. "Countess! I am to call you Lady St Clair, I believe?"

"You will make me blush," Catherine complained. "You have called me by my Christian name for as long as I can remember. Must you be so odiously formal?"

"Only because your noble demeanour requires it, my lady," Robin said, bowing exaggeratedly over her hand.

"Dreadful man, your brother," Catherine said to Melinda, who frowned at him.

"Robin, I am sure that you have a dozen buyers and sellers of horseflesh in one of the rooms upstairs, all haggling furiously. We will not keep you. Catherine is wondering if you know where Sir Lyle might be. You saw him yesterday, did you not?"

"I did. We had a good ride over his estate. But I believe he is now in Bath."

"He is not in Bath," Catherine interjected.

"Ah! Well then, I know. He was talking about a ship that is due in to Dover shortly. That will be where he has gone."

"Oh, no!" Catherine exclaimed.

"You could send him a message," Robin offered.

"I could, I suppose." Catherine rose from her seat. "Thank you for the supper, Melinda. And you, too, Robin."

"Is this message very important? The one from the captain?"

Catherine looked at Melinda blankly before realising that she had invented this convenient lie herself. "Yes, very," she said.

"Perhaps Sir Lyle will return soon," Melinda said.

"Perhaps." Catherine smiled. "Do not worry about it. I am sure all will be fine."

All will be fine, she repeated to herself as Lydia's sturdy arm helped her up into the carriage.

All will be fine, she repeated to herself as the carriage jerked away into the dark.

All will be fine.

It was beginning to rain, a miserable autumn rain that promised more damp and mist, by the time she arrived back at Wansdyke. She sat down in the library to write a note to Sir Lyle, addressed to him care of his ship in the port of Dover, and sent a messenger off with it immediately.

Then she waited.

SHE WAITED FOR A FULL WEEK BEFORE HE ARRIVED, DIRTY AND sweating, on horseback. She had just had a note from Jocelyn. She passed it to Sir Lyle without a word.

He took it and read it silently. Then he looked up. "I am sorry I could not come sooner. As I said in my letter, there were problems with my cargo. Still, it does sound as if the captain is being treated fairly well, all things considered."

"Considering that he is under investigation for a murder he did not commit," Catherine said bitterly. She motioned to Sir Lyle to sit down, which he did gingerly, trying not to get grime on the damask-covered chair. "They have no notion of justice."

"Ah but they do." Sir Lyle gave her a hard look. "I have spent many hours in the company of sailors this past week. I assure you that justice amongst seafaring types is harsh and swift. The fact that Avebury is being given the freedom to stay in his own quarters and the opportunity to participate in his own investigation is … well, it is extraordinary. It only shows what a good opinion they have of him. It is likely they feel a need to show Lieutenant Bright's family they are investigating his death, but that they also have no desire to cause Avebury any grief."

"Do not toy with me, Sir Lyle. I know how grave the situation is." Catherine hoisted herself up from the chair. She saw Sir Lyle's expression. "Yes, I know," she said irritably. "I am large and unwieldy and should not be troubling myself with matters too complex for my female mind. The cooler months are upon us, and I am fast becoming exhausted and demoralised. It is enough that I have waited this long for your reply to my letter."

"But what do you expect me to do, Lady Catherine?" Sir Lyle's question was gentle.

"Avebury told me to call upon you should I have need."

"Did he now?"

Catherine looked at him sharply, but his expression was bland. "Yes. And I do not know why, except that perhaps you are better acquainted than I assumed."

"We are both men with our fortunes at sea, Lady Catherine. We have an understanding. Nothing more."

"You are lying," Catherine said, trying to control her anger.

"What a harsh mistress you are," Sir Lyle said mildly. "I ask again, what would you have me do?"

Catherine walked slowly in the direction of the French doors. Her gait was becoming more and more awkward as the growing child caused her weight to shift. The doctor had warned her to avoid risking a fall that might harm the unborn child, so she had curtailed her walks and was more careful than usual on the stairs. Her health was good, but she directed every ounce of her energy toward her child, and there was none left to spare.

"I want him freed," she said.

"And how would I do that?"

"You have your ways. I know that you do."

"What makes you think so?"

"You know that world – the world of seafaring men."

"And why would I be more capable than you would, O Countess? Daughter of the Earl Delamare? Countess St Clair of Wales?"

"You mock me cruelly, Sir Lyle." Her voice caught. "I love him, you know."

"That does not surprise me, although I would have made you a better husband."

"We will not discuss it. It was … improper of me not to decline your offer immediately."

"Oh, ho?" Sir Lyle laughed harshly. "And now you expect me to do something for you for no compensation at all?"

There was a deep silence. A breeze blew gently through the barren shrubbery outside, only the occasional leaf rolling by. The laughter of the servants echoed down the hall. Someone was telling a joke.

The quiet was brittle and ready to crack.

"Forgive me," Sir Lyle said into the silence. "It is my cursed male pride. I envy Avebury. He has what I do not."

Catherine half-turned. "If you will not help, I will go to London and handle it myself."

"That would be a most foolish course of action."

"It would be my only recourse. Beaseley has done all he can. Perhaps I can do more."

"If it is the only way to stop you, I will do whatever I can to help. You cannot wander around the halls of the Admiralty in your condition. You will hurt him more than you will help."

"I thought I was the Countess St Clair? All-powerful?"

"Forgive me. I was rude. Your refusal of my hand left me bitter and angry."

"Would it not be natural for a wife to support her husband?

184

Why would it be so strange for me to try?"

She felt him come up quietly behind her. For a terrible moment, the air crackled; she thought he would embrace her, put his arms around her shoulders. She stiffened. But the gesture did not come.

"You are an impressive female."

"I only love my husband."

"You try to control the winds of fate."

"I will not let events I neither know about nor care about ruin my life. Or the life of my child."

"Tell me, Lady Catherine. Does Avebury know that you love him?"

"Why-why ..." The words would not emerge. "Why, of course, he must."

There was a rustling noise as Sir Lyle moved away. "Good," she heard him say softly. "Very good."

She was afraid to turn around. She was afraid that he still meant to refuse her. She stared out of the French doors into the distance.

Eventually, she heard him open the door and leave.

A note arrived the next day:

My lady, I am off to London. I will do my best. Do nothing foolish. L.

She had almost breathed a sigh of relief when another note arrived, this one from LaFrance.

He was going to offer "limited private showings" of the portrait to men "of the first circles," he wrote. This would not harm her in any way, he assured her, since no one was likely to know what she looked like – given that she had spent so much of her life in Bath and its environs. He wanted to use the portrait to amass a steady income from a well-paying clientele. Of course, he had no intention, absolutely none, of selling it.

Catherine called up to Lydia. She was to pack immediately for a trip to London.

CHAPTER 28

Sir Lyle arrived at his London house in the dead of the night to find a guest awaiting him. He was not surprised, for he had asked the small, weedy-looking man to meet him.

"I need all the information you can gather on Jocelyn Avebury. Captain, Royal Navy, recently married to the Countess St Clair. There may be some confusion about the countess – she is the daughter of the late Earl Delamare, and her title comes to her through the maternal line."

"Ah, one of those." The little man cocked his glass of whiskey at him.

"Yes. I expect you are familiar with such titles since they are more common in your part of the world."

The man inclined his head. He was Irish.

"There is something a little odd about Avebury. I would like you to find out what it is. He is accused of murder. He is not guilty, of course, but an investigation was called for, nonetheless."

"Is he one of your contacts?"

Sir Lyle laughed shortly. "No, which is a shame, since he is rumoured to be a smuggler. In that respect, he is as straight as a die, a thoroughly honourable man. Not at all like the ones I am accustomed to dealing with."

"Then the problem—?"

"I don't know. There is something odd about his accent, his behaviour. I want to know who his people are, how he came to join the navy. Everything."

The little man put down his glass. He nodded. "That should not be difficult."

"Perhaps." Sir Lyle rubbed his forehead. "It depends on what he is trying to hide."

WHY DON'T THEY JUST HANG ME?

The thought entered his mind over and over again as he peered through the clouded windowpane at the street outside. Smart carriages rolled by, street urchins screeched and threatened the traffic that seemed about to squash them at every turn. After the quiet of Wansdyke, the din was bewildering. It seemed bizarre to react so when he had spent several years of his young life on streets much like these. But that boy had come to the ruckus of London from the tranquillity of Yorkshire, and had then left for the relative quiet of the sea. Noise should have played a bigger part in his life than it had.

The rooms were rented and plainly furnished but much nicer than those he would have chosen before marrying Catherine. Marriage to a peeress, he reflected bitterly, had made him proud.

In point of fact, he had selected them because he was reluctant to embarrass the golden-haired, steel-nerved beauty who had got herself with child by a slippery fellow like Sir Lyle and then convinced a sailor to give the baby a name.

He was never going back to Wansdyke.

But when would she realise that?

She was a fool! She had thought to gain an earl by simply

standing up with him in church. She had thought to be revenged on her cruel father. She had thought to win the respect of society. She would gain an earl, possibly. But nothing else.

He regretted the marriage. He, too, had been a fool. But what had motivated him? A ship. Escape to the sea. He had thought she could extricate him from his troubles, somehow get him a ship.

But she claimed to be in love with him. He snorted. If she were, she truly was a fool.

And what on earth was wrong with Sir Lyle? Was he such a scoundrel that he would take away a maiden's innocence and then refuse to marry her? What made Catherine Claverton such a poor bride? Had he been put off by her leg? If so, then Sir Lyle was a fool as well.

Damn it all to hell! He loved her, God knew. He loved her desperately, for her strength and her fire and her passionate hold upon life.

Restlessly, he pulled away from the window and paced before the fire. A pot of tea sat, untouched, on a tray. A collection of political treatises lay beside it.

They were taking so long, taking such care over this so-called investigation. A slight acquaintance, whom he had come across while pacing the halls of the Admiralty, told him that the family of Lieutenant Bright had complained to those as far up the chain of command as they could reach – and they were wealthy and powerful. "It's a plague of red tape," he had said, "but you'll be cleared soon enough, my dear fellow."

Right.

There had to be more to it than there first appeared, Jocelyn thought again and again. There simply had to be more. Since the botched-up Indian commission, the confrontation with Bright and the brawl in Gibraltar everything had come crashing down. Something that didn't fit in with the orderly pattern of sailing life was needed to explain why it had happened all at once.

He had been waiting for it, he thought. Waiting, and waiting.

He had known all along that he couldn't maintain the farce forever. What an idiot he had been! Had he been intelligent enough to leave the navy with his fortune, to hide from the all-seeing eye of His Majesty's commanders, perhaps he would have been safely ensconced on a country property by now. With a roly-poly wife and a pack of children.

No, it had been bound to come out at some point. It had merely been a matter of time.

Would they hang him?

Were it not for the public humiliation involved, he would almost welcome that. It would be like coming full circle, coming home. A relief, of sorts.

But he couldn't bear the thought of what it would do to Catherine. It would rip the soul right out of her. And, even if the child were not his, he had no desire to do to a child what had been done to him. The thought of the heavy burden his public humiliation would place on a baby's shoulders made him feel queasy.

He wondered if the baby would be an earl or another golden-haired countess.

He wondered if there was any possible way for Sir Lyle to rescue the child.

Catherine's letters had been just like her, full of fire. Pages and pages of descriptions of the things he liked best about Wansdyke, the movements of the baby. No tears, no plaintive requests for his return. At the end of each letter, the same sentence:

I await your return with all my heart. C.

He had saved the letters, tying them in a neat little bundle with a blue ribbon he had bought for the purpose. *I'll leave them to the baby,* he thought vaguely.

~

"Captain Avebury, do you say that you speak the Hindu tongue?"

"Yes, sir."

"Did you acquire it through self-study?"

"Yes, sir."

"Do you have a particular interest in the country?"

"No, sir. I enjoy languages and, while on board, I made a study of as many as I could find texts for."

"What other languages do you speak?"

"Arabic, Malay, Spanish, and extremely poor Chinese – the dialect of the southern coast. There was a Chinaman on one of my commands."

"Yes, yes. We have noted that from the lists. Now, was this Lieutenant Bright also a studious fellow?"

"No, sir."

"Did he not accompany you about your business in the port of Bombay?"

"No, sir. I took with me some able seamen who were familiar with the local traditions."

"So Lieutenant Bright had no direct knowledge of your activities ashore?"

"That is correct."

"When you received word that Jonathan Waters – Viscount Roland – was trapped in the city, you left to search for him, without informing your lieutenant."

"That is correct."

"Is that usual?"

"Perhaps not, sir. But Lieutenant Bright was thoroughly occupied with the loading of provisions, and we were well aware of the time for the rendezvous." Hesitation. "I take full responsibility for the missed rendezvous, sir."

"I realise that, Captain Avebury. We appreciate your willingness to accept responsibility. What we are trying to understand here is Lieutenant Bright's accusation that you kept your movements in Bombay a secret, and that you rewarded the able seamen for doing the same."

"That was not true, sir. I understood from Viscount Roland's man that he was in trouble, and I went to investigate. That was all."

"Were Lieutenant Bright's accusations believed by any of your crew? Any at all?"

"I do not believe so. At least, I believe the subsequent brawl was due in part to Lieutenant Bright attempting to convince the crew that I had delayed the ship on purpose to sabotage the intelligence effort."

"An unfortunate incident."

Shuffling of papers, squeaking chairs.

"Captain Avebury, I must enter a line of questioning that may be uncomfortable. It concerns how you came to join the navy."

"Yes, sir."

It was over, Jocelyn thought. Once he had answered these questions, it would all be over. He tried to keep his breathing even, slow. He meditated on each breath, paying careful attention to filling his lungs so that he did not become faint.

"You were assisted by ... an uncle, I believe."

"Actually, he was a distant cousin, although I called him uncle, sir."

"How old were you?"

"Twelve, sir."

"And your parents? They did not object?"

"They were dead, sir. I was the ward of another cousin, an attorney-at-law in London."

"Did you have no wish to apprentice yourself to this cousin, the attorney-at-law?"

"He had several children, sir. The house was cramped and circumstances were difficult."

Jocelyn waited. But, amazingly, the question he dreaded did not come. He waited and waited. It was not asked. At least not out loud. But he could imagine it – and what might follow – all too clearly:

What happened to your parents?

My mother died of fever and my father was hanged, drawn and quartered as a traitor when I was seven. I was passed to a reluctant cousin in London who finally got rid of me by changing my name and sending me to sea. Better that a child drown than that his traitor blood taint them all.

Long live the King! I would give my life to defeat His Majesty's enemies. What a dreadful irony that three faithful subjects were executed because I was late to a rendezvous – late because I was rescuing a good-for-nothing officer from certain death in a Bombay brothel. I did indeed keep my business in Bombay a secret – because I knew that my senior officers would discourage my effort to save Lord Roland. I had no desire to be involved, but nor had I any desire to let a young Briton die.

But that was before I knew that Lord Roland is the half-brother of my enemy, Sir Lyle.

Sir Lyle the fornicator and fatherer of bastards. Violator of my wife. False friend extraordinaire.

CHAPTER 29

*T*hey travelled at night. Catherine did not tell Beaseley where she had gone, and left word with her household that she was visiting a desperately ill friend in the country. She and Lydia hired a conveyance at an inn just beyond the edge of town and, upon their arrival in London, went directly to a modest boarding house known to Lydia. No one there would recognise Catherine or ask questions; indeed, most of the other patrons were engaged in shady business of their own, and were as disinclined to notice their fellow travellers as they were willing to be noticed themselves.

Catherine was exhausted by the time they arrived. Without the comfort of her own well-sprung carriage and perfectly matched team of horses, she had been jolted and jostled and was nauseated and nearly delirious with fatigue. Lydia was heartily against the journey from the start, but set about her duties with the ferocity of a whirlwind when she saw that her mistress would not be dissuaded. At the boarding house, she ordered meals and changed the sheets on the beds before sending Catherine to her room with strict instructions to bathe and rest.

But Catherine was too nervous to relax. She paced, one hand

braced against the small of her back as she lurched from side to side, her leg buckling. It was early December. There were still three months until the child was due, and she was already so heavy and uncomfortable that she could not imagine worse. The doctor had said apologetically that it was on account of her bad leg she felt so uncomfortable and unsettled, but she was sure in her heart that there was something more.

Jocelyn. She wanted him back with a feverish intensity that became a dull ache in her heart. In her letters to him, she disguised her despair and her fear. She would not burden him with her love. After all, he had married her only to give her an earl and to go back to sea. She was sure that he loved her, but she would not make him say it. It would be enough if they could be together – if not for always, then at least occasionally.

And she would not allow the likes of LaFrance to jeopardise her almost-happiness. The portrait had been a stupid mistake of her youth. She would make him give it up. She had as much money, as much patience, as much determination as the task required.

For days, she waited while Lydia tried to contact the artist. He had left his previous quarters in a less-than-genteel part of London for a more respectable address. When Catherine heard this, she was momentarily terrified that he had already procured a patron on the strength of the portrait, but it turned out that the move had actually been intended to help solve the problem of his miserable finances. Although he had incurred a great deal of debt and expense, he felt his new quarters would allow him to show his paintings in a better light. In the hope of attracting a wealthy patron, he was also throwing extravagant parties that were way beyond his means.

But, as far as Lydia could discern, he had not yet revealed the existence of the portrait. There was no gossip about it – and Lydia had some expertise in ferreting out such information. Catherine watched with considerable sadness as she donned her finery and drenched herself with scent before heading into not-so-genteel London society: an exciting world that, to a neglected young girl with a twisted leg, had once seemed full of mystique and romance. Now it merely seemed sordid and scary.

A week into their stay, Lydia told Catherine that she had finally got hold of LaFrance.

"He knows we are here," she told Catherine.

"What else does he know?"

Lydia shrugged. She poured them each a cup of tea and carried it over to the table from the buffet. "He is a sneaky creature. I am sure he knows why we are here."

"You spoke to him?"

"No. But one of his friends relayed his greetings, so he knows we are here and will see us."

Catherine put her napkin on the table, her appetite suddenly gone. She had slept poorly and, lately, had been able to put very little weight on her bad leg, making walking next to impossible. Now she knew that confrontation was at hand, she had to be strong. She had to procure that portrait, no matter what the price.

"We will call on him today. I would assume he and his set do not make many morning calls, so he will probably be alone."

Lydia looked dubious. "I do not know if we should attempt to meet him alone at his apartments."

"What else are we to do, then?" Catherine exclaimed in irritation. She pushed her chair back from the table and held out her hand for assistance. "He knows we are here. He must know my condition. Surely he does not suppose that we are in London merely to make social calls. I will veil myself, and we will take a hackney. No one will see us."

"Yes, my lady," Lydia murmured. She wore a little frown, which annoyed Catherine.

"Do not desert me now, Lydia!" she said forcefully. "I have no one who can help me."

"Perhaps the captain should be the one to speak to him," Lydia murmured.

Catherine's knuckles grew white. She felt her nails biting into her palms. "No!" she managed to choke out. "He must never know."

Lydia slanted a glance at her as she led her to the door of the dining room. "He has his own burdensome past, my lady. Perhaps he will forgive you yours, if you forgive his."

At this Catherine stopped. "Forgive? There is nothing for me to forgive." She paused. "You are saying that there is yet something in his past that we do not know about."

"I am sure of it, my lady."

"I neither know nor care what he may have done. Surely he must know—"

"And he may be saying just the same about you, my lady."

Catherine shook her head. "What I have done is unforgivable," she whispered. "Utterly. But by this evening, I will have made sure no one can ever find out."

JOCELYN WATCHED AS THE ADMIRALS FILED INTO THE ROOM, THEIR boots clunking heavily against the floor. All was solemnity and pomp. He stood at his place, next to the witness seat in the centre of the room. It was a small chair, barely tall enough to contain his long frame. He assumed it was meant to be uncomfortable to remind those who sat in it that they lived only at the pleasure of the Crown.

He didn't need the reminder, he reflected. They owned him, and he was glad of it. A daily existence not circumscribed by the navy was painful. *I should not be allowed to run my own life*, he thought. *I am competent only when under someone else's command.*

"Captain Avebury, we regret the need to bring you in for yet more questioning. This is not a formal court martial, of course.

We wish merely to understand the unfortunate incident in which you were involved, and the subsequent mysterious death of Lieutenant Bright. We hope to finish with this affair as quickly as possible." The admiral leant forward. "In fact, we are quite sure that all will become clear today."

Today! For a second, Jocelyn felt the muscles of his body tense in an involuntary spasm. He felt a cramp in his calf. He suppressed the urge to reach down and rub his leg.

"After you give testimony today, Captain Avebury, we would ask that you remain in town until called to hear the final report." The admiral looked at him meaningfully. "We will announce at that time whether formal disciplinary action will be taken."

Formal disciplinary action.

He could hear the roar of the crowd. The squalling of a child, a mere infant, crying.

And Catherine – would she weep? Or would she lift her lovely chin in defiance and don widow's weeds without batting an eyelid?

She loved him. But, in this life, love would serve her ill – as it served all who dared to depend upon it. Love was not useful. Nerves of steel, ruthlessness – those were truly useful qualities. What was love? Nothing but a cloak for lust. An emotion that was only sanctified by the social convention of marriage.

He wondered again how Sir Lyle could have trapped her so effectively. Did he hold something over her? How could he not fear recriminations for his refusal to marry her?

Jocelyn's mind spun ever larger stories, devised ever more fanciful theories. A night of passion between two strong-willed people, with love never a possibility. An unintended conception. An abominable refusal to marry the mother or to acknowledge the child. A plausible story woven around a hapless sea captain who would marry a countess for his own desperate purposes.

If she had told him the truth, would he have agreed to marry her?

He was still pondering the question when the admirals asked him, for the third time, to give his version of the missed rendezvous out of Bombay. Exhausted, he began again.

"We left port two hours late—"

THEY LEFT FAR LATER THAN SHE WOULD HAVE LIKED, BUT IT COULD not be helped. She had discovered she had nothing appropriate to wear, nor had she a veil that would fully conceal her face and hair. She sent Lydia on a hurried excursion to find something – but not, of course, from Catherine's usual modiste. All Lydia could find was a voluminous cloak in navy blue and a matching veil, which she spent an hour adjusting so that it would not slip from Catherine's head. Lydia insisted they take every precaution and, fearing that Catherine would be recognised, she forced her to walk some distance from the boarding house – slow and tedious as the short journey was – in order to hail a hackney.

"This will attract far more attention," Catherine panted, trying to keep the cloak together in front as she lurched and jerked her way down the street.

"I apologise, my lady. But no one will look at us when we are in a crowd. However, if someone sees us hail a cab – that would be disastrous."

Catherine did not reply. It was too hard to talk, and the air was so cold that it made her lungs hurt. The weather was bright, the sky cloudless and blue. The gardens at Wansdyke would be empty and forlorn at this time of year and the gardeners occupied with indoor tasks. She wondered whether the grooms were exercising her horse properly. Her head ached, and her back ached.

"Wait," she gasped, holding her hands to her swollen abdomen.

"Is something wrong?" Lydia asked immediately.

"Just – just a spasm. They come and go."

"My lady, we should abandon this foolishness. Let me talk to LaFrance. Perhaps—"

"It will make no difference, Lydia, don't you see?" Catherine threw her head back and grimaced. "Good God! I do not think I can walk any further."

"Are you in pain? Shall we go directly to a doctor?"

"No, no. No pain. Just a spasm. They came from time to time at Wansdyke, as well. They are nothing to fear. But my leg … I cannot go further."

Lydia promptly hailed a passing hackney and, with some difficulty, handed Catherine up into it. She gave the direction to the driver and said to Catherine, "Are you better now?"

"Much, thank you."

"We will need to get off before LaFrance's."

"Oh, no," Catherine moaned. "Lydia, I cannot."

"We must, my lady." Lydia lowered her voice, obviously concerned that the "my lady" would be overheard. "We cannot be seen alighting in front of that place."

"As you wish, then," Catherine muttered. "We will not need to do this again. We will be on our way back to Wansdyke tomorrow."

Lydia leant forward to attract the driver's attention, while Catherine tried not to groan as the next spasm began. Occasionally, she felt as if an enormous vice threatened to squeeze the breath out of her entire body. It never hurt, but it left her exhausted and momentarily unfocused. She asked a concerned maidservant who had happened to witness one such spasm at Wansdyke what they might be. The woman had volunteered that they were probably the normal contractions of late pregnancy.

"But you should see the doctor, my lady," the maid had added. "It seems far too early."

And then all had been forgotten in the haste to get to London.

The hackney was slowing. Catherine tried to bring her mind back into focus, reminding herself she would need all her faculties to deal with the wily LaFrance. She peered out, trying to get a sense of the neighbourhood. It was pleasant enough: a quiet little street, a little too far out to be considered really fashionable, populated by comfortable-looking matrons examining the latest arrival in the window of a milliner and making purchases in a bookshop. Not quite bourgeois, she decided, but appropriate for the men who would keep company with LaFrance: a society good enough to look respectable, but not good enough to be noticed.

Lydia descended quickly and paid the driver before turning to assist Catherine, who clung to her heavily. The man watched, his expression impassive.

"Seems it's all bit too much for the lady," he offered. Lydia gave him a freezing look. He shrugged and called to his horse to walk on as they turned their backs on him and began their slow trudge to LaFrance's door.

Catherine struggled to keep pace with her companion. The cold cut through her gloves and boots and hat, and she could feel frozen strands of hair cling to her cheeks as the moisture from her breath swirled behind the sheer fabric of her veil. Her chest was beginning to feel hot and hollow.

"Lydia, slowly," she gasped.

"My lady, if we do not hurry, I am afraid we will never get there."

Catherine conceded the point with a miserable nod. Lydia was right: if they took too long, her strength would fail entirely. She tasted bile in her throat and wished she had eaten breakfast after all. She desperately wanted a cup of tea.

Lydia consulted a scrap of paper that she had withdrawn from her reticule while Catherine clung to her, panting.

"It is that one," Lydia said, nodding in the direction of a modest-looking terraced house. Catherine followed her glance. Four large stone steps stood before the door.

"Oh, no," she moaned, but Lydia was already pulling her along, steadily, steadily. So she bit her lip and grunted, the veil clinging stickily to her face. When they reached the steps, Lydia pulled her stoutly up – she had to bear nearly all of Catherine's weight as her knees had buckled and were almost refusing to move.

Fortunately, a servant had seen their struggle up the steps and he hastened to open the door to admit them. Before he could do more than give them a startled look, Catherine said, gasping, "I am here to call on Monsieur LaFrance."

She had no wish to reveal her identity, but one look at her dress, and another at Lydia, told the servant she was quality. He admitted her without a word.

CHAPTER 30

*L*aFrance was in his studio, and he requested his guest to wait on him there. The impertinence, she thought furiously. How dare he demand she attend him in his workshop! It was as if he were eager to remind her of the youthful foolishness that threatened to ruin her happiness. *Never mind*, she thought. *It will all end here and now.* She had Lydia wait in the drawing room; although Lydia had been with her for many years and knew LaFrance well, she had no desire to make the encounter any more public than necessary.

LaFrance's studio was on the first floor and spread across the full width of the back of the building. When Catherine entered the room, she could immediately see why he had chosen to work in it. The light that glowed was fresh from the icy-blue winter sky. She could do no more than blink at first, trying to see past the shadowy shapes of furniture.

"Lady Catherine. Or perhaps it is now Lady St Clair?"

She started, steadying herself against a large and extremely ornate sideboard. In spite of her determination to remain calm, the sound of his voice sent shivers up her spine.

He was standing at the far end of the room, slightly to her left.

He wore only skin-tight breeches and a shirt with an open collar. His sleeves were rolled up exposing well-muscled forearms – a stark contrast to the slender white fingers that held a cup and saucer before him.

Catherine opened her mouth to begin the imperious speech that she had planned, but the words flew out of her mind. LaFrance cocked his head and smiled at her. Good God, he was handsome. He had an athlete's grace and sculpted body, a finely chiselled face, a shock of golden-brown hair and deep brown eyes. She felt her heart race as his assessing gaze ran up and down her body. Her cheeks warmed, and she looked away, uncomfortable.

"What a pleasure, my lady. I must say that I did not expect you to pay me a visit." The voice was smooth, mellow, with a slight French accent: a sound she recalled from so many years ago. It startled her to realise that she had never forgotten the caressing feel of his voice.

"You knew I would come," she said quietly. She raised her head, this time determined not to look away. LaFrance was examining the contents of his cup. Slowly, he walked over to put the cup on a table near a south-facing window. He pulled a shutter across, removing the glare and darkening the room slightly so Catherine could see him a little better.

"I was not sure. I thought perhaps your husband? A friend? Someone else? But you yourself – that I did not expect." He turned. "But you should not be on your feet. Come, sit with me. Share my breakfast."

Catherine remained standing. "You know why I have come."

LaFrance shrugged. "I will sit, even if you do not." He sank into a chair and looked up at Catherine expectantly. "We are friends, no? Friends of long standing?"

Catherine opened her mouth and then closed it. She shook her head. She had hated him, hated him viciously for intruding upon her happiness. But now that she was here … no, she could not hate him. He had been there when she had no one.

"Friends," she said reluctantly. "We were friends once. But what you are doing now threatens our friendship."

LaFrance nodded gravely. "*Ah, oui.* I am so sorry."

"Stop it, Michel."

"I cannot, *mon amie*. Impossible. I am not a countess. I need to eat."

Catherine looked about the room. "You are doing quite well," she said, cynicism creeping into her voice. "Is this new dwelling the result of our … our friendship?"

"This?" LaFrance gestured with his hands. Catherine noted again the long, thin fingers, the fine white palms. "No. In fact, I have only been here for two months. This place belongs to another … friend."

Catherine started forward. "You have not shown anyone the portrait?"

LaFrance shook his head slowly. "No one has seen the portrait." He gestured toward a far corner. "There it is. No one has seen it. But I know not what else to do. I cannot float from house to house, party to party, living on my winnings from gaming and charity. I am an artist, my lady. I live to create." He was watching her narrowly. Catherine willed herself to remain impassive.

"I am sorry as well. But if you need a patron, I can be of assistance. Despite my … my infirmity, I have the St Clair name, the Claverton name. I can help—"

"Ah, but you do not understand." Restlessly, LaFrance jumped up from his seat in order to pace between his easel and a desk that stood in one corner of the room. Catherine moved forward, trying to catch a glimpse of the papers on his desk. They appeared to be sketches of a woman in an ostrich feather hat and a dress cut low at the bosom. The subject was twisting her shoulders in a way that served to accentuate the line of her neck and shoulders and the cleft between her breasts.

"You see my sketches, my lady?" LaFrance picked them up. He held them out to her. "This is what I have been working on."

"They are lovely," Catherine said. "Who is your model?" She flushed hotly, realising the undercurrent of the question.

"No one." LaFrance dropped the sheaf on his desk again. His shoulders sagged. "No. I have not used a model in a very long time. I use my imagination." He raised his eyes to hers. "There was a brilliance in my portrait of you," he said baldly. "That brilliance – I have tried to capture it once more. And I have failed."

Catherine felt her palms grow cold with sweat. "That is ridiculous. We were young – you were young. You have a long life ahead of you in which to paint, to capture the … the essence of life as you see it."

LaFrance's gaze held hers. "Have you seen it? My masterpiece?" he asked softly.

Catherine felt her chest grow heavy. Another spasm was beginning to tighten about her like a belt. She took a step forward in order to grip the back of a large chair. Wordlessly, she shook her head.

"I did not finish it until you had been gone for several months," LaFrance said. "There was much emotion – much in my soul that I needed to express. After all, I was heartbroken."

"There was nothing – nothing to be heartbroken over," Catherine said coldly.

LaFrance watched her for a moment. Then he shook his head. "You would not understand, perhaps. But to capture innocence and womanhood at the same time – to capture fear and courage – to an artist it is like an invitation to witness Adam and Eve in the Garden."

"You exaggerate," Catherine said. She attempted to laugh, but another spasm was gripping her, and she looked away, trying not to grimace.

"If there is any hope for me as an artist, it lies in that portrait," LaFrance said. He looked in the direction of a stack of paintings leaning against the wall on which the sun still fell. Catherine followed his glance.

"Surely, you do not keep it there, where anyone could find it!" she gasped.

LaFrance walked over to the stack and pulled aside a velvet curtain that hung next to it to reveal a framed canvas with a blue silk cloth draped over it. He reached out to pull the cloth away.

"Stop!" Catherine cried. LaFrance stopped. He looked at her over his shoulder.

"I have no wish to see that ... that thing," she gasped. She was out of breath, as if she had run all the way from Wansdyke, and the tight band about her middle was squeezing again. She grasped feebly at the seat before her then let go to totter in LaFrance's direction. He gave her a quizzical look.

"Are you all right?"

"I am fine – would be fine –" she said hoarsely, "if you would just let me buy that portrait from you."

LaFrance stiffened. "No. My answer is firm. This portrait will show the world that I am a man of talent. I cannot let it leave my hands."

"Michel, I beg you. If you hold – if you ever held – any affection for me. Please." She limped unsteadily to where he stood, stiffly guarding the silk-draped shape. "Please. My reputation, my child's reputation – my marriage." Her voice cracked on the last word.

LaFrance reflected for a moment. The harsh contours of his body seemed to relax slightly. "And what of this sudden marriage, my lady? Do you love this man?"

"I do love him. But he will not love me in return if he ever discovers this portrait."

"I would never divulge your identity."

"I know you would not want to, Michel. But someone might

force you. Or find out somehow. Surely you understand my predicament." Catherine wrung her hands. "I am no longer the crippled and forgotten daughter of an earl whose title is reverting to the Crown. I am the Countess St Clair, and my son will be the next Earl St Clair. My husband does not care that I have a withered leg. Do you not see? I might be happy – I might be happy, like any other woman." She was weeping openly now, the tears trickling down her cheeks as she spoke. "You would ruin me, Michel."

LaFrance turned away. He seemed to contemplate her words, to turn them over in his mind. "You broke my heart," he said finally.

"I am so sorry. I did not mean it. I was very young. And I was terrified. I did not believe that anyone could ever love me."

"But I, I loved you," LaFrance said bitterly. "My poor soft heart was bruised beyond recognition by the harsh way you dealt with me. All that I had of you was the portrait."

He lifted a corner of the silk as he spoke, and slowly drew it away. Catherine lifted her head, the brightness of the blue winter sky reflecting off the wall and glittering through the tears that clung to her lashes. What she saw made her catch her throat, bite her lip until it bled.

"There it is, my lady. This is what I have been protecting with my life. It is worth more than your entire estate, more than the wealth of all the crowned heads of Europe. It is my brush with brilliance. I will spend my life attempting to meet it again." He looked at Catherine, his face filled with pity. "I will never give it up."

"Oh, Michel!" Catherine said. She tried to speak, but no more words came. She stared at the portrait, feeling the vice beginning to grip her again, her pulse race. It was indeed a spectacular portrait – a far cry from the sheaf of pleasant sketches on his desk. She had never seen anything like it. She stared at it until her eyes hurt.

This was it, then. She turned away and lumbered to the door.

"My lady," LaFrance called. She ignored him, the tears streaming steadily down her cheeks as she opened the door and let herself out into the hall. Once there, she leant heavily against the door and wept silently, half-hidden in the dark shadow of the doorway. Her body shuddered, and she twisted her veil in her hands until it was a sweaty sodden mess.

I did not know, she thought. *I did not know this about love: that it could lead to such desperate despair.*

She had not loved him. He had shown her what it might be like to be a woman, a whole woman. But she had not regarded him as a human being with feelings. And that misstep would be the ruin of any happiness she might ever have had.

Unless she were to murder him, to burn the house down, she would never get the portrait away from him. And she could not grant him the brilliance he sought to retrieve, it could only well up within him. He needed to seek it, he needed to find his muse for himself. And he would hold that portrait fast until he drew his last breath.

It was time to leave London and return to Wansdyke.

From there, to Wales – far from any society.

But she had one last duty to perform.

JOCELYN WAS CONTEMPLATING A TEMPTING DISPLAY OF BAKED goods in a window when his attention was caught by a lumbering navy-blue form clinging to the elbow of a young woman. The lumbering form was heavily veiled. But he recognised it in an instant. Catherine.

He watched as they laboured to make their way down the street. The bustling crowds paid no attention to them. They stopped once, twice, and Lydia murmured something to Catherine. Was Catherine in pain? Was she ill? He was tempted, so tempted, to rush over and offer assistance. But something, some poisonous inner voice, forced him to stay put.

They climbed into a hackney and sped away. Jocelyn turned away, the baked goods forgotten. Catherine knew his direction in London. She could find him if she chose to do so. She had not mentioned any plan to visit London. So what could she be doing in town – in her condition?

The thought of Catherine and her round belly both saddened and aroused him. He turned into the wind and began to trudge in the opposite direction to that taken by Catherine's hackney.

CHAPTER 31

*H*e'd had a most satisfying run of luck at faro. Generally speaking, Sir Lyle was not a gambler and he disdained the dandies and fools who thought that the various gaming hells about London were the very apotheosis of adventure. The idiots led such sheltered lives that they did not have the faintest clue about true risk, true danger. He would love to see some of them sail through a storm on one of his ships. Just once.

But, since he was in London …

Sir Lyle slowly swirled the port in his glass. It had a pleasing aroma of cherries and dark wood. Although not nearly as good as the vintage he procured for himself, it was perfectly acceptable.

He snorted, a little irritated. It wasn't as if he really wanted to be in London at all. He was extremely busy, and his man of business in Dover was sending him frantic message after frantic message. It was difficult, dealing with a ship and its cargo from a distance. He loathed the fact that he was not there to personally supervise activities in port.

He was not, however, concerned about being found out. Too many important officials were in his pay for that to happen.

He turned his mind to Jocelyn Avebury's sorry predicament.

Pity that he could not risk involving any of his connections in the affair.

He had done some digging around: not content to sit still and wait for his Irish friend's report, he had taken it upon himself to follow Avebury's hearings and to try to find out how he came to be in the navy. There actually was something quite strange about the captain. He appeared to have no family, no friends, no connections of any kind – respectable or otherwise. He came from Yorkshire, London, Scotland – Sir Lyle's naval contacts had offered all sorts of guesses about Avebury's family and origins. The only vague consensus was that he had entered the service through the good graces of a well-connected relation, although no one seemed to know who that relation was.

It would help, Sir Lyle thought tiredly, if he could see the man's files. But that would take time, and some finessing. It hardly seemed worth it.

He stood abruptly, went over to one of the tall windows and pulled back the dark red curtains. The moon glimmered through the sleet, scattering sparks of light over the cobblestoned streets. Snow from an earlier shower had collected here and there, but it did not seem there would be any more.

Why do I do this to myself?

The answer was one that he did not want to consider. Because he loved her. Loved her still. "What kind of a fool am I?" he muttered with a grimace.

He turned away from the window, downed the rest of his port, and slammed down the glass down so viciously that it shattered, imploding in the palm of his hand. He ignored the pain, shaking the glass easily from his fingers. Worse things had happened. He drew a handkerchief from his pocket and dabbed lightly at his hand. Little flecks of blood appeared on the snowy white linen. He tossed it onto the table beside the mess.

A soft knock at the door. Sir Lyle crossed the room to procure another glass. "Come in," he said over his shoulder. He sloshed the rich red liquid into the glass, slightly spattering the marble tabletop.

"Have I come at an inopportune moment?"

"You have a talent for poorly timed arrivals." Sir Lyle picked up a second glass. "But I suspect that is due to your trade. You specialise in a most distasteful art. I assume that you will not have port, my fine Irish friend."

"I am not so proud, Sir Lyle. I will always drink with a friend."

Sir Lyle muttered as he inspected the decanters. He selected one. "I regret to say that my whiskey seems to have gone missing."

"We finished it, Sir Lyle. The last time."

"The last time – ah, yes. The last time." Sir Lyle let out a bark of laughter. "I barely remember. I should never have attempted to outdrink you."

The man removed his coat and gloves and placed them on a nearby table. Sir Lyle handed him his drink. "What, did my butler not take your coat?"

"Your butler is asleep, Sir Lyle. There are not many hours till daybreak."

"I will not ask, then, how you managed to enter."

The man cocked his head. "You should know better." He raised his glass in salute before downing the drink.

Sir Lyle walked over to the fireplace and bent to inspect the cheerful orange flames before turning to look at his guest. "Well?"

"It is a long story."

"I have time. But let me ask you something first. Is the man honest? Or was I mistaken in his character?"

The man gazed into his glass, rolling it between his palms. There was a pause. Then he laughed. "A difficult question, Sir Lyle."

"Never. A man is either true or he is not. I believe I know how to judge character – if I did not, I would be dead – but I want to know. Was I wrong about Avebury?"

"Life is filled with grey, Sir Lyle. All is not black or white."

"Yes, yes, I know what you think," Sir Lyle said impatiently. "Rubbish, all of it. I know what I know. If I was mistaken in Avebury—" If I gave Catherine up to a lying sailor, he finished silently, I will kill him myself. And ask God to rot all lying sailors.

The Irishman heaved a deep sigh. "As I was saying, Sir Lyle. That is a difficult question. And you do not pay me to philosophise. I merely investigate."

"Out with it, then. Avebury – liar? Saint?"

"We might as well start at the beginning. Randall."

"Eh?" Sir Lyle had been raising his glass to his lips, but he stopped, his drink sloshing over the rim of the glass.

"His name is not Avebury at all. His name is John Randall."

CHAPTER 32

*H*e overslept yet again – the victim of fevered nightmares – and woke a sodden sweaty mess between the unstarched sheets in his rented bed. He wiped his neck with the corner of one of them, then squinted into the sunlight, trying to gauge the hour. He felt as exhausted as if he had been running all night.

He was also extremely aroused. Disgusted, he looked down at the evidence of his preoccupation. After years at sea and years of controlling his urges between discreet visits to a certain lady in Gibraltar he thought such wakings were long in the past, something for younger men. But his brain was again a mass of urges and fantasies and obsessions. And they were let loose in his dreams with an explosion of colour and smell, feeling and taste.

"Kate," he said aloud. He thought of her long blonde hair, how it was always getting in the way when they made love. He would spread it lovingly over her body, teasing her, kissing her. He took great delight in running his fingers through it; he had never had such a fair-haired lover before. She was so tremblingly fresh, salty and young. She never had the faintest whiff of an experienced woman about her, despite her efforts to maintain a damned air of confidence.

"Funny how easily we are deceived," Jocelyn muttered. He swung his legs over the side of the bed and rubbed his face. Had to stop thinking about her. Had to stop before it drove him to desperation. And it would be extremely poor form to be found wandering the streets of a questionable neighbourhood in search of a certain kind of commerce while the Admiralty was deliberating his fate.

It would be another dreadful day of waiting.

Over his breakfast, he wondered whether Catherine was still in London. He wondered yet again why she had not said anything about coming to town. He wondered, reluctantly, whether she planned to visit him.

A maidservant knocked and opened the door, interrupted his reverie. "There's a Sir Lyle Barrington here to see you, sir." Startled, Jocelyn jerked to his feet, his napkin falling to the floor.

"Do not get up," Sir Lyle said from the doorway. "I am sorry to interrupt your breakfast."

"Not at all," Jocelyn said. He gestured at the table. "You will join me, of course."

"I will have some coffee, thank you. But let me serve myself." Sir Lyle wandered over to the sideboard. Jocelyn sat back down.

He watched Sir Lyle walk over to a front window and inspect the street before him. Under heavy skies, with snow likely to fall soon, matrons and delivery boys hurried along the steep incline of the street. Sir Lyle sipped at the coffee and made a face. "How do you stand it, Captain? The coffee. It would never be tolerated on one of my ships."

"Is it so bad?" Jocelyn replied mildly. He watched as Sir Lyle circled the room, sipping at his coffee and examining the pleasant furnishings with feigned interest.

"Do you not long to be at sea, Captain Avebury?"

"Why are you here, Sir Lyle?"

Sir Lyle's back stiffened slightly. He turned. "Are we not to allow ourselves a few moments of polite chat?" His voice had gone quiet. "I understand that you are a man of honour, and you appear to disdain me as a man of business. Still, I am accustomed to a certain amount of politeness – a façade, if you will – when I am amongst gentlemen."

Jocelyn watched him impassively.

Sir Lyle put down his cup, his hand steady. "Never mind. I do not understand what you have against me, but I know the pressure you face at this time in your career."

"What of it?" Jocelyn rose slowly from the table. "What do you know of it, Sir Lyle?"

"I am a seafaring man, Captain Avebury, much as you are. Oh, I do not pretend that my life is as honourable as yours. I trade in something ... er ... tasteless, shall we say?" Sir Lyle laughed, but he did not sound amused. "People may make of that what they wish but I have a great deal of money. I have land, mansions, horses, ships – I have a great deal of everything there is to own. The very people who condemn my work would be the first in line if I decided to give my assets away."

"Your point, Sir Lyle?"

"My point, Captain Avebury, is that 'honour' is a very strange word. The ones who are most protective of the notion that 'honour' is above all else are the very people who have something to hide."

Jocelyn was very still. He felt rather giddy, almost relieved, as the blood rushed out of his head. Beads of sweat suddenly appeared at his hairline.

"Your behaviour in Bombay displayed a great deal of 'honour,' Captain Avebury. Your reluctance to leave behind an officer of His Majesty's Navy, despite your schedule. Your insistence upon taking all the blame, accepting sole responsibility for the missed rendezvous. All truly the behaviour of a man of honour. Your record is spotless. It is with the utmost reluctance

that the Admiralty holds these hearings: had the good lieutenant's family not insisted on a full investigation, you would
not be here now."

"Say it," Jocelyn said quietly. "You have something to say. I
would hear you say it."

"I am not a man of honour, Captain Avebury. But I am exactly
who I say I am. Can you say the same?"

There was silence. The two men stared at each other.

"What do you want with me, Sir Lyle? Are you determined on
my ruin?"

Sir Lyle drew back sharply. "I have made it my mission to save
you from a folly which was not your own," he said icily. "I do not
know whence you arrived at such a notion."

"You keep appearing, Sir Lyle. And every time you appear, you
remind me that I am ... indebted ... to you." Jocelyn spat out the
word with difficulty. "I neither understand nor desire the debt,
and I do not know what sort of favour you imagine your friends
in the Admiralty can offer. I beg to be left alone."

"You are a very strange man, Captain. I thought it was understood. My brother – and hence his family – is in your debt. My
wish is to be of assistance. You saved his life, and my mother's
sanity."

"I did nothing to incur your gratitude. I wish to be left alone."

Sir Lyle shook his head wonderingly. "I do not understand.
What is the source of your bitterness, Captain Avebury? Why do
you loathe me?"

The fire popped then gave a long hiss. Sir Lyle walked over to
pick up the poker, and attended to the flames, laying a new log
onto the red-orange mass. Jocelyn walked away from the table,
his appetite gone.

"Is it Lady Catherine?"

The question hung in the air. It was muffled; Sir Lyle was still
crouched before the fire. Gazing absently at the poker, rubbing
smudges of ash from the shiny metal, he spoke again. "Tell me,

Captain Avebury. Are you angry because I continue to maintain the semblance of a friendship with your wife?"

Jocelyn clenched his fists, then released them. He felt as if his heart had risen into his throat and it threatened to burst there: his pulse thudded heavily in his mouth. He ought to say something, to tell Sir Lyle that he knew about the child. That he knew just how dishonourable he was. But was it possible that Sir Lyle knew nothing? Was it possible that Catherine, his strong, sturdy princess, had tricked Sir Lyle too?

He found himself with nothing to say.

Sir Lyle looked at him over his shoulder. "I see now that my friendship with Lady Catherine causes you displeasure. I assure you again that I mean only to help."

The throbbing ebbed slightly. Jocelyn fastened his gaze on Sir Lyle, trying to appear indifferent. "It is none of my concern."

"Lady Catherine sent me here, you know." Sir Lyle rose. He went over to where his now-cold coffee sat, and frowned at the cup in distaste before turning back to Jocelyn. "She is beside herself with worry."

"Worry?" Jocelyn shook his head slightly, as if to clear cobwebs.

"Aye, worry. She wants you out of this mess, and will do anything to ensure it." Sir Lyle gave him a hard look. "She took a great deal of trouble to locate me. I was in Dover, overseeing a particularly touchy crew. Cargo of considerable value. I am sure you understand. But nothing short of my immediate attendance would please her – followed by assurances that I would come to London to ensure your safe return to her."

Jocelyn felt his mouth go dry. Sir Lyle was in London because of him? Because Catherine had … asked him to help? He saw the truth in Sir Lyle's frank stare and his legs weakened. He sat down.

Sir Lyle was in love. He was in love with Catherine. There was no mistaking it.

But then, why? Why the hiding, the subterfuge? Was there something so thoroughly unacceptable about Sir Lyle that meant Catherine would not consider marrying him? Was Sir Lyle unwilling to bestow his name on an innocent child? And could Catherine be in London to meet Sir Lyle?

Jocelyn could not bear it. He rubbed his temples with his fingertips, shading his eyes from the too-bright morning light. Faint memories tugged at the edges of his mind.

On the day he first visited Wansdyke, he had come across Sir Lyle leaving. And Sir Lyle had laughed, told him to marry Lady Catherine.

He remembered his own confusion when Catherine had brought up the subject of marriage. He had at first imagined that she had meant to marry Sir Lyle. Because Sir Lyle had appeared for all the world to be a lover scorned.

There was something else there, something too big and complex for him to fathom. Catherine was almost certainly in London to see Sir Lyle. And, whatever he claimed, it was probably not to beg Sir Lyle to help exonerate him.

"I have a few friends amongst the officers of the navy. Lady Catherine was most anxious that I use my influence to the fullest extent. And so, here I am." Sir Lyle leant forward. "But I was not going to take any chances. I did not want to become involved in a story I only half knew."

"So you had your people investigate me."

Sir Lyle laughed. "People? I don't have my own 'people', Captain! My business is a very solitary one. But yes, I have access to those who will perform tasks for the right price."

"And you have found me out." Jocelyn spoke with his head still in his hands. He could not bear the glare of the low sun streaming through the windows – or the sight of Sir Lyle's face.

"Does Catherine know, Captain?" Sir Lyle asked the question quietly.

"No, she does not."

"Were you planning to tell her?"

"Is it any of your concern?" Jocelyn lashed out. He raised his head, squinting. "You have done enough to repay your gratitude, do you not think? Perhaps you could finish your work by telling Catherine about my past. Were you not planning to meet her after seeing me here?"

"Here? In London?"

"Oh, surely, Sir Lyle," Jocelyn said acidly. "You cannot pretend that you do not know she is here!"

"I know no such thing, Captain. I swear it. My honour may mean nothing to you, but I swear that I know nothing of her being here." Sir Lyle swung around on his heel and paced to the far end of the room. Jocelyn could see the muscles in his cheek working. "Damn it, I told her not to travel. She is in far too delicate a condition to—" He cut himself off suddenly, swinging back around to look at Jocelyn. Jocelyn felt his stomach lurch.

"Sir Lyle. Is she … is she all right? Is … is the child well?"

"She is very tired, Captain. Worn out. I hope that she lasts until her confinement. I speak frankly, and hope you will forgive me. But she does not seem to be at all well." Sir Lyle paused. "She worries about you. And, what's more, her leg … you know. It pains her. And the child grows."

"Thank God for that," Jocelyn breathed.

"Aye, thank God. But the additional weight on her leg – it makes things difficult. Damn it all to hell! I told her not to travel. What can she possibly be thinking? I told her I would come and do my best, and I have." Sir Lyle was muttering to himself, not paying any attention to Jocelyn. "There is nothing she can do. Surely, if there is anyone she could speak to at the Admiralty, she has already done so. If not, she would have told me—" He stopped suddenly and looked sharply at Jocelyn.

"Captain, your secret is safe with me. I have no desire to expose you. Is there some other reason Lady Catherine could be here? Some business I do not know about?"

Confused, Jocelyn spread his hands apart. "Nothing, to my knowledge," he said.

"No relations, no hidden bank accounts? No solicitor to speak to?"

"Her man of business comes to Wansdyke if he needs her, and spends much of his time at Albrook, working on the transfer of the estate. There is no reason for Catherine to be here at all." *Unless it is to be with you*, he added silently, and watched Sir Lyle frown in contemplation. Perhaps he was wrong. Or perhaps Sir Lyle was an excellent actor.

"Captain, I assure you again, I know nothing either. She did threaten to come to London and beg the Admiralty's indulgence herself, but I was sure I had dissuaded her. Such efforts would have resulted only in embarrassment. I had no idea she was here until you spoke."

"I saw her," Jocelyn said reluctantly. "I saw her not far from here, with her companion Lydia Barrow."

"The infamous Miss Barrow," Sir Lyle said dryly. Sir Lyle laughed at Jocelyn's questioning look. "One day you will hear Miss Barrow's story – if you have not already. But right now, I need to attend to some business which cannot be delayed any longer. Have a pleasant morning, Captain."

"Sir Lyle – I apologise. I beg your pardon for my rude behaviour."

"Do not fret over it, Captain. I am used to much worse." With a brisk nod, he took his leave.

Jocelyn put his head in his hands again. His secret was out. It was only a matter of time before it came to Catherine's ears. He would have to tell her himself, as soon as he heard the Admiralty's verdict.

Sir Lyle loved her. He would take care of her. It gave Jocelyn a perverse sort of comfort to understand just how deep Sir Lyle's affections ran. If he could not be around himself, Sir Lyle would be. He still could not understand why Sir Lyle would not admit to fathering the child, but perhaps he was protecting Catherine's name.

Ah, Kate. His golden-haired countess. He wanted to believe that, when all this was done, they could be together once more. He knew better, of course. He would go on his way. She would go on hers. She was too independent to tolerate a man controlling her. And, despite Sir Lyle saying she worried about him, he knew that nothing was more important to her than the baby earl who would allow her to feel she had triumphed over the Claverton indifference. And he did not know, he truly did not know, if he could raise another man's child.

Jocelyn looked up at the mantelpiece clock. It was still early. He had the entire day with nothing to do but await word from the Admiralty. And tomorrow, the waiting would begin again.

He could barely stand it.

He rose, paced around the room. He stopped to pour himself a lukewarm coffee, swigged it back in one gulp. Sir Lyle was right – it really was not very good. He slammed the empty cup into the saucer.

Should he search for Catherine? She was here somewhere, somewhere in this city. As good as alone, and not in good health. Never mind the fact that the child was not his. He still wanted her happy and well.

He couldn't think where to start. It was obvious that she had not wanted anyone to recognise her. She would not, therefore be staying at Claverton House, and probably would not want to rely on any of her friends in London – heavy with child, she would surely want to avoid the gossip and stares of society.

Sir Lyle had seemed truly surprised at the news that Catherine was in London. Perhaps—

He was ashamed of the thought, but he hoped that Sir Lyle would find her. And he hoped that, if she needed help, Sir Lyle would tell him.

SIR LYLE WALKED BRISKLY, TIGHTENING HIS COAT AGAINST THE bitter wind. He had left Avebury's rented accommodation far behind, and was nearing the Admiralty. He had a few favours to call in. He had been hesitant about pursuing this route but, if it was the only way to keep Catherine from further folly, it was necessary.

Catherine was in London. He wondered how Avebury had discovered her, how he had managed to get a glimpse of her in such a large and busy city. He grinned wryly. Well, he was her husband, after all. It would not be strange for him to keep a watch on her movements.

And yet it was clear he had assumed Sir Lyle knew more than he did.

Sir Lyle shook his head. There were secrets that would tear their marriage asunder. He would not be the one to reveal them. They would each have to own up to their own guilty pasts.

What could Catherine possibly have come to London to do?

He would find out. He would not have to look for long; a countess heavy with child could not go far without being noticed.

CHAPTER 33

*S*ir Lyle completed his subtle inquiries at the Admiralty and, as soon as he returned from his expedition, sent over a generous donation of smuggled brandy. He cautioned the delivery boy to handle the barrel with particular care, and to deliver it directly into the hands of an upper servant. It would be understood. It was not the first time.

Blast those stiff-necked sailors! he thought. *Avebury is worth ten of them, and they know it.*

He had made no threats, and did not mention the captain's name once. But he had made his interests known, and was sure the gentle exchange of pleasantries with various officers of His Majesty's fleet would have some result. At the very least, he had shown them he knew what they were, and now they feared him. He was usually reluctant to let anyone hang for their weakness but, in this case, he would act. It would be the last time he did something for love rather than money, however.

But tonight he was going to forget his troubles. He was going to forget Avebury, his damned cargo in Dover, the fickle Lady Catherine – everything. He was going to enjoy himself a little. After an early dinner at his club, he indulged in a quick and mindless game of cards. Finding the competition lacking, he strolled over to the residence of a certain widow who promised good company, good food, and the utmost discretion.

Celia Farnsworth had expensive tastes and, when her dull husband of twenty years had done her the favour of dying, she had invested her energy into generating money to spend shopping abroad. Her home was too elegant, too tasteful, to be considered a brothel. The ladies who worked for her were genteel. Most were impoverished and all were beautiful and smart. None remained against their will. They could not frequent the card parties and assemblies of the ton without creating considerable discomfort amongst the male population – they were known to too many of them – but lived discreetly in a dignified fashion. The source of their income apart, they would not be an embarrassment to any gentleman and, in fact, it was not unknown for a naïf young man to fall in love with one of the ladies and decide to spirit her away to Gretna Green.

Sir Lyle had not paid a call to Mrs Farnsworth's establishment in quite a long time but she greeted him fondly and invited him to join her for a glass of wine. He obliged for a while, chatting amiably about unremarkable topics, but he eventually excused himself to take a turn around the small but lovely garden while he smoked a cheroot. When he came indoors, he went upstairs. He surveyed the works of art that lined the corridor and noted with amusement that Mrs Farnsworth had expanded her collection of Chinese pottery. He had been instrumental in securing some of her most prized pieces, and her gratitude was, she said, boundless. He wondered, as he strode toward the end of the hall, what she considered to be an appropriate quantification of boundless.

He entered the room at the end of the corridor without knocking, and shut the door behind him. He paused. His eyes adjusted slowly to the dim light within, and fell on the glow of a candle at the edge of a night table.

A young woman turned. It was hard to see her face in the candlelight, it, but Sir Lyle could make out a tumble of long fair hair, caught up and loosely twisted into a careless knot. Curls that sprang free dangled beside her cheeks and down her back. She was dressed in a plain white dress with a blue sash, as if she were a virtuous girl making her London debut. She was not Catherine, but she could have been – were it not for the curls. She picked up the candle and held it near her face. Sir Lyle gave a startled gasp. Her eyes were the right shade of blue.

"Do I remind you of someone?"

It was a moment before Sir Lyle understood that she had spoken. Her voice was not Catherine's although, for some reason, he had expected it to be. It was much higher and had a clipped London tone.

"I can see it on your face," she continued. "Someone else once told me that I was the image of perfection, but merely the image. He said he had seen perfection itself, and told me that I was not nearly as beautiful. I wish I could see this perfect beauty for myself."

She walked over to Sir Lyle and put the candle down at the door. Gently, she offered her hands, and he managed to move forward to take them.

"I can be whoever you wish," she said softly.

"You cannot," he whispered.

"I will try." She led him to the bed, but he stopped her. He pulled his hands free.

"I dislike fantasy," he said bluntly. "What is your name?"

The girl cocked her head. "What would you like it to be?"

"Listen to me," he said. "You cannot be the girl in my heart. So you may as well tell me your name."

She inclined her head. "Mary." Curls bounced forward to cover her cheeks.

"Mary, then. I am afraid I am not here to play games, even if the other gentleman chose to do so." He sat on the edge of the bed and began to remove his boots.

"He called her Angelique," she said wistfully. "She sounded so very beautiful and so very perfect. He said that he knew every inch of her and that she was without blemish, like a fine piece of porcelain."

Sir Lyle stood to remove his shirt. "That does not sound very likely to be a real person."

"Indeed she was," Mary returned. "The man wept bitter tears. I was never so moved in my life. He was an artist, and he had painted her portrait. He said he would never sell it, but it was his masterpiece." She giggled. "I wish I had such fortune. Imagine being perfect, the subject for an artist's masterpiece!"

Sir Lyle did not reply. He turned to Mary and deftly untied her sash. She willingly removed her dress, and he reached out for her.

It took more work than he had expected. He was distracted: thinking about the day, thinking about the captain, thinking about Catherine. He needed the comfort of a soft feminine body, generously offered, but Catherine's image danced before his mind whenever he tried to turn his thoughts to the woman in his arms. Eventually, the image aroused him. He thought of the inches of her that he had come to know in the garden in Wansdyke – her lovely pink mouth, her smooth white neck, her generous bosom.

He looked down at the woman beneath him, her glossy blonde hair spread over the pillow, her smooth skin glowing in the dim candlelight. Her stomach was so flat, so girlish. Catherine's would never be like that again. He suddenly had an urge to please this woman, this Mary – was that her real name?

He did not normally bother about anything other than his own satisfaction when he came to visit these ladies. He gave generous presents, and occasionally maintained a relationship with a fortunate young woman for several months in a row, but he made no pretence of being there for any reason but to assuage his own needs.

Today, he felt curiously empty, yearning for more than a physical solution to the ache in his soul. Catherine loved her captain. Avebury loved Catherine. They had created a child. If only they could get past whatever blocks their hearts put in the way of each other, they might be truly happy in the eternal way of lovers the world over.

For the first time, Sir Lyle realised that he himself was not soulless, heartless. He was able to imagine something good in the core of his being without cynicism. He was able to give Mary pleasure, to love her with tenderness and generosity. Afterwards, he wondered that he had wasted so many months grasping at a memory, at something only half-real. This was real. This was real, and it was far more pleasant than the bitter half-truth of the past.

The candle was out.

"This Angelique," he said suddenly into the darkness. "Who was she? The painter's Angelique."

"I do not know. A noble lady, to be sure. The painter is a man I know well. He does not come often anymore because his circumstances are reduced. But he is a gentleman, a Frenchman by the name of LaFrance."

CHAPTER 34

*I*t was still early when he left Mrs Farnsworth's, promising to give her her choice from a new box of treasures that was being unloaded in Dover. To the fair Mary, he gave his Chinese enamelled snuffbox. She was delighted. But he knew he would not see her again. She reminded him too much of what he could not have, and should not want.

He hailed a hackney and went directly to a small house on the far side of town that Mrs Farnsworth had described. She had, upon questioning, admitted to knowing Monsieur LaFrance well. She pointed out a painting, a pleasant rendering of a girl in a garden, which was of his creation. Sir Lyle, casting a critical eye over the work, thought it showed talent – but nothing spectacular. He wanted to see for himself a man who knew perfection, who wept bitter tears over a masterpiece.

He rapped boldly at the artist's door. When the servant answered, Sir Lyle offered his card and was shown to a drawing room.

He waited. The clock ticked the minutes by. Restless, he rose and went to look out of the window. The street was dark and empty. There was no activity in this unfashionable district at a time when other parts of London were bursting with gaiety. The house itself was shabby, the furnishings old and faded. It had the neglect of rented accommodation, much as Captain Avebury's rooms had.

"Good evening." Sir Lyle swung around. A man had entered the room and shut the door behind him. He was unassuming in appearance, with a boyish face and curling golden-brown hair. He was in evening dress, as if he had just returned from a party. Sir Lyle's eyes were drawn to his hands, which held a cloth. Slowly, slowly, the man rubbed the cloth over and about, over and about his slender white fingers. The artist wore a ring with a deep-set ruby.

"I have interrupted your work?" asked Sir Lyle abruptly.

"Not at all. I was cleaning my studio." LaFrance's accent was slight.

A long-time refugee, thought Sir Lyle. "I hear you have a portrait that has not been sold. A portrait of a lady you call Angelique."

The movement of LaFrance's hands slowed perceptibly, although his expression did not change. He gazed at Sir Lyle, continuing to rub his hands slowly.

"I would like to see this portrait."

"It is not for sale."

"Perhaps I will be able to change your mind."

"It is not for sale. May I ask where you heard about my work?"

"You are well known in artistic circles, Monsieur LaFrance."

LaFrance inclined his head. "I thank you for that. Unfortunately, I know it is not true."

"Shall we say, then, that I would prefer to be discreet."

LaFrance shook his head. He gave a crooked half-smile. "If you are talking of the painting that I am thinking of, it has never been seen. I do not know who spoke of it to you, but it has never been seen."

"Never?"

"Never." LaFrance ceased rubbing his hands with the cloth. His arms dropped limply to his sides. "However, I was planning to show it to a select few tomorrow evening."

"I thought it was not for sale?"

"It is not. But it is my masterpiece. It is all I have to show what I am truly capable of creating – given the right ... inspiration."

"And your inspiration? Is she no more?"

LaFrance shook his head. His glance fell. "No."

Abruptly, he turned. "You might as well see it," he said over his shoulder. It sounded as if he were saying the words with considerable effort.

"Wait, Monsieur LaFrance."

LaFrance paused, but did not turn.

"If you have no plans to sell this painting, may I ask what compels you to exhibit it?"

LaFrance laughed grimly. "Well might you ask." He rubbed his eye with one hand before continuing. "I am looking for work. Work that is worthy of my talent. Work that will get me out of this bourgeois hellhole." He shrugged. "I have had few worthwhile commissions in the past few years. And none that have allowed me to show my true abilities. So this is my last hope. I can show those who might give me the chance to create truly important work, that I have the artistry, the technique that is necessary."

"You need a patron."

"*Oui.*" For a moment, LaFrance seemed as if he might say more in his native French. But he shook his head. He motioned with his hand. "You will follow me, Sir Lyle?"

Sir Lyle followed him down a corridor to the back of the house. LaFrance opened a door and led him into a vast room, dark but for the feeble light produced by the nub of a candle on a desk in one corner and the welcoming glow of the fireplace. Several sketches were carelessly scattered across the top of the desk, along with a charcoal pencil that had been broken in two. LaFrance swept the sheets away, allowing the bits of pencil to fall to the floor.

"I am sorry it is dark," he muttered. He picked up the candle nub and dug around in the desk for a longer one. He lit it and crammed it into a sconce. He walked over to the opposite wall and stood for a moment, hands clasped. Sir Lyle could see draped stacks of canvases leaning against the wall.

"May I assist you?"

LaFrance shook his head. "No," he said softly. "No, I will bring her to you." He reached for a single frame draped in dark blue silk, set apart from the rest. Lifting it gently, as if it might crumble in his hands, he brought it over to an empty easel.

He removed the drape.

Sir Lyle blinked, then stared hard. It was at first difficult to see. The room was dark, and the candles guttered and danced, creating long shadows that flicked dark tips across the canvas. LaFrance handed Sir Lyle the one from the desk.

"Please be careful," he said tonelessly. Then he wheeled around on his heel, sat down and put his head in his hands.

Sir Lyle approached the painting. It was a nude, a lushly rendered oil of a young woman. But it was unlike any painting he had ever seen. The woman sat simply on a sofa; one leg drawn up under her, the other stretched out in front. She looked away from the viewer. One hand rested on the folded leg, the other arm was stretched out to the side, hand palm-down, fingers splayed, nails digging into the back of the sofa. A simple white sheet was carelessly draped over her lap, but there was no pretence of modesty. If anything, the drapery drew the viewer's eyes directly to the beautiful sweep of her naked body, from her face and tousled blonde hair to the nakedness that the sheet stubbornly refused to conceal. Everything was exposed, there was nothing left to the imagination.

Sir Lyle stared, unable to tear his eyes away. A rosy flush

swept up the length of the woman's body to her neck and her cheek. Her just-visible lips parted, the woman seemed both tensed and relaxed, as if she had suddenly realised she should hastily leave her lover's bed but was too sated, too pleasantly aware that she was somewhere safe while the world beyond the bed was cold and cruel.

Sir Lyle raised the candle. He could see why LaFrance might have remarked on Mary's resemblance to the model. But Angelique was indeed more perfect, more exquisite. Her breasts were rounder, perfectly placed on a narrow torso above a slim waist. There was a delicacy, an intrinsic modesty, of the sort that Mary's brash sensuality mocked but could not diminish. What was truly brilliant was that LaFrance had captured the passion of a moment when most men would no longer be paying the least attention. This was a loving portrayal made by a man who wanted to pleasure a woman, who would bring her to the height of passion with no regard for his own needs. It was a sacrifice, this kind of worship.

"You love her," Sir Lyle said into the darkness behind him.

"*Oui*. But she is a dream."

"A dream?"

"The woman is not she whom you see here." LaFrance raised his head. "She is all fire and ice, passion and cruelty. I painted what I wanted to see."

"But you saw her in your heart."

"I did. She was unattainable, a lady of great consequence. She was just a girl in many ways, but beyond my reach."

"Why would someone of such consequence allow this portrait to be painted?"

"She felt ugly."

"Ugly? You jest, Monsieur LaFrance! No woman who looks like that—"

"I am serious, Sir Lyle." LaFrance stood up slowly, and came over to join Sir Lyle. Looking at the portrait appeared to pain him; he focused his gaze into the distance beyond a corner of the frame. "We were introduced by a mutual friend. She was shy, ill at ease. She was not in society often because of a deformity – the hidden leg is twisted. But her face – such an angelic face! And I could see the passion in her eyes. I knew I had to paint her. But she came to sit alone. And she told me that she would never be loved, because she was so ugly. *My God!* I thought. *This cannot be right.*

"I did many sketches. I was quite content to draw her face – I think I loved her already. Then, one day, she asked if I could make her beautiful in a portrait. I did not quite understand – I was less confident of my English in those days. But I came to understand that she wanted to become my lover. I did not want to permit her to do this. It is against my way of doing things to become involved with a subject. And she was an innocent girl in many ways. But I was already so in love with the ideal of her that I permitted her to shed her clothes."

With great effort, LaFrance shifted his gaze to the portrait. A muscle worked in his cheek. "I taught her many things about the arts of love, but I did not … take her. It seemed wrong, debauched. But she wanted everything. And she despised her virginity. So, at the very end, she became my lover."

Sir Lyle had been standing at a little distance from the painting, but now he stepped right up to it. He gazed at the little indentation above the pink upper lip, at the curve of the chin, at the fine straight nose. There was no mistake.

It was Catherine, mere moments after a passionate interlude. He had never seen her thus, and never would. But oh, how he had dreamt, how he had imagined!

It was Catherine, portrayed with the perfect body that she yearned for so badly.

Catherine, able to enchant with charms she never believed she could command. Embracing a passion she had never realised a crippled girl could experience.

Catherine as Angelique.

He wanted to laugh and to weep at the same time. He had known only the strong Catherine. He had never realised what it had cost to attain that strength.

"She captured you," he said softly.

"She captured me, Sir Lyle. I was heartbroken and she was gone. She had never mentioned any interest in the portrait, and I was so enthralled that it did not occur to me that I might not create another such work." He threw up his hands. "But I never reached this level of artistry again. I have struggled on, hoping that someone will recognise my talent from my other pieces."

"Why have you never yet shown the painting?"

"I could not. It was sacred, this proof that I had the mastery." LaFrance smiled a little. "And I was proud. I thought that my talent was in my hands and my brain, not released by my subject. I finally contacted her, desperate, last spring. I needed to warn her that I planned to show the portrait. She was upset, and tried to buy it from me. But, you see, without it, I cannot show what I am capable of. I need the portrait to find a patron who will respect my talent."

Sir Lyle lowered the candle and turned to him. "I will be that person. But, in return, you must sell me the portrait."

"What are your terms?" LaFrance sounded suspicious.

"I own a vast fleet of merchant vessels and trade in many goods. Antiques, statuary, paintings – amongst other things. I will be leaving shortly on one of my ships bound for the Americas. Join me, and I will make you a rich man."

"The Americas? What would I do in the Americas?"

"Paint portraits, Monsieur LaFrance. Wealthy landowners in Charleston would like to be memorialised as their forbears were in England. There are few artists, and none of your calibre. You would become the only acceptable portraitist for the wealthy." Sir Lyle strolled over to the desk and put down the candle. He bent to pick up a piece of charcoal from the floor. "I will fund this venture generously. It amuses me, in fact, to do so. I appreciate good art, Monsieur LaFrance. But stay in London and your masterpiece will lead you into trouble. Angelique will not rest until she destroys it. And everyone who sees it will talk." He nodded in the direction of the portrait, then bent to scrawl a figure on a stray sheet of paper. LaFrance's eyes widened.

"You may draw this amount tomorrow afternoon from my banker. I will tell him to draw up a contract so you know your interests are protected. Start packing your belongings. The ship will leave within the fortnight, and I would like to see you on it. Have you any family you would need to accompany you? No? Then it will all be very easy to arrange."

"Why? Why do you do this, Sir Lyle?"

Sir Lyle's eyes slid over in the direction of the canvas again. "I am a patron of the arts, Monsieur LaFrance. And I am … shall we say … looking for adventure. Right at the moment, a trip to the Americas will suit me very well."

"But the portrait?"

"I am not sure. I think I may take it with me. As a reminder."

"A reminder?"

"Of perfection."

CHAPTER 35

*S*OLD. Catherine sat back in her chair. A dozen dizzying images flooded her mind as the note fluttered to the floor.

Have no concern, dear Lady St Clair.

I am off to seek my fortune in the fair city of Charleston, thanks to the kind patronage of a man who wishes to remain anonymous. In exchange, he has purchased my greatest work—

Lydia made a move to pick it up, but Catherine stayed her with a motion of her hand, shaking her head wildly. *It cannot be true, it cannot be true, it cannot be true,* ran the panicked recitation in her mind. *The portrait, sold!* All chance of happiness was over. With the portrait beyond her control, she would have to live with the fear of discovery forever. And if Jocelyn should chance to hear of it—

She rose suddenly. "I must go to see the captain."

"I will call a hackney at once," Lydia said, rising.

"I want to go alone."

"Alone! You cannot, my lady."

"I must." She turned to Lydia. "Hire a coach. I will go to see Avebury, and, when I return, we will head to Wansdyke immediately. While I am gone, collect my things. And send a message ahead to Wansdyke. Tell Clara to pack for a long stay and get them to ready my coach."

Lydia paused on her way to the door. "We're to travel on, my lady?"

Catherine drew herself up. "Yes," she said. "To Wales. To Castle St Clair."

THE CARRIAGE SLOWED, THEN STOPPED, BEFORE A COMFORTABLE-looking home on a modest street near St James's Park. Catherine peered out of the window at the place where Jocelyn was living, thinking of the many letters she had written to this address and how she had never been able to imagine it. She stared until her eyes began to water. Blinking, she eased herself out of the carriage seat. The coachman, a fatherly sort, held the door and helped her down.

"I shall not be long," Catherine said. He nodded, and stepped back to watch her grip the rail beside the two shallow steps. She hesitated, then rapped at the door. It was answered almost immediately by a buxom young maid.

"Good day," Catherine began. She could not help it; her eyes wandered, taking in the sturdy, sensible curtains, the dun-coloured rug in the hall. A plain table with two drawers stood behind the bewildered-looking maid.

"Ma'am?"

"Yes." Catherine jerked her gaze back to the girl. "I am here to see Captain Avebury. Is he at home?"

"Yes, ma'am. Will you come in, please?"

Relieved to be out of the cold, Catherine followed her into the house. She stole a look across the hall and glanced up the stairs. All was silent.

"If you please, your coat, miss." The maid took Catherine's cloak. "Who shall I say is calling?"

"I beg your pardon," Catherine said hastily. "Here is my card."

The maid looked at it, and her eyes widened. She dropped a funny little bob that barely passed as a curtsey.

"This way, please, my lady."

Catherine followed her down a short hallway to what appeared to be a drawing room. The maid knocked at the door.

"I'm on my way out," Catherine heard him say in his calm, low tones. Her heart seemed to rise in her chest, threatening to choke her. She put a hand on her swollen abdomen. She might have expected the child to be performing his usual antics, but all was quiet in the womb. "That's your father," she was tempted to say out loud.

"You have a visitor, Captain." The maid had opened the door. She gestured for Catherine to enter. Slowly, Catherine moved forward. For the first time, the maid noticed her limp, and her face registered surprise and sudden pity. She quickly offered her hand for support, but Catherine reached out to lean heavily against the doorframe.

"Leave us, if you please," she said quietly over her shoulder. Speechless, the maid bobbed a curtsey and backed away.

Jocelyn was bending over a chair upon which his uniform jacket had been draped. He held a needle in his right hand and was engaged in making a minor repair to the braid. Catherine stood watching him.

"Are you forced to do your own mending? Or is this another sailors' skill of which I knew nothing?" she asked. She saw the jolt that her words sent through him. He knew her immediately, but did not turn for a moment. He was collecting himself, she thought. For one impossible moment, she was convinced that he loved her. He had to, she thought desperately.

He turned. "Kate," he said softly. "You should not be here."

There was a wariness in his beautiful blue-grey eyes that stopped her from replying.

Why, he doubts me, she realised. *For whatever reason, he has found reason to doubt me.* She hobbled slowly across the room. She ran out of breath long before she reached him, and leant panting against a sturdy but ugly chair. "I am well," she said.

"I am glad." He looked at her, his eyes travelling slowly over the bulk of her frame from head to toe. She felt her cheeks flush.

"Your son is very lively," she said, placing a hand over her abdomen. "He does not like to be still."

He nodded. His eyes, which had been gentle, grew shuttered and dark. He looked away.

"What is it? Jocelyn?" Catherine took an involuntary step toward him, then grabbed the chair for support as her leg threatened to give way.

"Are you here to see me?" he asked bluntly. He returned to the mending of his coat.

Confused, Catherine pondered the question. To see him? Why else would she be here?

"In London, I mean," he added.

"I-I came with Lydia."

"That is not what I asked, my dearest Kate." Jocelyn straightened. He viewed the coat critically, then turned to replace the needle in the sewing basket beside him. He turned to face Catherine once more.

"You should not be standing," he said. He offered his hand, and gently guided her to a worn sofa in front of the fire. He stood himself at a little distance with one arm on the mantelpiece.

"It seems that walking has become difficult," he observed.

"It has. But I had to see you, Jocelyn. I—"

"So you came to London to see me?"

Catherine took a deep breath. "No," she admitted. "No, I did not."

"Admirable honesty," Jocelyn murmured. "I expected a different answer."

"Jocelyn, what is wrong? Why are you behaving this way?" Then a thought struck her. "Have you heard something? Any news?"

"No, nothing," Jocelyn said. He shook his head bitterly. "The Admiralty will take as long as their lordships please to decide on the disposition of a man's life."

"You will be acquitted," Catherine insisted. She leant forward, bracing herself with her hands. "They know you had nothing to do with the lieutenant's murder. They must."

"They will do as they please," Jocelyn said tonelessly. He glanced at her. "Are you here to tell me the truth?"

The truth? Catherine stared back at him in dismay. Was it possible that Jocelyn—?

No, he could not know. There was no way he could have found out about LaFrance. No one had seen the painting but for the purchaser – and he was taking LaFrance to Charleston. And, those two apart, only Lydia knew about the painting. She would never tell. So what could he be referring to?

"I see from your face that you did not expect such a reception." Jocelyn smiled faintly. "But I have known all along that something is not right."

"Jocelyn, dearest. I do not know what—"

"Do not lie to me, Kate." He turned to the fireplace, knelt down, poked aimlessly at the coals. "I have a peculiar dislike of lying. It is an inconvenient aspect of my character. I am hopelessly honest. The result of many years of enforced lying, I suspect."

"Jocelyn!" Catherine made as if to stand, but she could feel the beginnings of a spasm tightening its grip about her middle. She tried to sit back into the cushions of the sofa, to breathe deeply. Sometimes she could ward off a bad attack if she concentrated hard enough. She tried to speak slowly and evenly. "I do not understand what you are speaking of, Jocelyn."

"You are forcing me to be coarse, darling Kate." Jocelyn rose and dusted off his hands, but did not turn to face her. "I so dislike being coarse."

Catherine was still trying to fend off the threatening spasm. She felt her irritability rising. What was wrong with this man? "I beg your pardon," she said stiffly. "Perhaps it is what I require, having only a weak female mind."

"I am glad to hear that your spirit is still intact."

"Well, mothers are forced to be strong."

"Yes. Your child will be fortunate."

She could hear the distance in his voice. Suddenly, she realised that what she had hoped against was to happen: she would have to parent her son alone.

She had always known that she could only count on herself. She had always known that no one would ever find her attractive, that no one would want to spend a lifetime near her.

She now understood that Avebury had, in fact, married her only so that he could be free. He had wanted her to use her influence to send him back to sea, and she had failed – partly because the quagmire he was in was too deep, but partly because she was reluctant to send him away. She loved him far too much. It was a weakness that could destroy her. It could destroy her son. The son for whom all she wanted was the earldom.

She had no ambitions for herself. She was a countess, a rich woman. She had a castle in Wales, money and properties all over England. Society be damned! The portrait be damned! She could exist alone if need be.

She needed no one.

She would always love him, but she would not beg.

She rose with difficulty. "I did not come to bicker with you," she said. "I am returning to Wansdyke. And thence to Wales."

His back stiffened. He wheeled around to face her immediately. "Wales? Where?"

"To Castle St Clair. I am going to make my son a nursery in his rightful home."

"Wansdyke is also his rightful home. Why are you doing it, Kate? It is foolish. In your condition, it is absolute madness."

"I am well, and my son is well. We will restore the castle, and he will call it home."

"Catherine." Jocelyn stepped toward her, his voice urgent. "Kate, it is the dead of winter. You surely see the foolishness of travelling at such a time, while you are expecting a child, to a castle which surely has not been inhabited for a hundred years or more."

"I am sure it is not that bad," Catherine said. She glared at him. "I must do it, Jocelyn."

She thought she saw a flicker of something – concern? hope? fear? – in his eyes. She felt it tug at her heart, but she stubbornly refused to heed it. *I have not come this far,* she thought, *to lose everything now. I will not allow it. I have never let society determine my fate, and I will not allow anyone, anything to do so now.*

No, not even love.

"You will not go alone, surely."

"I will take Lydia, I suppose, and a man or two."

"Kate, I beg you! It is sheer foolishness."

"What right have you to stop me?" she shrieked suddenly. She turned away to hide her tears. She coughed, rubbed her face.

"Aye," she heard him say. "I have no right." He walked over to the far side of the little room and stood quietly while she tried to compose herself.

"Jocelyn," she said finally. She did not turn to face him. "Jocelyn, please listen to me. I need to go away. I need to consolidate my son's legacy, to give him a start in the world. There are … reasons – good reasons – I cannot do this at Wansdyke – or here either. And it is important that I leave immediately.

Perhaps when our son is older, he and I will be able to return. This is what I came to tell you." *And that I love you,* she added silently.

It hurt to love people. They expected more than you could give. She did not know what kind of honesty Jocelyn Avebury was demanding, but she was not going to give it.

She started toward the door.

"Wait!"

She paused and looked over her shoulder.

"We may not see each other again."

She acknowledged this with a little nod of her head.

"I still wish to recognise the child." She cast him a puzzled look. He went on. "I married you in good faith, to give you an earl. Do you expect the boy's father to claim him at some point?"

"The boy's father," Catherine repeated dumbly.

"Yes. No doubt you will give him my name – unless you choose to make his father acknowledge him."

Catherine shook her head, confused. But then she saw the sheen of sweat on Jocelyn's forehead, and she knew. Oh, God in heaven, she knew!

He thought the child was not his.

Her reticule slid to the floor.

"Jocelyn," she croaked.

"Spare me your explanations," he said. The words were obviously painful for him to utter. "I merely wish to know whether my recognition of the boy would be welcome. I try to be a man of honour, you know. And I married you to give your son my name."

"Jocelyn, you misunderstand," she began, but he silenced her.

"I don't know what prevents the boy's father from stepping forward. He loves you, you know."

"Loves me?"

"Aye, he loves you, fair Kate. I see it in his face when he speaks of you."

"Jocelyn," Catherine said, panicking. "Jocelyn, you must explain. Of whom do you speak?"

"Do not make me say his name."

Catherine looked at him, and her pleas died on her lips. Was he referring to LaFrance? Had he somehow discovered the portrait and deduced that the artist was once her lover? But she had not seen LaFrance for a very long time – far too long to be able to accuse him of fathering this child.

"I don't know what you are saying, Jocelyn. Please, I speak the truth."

"I am no fool, Catherine. You did not come to our wedding bed a virgin." He said the words softly, reluctantly.

Catherine felt a spasm starting. This time, it came with the ferocious intensity of thunder, and she gasped and clutched her belly. Jocelyn leapt to her side to guide her to a chair.

"No," she whispered. "No, I cannot walk." She slid to the floor, breathing hard. He put his arms around her.

"Grip my arms," he whispered. "Grip tightly if you must. And breathe as deeply as you can. Do not open your mouth, or you will grow faint. That's better."

Catherine held on to one sturdy arm and tried to breathe. "You... you will ... be ... black and ... blue," she panted.

"Not to worry," he said. He put his hand on her belly. "This is not a good sign, is it?"

"It happens," she said with effort. "For one ... such as I ... it is merely ... inconvenient."

"Kate, if this happens during a winter journey to Wales—"

"I must go, Jocelyn."

His hand fell away. "Of course," he said. The sound of his voice was brittle.

"But why do you doubt me, Jocelyn?" The spasm had passed. She opened her eyes, and saw the stern lines of his jaw, of his nose, the profile strong and comforting above her. She felt secure pressed against his chest with his arms wrapped around her –

she knew that it would take a supreme effort to leave this warmth.

"Oh, Kate."

For a moment she thought he would tell her. His arms tightened around her for a moment.

But then he said coolly, "It was rather hard not to doubt you."

Catherine nodded. She took a deep breath. "There was someone – someone before you." She could tell he was about to interrupt her, so she placed her fingers over his lips. "Please. Please let me finish."

She waited until he gave a grim little nod. "I was a young girl, Jocelyn. My father had sent me to Wansdyke to live out the rest of my life alone. I— no one wanted me." She coughed, clutched at her stomach again, but shook her head when Jocelyn began to speak. "No. No – let me finish. I was not out, you know. There was no ball, no season for someone like myself. I was not considered marriageable. I had very few friends. And I dreamt that, someday, a man would find me beautiful and desirable.

"On a visit to London, I met a man. I did not prize my innocence – then. But that was years ago! This child is yours, Jocelyn. He can only be yours."

"But can you deny Sir Lyle is the father?"

"Sir Lyle?" Startled, Catherine looked up at Jocelyn. The sturdy lines of his face remained stony. "Jocelyn, did you not hear me? This child is yours! I have never— Sir Lyle has never been my lover, Jocelyn! I cannot imagine why—"

"He loves you, Kate. And you have secret … dealings with him. Can you deny it?"

A little memory tugged at the corner of her mind. A fichu, fluttering to the ground. The warm sun of early summer on her neck and her bare breast. Sir Lyle's gentle mockery.

She felt her face flush in a sweep of colour.

"Sir Lyle asked me to marry him," she said stiffly. "I thought for a time that I might. But, in the end, I refused him. I chose you.

I could have married him, Jocelyn. Do you not think that I would have, if I were carrying his child?"

She saw a wave of pain flicker over his face and he covered his eyes for a moment. "I do not know, Kate. I do not understand his motives – or yours, for that matter. I only know that you were not an innocent maiden on our wedding night, and that you share some secret with Sir Lyle." He smiled sadly. "I never assume anyone is only what they seem."

"I am what you see, Jocelyn. I am nothing more." Catherine drew back her skirts to show her twisted leg, thin and weak next to the bulk of her abdomen. They contemplated it together, then she raised her eyes and met his.

"Do not ask me to tell you more, Jocelyn. You will not like what you hear. But the child is yours. I swear it."

The moments ticked by. She felt his arms loosen.

He sighed heavily. "I, too, have something to say."

"Do not say it!" Catherine exclaimed. Something dark and heavy pulled at her heart. She turned, burying her face in his shirt. "Please do not," she whispered.

"I must tell you, Kate. I may not see you again. I am a hypocrite, and a liar."

"Do not say it!" she cried. She beat at him with her fists. "I cannot stand it!" Her voice broke. "I cannot stand any more," she moaned. She began to weep, her shoulders shaking.

Jocelyn held her close. She felt his heart beating, a steady movement which calmed her. His breath tickled her hair, warming her through.

"Who would have known—" she heard him murmur, then sigh. "Who would have known, indeed."

She pulled away and lifted her face up to his. She kissed him tentatively, then with more passion. He yielded to her, the warm, easy lines of his lips melting into hers. She felt new tears seep from the corner of her eyes. She knew she would not see him again.

"Know this, my love," she whispered. "Just as you saw past my lame leg, I saw into your heart. I know what you are. You could not have lied to me, even had you tried."

He briefly gripped her so tightly that her breath failed, but he let go just as quickly. With his support, she rose, stumbling as she did so. He caught her easily and held her close.

"I will not forget those words," he said. Catherine thought she heard a tremor, but could not be sure. She nodded.

"You will be careful."

"I will. I am carrying our son. I will not fail him."

"God be with you."

"And with you." She wiped the tears away and tried to smile. "I am strong, Jocelyn."

"You are that, dearest Kate."

"I will pray for your quick return to sea." She turned, and hobbled slowly out of the room.

CHAPTER 36

*A*fter the door shut and the clop-clop of the horses' hooves had faded into the distance, Jocelyn stood watching the door. Its outline wobbled and melted into a white mass of nothingness.

It was his child. She carried his child.

There was the tiniest bubbling spring of joy somewhere in the deepest regions of his heart.

His child. His son.

Jocelyn reached a finger into his collar. He was suddenly rather warm. He reached awkwardly behind him with one hand, felt around for a chair, and sat. While the room was now sitting straight in his mind, its corners still wobbled and danced with alarming facility.

He closed his eyes. He could feel the press of a crowd on him, howling for blood. His youthful dreams had been haunted by the idea that he had been able to smell, actually smell, the blood of his father when they tore him open. It was ridiculous, of course, but he had been so small he had not known what he was hearing or seeing or smelling.

Now he could be someone's father. He could guide the life of a new human being.

Or he could vanish forever, go to sea and be a mere shadow in the child's life.

He raised his head, looked over at his proud Navy coat. It was escape, this yearning to be at sea, commanding the fates of hundreds of men. Here on land, it seemed he commanded nothing. But he had the chance to raise a child.

However, did he want to subject a child to … someone like him?

He made a sudden move to stand. The room was too warm. He went to retrieve his coat and stood uncertainly with it hanging from his hands.

A knock at the door. He turned, in his haste knocking over and shattering an ugly statuette. His heart pounded.

Kate, he thought. *She has come back. She will ask me to go with her to Wales.*

"Yes," he called, trying not to let the urgency in his gut overwhelm him.

He took a tentative step toward the door.

It opened.

"Captain? A message for you." It was the maid. She looked at the shattered statuette in surprise.

His heart sank. "A message?"

She held out a tray, then, when he had lifted the paper, bustled off to take care of the debris.

Jocelyn slit open the message.

Captain Avebury, greetings.

I would be honoured to see you once more before I voyage to the Americas—

The Americas! His heart suddenly seemed to skip a beat. He would give anything, anything to get out of his predicament and sail off—

No! No. No, it was not what he wanted at all. Not at all.

He crumpled the note in his hand and stared at it. He had not the least idea what he did want.

Had Sir Lyle mentioned a trip to the Americas? No. He would certainly have taken notice if he'd said that. So he had not, Jocelyn decided. He wondered briefly what business took Sir Lyle in that direction.

Sir Lyle held the key. That much was fact. He held the key to whatever it was Catherine was hiding from him. And Sir Lyle alone knew what had driven him to help a man whose life was based on deception and dishonour.

WHEN HE KNOCKED AT SIR LYLE'S DOOR THAT EVENING, HE WAS IN dress uniform. A few snowflakes were fluttering about, but the wind had died down and it seemed much too cold for real snow.

He thought of Catherine, on her way to Wansdyke and thence to Wales. No matter how lushly appointed her carriage, it would still be chilly and uncomfortable. And the spasms – he knew nothing of what happened to women expecting children, but he thought they could not be right.

The butler who admitted him spoke gravely and with respectful admiration for his rank. He would show the captain directly into the library, he murmured. Sir Lyle was there chatting with another well-wisher. He led Jocelyn across the hall and along a short corridor toward a beautiful pair of heavy doors. The butler pulled one open.

Jocelyn walked in. Two men stood at one side of the large library beside a bank of windows. It was dark outside, but the light leaving the window illuminated fat flakes of snow floating down; only a man born and bred in Yorkshire would know those flakes would not settle, he reflected. It was just a flurry.

Sir Lyle stood talking gravely with a handsome youth,

someone Jocelyn did not recognise. As he entered, both men turned in his direction.

He walked toward them, his boots clicking loudly on the polished wooden floor. The two men had been examining something propped up on a stand; indeed, they had positioned the lamp so the light fell directly on it.

He had no time to control his reaction. He stepped toward the picture and suddenly, the wind was kicked out of him. The image hit him full in the face. He gasped.

Catherine.

Catherine as he knew her, as he loved her. Long white fingers, her nails digging into the rich red fabric beneath her. The little indentation above her lip, the spectacular blanket of fine blonde hair, the precise colour of her nipples.

He automatically sought and found the tiny mole on her right side, on her pelvis.

He staggered, then lifted a hand, accusingly. He pointed at Sir Lyle.

"You—" he choked. His voice felt like raw blood in his throat. He felt as if he were breathing through a curtain of smoke – a thick, waterlogged smoke, like that of a shipboard fire.

"Wait. Things are not as they appear." Sir Lyle stepped forward, a hand held up in warning.

"You bastard," Jocelyn spat out. "Jesus, Mary, and Joseph! You damned bastard. Did you threaten her? Blackmail her? Humiliate her?" His carefully controlled accent and diction threatened to fail for the first time ever. Choice Yorkshire language sprang to his lips. He suddenly knew quite positively that he could murder both men in the room, with bare hands if needs be.

"It is my work." The other man spoke. He had a slight accent. He wore a puzzled frown.

Jocelyn turned on him. "So this is about money? How much do you want? I will give it to you, however much it is."

"It is not for sale."

"I will buy it or I will take it. You may choose." He felt his fists clench involuntarily. Ah, so this was rage, the rage that caused men to punch each other. It felt sick, dizzying, nauseating. Would beating these men to a pulp give him any relief? He didn't feel well now. The young one he knew he could kill quickly. He was not so sure about Sir Lyle.

The man with the accent looked helplessly at Sir Lyle. Jocelyn advanced a little closer, his gaze fastened once more on the painting. It really was her, the likeness was unmistakable. He had seen her sit just so, many times.

"You were her lover," he said, not taking his eyes from the painting.

"She was my life," the stranger said softly. "But she did not love me. She left me as soon as I completed this portrait. She was selfish. She wanted me for her own ends."

"She is my wife. I demand that you give me this painting."

"I have bought it, Captain Avebury." Sir Lyle spoke quietly. The popping of the fire almost ate his words.

"You?" Jocelyn looked up.

"Yes. And tomorrow Monsieur LaFrance leaves with me for the Americas. We go first to Charleston where Monsieur LaFrance will begin a brilliant career as a portraitist. I expect to sail on, through the West Indies, to Brazil."

"What—?" He cleared his throat. He did not want to hear the answer, but he needed to ask. He prayed that Catherine had not lied to him.

Oh, Kate, my love. Is this what you hid from me?

The child, the child. My son. It is my son after all. Now there can be no doubt that she was telling the truth. Because her secret had nothing to do with our child.

He saw the artist turn to Sir Lyle with sudden keen interest.

"Yes, I admit it," Sir Lyle said. "I know the woman. I was not certain at first, but I guessed." He smiled briefly, turned to the artist. "Your description of her leg convinced me. You may rest assured, Captain, that, until Monsieur LaFrance told me his beloved model limped," he gestured at the painting, "I had no idea who she was."

"And now I am taking it." Jocelyn made a move toward the portrait. He glanced toward the two men but neither seemed inclined to stop him.

"You might prefer me to keep the painting, Captain Avebury." Sir Lyle nodded at the canvas. "You would not want it to fall into the wrong hands."

"She worked so hard to hide this from me," Jocelyn muttered. "And all along, I thought—"

"If you wish, I will take it with me," Sir Lyle continued. He shrugged. "To tell the truth, I was planning to … er … dispose of it after leaving England, anyway."

"Oh, you cannot be serious!" LaFrance cried. He looked from one man to the other. "Do not destroy it," he begged.

Jocelyn looked at him. This man had been Catherine's lover. He had imagined he would feel intense hatred for anyone who had known her as he had but, now the time had come, he felt sorry for the artist. He could see immediately that he was someone Catherine would have had no use for once she had achieved her objective, once she had had the chance to feel beautiful. The painting had done that for her – and the attention of LaFrance meant she had attained more proof of her beauty than she had imagined possible. But, once her confidence had been bolstered it would not be shaken and she needed him no longer.

"Had you intended to keep it?" he asked LaFrance.

The artist shrugged, looked away, embarrassed. "It is all I have."

"You do not need it," Sir Lyle said. "I have told you, there is nothing in London for someone of your talent. You must travel, earn your fortune. Captain Avebury will tell you the same. Eh, Captain? Leave England, go abroad, accumulate riches. Return and set up your nursery." He glanced at the mantel clock. Jocelyn followed his glance.

"Catherine is going to Wales," he said bluntly. "I must stop her."

"Wales? In her condition?"

"To Castle St Clair. She is trying to escape the disgrace which would have followed the exhibition of this painting."

"Have you spoken to her?"

"I have. But she said nothing about the portrait. Still, I know her. She is trying to protect the child from her disgrace. She fears she has ruined the child's life."

"She is being foolish. But no one can stop her now."

"I will head to Wansdyke."

"But you are waiting for the decision on your case—"

"I will seek permission from the admirals."

Sir Lyle moved to cover the painting with a large silk cloth. He nodded at it. "I will make sure that the painting is delivered to Wansdyke, then. I will crate it. No one will see it."

"No, I will take it to Wansdyke myself. I need to stop her from embarking on this foolish journey. If I don't arrive at Wansdyke in time to stop her, I will continue on toward Wales. Perhaps I will catch up with her on the road."

"I am afraid you will not have time," Sir Lyle said softly.

"What do you mean?" For an ominously silent second Jocelyn wondered—

The door opened suddenly. The three men turned to see another three men in uniform pushing their way past the distressed servant. Jocelyn turned to Sir Lyle. "You bastard!" he croaked.

"It was the only way I could save her, you idiot," Sir Lyle hissed.

"Jocelyn Avebury, captain of His Majesty's Royal Navy," one of the men called. "We are commanded to place you under arrest."

Jocelyn felt a queer relief that he had worn his full dress

uniform. It would have been disgraceful to be arrested in a dressing gown, for example, or farm clothes.

"The charges, gentlemen?" he said, keeping his voice calm.

"Misrepresentation, lying under oath. You will please accompany us immediately."

Jocelyn looked at Sir Lyle. "You lied," he said. "I thought you were going to help me, for Catherine's sake. But instead you betrayed me. Do you hate me so much? Are you scheming to take my place?" He paused, then added bitterly, "The child – the child is mine."

Sir Lyle looked incredulous for a moment. Then he started to laugh. It was not a nice sound. "I had to, Avebury. She needs you. And you would have left her, gone to sail the seas. You can't leave England now. And, even if you do not end in prison, you will certainly not get back to sea."

"I would not have left them."

Sir Lyle shrugged. "Perhaps. You are a sailor, and all sailors long to be at sea. Catherine needs you here. This is the best thing for her and for the babe – to have you here in England."

"She does not need a convicted criminal for a husband," Jocelyn retorted.

Sir Lyle smiled. "As ever, no choice is ideal. That is life, eh, Captain Avebury? It is what I could do."

"For her," Jocelyn muttered.

"Yes. For her."

Sir Lyle extended his hand. "Will you bid me farewell?"

Jocelyn looked at his hand for a long moment. Finally, he took it. "Farewell." He turned to LaFrance. "A safe journey." Then he straightened his jacket and walked to the far side of the room, where the men waited. "Gentlemen, let us go," he said.

For a long moment after they were gone, the only sound was the popping fire. Sir Lyle retreated to one end of the room to pour himself a glass of wine. LaFrance sat in a chair, gazing blankly at the shrouded canvas.

"But they will be apart," he said suddenly into the quiet.

Sir Lyle finished his glass and poured himself another. "Not for long. And when Avebury is free, he will really be free. No more secrets." He looked at LaFrance over his glass. "As far as I know," he added, and laughed.

CHAPTER 37

The journey to Wansdyke was slow.

For one thing, the weather was much colder: the occasional fall of snow made the horses hang back and ostlers and innkeepers slower to respond to Lydia Barrow's urgent entreaties. For another, Catherine felt simply unable to travel as fast as she might have. The jostling of the carriage kept her awake through the night and, exhausted, she was too tired and ill to eat. When, after over a day spent on the road, they finally reached Wansdyke, Catherine overruled Lydia's anxious objections and said that they would continue on to Wales that same day.

"I will be fine after a short nap, and so will you," she said firmly. "Kindly have the staff put the furniture under the holland covers and prepare to close Wansdyke for a time. They should have already begun, so I expect it will not be too onerous. Henry Coachman and his boy should come along; they will be able to see to the stables at Castle St Clair. We have someone who is Welsh, do we not? An under gardener? He may wish to accompany us. I will leave the disposal of grounds to his imagination if he would like to be in charge."

"My lady, I—"

"We will have a cook and chambermaid from the village. And I have no need of a butler. Perhaps a couple from the village will serve as housekeeper and valet to—" Catherine caught herself, shook her head. She pressed her lips tightly together. There would be no need of a valet. Avebury would not be in residence. "We will manage delightfully. Have Clara prepare a bath for me, Lydia, and see if there might be a dress that has not been put into a trunk."

She had never been to Wales. She had no clue what to expect. And, she imagined, were she an ordinary person, that would terrify her out of her mind. *But I am the Countess St Clair*, she reminded herself. *I am not ordinary. Thank you, Papa, for making sure that I could bear any cruelty, any difficulty life might bring.*

After her bath, she dashed off a short note to Beaseley, outlining her plan to give birth to the new earl in Wales. She left instructions regarding Wansdyke and her Bath apartments, and requested that he handle her financial obligations. She would need him to forward funds to her in Wales as soon as possible.

She then wrote a quick and apologetic letter to Melinda, attempting to explain her departure by saying she wanted to bear the child in Wales on what would one day be his estate, to prepare the castle for habitation, and so forth. It was a dreadful accumulation of lies and misleading statements, and she was glad when she had done with it. Having folded up that note and addressed it, she hesitated before taking a fresh sheet of paper.

Dear Jocelyn, she wrote.

Then she crumpled up the page and tossed it aside.

"Can't," she said aloud. She pushed herself away from her desk and heaved herself up and out of her seat. She limped over to the bed and stood there for a moment clenching the sheets in her fists. She raised her head. The child was stretching, bouncing, pushing at her from inside.

"I promise you," she said hoarsely. "I promise you the life that you deserve."

THE WEATHER WAS OVERCAST, WITHOUT SNOW BUT BLUSTERY. Catherine spoke briefly to the gathered household staff from the grand staircase that spiralled down to the hall. She gave final instructions to the housekeeper, granted the butler's wish for a holiday, promised a bonus to the underservants and apologised for her abrupt departure. Then, leaning on Lydia's arm, she descended the stairs in as regal a fashion as she could manage.

They did not get very far that day. Not only were they exhausted, but there was also some confusion about which way to go. Catherine wanted to take the most direct route through Bristol and on across the Severn. She was feeling most unwell, and Lydia agreed with her that it seemed unwise to spend extra days on the road. However, the coachman and the Welsh gardener's boy felt that a more indirect route – via Gloucester – would be more manageable. A December crossing was likely to be unpleasant in any sort of weather, and the shorter one further upstream would be much easier. The Gloucester road was well-travelled, so it would be possible to stop frequently if bad weather or exhaustion made it advisable. But taking the land route would add days onto their journey ...

In the end, they agreed to go via Bristol. It was likely they would be able to find a ferry or ship that would take them not just across the river but as far as Newport.

Ironically, it was Lydia who was violently ill during the crossing. The Bristol channel was rough, and icy winds whipped about them, but Catherine felt a perverse relief on leaving English soil behind. Would she ever be able to return to Wansdyke, she wondered. Would she be able to bring the heir to the St Clair earldom to London to take his place in society? Or would her disgrace taint him permanently?

Would her son ever see his father?

The child stretched itself out so far that she felt she had

hardly any room to draw breath. A wave splashed over the deck where Catherine stood, and she stepped back automatically. How odd, she thought wryly. It was easier for her to navigate a swaying ship in bad weather than it was for her to dance in a stable ballroom with a level floor. She compensated automatically for the roll of the deck under her feet, and did not feel as unbalanced as the other passengers did. So long as she could clutch a rail or some other support, she managed perfectly well.

She mentally planned her arrival at Castle St Clair in the minutest detail. She was sure she would be able to hire villagers to work in the castle: at the very least, she would need a cook and a maid, and help in the stables. Right now, in winter, it would be hard to get any external work done, but surely there would be carpenters and a blacksmith who could do what was needed indoors. It would probably take a while to make the place smart, or maybe even comfortable, but she was sure she could do it – and manage meanwhile.

The wind was biting. The rising mist was very deceptive; it made it seem as if they were enveloped in a warm cloud when, in fact, it was freezing. She shuddered as they began the slow descent from the ship, and Lydia pulled her closer. Her limbs were stiff. Her knees creaked. Nonetheless, she had to take charge, so she raised her head and scanned the questionable-looking crowd on the dock. She did not see anyone else from her party and she pressed Lydia's arm. "Where are they?" she asked

"They will have gone to see to the carriage. And they might also be seeking provisions. We may be able to buy little or nothing on the way to Castle St Clair."

"But the village," Catherine said quickly. "There is a village."

Lydia nodded.

They hesitated at the bottom of the gangway finding themselves amongst a crowd of drably dressed pedlars and longshoremen. They all spoke Welsh, which was disconcerting, although they were polite and did not stare. Commendable, thought

Catherine wryly. It would have been rather unfair to ask people not to stare at a cripple who was so heavy with child.

The spasm came as she waited for the carriage. Its sudden violence astounded her, and she dropped to her knees in the mud before she could even gasp. There was no pain – just the sensation of her breath being squeezed out of her. She opened her mouth to speak but found she had no voice.

Lydia was beside her in a moment, as were countless other people.

"Stand back, please," she heard Lydia say. "Stand back – my lady is unwell."

The swell of voices in her ears grew louder. She was finally able to gasp. Her belly seemed to shudder, and she grasped at it protectively.

"No!" Her voice creaked and ended in a wail.

"Has she eaten?" A woman's voice. It was the only voice she could understand. The rest were an incoherent babble of concern.

Lydia replied, but her voice was lost in the roar of noise.

Two strong arms were put around her, warm like an embrace.

"Easy, my lady." It was the woman. "My son is going to lift you. I am holding your skirts. You will be comfortable soon."

"I am all right," Catherine panted. "Must … must hurry—"

"You can rest with me. My house is over there, on the high street. You'll be on your way in no time."

The vice grip around her middle was lessening. "Please," Catherine begged, lifting her head. Her hair had fallen from its pins and was pasted onto her face with a sheen of sweat. She pushed the strands out of the way as best as she could, and looked up at the woman who had spoken to her. She was middle-aged, brown-eyed and brown-haired, and wore a rough brown cloak. Brown from top to toe.

"I have to go home," Catherine whispered.

"And where are you going?" The woman turned to Lydia, but

Lydia remained silent. The woman looked around the silent crowd, and said something in Welsh. When no one replied, she repeated herself a little more loudly, and with shuffling feet, the crowd began to disperse.

"That's better," the woman muttered. She turned to Catherine. "My dear," she said, her voice softening. "You will go nowhere today. You might as well come home with me."

"I cannot," Catherine said, trying to push the arms away. "I need my coach. I am going home. Oh!" She bent forward again.

"Are you in pain, my lady?"

"No," Catherine groaned. "No …I …the babe—"

The woman in brown put her hands on Catherine's belly. She looked over at Lydia.

"February?"

"March," Catherine said.

The woman looked back down at her. "No," she said quietly. "February, to be sure. And it's likely to be January, if you don't come home with me today." She said something in Welsh, and strong hands reached over to lift Catherine up. She whimpered slightly, but allowed herself to be lifted into her waiting carriage. Lydia climbed in after her and beckoned, but the woman glanced at the crest on the doors and shook her head.

"The high street, at the top of the hill," the woman said to the coachman, who nodded and shut the door. She turned and walked over to a waiting gig, where her son now sat holding the reins of an old cob.

THE HOUSE WAS LARGE AND COMFORTABLE, CLEARLY THE dwelling of a prosperous merchant or tradesman. It stood alone at the top of the high street that was paved in tidy cobblestones.

The woman in brown emerged with her son – a stocky, silent

fellow of not much more than twenty. Together, they helped Catherine down from the carriage.

"I am grateful for your kindness. But I cannot stay. I am travelling north, and I need to make some progress before the day is done."

"She is the Countess St Clair," Lydia murmured.

"Indeed?" The lady in brown looked at Catherine, her face suddenly grim. There was an awkward pause.

"I am going to Castle St Clair."

Silence.

"It is—"

"I know where it is."

Catherine drew back. She looked at Lydia for help, but Lydia was folding and refolding a handkerchief.

"It is a long journey. And hard."

"But it is where I must go," Catherine protested. She looked from the woman to Lydia and back again. "I am sorry, madam, but I do not know your name."

"Mrs Owen, my lady." The woman in brown nodded at her son. "My son will help see to the horses. You must come in."

Catherine could find no polite way to refuse. With reluctance, she entered the house and was shown into a surprisingly large and lavishly appointed room. She sank into a chair, and was immediately overcome with fatigue. For a moment, she thought she would fall asleep just where she was.

"You will have something to eat."

"Thank you," Catherine said, her voice failing. "But I—"

"You will not get to Castle St Clair today, my lady. And it would not be wise for you to travel by night."

"You do not understand me, I fear," Catherine said. She was beginning to feel exasperated and trapped. "I own Castle St Clair. I have come to take up residence."

"You will forgive my rudeness, my lady. I know a little bit about birthing and I know you would not like to bear your child at Castle St Clair. The journey alone is long and rough. And, when you get there—"

"I will have help!" Catherine exclaimed. "There is a village—"

"You may not find much help," Mrs Owen said, rising. She took a tea tray from the hands of a curious maidservant and dismissed her before sitting down once more. "You are English. The villagers may not think well of you."

Catherine protested, "But I mean to hire them! I will not cheat anyone."

"Being cheated is not what they will be concerned about, my lady." Mrs Owen's voice softened. "Come, here is something to eat. You must keep up your strength. Tiring yourself does the child no good. After you have eaten, we will talk about your journey. My son says your horses also need some rest. Let us not get ahead of ourselves."

"I do not like to impose—"

"You do not impose, my lady." Mrs Owen rose. "I will speak to your coachman about the route he proposes to take to Castle St Clair. He is English, I think? He may not know the best way—"

"The boy," Catherine interjected. "He is Welsh. We had thought to follow his directions."

"Then I will speak to the boy. But rest and eat a little, build up your strength. And do not think you will travel on tonight. It is already too late."

With this, Mrs Owen left.

Catherine looked helplessly at Lydia. "This is terrible."

"But she is right." Lydia hesitated. "And she is likely to be right about the village, too."

"What, that we will find no help?" Catherine felt a sudden chill. The thought had not even occurred to her. To have a child with no help in the cold, wet Welsh spring – it was a dreadful thought.

"It cannot be true," she said slowly. "Why would the villagers refuse to work?"

"Because, my lady," Lydia said nervously, "because we are English, and they are Welsh."

Catherine felt the fear wash over her again. Impossible, was her first thought. But she suddenly had a dreadful premonition that Lydia was right. The castle had been uninhabited for a very long time. She had no idea what the previous St Clair lords might have been like. She knew nothing of St Clair family history. Had they been bloody? Cruel? Dishonest? She had no way of knowing.

To her growing despair, she realised that the only house she knew was that of the Clavertons. The Delamare earldom, which had rejected her – and which she had proudly rejected in turn – was, nonetheless, the only history she had.

She felt as if someone had kicked the wind out of her. All this way. She had come all this way to give her son what was his. And now she realised that she did not know exactly what she was giving him. It could be a most unwelcome gift. To be despised by those around you, to be tainted by a history for which you were not responsible – it was a horrible thing to do to a new life.

The St Clair earldom was no simple gift, she thought.

But I have no choice. I am here. I cannot return to Bath, or to Wansdyke. Avebury does not love me as much as he loves his ships. And Sir Lyle – I have dragged him through the dirt, too. He will not save me now.

When Mrs Owen returned, Catherine spoke calmly. "Mistress Owen, I will gratefully accept your offer to stay here tonight. You are right – I am fatigued, and the spasms come when I am fatigued. But tomorrow I must leave, and I beg your assistance in finding the best route."

"Your gardener's boy knows the way," Mrs Owen replied. "I have spoken to him, and he will guide you along the river. Do you know Abergavenny? No? You will be travelling along the edge of the mountains, and Castle St Clair is beyond Abergavenny." She shook her head. "I would not have thought it wise for you to travel so far in your condition. It will be slow going." She looked sharply at Catherine. "And your husband? When will he join you?"

"He is not joining me," Catherine said. Her voice was calm. "He is an officer with His Majesty's Navy. He will be at sea."

"And these spasms? Do they come often?"

"Often enough," Catherine admitted. "But only when I am extremely tired, and the child does not seem to be in danger."

"You can expect this child in February, my lady. Forgive me for saying so, but—" Mrs Owen shook her head and glanced at Catherine's belly.

February. How could that be? That would mean – Catherine counted absently – an image of Jocelyn in shirtsleeves, silhouetted in the light of her bedroom window at Albrook, entered her mind.

This child is anxious to be born, she thought. *He will take the first opportunity to arrive.*

She would make sure he was safe.

She rose with difficulty. "I thank you for your help. If I might be so bold—"

"I will take you to your room, my lady."

CHAPTER 38

*J*en Owen was a widow. Her husband had been the apothecary, and had left her a reasonable sum. Thanks to that, the assistance of several sons, and occasional work caring for the sick, she was comfortably off. She did indeed know quite a bit about midwifery, and so she pulled Lydia Barrow aside. "You do realise that you will have to manage the birth when the time comes," she said gravely.

Lydia was not fearful by nature, but this shocked her.

"Will there be no one to call on?" she asked, in horror.

"You can try getting a message to me. If I hear from you, I will come. But you should not expect any other help. I suspect that men will not allow their women into the castle – even if some of the carpenters are prepared to work on it."

"But the danger of it! Will there be no one to protect us?"

Mrs Owen shook her head. "We are not so horrible, you know. I cannot think that a Welshman would attack a household of ladies. It is not the way we are. But they will not hold you in any affection. Listen to me. I have family in Abergavenny. If you can get a message to them, they will find me. I will come as quickly as I can."

THE JOURNEY WAS ROUGH. CATHERINE WAS RELATIVELY WELL-rested, they had provisions, and the horses were fresh. But the weather was foul – wet and cold – so it took all of a hard day's travel to reach Abergavenny. Catherine was grateful that it did not snow. Their route wound along the edge of the mountains, and she could see the crags above the road, snowy and grand. At another time in her life, she would have found them enthralling, uplifting. Today they were terrifying.

In Abergavenny, they found an inn where they were able to spend the night. They were up early the following day and pressed on through a damp drizzle that turned into wet snowflakes. The snow soon gave way to a depressing fog. There was no scenery to admire – they could barely see beyond their immediate path.

As the afternoon light faded, the horses seemed to get slower and slower. Finally, they stopped. There was absolutely no sound, no motion. Having been rocked continually for two days, Catherine was momentarily taken aback, as if being still was about to make her seasick. Lydia rapped at the door. No response.

"This is ridiculous," she muttered. She threw open the door and, suddenly, they saw what had made the coachman stop.

Castle St Clair. It seemed to be a giant shell – an utter ruin.

IT WAS A MUCH BETTER PRISON THAN THE SORT JOCELYN HAD imagined: not a dank cell, but a sun-filled room. But it was still confinement. The windows were so high he could not see out. The door was kept locked. Meals were brought, but no conversation offered.

It felt like death. He would prefer death, he thought, to this endless waiting. But he was a navy man through and through. Whatever his superiors demanded of him, he would do.

His mind turned to Kate and the child. She would be in Wales by now. He wished her Godspeed, and good health. He hoped someone would tell him when – and if – the child was born safely.

On the fourth morning, the door opened. It was Beaseley.

"Sir." Jocelyn rose.

"Captain Avebury." Beaseley looked over his shoulder at the guard on duty, and dismissed him with a nod. The door shut.

"I confess, I have always been rather ignorant of naval procedure." Beaseley kept his voice light. "I was told of your arrest the morning after it occurred. But I had some trouble getting in to see you." He shook his head. "You are quite a troublesome young man."

"I am sorry." Jocelyn sat again. He gestured toward the only other chair in the room, and Beaseley also sat.

"What am I to call you?"

Jocelyn shook his head. He did not meet Beaseley's gaze.

"The admirals seem to be having the same problem. What do we call the golden boy of the Royal Navy – the one who would have been on his way to Spain by now, if— Ah, you look startled? Do you suppose me so ineffectual that I would have had you taken to London for questioning without assurances? I insisted on a return for making you available for the interminable hearings of the committee looking into Lieutenant Bright's death. A ship. A rather nice ship, as I recall. And an easy and potentially profitable tour of the Mediterranean." He sighed deeply. "Why on earth could you have not stayed out of trouble until then?"

Jocelyn shrugged. "It was bound to happen, Mr Beaseley. I am not Jocelyn Avebury. There never was, never has been, such a person."

"Fie, Captain Avebury! You are talking rubbish." Beaseley rose and rapidly paced the little room. "No man is who he says he is.

No man is what his parents say he is. Do you take my meaning, sir?" He pointed toward the door. "Do you know that there are piles of paper in the Admiralty testifying to your bravery and courage in the face of great danger? I know who you are, Captain Avebury, as do the admirals – we all know what stuff you are made of!"

"But that is to no purpose, Mr Beaseley. I would not be here were it of any use."

"Nothing is that simple, Captain Avebury," Beaseley retorted. He stopped pacing. "You have got to tell me everything. Then I may be able to comprehend who benefits by you being here."

Jocelyn laughed: a short, harsh laugh. "Do you not know why I am here, Mr Beaseley?" He rose. "I thought you understood very well on the day I married Lady St Clair. Do you not remember? You were willing to procure a licence without seeing any of my papers. Surely you knew."

"Quite honestly, Captain Avebury, I do not know why you are still here. I am rather proud of what I was able to persuade the Admiralty to do for you. Everything was all ready. All that was required was your testimony. So I ask again, why are you here now and not at sea? How did you turn all my careful plans upside down? Do you think no one knows there is something you hide about your past? No one cares, Captain Avebury!"

Jocelyn stared at him, perplexed, beginning to realise that Beaseley was beside himself; he truly expected Jocelyn would have been long gone from London by now. "But – but I am here accused of misrepresentation—" he stammered.

"And what of it?" Beaseley demanded. "They are not fools, these men. When your distinguished record and impressive accumulation of prize money came to their attention years ago, they will have scrutinised your records closely. Do not underestimate the Admiralty, Captain Avebury." He walked over to the chair again, and sat down. He produced a handkerchief from his breast pocket, wiped his forehead, blew his nose, and delicately replaced the handkerchief.

Was it possible? Jocelyn saw the room blur before his eyes. He tipped his head back to look up at the windows, as he had done so many times since being brought here. Rare January sunshine poured through. He squinted, then shut his eyes. His head was pounding.

Was it really possible? He was beginning to realise that self-pity had blinded him to what surely must be the truth – the Admiralty had known all along that, whoever he was, he was not Avebury. And yet they would continue to use him for their own purposes. Had they wished it, he would have been found out long ago.

A weight was lifted from his heart, from his shoulders. It flew away on gilded wings, leaving him dizzy and light-headed. But he was free, truly free, for the first time in many long years. And what sorrow remained in his heart was for Kate and the child.

His thoughts travelled to Wales. Was she safe in Castle St. Clair?

"You are going to tell me your story from the beginning, Captain Avebury. The truth."

The truth. He opened his eyes, directed his gaze at Beaseley. He pulled himself back to London.

"I was born," he began, "twenty-nine years ago in York. My father was a prosperous doctor. My mother was the daughter of a squire. She died when I was very young." He hesitated, continued with difficulty. "My father was a political malcontent. He held some rather extreme views – I wish I could tell you what they were, but I was much too young to know what he was about. He was condemned as a traitor and executed when I was seven."

"You were sent to relations in London."

"Yes. My mother's family. I went to several different places, but eventually found a home with a distant cousin. He was an old gentleman who had a large family – another boy, another son, was no trouble to him. But they wanted nothing to do with my father's disgrace." Jocelyn looked down at his hands. "They can scarcely be blamed for feeling that way."

"So these people gave you a new identity."

"That is correct. Since there were so many children, it was actually not very difficult to pass me off as a country cousin called Jocelyn Avebury. No one knew one of us from the other anyway."

"Was there any outright fraud?"

"As in money? Papers?" Jocelyn laughed. "You really are a solicitor, Mr Beaseley, if such things concern you more than fraud of the spirit! No, no, do not try to deny it. I will tell you what I know: as far as I can tell, there was no forgery. No fabricated baptismal certificates or such like. I believe that the old gentleman asked a favour of a friend in the Admiralty who took his word that I was an orphaned country cousin. My real name is John Randall, but I have never gone by it since I came to London. It feels like the name of a stranger now, but it is mine. If you check the register of a certain parish in Yorkshire, you will find me."

"You will pardon me for saying that all of this is a tempest in a teacup."

Jocelyn lifted his hands helplessly in a shrug. "You might say so. But here I am."

Beaseley was gazing up toward the windows. "Someone," he mused, "has changed his plans. We need to know who has done so, and why. Captain Avebury," he said, suddenly turning his gaze on him, "have you any enemies? Those who envy your advancement, your fortune?"

Jocelyn shook his head. "None," he said. "Lieutenant Bright was an impressive officer, and would have gone far. I thought highly of him, and was very much shocked when he made accusations against me. And the brawl … I arrived too late to save him but, had I been there from the beginning, I would have prevented it, I am sure. My men were extremely loyal. Not a malcontent amongst them. Their reaction to Bright's treachery was too swift."

"Others? Not on your ship?"

"No – no, I cannot think of anyone who would wish me so ill as to—"

He suddenly remembered. It seemed to be an irrelevant detail, but he could not shake the feeling that it was somehow pertinent. Beaseley saw the change in his expression.

"Well?" he pressed.

"There is one person – not an enemy, you understand. But we had an encounter that might be considered unfortunate—"

"Out with it, my boy. Speak!"

"Roland. A lieutenant aboard the Majestic."

"I recall hearing about Roland. Viscount Roland, I believe? You saved him from some trouble with natives in Bombay. You were then late to a rendezvous."

"Yes," Jocelyn said, grimacing. "That is where the trouble began."

"And why would Lord Roland wish you ill?"

"I don't know. He lost a finger in the fight – the fight in the brothel where I found him."

Beaseley snorted. "Surely he cannot regret the loss of a finger when he might have lost his life!"

Jocelyn got the words out with difficulty. "Lord Roland is the younger half-brother of Sir Lyle Barrington. Sir Lyle has vast shipping interests – trade interests. He thanked me personally, in fact, for saving his brother. I thought it was odd at the time – I did not really understand what he was thanking me for."

"I am a little acquainted with Sir Lyle," Beaseley cut in. "Any relation of his is likely to get up to no good, I imagine. Lord Roland, in particular. He is someone who does not belong in service to the Crown, I can assure you. His mother must have gone to some expense to secure his position. But tell me, Captain

Avebury. Why on earth did you risk your assignment by going to find him?"

"I could not let him die," Jocelyn said simply. "And I knew that he would. There was no way that he would be allowed to leave. If I may speak rather indelicately, sir, he was smoking opium and had made himself rather unpopular with the – the ladies. The men of the district were prepared to kill him. I did not want to see a uniform belonging to His Majesty swinging in the wind. His own captain was reluctant to go after him. He did not speak the native tongue, which I do. And I was his captain's senior. I was not going to send men into a situation where I was not prepared to go myself. So I went."

Beaseley rose from his seat. "There is something very strange about this story, Captain Avebury. And I mean to find out what."

"Lord Roland is serving aboard the *Surrey*, I believe."

"No, I do not think so. The *Surrey* has been moored at the Nore for repairs since last November. He is probably in London. And I will find him."

Jocelyn rose. "Mr Beaseley, I appreciate your assistance. Can you – can you tell me why I am here? Am I awaiting trial? Am I truly under arrest?"

"The ways of the military are very strange to me, Captain Avebury. I tell you, I do not know their justification for keeping you locked in this room. But I will demand answers, and return with them. That I promise you. You are to leave everything in my hands, and do not under any circumstances execute any ridiculous plans of your own devising! Is that clear?"

"Very clear," Jocelyn said. "Thank you. And, Mr Beaseley – have you heard from Kate – Lady St Clair?" His heart pounded. *When I get out of here, I am going to find her. Even if she will not come with me, I want to see my son. He will bear the name of Avebury, by God! He deserves to at least once see my face, the face of a man who remade his past.*

Beaseley slowed his steps. He turned from the door. "No," he said quietly. "I have not. I am sure she will need my services soon. But I have not heard anything."

"Will you tell me when you do? And – and tell me if there is something, anything—"

"Absolutely." Beaseley turned back to the door. He rapped on it, and it was opened immediately from the other side. "Good day, Captain Avebury."

The door shut behind him.

Oh, Christ Almighty! He might be free, truly free. If it were really true that the Admiralty had known, had forgiven him long ago … if it were really true that they were going to give him a ship to Spain ….

But if it were really true, what was he doing in this damned room?

Kate, my love.

He hoped that Beaseley could work quickly.

CHAPTER 39

She had never seen such high mountains in her life. They took her breath away. They terrified her. But she had little time to gape, to forget the damp snowflakes swirling about her, for the coachman and Welsh gardener's boy were standing awaiting her instructions.

She finally found her voice. "I know the castle is not as empty as it appears, there have always been custodians. I wrote to them in the autumn saying I intended to take up residence eventually." Her voice trailed off as she realised that she had never had a reply. She had thought nothing of it, but she knew now that she ought to have taken the lack of response as a warning.

The St Clairs were not welcome.

Catherine turned to the coachman. "Ride into the village and trouble the keeper of the nearest inn for advice. Tell him that I will pay him handsomely if he has a servant he can lend us. And I will compensate the servant well. We also need provisions. To see us through to tomorrow, at least."

"My lady," the coachman replied, "might I take Thomas with me? They might receive him better – with him being Welsh."

"Go ahead. But return quickly. Lydia, we have to find shelter.

277

We will all spend the night in whatever room is most easily and quickly heated." Catherine made a move to descend from the coach, and winced as her aching back reminded her that she had not changed position for several hours. Once Lydia had helped her down, she stood, hand pressed against the small of her back, marvelling at the great stone hulk that stood before her.

That, she thought, was what the St Clair earls had left her. That, and the hatred of the local folk.

What on earth could they possibly have done to make themselves so unpopular? She did not really want to find out. But she was here, and she had no choice but to manage. She could die, or she could save her son.

The hall appeared to be clean and in excellent condition. It would be hard to heat, however, and Catherine pressed on into the depths of the castle, trying to block the image of the ruined towers above her from her mind. The other rooms on the ground floor were cold and damp. Were any of the upstairs rooms habitable? She shook herself. Right now, all she needed was a single room, no matter where it was.

A suite of rooms off the kitchen seemed intact. There was firewood aplenty, mattresses with clean ticking, and a neatly folded pile of bedding suggesting the custodians might have lived in them. Lydia sniffed cautiously at the sheets before deeming them acceptable for use.

She made Catherine sit. "You are not going to be of any use if you swoon," she said firmly.

Catherine sat. She looked at the neglected furniture, the feeble beginnings of a smoky fire, and thought about the useless contents of her trunk. She said suddenly, her voice thickening, "Lydia, I am a fool."

There was only the slightest trace of hesitation in Lydia's movements. She continued to bustle about the room.

"I never should have come."

"We do what we must."

"This is all because I am a fool." Catherine's voice rose until it cracked painfully. "Oh, Lydia. I have been so stupid! I have done so many things of which I am ashamed. I need to set my life in order but I hardly know where to begin. And now I have risked myself, my child, any decent future, all because ... because ..."

She could not finish. She buried her head in her hands. For a moment, all was silent but for the crackling of the fire.

"I should have told Jocelyn the truth about LaFrance and the portrait. He might have forgiven me."

"Captain Avebury is bedevilled by his own past, my lady. You were not alone in practising deception."

"You did tell me to be honest," Catherine whispered. "I should have listened. Instead, I was stubborn. I was stupid. That is the real reason I am in this unhappy state. Not my father, not the world. It is I who manage to complicate my own life, every time."

Lydia came and knelt beside her. She took her hand. "My lady. Forgive me. I wish to be honest with you." There was a long hesitation. She squeezed Catherine's hand for a moment, then looked up at her. "I know better than anyone what it is like to be born in disgrace. No, no – do not stop me. Your kind words cannot erase the fact that I was unwanted. My own mother would have nothing to do with me. And having a duke for a father was certainly not an advantage for me." Her voice grew bitter. "I was the consequence of a moment of reckless passion."

Catherine looked at her mutely. "At least you were conceived in passion," she said.

The two women looked at each other for a long moment. Suddenly, they began to laugh. They wept and laughed, holding on to each other, until they were exhausted.

"Only you could turn my bitter past into something worthy of laughter," Lydia gasped, wiping her eyes. "My lady, I do have something to say. You have done what you think best for your child. We all have things in our past we would rather not consider. You faced your past bravely, and you fought that battle well. Now it is time to take up the banner once more and claim this castle for your son."

"I do not know if I want it anymore," Catherine said. She looked at the cold stone floor, the cold stone walls. "They hate us here. I never thought I would say this, but perhaps it is just as well that I am – was – a Claverton. The Clavertons were good to their tenants. My father was an excellent manager and a kind landlord. He may not have been kind to me, but he was fair and generous to his servants and tenants. Perhaps I will find that I would rather my son were not the Earl St Clair at all. Perhaps I should have run away to – to wherever it was Avebury is from. Yorkshire."

Lydia bowed her head. Catherine sighed. "My complaints are of no use; they will merely make us morose. I am glad that Thomas drew some water before he left with the coachman. If you will bring it through, I think I shall wash and have some bread before retiring. Tomorrow we must begin work on this place." She shrugged gloomily. "We will do what we can. We cannot return to Wansdyke now."

THE CUSTODIANS APPEARED THE NEXT MORNING. THEY WERE AN elderly couple, farmers who lived further along the road, beyond the fields and woods of the St Clair estate. They were friendly, but Catherine could see that they were uncomfortable with both the idea of a St Clair heiress and her advanced state of pregnancy. When she tried to persuade them to work for her, they begged forgiveness. They were farmers, they said, fortunate enough to have their own land to till. They did not want to put their land or animals in the care of others. They were extremely sorry, but they could not fill posts in a St Clair establishment.

The old woman left a basket of fresh rolls and butter as a gift. Catherine pulled out a couple of rolls and handed one to Lydia.

"I suspect," she said, "that the only reason they agreed to act as custodians was that they were afraid to refuse the person who asked them. My grandmother, perhaps. Certainly someone they hated and feared."

"Now, now, my lady. You have no reason to think so."

"I have a very good instinct for half-truths," Catherine said dryly. "A consequence of my upbringing, I suspect." She ripped her own roll in half. "Now we are in a bind. We need help. Henry Coachman can manage quite well with the horses, and it seems there are men who are willing to work on repairing the castle – although outdoor work will have to wait until better weather. That Thomas is Welsh – and that we are not concerned about cost – has certainly helped get us those. I will write to Beaseley to arrange the funds. "

She discovered she wasn't hungry and, not eager to waste food, she tucked the remainder of her roll back into the basket. She brushed the crumbs from her hands. The remaining problem, of course, was one she had left unsaid. As Mrs Owen had foretold, there appeared to be no women prepared to work in the castle. And, as Catherine's confinement approached, they would need the help. She would also need a midwife. She had not plucked up the courage to send for the village midwife – yet. She was afraid of being rejected with yet another pleasant excuse and then having to confront the urgent reality that stemmed from her folly.

If no woman in the village would come to help her, what would she do?

Should she return to Wansdyke, and to certain disgrace? Could she even survive another journey?

∼

CATHERINE MASSAGED HER TEMPLES WITH HER FINGERTIPS. SHE had no time to sit and worry: Henry Coachman was on his way back from the village with a cartload of lumber, the blacksmith's son and a journeyman carpenter who was to hang doors and look at the windows. She had never in her life had to carry out menial tasks, but now it was imperative that someone make sure there was water and food, and that the few rooms they occupied were reasonably clean. It was next to impossible for her to sweep or do the washing and, in any case, Lydia would not allow it. Instead, she sent into Abergavenny for cloth and managed to fashion several plain heavy curtains to hang over draughty windows and doors.

They gingerly spread into a few more rooms, giving Henry Coachman and Thomas a private space in which to live and sleep. Snow fell, and January slithered into February. The villagers were undaunted by the weather – they appeared, ready to work, no matter how slippery the road. They were polite, and seemed happy to have the work. Many of them were farmers in the good months of the year with little chance of employment in the winter months, so the opening up of Castle St Clair was good news for them, even if they did not care to be friendly.

And still, no women came. Once in a while, a workman would offer a gift of food that, Catherine suspected, had been sent by his wife. She accepted these with as much dignity as she could muster, but it was not easy. The silence of the women of the village, the lack of talk about the imminent birth of the next Earl St Clair, was deafening.

Catherine wrote a note to Beaseley outlining her financial needs and asking him to ensure all was well at Wansdyke. She wrote a few genteel lies about the state of Castle St Clair, then considered asking about Jocelyn – but decided against it. She believed he was at sea. She was sure he would have gone back the moment the hearings were over. Especially as Sir Lyle had promised to help – and she assumed he could act where Beaseley could not.

She did tell Beaseley she needed servants. Anyone would do.

The villagers were – she hesitated. What to tell him? If he knew her true predicament, he would certainly insist that she return immediately to Wansdyke. And she did not feel capable of admitting that she had no midwife, no doctor to help her child into the world.

In the end, she asked only that he locate a nurse for the child, and that he do so quickly, as she wished to prepare the nursery.

The nursery, she thought grimly as she handed the letter over to Thomas to take into the village. What nursery? None of the upper rooms were usable.

Lying, an activity in which she had never before hesitated to engage, felt more and more dreadful. It seemed that one had no need to lie – unless one was trying to keep loved ones from finding out truths they would rather not know.

Her entire household lived in a few downstairs rooms, and it was stifling. She would take a walk, she thought. She had not tried to walk far outside in the snow. It was time she took a look at the grounds of Castle St Clair.

Lydia was taking delivery of supplies and supervising their storage in the cellar. Catherine pulled on her wrap and limped toward the hall. She could not pull the heavy door open. Disheartened, she made her way clumsily across the stone floor to a side door. It had been left ajar when Lydia had gone out to inspect the delivery. Catherine slipped through and out into the bright February afternoon.

Most of the snow had disappeared. Thomas said it was a mild winter – for Wales – and indeed, it did almost seem warmer outside than in the castle. Catherine lifted her face to the sunlight. There was a very slight breeze, but the air was not too cold.

She pulled her shawl more tightly about her. She had not had a bad spasm for a little while now, she reflected. Her belly seemed to tighten in response. "Thank you very much," she said sarcastically. "I suppose you will remedy that now." She did not feel unwell, precisely, but a bit queasy and nervous. Fresh air, she thought. The fresh air would take care of that.

She followed the stone wall around the castle for a while then headed across what seemed to be a snowy field. It was once a landscaped garden, she realised, but there were patches of snow in the shaded hollows and it had not been maintained for a very long time. Once, designing a garden would have pleased her. Right now, the thought of it exhausted her.

She paused, breathing hard. She really did not feel at all well. Had she forgotten breakfast? She considered for a moment. No, she had eaten lightly, but Lydia had made sure she had taken something. Catherine closed her eyes. She could feel her forehead beading with sweat and growing chill in the breeze.

"I had better go back," she said aloud. But she could not make her feet move in the direction of the castle. She wanted to rinse her mouth, cleanse her palate. She reached out to pick up some snow, and toppled over heavily onto her knees. She grunted in surprise.

"You fool!" she muttered breathlessly. With great difficulty, she pushed herself up again, but her wrap was soaked.

That was it, then. She would have to go back. She could not be outside in February with her clothes soaking wet.

Suddenly, she realised something about the situation was wrong. She paused. The silence hurt her ears.

And she knew with calm dread what was wrong.

Her skirts were wet. And they were warm, not cold.

Her waters had broken.

"Dear Lord," she whispered. She had not prayed or been in a church for a very long time. But she suddenly felt certain that, if there really were a God, He was here in Wales.

The trouble was, He might be laughing at her.

"Please help me," she said, her voice breaking. She began to move slowly toward the castle. Her breath quickened, and she was very tempted to sob, but she knew that if she began to weep she would never stop. She needed to be strong, for the child.

Of all things, she suddenly thought of Jocelyn.

If he were here with her, he would have that calm sea-captain expression on his face. He would not panic. He would probably say something funny and make her giggle. He would pick her up and take her into the castle.

"And then—" she said out loud. She stopped. She looked about her, at the mountainous peaks in the distance, the snow-patched fields in between. "And then what?"

I'll do it alone, she thought. *I'll do it alone if I must, but I will do it.*

Another faint cramping sensation. Ah. So the nausea was not the result of a missed meal after all. It was the child, saying that he was ready.

I am ready, too, thought Catherine.

CHAPTER 40

*T*he silence from the Admiralty was intolerable. What could they possibly be thinking? Had Jocelyn not known that his secret had never been a secret, he might have thought they were preparing to court martial him and sentence him to death.

But he had a new reason to live, and so he was impatient with every day, every hour, every minute of waiting. Beaseley did not come. And neither did any representative of the Admiralty. Nor any letter from Catherine. And there was no word from Sir Lyle.

He was suffocating, choked off from everyone who might tell him whether his love was alive or dead, whether his son lived. And, for the first time, he was aware that his legacy meant something. Living meant something. Having the blessed opportunity to remake oneself – it was like Easter morning: it was no wasted life, no wasted death. He was reborn, and he meant to make it matter.

For the final piece of the puzzle he had only Beaseley to rely on. But this, too, was novel. The very idea of relying on someone to save you! Nor was it in Jocelyn's nature to accept that a person might offer charity not because he wanted anything in return, or because offering assistance would be an advantage to him, but out of respect. Beaseley was devoted to Catherine. And he trusted Jocelyn.

Trust. Ah, fleeting trust! He had not understood its nature. His men had trusted him – he had trusted his men. But that trust was not free: the men on board were not there willingly. And Jocelyn himself felt he had been merely acting a role, reading his lines on a stage. But now he did understand what it was to trust, and he thanked God for it.

The only issue was how to escape these four walls. They were now the only thing between him and Wales.

When, finally, the guard said he had a visitor he was ready. But it was not Beaseley.

It was a gentleman of about twenty-five, with carefully curled hair. Jocelyn stared in amazement at the yellow silk pantaloons and snug coat. The man carried a silver-headed walking stick. He was missing a finger.

"You do not remember me, my friend?" The gentleman simpered and bowed in an exaggerated fashion.

Jocelyn found his voice. "Forgive me … er … Lieutenant – Lord Roland. I did not recognise you. Are you not required to be in uniform?"

"Dreadful things," the viscount said, his mouth forming a moue of distaste. "I loathe uniforms. They do not suit me. You, however, Captain Avebury, are a man with a fine figure. Uniforms look well on you." Lord Roland walked around the room, and poked the pallet in the corner with his cane.

"Good God! Are they making you sleep here, Captain Avebury?" He shook his head, and circled back to where Jocelyn stood. He sat down, then looked annoyed. "How uncomfortable. You don't even have a decent chair. I wonder if Lyle knew what he was getting you into. A gentleman should not have to put up with such conditions."

Jocelyn tensed. "You refer to your brother, of course."

"And who else?" Lord Roland gave a little snort. "He gets his fingers into every pie – and botches everything. He ought to learn to leave well enough alone."

"Perhaps he worries for your welfare, Lord Roland."

"Ha!" Lord Roland wiped his nose elegantly with a lace handkerchief, then returned it to his pocket. He looked up at Jocelyn. His eyes were sharp. "Lyle has a twisted notion of loyalty." He shrugged. "Perhaps I am not enterprising, perhaps I do not own fleets of ships. But neither do I indulge in wild and fruitless chasing after women or respectability. Then again, I do have the title he lacks and that has always been a sore point."

What the hell are you talking about? Jocelyn thought. He felt like grabbing the man and shaking him. Instead, he leant against the wall and dug his fingernails into his palms. He said nothing.

"Well? Are you not curious?" Roland eyed him up and down, clearly disliking what he saw.

Jocelyn hesitated, struggling with himself, not wanting to give the man satisfaction. He gave up. He wanted to know. "Why are you here, Lord Roland?"

Lord Roland smiled. "You are a patient man, Captain Avebury. I have no doubt you will be Admiral Avebury soon enough, you have that certain … smell. I have never been able to figure out what it is. The smell of authority, perhaps. Control. That of the dog the others gather around when looking for direction. Do you hunt?"

"No, I do not."

"Ah, then the example is lost on you. Never mind." Lord Roland examined his nails for a long moment, appearing to contemplate them intently. Eventually, he smiled, then looked slyly up at Jocelyn. "You realise that you are here because of Lyle." He waited for a reaction, but got none. "You are hard to impress," he complained.

"I am merely waiting for you to explain yourself." Jocelyn spoke carefully. His heart was racing.

"Well, then, I shall." Lord Roland rose, paced over to the pallet, grimaced and turned around again. "I would not mind seeing him ruined, to be honest. That is why I am here."

"To see your brother ruined? I do not understand."

"Mind your words," Lord Roland said sharply. "He is only my half-brother! He has always despised me yet he looks after me – in a rather odd way – all the same. I do not need him, but he is always there, hovering."

"He was not there in Bombay." The second the words were out of his mouth, Jocelyn regretted them. He had not meant to bring up the trouble in Bombay.

"Ah, but Captain Avebury, he was! Think!" Lord Roland beamed. "Where do you suppose Lieutenant Bright got his rumours from?"

"What? What rumours?"

"Oh, Captain Avebury," Lord Roland sighed. "You are very frustrating. Try again. The rumours that caused Lieutenant Bright to accuse you, in front of your crew, of smuggling and deliberately missing your rendezvous. The rumours that started the brawl and caused your sailors to kill a man. Did you think, in your innocence, that the rumours of your opium trading had begun for no other reason than envy of your vast personal wealth?"

"I-I-I did not know where Bright had heard such wild tales," Jocelyn stammered. "They were utterly unfounded, and I had no idea why he seemed so sure of them."

"Lyle has men working for him in every major port, my friend. He was loading a very large cargo that day – in the worst possible place. Your aptly named Lieutenant Bright connected a series of observations to reach the conclusion that you were a smuggler when, in fact, the smuggler was Lyle." Lord Roland smiled. "Lieutenant Bright did an excellent job putting together the information he had gathered, but he came to the wrong conclusion. He was very sure of himself, as foolish young lieutenants often are. And he was a fool indeed to fight when his honour was questioned by common sailors."

"Wait," Jocelyn said. "I do not understand. Do you mean to say that Bright had gathered enough information and heard enough rumours to accuse me of smuggling – when actually the real smuggler was Sir Lyle? But where was Sir Lyle?"

"Taking shipment of his goods, of course, but safely out at sea. When he heard about the … er … incident that you so graciously intervened in on my behalf, he was extremely cross. At least, he was cross with me: I had been a very naughty boy. But he was grateful to you, not only for saving my life but also for taking the blame for his activities."

"I see," Jocelyn said slowly. "That is why he sought me out on my return."

"Lyle is very strange, Captain Avebury. To make sense of what I am telling you, you need to understand how his mind works. He is very conscious of his lack of status, yet, I will concede, his morals are unimpeachable. The ethics of his code of conduct are difficult for gentlemen like us to understand. But it has its own logic. So, when we were sent back to England, he felt compelled to rescue you from a situation where you were being wronged."

"But-but how? How could he rescue me?"

"He arranged to have Stephen Bright murdered."

"Lord Roland, that is an outrageous suggestion!"

"It is true." Lord Roland shrugged his slim shoulders and turned away. He looked up at the windows above, then slanted a glance toward Jocelyn. "I have no proof, and I am sure no one does. But it has all the hallmarks of Lyle's handiwork. An invisible poison, deftly administered. Probably in food. Fast-acting, tasteless, invisible. I expect he believed there could be no hearing without the accuser. He was wrong, of course, and that must have frustrated him terribly."

Jocelyn's mind was reeling. Sir Lyle, a murderer! It was impossible.

But then, he was beginning to understand Sir Lyle's twisted morality. The man had a fixation with honour. Gentlemanly behaviour. Codes of conduct. His notion of honour was warped – very different from Jocelyn's understanding of the word. But it was honour nonetheless.

And what about Catherine?

He opened his mouth, then checked himself. He was not sure he wanted to ask. But Lord Roland read his mind.

"He loved her, you know."

Jocelyn did know. He nodded.

"He has loved her for a very long time, but said nothing. He imagined he was not gentleman enough to interest her and that her father would never permit such a mésalliance. And so he waited until her father was on his deathbed to declare his interest. When word of her title became public, it gave him another reason to woo her." Lord Roland again twisted his mouth into a grimace. "I am sure I do not know why he was so intent on marriage. It is more trouble than it is worth. But he loved her."

"Then why did he not say so?" Jocelyn asked. He flushed at Lord Roland's inquiring look. "I am sure she thought he wanted to marry her for the title, not for love."

Lord Roland lifted his hands in a gesture of helplessness. "Why indeed? And yet, I know he loved her. He loved her through all the years he spent sailing the seas waiting for her father to die. He must have thought she would not consider him for a moment. And it seems he was right." He eyed Jocelyn shrewdly. "She married you, after all."

He moved toward the door. "Now you have the whole truth. I have wanted to see you – to thank you for sacrificing yourself in Bombay. It was the act of a true gentleman. And now that you have the whole truth, you can discredit Lyle openly and be out of this place. I am sure the admirals will believe you. They know about Lyle's dealings, but have not been able to catch him in any criminal act or to find anyone who will speak against him. If you

do so, they will make it impossible for him to return to England."
He rolled his eyes distastefully. Then he paused, and turned.
"Don't bother thinking that you can somehow implicate me in
this whole mess. I admit to being rather stupid in that Bombay
hellhole, but the opium smuggling – those are not my crimes.
And certainly not the murder."

"I did not think it for a minute, Lord Roland. But wait – you
have not answered the main question." Jocelyn took an anxious
step in his direction.

Lord Roland raised his eyebrows dramatically.

"Why am I here? Why would Sir Lyle attempt to pin the blame
for his crimes on me, if he is such a man of honour?"

At this, Lord Roland burst into laughter. "My dear Captain! If
you need to ask me such a question, then you are worn out
indeed! You need to leave this place, have a bath and a meal, sleep
a while in a proper bed – the answer is obvious, is it not? No?
You poor man. Then I will spell it out for you. Lyle and the
Admiralty … there is an uneasy understanding. Do you take my
meaning? He has friends, highly placed friends. They do not
particularly enjoy the friendship, but there it is. He has asked
them to make sure that you do not leave England. And so, here
you are, on the verge of expulsion from the navy."

"To make sure that I do not leave England," Jocelyn said
blankly. He looked at Lord Roland.

Then the impact of the words struck him.

To make sure that he did not leave England.

To make sure that he did not leave Catherine.

Sir Lyle had made sure that he would not leave Catherine.

A final gift, the ultimate gift, to the woman he loved.

CHAPTER 41

The pain was mild. Uncomfortable, annoying, but mild. Catherine could well tolerate it. After a lifetime of hobbling about, it seemed ridiculous to her that women whispered about it and men panicked.

"The child is coming, Lydia." She made the announcement simply as she limped into their shared room. For a split second, she saw an expression of panic cross Lydia's face. "I will be fine," she continued reassuringly. "I am not in pain."

A wave of discomfort made her stop and press her hands against her belly. Lydia started toward her, but Catherine stretched out her arms, warding her off. "No," she said quietly. "I have told you, I will be fine. There is bound to be some pain, but right now I can manage. I need you to prepare some linen. And I would like privacy. Henry and Thomas will have to sleep elsewhere tonight."

"I will send them to the village," Lydia exclaimed. "They can seek help, too. Surely someone will come."

"No," Catherine said with force. "Absolutely not. I cannot afford to lie here and wait for assistance. No one will come, I am certain. We will have to do this alone." She put a hand on Lydia's

293

arm. "You are the only friend I have," she said quietly. "I know what this will cost you and I promise I do not ask it lightly." She turned away and limped slowly to the far wall and pushed her hands briefly against the cold stone before turning again.

"Go," she said, her voice calm. "I will cope."

Lydia left.

It was slow. For hours – through the dusky light of the February afternoon and on into the inky black night – nothing seemed to happen. Catherine paced and sat, paced and sat. She had absolutely no appetite, though Lydia tried to feed her. Henry and Thomas had gone, she did not know where. She felt tremendously unwell. Occasionally, the vice-like grip of a spasm consumed her, but it was still more annoying than painful.

At about midnight, she gave up waiting and went to bed. She could not sleep well, though she was exhausted. She slipped easily from wakefulness into fitful slumber and back into wakefulness. Her dreams were odd: vivid and colourful and disturbing. She and Sir Lyle ran easily across the fields at Wansdyke, hand-in-hand. They collapsed into the grass, laughing, and began to make passionate love. Catherine then found herself staring into the dark, her hands gripping the edge of the straw mattress. Pain had awoken her, but she was disoriented, half her spirit still at Wansdyke.

She awaited the next spasm with trepidation, but it did not come. She wondered if Sir Lyle had managed to help Jocelyn. Dreaming of him was bizarre – she had never loved him. She should never have let their affair go as far as it had. It was cruel. She had thought their liaison almost a game, but it had not been a game to him.

She closed her eyes. Her mind wandered. She thought of the night she had searched Bath for Sir Lyle. And of how he had come to see her at Wansdyke in response to her letter. He must have held her in some affection, she thought hazily. He had always been there to help her – even though she would not marry him. She wished him well, wherever he was, as a knot of pain started in her belly and spread tense fingers across her back.

This time, it hurt. She woke out of her half-sleep with a gasp.

Lydia was beside her, trying to bathe her face, but Catherine pushed her away fretfully.

"I don't want to be touched," she complained. The pain subsided.

"Would you like to walk, my lady?"

"No," Catherine said peevishly. "I want this to end."

"It will end," Lydia said soothingly.

Neither of them spoke for a moment. The darkness somehow finished the thought for them. It certainly would end – the question was how.

Early morning arrived. Dark and damp. Lydia kept the fire burning well, but the edges of the room were not warm: the stone wall could not absorb enough heat from the fireplace.

The contractions were beginning to hurt. They were also lasting longer. Catherine tried not to weep, but she whimpered as the pain became urgent and forceful. At least there were blissful dark periods of rest between them.

Catherine discovered something about herself. It was the anticipation of pain which could nearly undo her. Actual pain, when it arrived, was almost welcome. She could handle it. It was unpleasant but, although she was tired, it was something she could get her thoughts around. However, she could not enjoy the pain-free minutes in between contractions. She hated that she had to sit and wait for pain, pain she continued to fear even though it was never as bad in reality as in her expectations.

Each time a contraction came, she vowed to remember what it felt like so that she could control her panic. And every time, she failed. When the pain died, her body reacted with pleasure and she could not bear the thought it would return.

The dawn came. And, with it, the first truly blue sky Catherine had seen in Wales. It was a brilliant blue that reminded

her of autumn days and riding through the fields at Wansdyke –
not the hazy blue of spring, the rolling mists of Jocelyn's eyes, but
a hard clear blue that she was surprised to find made her yearn to
see the mountains surrounding the castle.

She could not, of course. She was fatigued beyond imagining.
The pains had become erratic. Some were the manageable sort
she had felt for much of the night. Some were vicious, with two –
even three – excruciating peaks. She was beyond tears, beyond
reason. She asked Lydia to fetch Jocelyn, and did not understand
when Lydia blinked and turned away.

"Please tell him to come," she said humbly. "He will come.
This is his son."

Dawn also brought Jen Owen, and another woman with her.
Mrs Owen strode briskly to Catherine's bedside, her strong
Welsh features stern and harsh. But her face softened as soon as
she saw her. "*Cariad,*" she said. She put down her large basket and
took Catherine's hand.

"*Croeso,*" Catherine said, smiling. "You see, I am not such a
barbarian after all. I can greet you in your own language." She
winced a little as she drew herself up on her elbows.

"You should not be lying down. Here, let me." Mrs Owen put
an arm under her to help her up. "A labouring woman should not
be on her back. It will hurt more. How long has it been, *cariad?*"

Catherine shook her head. She bit her lip and tried not to cry
out as pain swelled over her and tightened her body.

Mrs Owen held her hand. "Squeeze my hand," she said quietly.
"It is bad, isn't it? Yes, I know. But I'm here now." She said something in Welsh over her shoulder, and her companion nodded
and vanished. Mrs Owen turned back to Catherine. "Alice is my
cousin. She lives in Abergavenny and sent me a message. It was
wise of your friend Lydia to send Thomas there."

Catherine turned her head to look for Lydia, but was overcome by another pain.

"Sit on the edge, my lady. My cousin has gone to make a tea

that will help you." Mrs Owen stopped speaking for a moment as Catherine gripped her hand. At the spasm's peak, Catherine moaned loudly. Tears seeped from under her closed eyelids.

"I meant to do it myself," she panted. "I meant to have enough strength to bear this child alone. I fear I will fail."

"You will not do it alone," Mrs Owen said firmly. "We will help you. Who would want to be alone to meet such joy?" She stopped. Catherine was weeping openly now.

"I am being punished," she wept. "I was such a thoughtless and selfish daughter. I did not even grieve when my father died. God has made me see what I am."

"God takes care of everything," Mrs Owen said, a note of finality in her voice. She patted Catherine's hand. "There is no use discussing God right now. We will talk of Him later. Now, see, I need to see where the babe is. Forgive me, but ..."

When she rose again her face was grim. "For someone who has laboured all night, you have a long way to go."

"No!" Catherine implored.

"I have seen many long labours. We will get through this one together. Alice and I have brought our herbs and Lydia has gone to the village to procure some other things for me."

"The village," Catherine said faintly. "They despise me there. I do not even know what my St Clair ancestors did to make them loathe me so."

"I'm sure I could find out and tell you." Mrs Owen paused. "But why? Why would you want to know, and why should you care? This is a new life, Lady Catherine."

A new life, Catherine thought. A new life. She wanted a new life so badly. As another contraction began, she thought of Jocelyn and how he was returning to an old life. Would he consider a new one, one that could include her?'

But first – Catherine gasped in pain – the portrait. Could she tell him about the portrait? Would he love her if he knew of her shame?

"I want to see him," she groaned.

"Him? Your husband?"

"His name – Jocelyn – Avebury – Royal – Navy—"

"Does he know about the child?"

"He knows," Catherine whispered. "He is at sea."

"Do you know which ship he is on? I can send a message."

Catherine shook her head. She did not know where Jocelyn was. Beaseley did not know. Everything, she thought as the pain engulfed her once more, was indeed in the hands of God.

CHAPTER 42

*J*en Owen was worried. She consulted her cousin, looked through her basket, held Catherine's hand and worried. The day stretched into afternoon and, still, the contractions that exhausted the countess failed to bring a child. They were too erratic, too weak. She feared the child would die, or that Catherine would take ill with fever. Mrs Owen dosed her as best as she could, but Catherine was weakening and began to drift into unconsciousness.

"Get up, my lady!"

Catherine's eyes fluttered open. She looked tiredly about the room. "I was at Wansdyke," she whispered. "Do not wake me." She closed her eyes once more.

Mrs Owen nodded at Lydia. Together, they lifted Catherine to a semi-stand. Catherine opened her eyes again.

"What are you doing?" she said, her voice edged with irritation.

"We are going to take a walk," Mrs Owen said firmly.

"A walk?" Catherine looked at her incredulously. "Do you normally ask ladies in this situation to walk?"

"If necessary, I do," Mrs Owen replied. She prodded Catherine, who took a step. Her knees buckled, and the ladies caught her between them.

"You know that I am lame," she said. "I cannot walk, even when I am not giving birth!" She began to laugh, but a spasm caught it short. She gasped and grunted, then began to laugh again.

"What an odd sound I am making," she said. She took another step. "It is not very appealing. I suppose it is fortunate that Jocelyn is not here to see me."

"I am glad you are in good humour, my lady. We are heading for that door."

"Are you kicking me out of my own castle?"

The two women helped Catherine to slowly hobble along. When they reached the door, Lydia threw it open.

"Look at that, my lady."

Catherine tried to look but the sky was so bright, it hurt her to open her eyes. She rolled her head back, trying to avoid the light.

"What is it?" she mumbled.

"It is Wales."

Catherine tried again to open her eyes. It was still too bright. She struggled. The fresh air was warmer than she had expected, far warmer than the cold wall next to her bed. She made herself squint into the light.

The snowy mountains reared up before her. Afternoon light slanted through the clear air, golden and mysterious, carrying that certain melancholy which tells of approaching dusk. The stone path sloped down before her to a drive that ended where tufts of green poked up from the white ground.

"The snow is leaving us, my lady," Lydia said. "Spring is early."

"A good sign," Catherine whispered. Her chin dropped down to her chest; she gave a tremendous shudder and collapsed into Mrs Owen's arms.

Together, the two women dragged her to the closest chair.

Lydia chafed her wrists. Mrs Owen bathed her face and called to her cousin to bring smelling salts, but Catherine revived with a start before they arrived.

"What happened?" she asked. The fog seemed to have lifted from her mind.

"You are having a baby, my lady," Mrs Owen said. "You must help now – you are almost done."

"Almost" turned out to be three hours and, it was nearly seven o'clock that evening when Mrs Owen delivered Catherine of her first child. It was weak, and cried for only a brief moment. Mrs Owen worried over the child while Lydia held Catherine's hand.

"You have a lovely daughter," she said gently.

"I know," Catherine said in a hoarse whisper. Her voice was nearly gone. "It is a girl."

"She looks like the captain." Lydia smiled. Her voice caught. "Very dark curly hair and grey eyes. Perhaps her eyes will change, but she will never have your golden hair and fair complexion."

Catherine turned her head. Her voice was muffled. "God punishes me, and now he punishes my child."

"Whatever are you talking about?" Mrs Owen's voice rose from the foot of the bed, where she was examining the child. "Hold your tongue, Lady Catherine. You are lucky to be alive, and to have a living child. Others are not so fortunate."

Catherine smiled slightly at the wall. "After all that I have sacrificed to get here, to be here, it is a bitter irony that she cannot be an earl who will carry the St Clair name."

"But you have a daughter!" Lydia exclaimed. "Your title can pass through the female line – she may become the next countess."

"Yes," Catherine whispered. She nodded. "Yes. And all I have done is pass my own curse to her. She is fatherless, just as I was, and her heritage is questionable. She will be alone with her title. Were she a boy, she could create a new dynasty. But, because she is a girl, she is alone."

"I do not understand what you mean and I must admit that I do not care." Mrs Owen approached the bed. She held out the bundle in her arms. Catherine shrank and shook her head.

"Your child needs you, Lady St Clair. You will have to nurse her – there is no wet nurse. She is weak after the long labour and may yet fail."

Lydia sat Catherine up. With great reluctance, Catherine held out her arms. Mrs Owen placed the child in them.

Catherine looked down at her daughter. She was so small, so very light. She seemed to be asleep. Lydia was right. She was the image of Jocelyn – she had his strong cheekbones and stone-carven lips, his dark curly hair.

Then her tears came. This was a helpless child, doomed to a fatherless existence. How unfair it all was.

"I promised I would not fail you," Catherine said, choking back her sobs. "I promised. It is not your fault you are a girl, any more than it was mine."

Jocelyn would have loved his child. She was sure of it. Memories flooded back so strongly that, as she closed her eyes, she felt she was breathing in the scent of grassy fields and sheep at Wansdyke. Jocelyn would have taken his little girl riding, even though he had such a lamentable seat himself.

Catherine giggled weakly in spite of her tears. This was Fate's revenge on all of them. It made no sense to protest or to fight.

She looked up at Mrs Owen. "Will you show me how to nurse her?"

CHAPTER 43

The Lords of the Admiralty at least had the courtesy to give him fresh clothes, the opportunity to bathe and the services of a barber before requiring his presence. Jocelyn went calmly. He had had many weeks to consider his testimony. He knew that Lord Roland would, by now, be on yet another ship, this one sailing toward the East Indies. Trying to explain Lord Roland's involvement would be a gamble – and not a wise one.

Jocelyn knew Lord Roland's counsel was sound: Beaseley was of the same opinion. The Admiralty would love to rid themselves of Sir Lyle. Those who felt themselves under an obligation would be happy to see him brought low. And those who disapproved of his dubious activities would be equally happy to see him taken to task for his attempt to influence justice.

"Go ahead, Avebury," Lord Roland had hissed. "Do it. The man who did this to you deserves to be locked up."

Destroying Sir Lyle would call for precision gunnery. But the reward would be great. Catherine. The child. A new command.

"Captain Avebury. We are quite displeased. What are we to do with you? And what are we to call you?"

"My name is Avebury, sir."

Rustle of papers. "It seems that is uncertain."

"Yes, sir. I entered the navy under an adopted name."

There was a pause. A brief, but surprised, pause.

"I was not proud of my father, sir. He was executed for treason when I was seven. My new family gave me a name that they felt would not hinder me in my desire to serve His Majesty."

"You disguised your connection to your father?"

"I did, sir."

"This is a serious matter, Captain Avebury. You still wish to be called Avebury?"

"I do, sir. It is the name under which I served His Majesty. I received my wounds under that name. I am proud to serve as an officer, no matter what name I use, but I would beg to be allowed to keep that which I have, I hope, distinguished, sir."

"I see." There was a whispered conference. "Normally, this sort of misrepresentation would demand a severe punishment, Captain Avebury."

"Yes, sir. I am prepared to take my punishment, sir. I only request, humbly, that I be allowed to remain in His Majesty's Navy using the name under which I have distinguished myself. I have a son, and would like to give him this name, a name of which he can be proud. I did not intend to deceive so much as to … remake myself, sir."

"You have a son, Captain Avebury?"

"Yes, sir. I believe so. Born this month. But I have not seen him. My wife is the Countess St Clair; her father was the Earl Delamare."

"Ah, yes."

More uncomfortable muttering. Then a delicate question.

"The matter in Bombay – there is a suggestion that Sir Lyle Barrington was involved. He is the half-brother of Lord Roland, Viscount Roland, whom you rescued."

Jocelyn did not blink. He had made his decision. It would be the honourable one. He was nothing if not a man of honour. He had that, no matter what his name, no matter what his crime.

"I would have known of any smuggling in our squadron, sir. I am confident that neither my ship nor Lord Roland's had anything to do with any smugglers."

"Then you do not suspect that Lord Roland held up your departure on purpose?"

"Absolutely not."

"And Sir Lyle? His involvement?"

"I only know the man very slightly, sir. And the only reason for my lateness to the rendezvous was my own inexcusable lack of judgement. I accept all responsibility."

"Your words are very touching, Captain Avebury. We heard them during the hearings on the Bombay incident, before Christmas. But you are here now on charges of gross misrepresentation and lying under oath. What say you to those charges?"

This was it. Jocelyn knew that he could offer Sir Lyle to them on a platter. They had brought his name up first. They were clearly waiting for him to speak against him. If he told them what he knew to be the truth about Sir Lyle, they would let him go. They would put out the call and Sir Lyle would be unable to return to England. His properties seized, his lines of credit frozen, perhaps. His affairs in disarray. But he, Jocelyn Avebury, would be free. All he had to do was to defend himself against Sir Lyle's accusations.

"I accept all responsibility for any ... er ... perceived misrepresentation. I await your decision, but humbly request permission to use the name Avebury and to remain an officer in His Majesty's service."

There was an annoyed shuffling of feet. "Listen, Captain Avebury," the impatient voice went on. "It is clear you have high standards when considering loyalty and ethics. But we are giving you the opportunity to do exactly what you have asked of us. To clear your name."

"I care a great deal about my name, sir." Jocelyn hesitated, choosing his words carefully. "Because it is a name that I have made myself, I perhaps take better care of it than others do of theirs. And I feel that I must maintain the highest standards to protect it. I do not think my actions or behaviour have shamed His Majesty or my country, and I would be pleased to indicate my absolute obedience in any fashion that you may require. Sir."

No one spoke. Jocelyn kept his eyes on the table in front of the admirals. He did not want to look them in the eye and seem impudent, but he did not want to seem weak or ashamed. *Strength*, he thought. *Strength will see me through.*

The wait was interminable. In the distance he could hear the sounds of city life. He wondered if he would be stuck ashore much longer. If he were, he would definitely go to Wales. He would find Kate and their son, and bring them to Wansdyke. They could have a beautiful spring. If the Admiralty saw fit to throw him out, he would become a farmer. He had always wondered what it would be like to till the land. He discovered, much to his surprise, that he could probably live with whatever decision the Admiralty saw fit to make.

"You have never given us cause to discipline you before, Captain Avebury." The words that finally came were spoken by the elderly admiral who sat at the end of the table and had remained silent throughout the proceedings. "I would recommend that your punishment involve another command."

"Sir?"

"Your record is exemplary. I cannot see that it would be in His Majesty's interests to let you go over a ... what? A tempest in a teacup?" Jocelyn looked at him sharply. The admiral gave him a shrewd look in return. Ah, so he was Beaseley's contact.

"Take yourself off to your ship. Gentlemen, are we agreed?" There was a general muttering. None of the others seemed inclined to object. The admiral in charge held up his hand.

"Are we unanimous, then? Captain Avebury has accepted

responsibility for the … er … misunderstanding over his name. You are dismissed, Captain. Oh, yes. The command." More paper-shuffling. "These are for you. You will find it an easy assignment." He smiled. "A task that will allow for the transport of a lady and a child to Gibraltar. Congratulations, sir."

Jocelyn stood up automatically as the lords began to file past. The elderly admiral was at the rear of the line. He nodded curtly at Jocelyn and, as he brushed past, muttered quietly "We'll get Barrington some other time."

CHAPTER 44

*H*e attempted to contact Beaseley but, with his mission accomplished, he seemed to have left London. Had he left news of Catherine? Jocelyn's heart turned over. There was no news –surely that was good news?

He went to Wansdyke and found it shut up. The few servants who remained told him that Catherine had travelled by coach to Bristol. He had no idea where Castle St Clair was. Catherine had said only it was near the border so she must have found a ferry.

He could not bring himself to search Wansdyke for the portrait, to turn it upside down, to raid the galleries and tear the holland covers from undisplayed paintings that slept gently in the dark. He wondered if Sir Lyle had carried it with him to the Americas, or whether LaFrance still had it, perhaps safely hidden somewhere. He wondered if Sir Lyle had delivered it to Wansdyke. That would have been generous – but no more than a fair exchange for what he, Jocelyn, had done for him.

Sir Lyle could not have known that the Admiralty would be willing to let him go. He would have assumed Jocelyn would spend some time in prison, or perhaps be given some low-level tasks to do in port, or be punished by being forced in some other way to stay in England. He would have thought himself clever: that his actions had forced Jocelyn to think of Catherine and that he, in turn, would force her to come to her senses by telling her the portrait was gone and that their son was safe from shame and humiliation. In fact, there was no way Sir Lyle could have guessed that the Admiralty would instead give him a ship and reward him handsomely for being who he was: a decent human being with friends in high places. "Laughable," he could imagine Sir Lyle chortling. "Ridiculous!"

Jocelyn made for Bristol. It was not hard to find a ferryman who remembered the St Clair carriage and its extremely pregnant owner. How many English countesses could there have been, driving through the January snow? The man told Jocelyn he had spoken briefly to the coachman and the Welsh boy and thought they had been going to head north through Abergavenny – but he was not sure. It was a good enough guess, at any rate.

The crossing was turbulent. Melting spring snows somewhere, he reckoned. The air was damp but warm, filled with the scent of budding trees. It reminded him of the warm spring night in Bath when he had first seen Catherine, and of the damp walks in the meadows at Wansdyke. Water, he thought, was part of his life. It seemed it was part of Catherine's, too.

He had to still his heart, calm his mind. She might not come with him. She was the Countess St Clair, and she was now installed at Castle St Clair with the future earl. What was the child for now? A viscount? Jocelyn almost laughed. It was ridiculous. No, it was appalling. How cruel to burden a child with the weight of ancestors long before he was aware of his own existence. But Catherine saw it differently. Nothing meant more to her, nothing in the world, than this earldom. She would do anything to protect it. He would have to be prepared, accept the possibility that she might send him away.

Jocelyn disembarked on the other side of the channel. A

group of farmers loaded crates for the return trip and chatted loudly in Welsh. They fell silent as he approached.

"I beg your pardon," he began. "I need to get to Abergavenny."

"Are you looking for a ride, sir?" One of the farmers, a young blond man, rose from a crouch. He wiped his sweaty brow with a brightly coloured handkerchief.

"I would rather not," Jocelyn admitted. "But I will if I must."

"The road is good. But it may be muddy and a bit difficult for a cart. You can get a mount in town. And you will reach Abergavenny quickly that way."

"That is excellent news. I thank you."

"May I suggest you take a bite at The Red Hen?" the man said. "It's very clean, sir. My sister runs it and the food is excellent."

"Thank you very much," Jocelyn replied. "But I need to get to Abergavenny as quickly as possible." He was about to turn away, but a thought occurred to him. He paused, then spoke. "In January, a lady and her carriage came this way. The lady was expecting a child. She had her maid and her coachman with her. Do you know anything about where they might have gone?"

"Yes, I remember her," the blond man said.

"She was ill," one of the farmers added.

Jocelyn felt his stomach lurch. He looked from one man to the other. "You mean she was lame?"

"No, sir. She was lame, but she was also ill. She collapsed, by here." The man pointed. The others nodded.

Jocelyn blanched. He knew it was possible he would not find Catherine at Castle St Clair – indeed, he knew it was possible he would not find her anywhere. But he had not thought it possible she might be dead. And what of the child?

The blond man added soothingly, "Mrs Owen, the apothecary's widow, took her into town. I expect she took good care of her. And she has not come back this way."

"Mrs Owen is a friend of my mam," said a third man. "The

lady can't have lingered long with her, or I would have heard. So she can't have been very ill and must have gone on her way."

"Right," Jocelyn said, breathing a little more easily. If something dreadful had happened, surely the news would have travelled back here. And now he had the name of someone who had actually spoken to Catherine, and possibly cared for her. Someone who lived nearby.

"I thank you all very much," he said, and turned in the direction of the town.

He found Mrs Owen's home fairly easily. The young maid who answered the door said that her lady was visiting relatives. Jocelyn was disappointed but persisted. Had there been any English visitors in January? A young woman who was expecting a child?

"You would be referring to the Countess St Clair," the maid said stiffly. "She was here briefly."

"Was she ill? Did she go to Abergavenny?"

The maid gave him a strange look. "Abergavenny? No, no. Castle St Clair is not in Abergavenny. It's past there."

"You know Castle St Clair, then?" Jocelyn pressed.

"Yes," the maid said. She hesitated. Jocelyn noticed that she was wringing her hands nervously in her apron.

"Is there something about Castle St Clair that I should know?"

"Are you intending to go there, sir?"

"I am."

The maid glanced up at Jocelyn hesitantly. She seemed to conclude that he was all right, even if he was English. She leant in a little closer and confided, "It's a ruin."

"Ruined? Ruined – how?"

"The St Clairs were chased away. And then the people of the village destroyed what they could. I have never been there. But the St Clairs were dreadful people, sir. Everyone in this part of Wales knows. They took high rents and used people badly."

"I see."

The maid added, "The countess insisted on going there, even though the mistress told her not to. I don't know what happened to her, but I don't expect she'd have had much help from the village."

Kate, with no one to help her! Kate, living in a ruin! It was unthinkable. "Can you direct me?"

"I can, sir. I beg your pardon, sir, are you … is the countess … your—?"

Jocelyn interrupted her. "You did right to tell me about the St Clairs. Now, can you direct me to the castle?"

By the time Jocelyn arrived in Abergavenny, he was a much better horseman. But time was pressing. How long could Kate possibly last alone in a ruin? And what of the child? And, if she had fled Castle St Clair, where would she have gone? Who would be with her? She was not at Wansdyke and no one there had heard from her. How would she care for an infant, alone?

He got his first glimpse of Castle St Clair at midday. The snowdrops were out, although the peaks of the mountains beyond were still snowy. The castle perched dramatically amidst breathtaking scenery, leaving no doubt that the St Clair family had chosen to command not just the best views but also the entrance to the valley. But it was indeed a ruin. All the upper floors had been destroyed.

As Jocelyn rode up the drive, he realised there was absolutely no way anyone could be using the hall and the great hall – both appeared to be completely blocked. He dismounted and rubbed his aching back, then secured his mount to a post. He began to walk awkwardly around the stone walls. It was slow – the castle was large, and his back hurt incredibly.

He struggled along the side, searching for an alternative entrance, but the only one he found was locked. Annoyed, he limped on round to the back of the castle whence a wet green field extended into the distance.

He could hear snatches of something on the warm spring

breeze – a human voice. He saw a wavering white smudge under a tree. And he was caught in a rush of memory – of the day he had walked from Bath to Wansdyke and had found Catherine struggling up the muddy hillside, singing a tune.

He knew, was convinced, that the smudge was Catherine. But what of her song? Was it a happy tune, or a sad tune?

CHAPTER 45

*H*e limped painfully toward the white smudge. As he came closer, he could make out long blonde hair flying free in the wind. She sat on a blanket, staring vacantly at the snow-capped mountains. She was singing something that sounded Welsh. A nursery song.

"Kate," he said. His voice choked, and he felt his chest tighten.

He saw her shoulders stiffen. She turned her head carefully. She seemed fragile, wrapped in a white garment that was far too large for her. Her blue eyes were wide, frightened. She did not look like herself. He suddenly realised that perhaps she no longer was herself. Perhaps she had gone mad. Perhaps she had lost the child. Perhaps she would never be the Kate that he had known.

"Jocelyn," she said. Her lips trembled. Then she smiled a little. "You have found me."

"Were you trying not to be found?"

"Not exactly. Although … although Castle St Clair is not what I had imagined." She gave a rueful little laugh. It sounded forced to Jocelyn's ear.

Again, he felt panic, almost from a distance – as if he were feeling the panic described in someone else's story.

"Kate, I must ask. The child—"

"'The child,' he asks." Catherine's voice was carefully neutral. "Are you here to see your son?"

"I am here to see you, Kate. And I am also here to see my son."

"Well." She turned away again. Her voice was careful again, studied. "So much has happened. I was foolish. Very foolish. I should never have come. I risked everything, and I have paid dearly."

Jocelyn had thought that this moment would be like the state of readiness before battle – adrenalin clarifying his mind, focusing his intent, an alert, steady hum in his chest. He would be wide awake, his hearing sharper than usual. But no.

Panic has its own set of sensations; it is a jealous master intent on domination.

He was once again a small child. The strong hands of a strange woman were forcing his head into her skirts so that he could not see the executioner's actions. He screamed into those skirts, feeling damp spread over the salty dirty cotton in his mouth as his spittle and tears soaked through. The hands swept him up, cramming his head into the crook of an arm, and he kicked his legs and screamed as the arms hauled him away from a sight that he would imagine for the rest of his life.

This was not readiness. It was fear.

He had never feared the loss of his own life, but faced with the loss of a child, a child who had no father but himself to mourn him, he was afraid.

For a long moment, he had no voice. Only his breath, harsh and hot, rasping in his throat.

Then she sighed, and her sigh seemed to release the pressure in his own chest. She bowed her head. He could barely hear her.

"It was … dangerous … for a little while. But it seems that we will be all right. I had a fever, along with everything else. And exhaustion." She laughed a little. "Exhaustion is my constant companion. But I am a servant here. It is a life I never imagined, that of a servant."

"Kate, look at me," Jocelyn said urgently. His voice sounded thin and high to his ears. He was light-headed, dizzy. Did this mean the child was not dead? Dared he feel relief? "Do not turn away."

There was a pause. Catherine did not look round. "Forgive me," she whispered. "It is very hard. To know one's folly. To admit it openly."

"None of us have anything but ourselves to offer. Your folly is no more, no less, than anyone else's."

He saw her shrug slightly.

"There is no need for you to be strong, Kate. Will you not let me take care of you?"

"And then?" Catherine shook her head. "You will leave. I can rely only on myself." Jocelyn could see the tension in her slim neck. "And I have made a desperate mess of everything."

"We will fix the mess. I will help you."

"It cannot be fixed, Jocelyn!" Catherine looked at him now. "Castle St Clair is in ruins. It cannot be fixed."

"Surely it can be fixed."

"No. Not with all the gold in the world. The people here – my family has done terrible things to them. They do not want the castle fixed. They refuse to help. And they do not want me here. But I have no other home."

Jocelyn took a step toward Catherine, but the stiff pose had upset his balance, and he staggered.

"Good God!" Catherine cried, reaching out to him with her hands. Jocelyn managed to catch himself on a low-hanging tree branch.

"It was the ... the journey," he panted. "I am still not used to riding."

Catherine looked at him, wide-eyed. Then she began to laugh. "No wonder, then!" she gasped. "You are a dreadful horseman – no one with any intelligence ought to let you near a horse—"

"Of all the insults," Jocelyn protested hotly. "I was quite good by the time I reached Abergavenny – although I admit I did receive quite a few offers of assistance."

"I am sure they were from people who could not stand the sight of you on a horse," Catherine laughed. "You need to stick to ships, Jocelyn."

"Yes! I am quite good at handling ships," Jocelyn retorted. "Unlike them, horses are stupid animals who won't do as they are told."

"Oh you ridiculous man! I already have a limp and I suggest you avoid anything that causes you to do the same. Stay where you belong!"

They laughed until they were spent. Jocelyn creakily lowered himself onto the damp grass and, for a moment, they sat silently. Then he reached out for her hand.

"Kate," he said. "Let me speak without interruption – for once!" he added, as he saw her opening her mouth. She shut it again. "Thank you. My love, Castle St Clair was never your home. It never was, despite your desire to make it so. It will do you and the child no harm to walk away from it. You can walk away from it today – tomorrow. I will take you both away, and we will start over."

Catherine was silent. She nodded once, then twice. "I was very foolish," she said in a small voice. "But you do not know everything. And, when you hear everything, you may not wish to take me away with you."

"Your name is Avebury, Kate. Catherine Avebury. You have my name now. There is no need for you to create another Catherine, to go anywhere else. I do not need anything from you but your love. I did not when your name was Claverton, and I do not want this castle or the St Clair name."

"I cannot return to Wansdyke, Jocelyn," Catherine burst out.

She pulled her hand away and covered her eyes. "I cannot return to London or Bath ever again."

"My love," Jocelyn said gently, "If you are speaking of the portrait – it is safe. It is wrapped in holland covers, hidden away amongst the worst of your Elizabethan ancestors, somewhere in the dark recesses of the attic, most likely. I know that no one enters the attic and returns alive, not even the servants." He smiled, then reached out to touch her cheek.

She flinched and dropped her hand, then looked at him, appalled. Her face had gone nearly as white as her dress. "How-how can that be?" she stammered.

"Sir Lyle extricated LaFrance from his predicament by taking him away to the Americas. And he made sure that no one else would see that portrait. I saw it at his home, quite by accident, the night I was arrested. He had me arrested, you know."

"Arrested!"

"So I could not leave England without taking you – and the child – with me. Do not look at me that way, Kate – all is well! I was due to sail for Gibraltar. I was offered a ship – a ship with quarters eminently suitable for travel with a lady – and a child." He paused, then finished. "But I declined."

"You *declined*?"

"I very respectfully declined." Jocelyn reached out again, locked his fingers with hers and firmly drew her hand into his lap. He hesitated. He had practised the words in his mind but, now that he was saying them, they felt strange. "Sir Lyle designed what he thought was the perfect life, for you and for me. I was to take you away so you could recover your dignity – something he thought would be more important to you than your life." He chuckled. "It is obvious something is, since you risked your life to get here." He waved his other arm toward the castle. "And he knows you have the power to give me a name to replace the one taken from me as a child. I would regain my place in the world."

"But you refused!" Catherine exclaimed. Her face reflected the horror he had felt in the chambers of the Admiralty when realised the consequences of his decision not to become the admirals' tool – not for love, not for money. They would have sent him to chase Sir Lyle down, and he was not going to do it. He would not be their executioner. Even if it meant he would never go to sea again.

"I refused," Jocelyn agreed. "Because I have a name. It's mine. I created it. I own it. And you have dignity. You never lost it. I have given you the name that I worked very hard to deserve. And you will bestow your dignity upon our child."

"I think you have gone mad," Catherine said, but her voice was calm.

"Perhaps." Jocelyn picked up her hand and kissed it. "Perhaps I am madly in love with you. Perhaps I am just mad. We can return to Wansdyke and become the mad sailor and his countess. We will be legendary."

Catherine looked about them. "In some ways," she said softly, "This place has healed me. My soul needed time. And this castle … it is the place of my ancestors but it is not mine. I feel as if I have spoken to this country with my heart."

"And it has forgiven you, dear Kate. You have done no harm. And your – our – child need not be burdened with crimes that are not his responsibility."

"Oh, Jocelyn." For a moment, Catherine could not speak. Then she lifted her face to him. A single tear trickled down her face. "We have a daughter," she whispered. "A quiet, dear little thing. When she looks at me with those great eyes of hers, I know she is doomed to a desperate life like my own – alone and father-less, the countess who should have been the earl—"

"You are talking nonsense," Jocelyn said. He grasped her hands tightly. "She is not you. And she has a father. We will make our destiny together." He dropped her hands, looked despairingly up at the mountains. "You need to know the truth. My name was not always Avebury. My father was executed for treason when I was a small child, I was sent to London to live with relatives and I entered the navy as a midshipman under the name Avebury. For many years, I feared that this would be found out and ruin me. But I know now that we make our own truth. I will tell our daughter so, and you will not stop me." He rubbed at his face in some exasperation. "I am tired. But I want to see my daughter."

"Wait!" Catherine cried. She held out her hands. "Do not take her from me," she begged, terror on her face. "When she was born, I did not love her at first. I admit it. But I love her now, and I cannot live without her."

Jocelyn looked horrified. "I would never do such a thing. But I must see her."

"Do not leave me," Catherine said. Her voice broke, her face dropped. A tear rolled down. "Do not leave me again," she said again. "I could not bear it."

Jocelyn grasped her hands and gently moved closer to her. "I will not leave you, I promise, light of my heart." He kissed her, then brushed the damp from her cheeks. He bent to kiss her again.

It had been a long time – too long. He was eager, and had not known how eager. He had dreamt about her, and was shocked at the degree to which he had memorised every plane of her face, the feel of her hair in his hands.

"What is this thing?" he murmured against her neck. He plucked questioningly at the white dress she had swathed about her.

"Oh!" she said indistinctly. "Oh, my clothes ... they don't ... fit."

He found her beneath the folds after all. Her breasts were full and leaking. She clutched again at the dress, mortified.

"You are utterly enchanting. But look, someone is coming."

Catherine turned, hastily belting her dress. Mrs Owen strode across the great lawn, holding a squalling bundle.

"I am late, my lady!" she called.

As soon as she reached them, she handed the bundle to Catherine and gave Jocelyn only a brief nod. Catherine pulled at the dress and put the child to her breast. There was immediate silence, followed by loud smacking.

"Well." Jocelyn looked up at Mrs Owen. "I would like to say that she may look like me, but I object to her table manners."

"Shame on you, Captain! How can you say such a thing?" Mrs Owen exclaimed. "There's a word in Welsh for someone like you, but I will refrain from using it."

"She does look like you," Catherine said. "She looks nothing at all like me. Or Sir Lyle," she said slyly.

"I apologise for doubting you," Jocelyn said. "I doubted myself, too – but that was deserved. I was very foolish."

"Ah, well." Catherine squinted up at Mrs Owen. "Men are."

As they watched Mrs Owen's retreating figure, Jocelyn put his arm about his wife. "You have not told me her name," he said.

"Gwenllian."

"You gave her a Welsh name? Could you not have called her something more predictable? Like Anne, or Mary?"

"Mrs Owen saved me," Catherine said simply. "She was the family I did not have. She had a daughter once. Gwenllian. She died as a child but would have been my age." She looked up at the mountains surrounding them. Gwen had stopped nursing, and was staring up into Jocelyn's face with interest. He reached out to touch one tiny fist, and found his finger being grasped tightly.

"Another countess, perhaps."

"Perhaps," Catherine whispered, her gaze not leaving the mountains.

"Yes, that would be a fine thing," said Jocelyn bending to kiss his daughter's forehead.

EPILOGUE

*L*ydia came round the bend of the castle wall, shading her eyes from the brilliant sunlight, pulling her wrap about her, a sealed note in her hand.

The messenger had only just left, and when Lydia saw the familiar scrawl of Sir Lyle's hand, she panicked and ran out to find her mistress. But there he was—Lady St Clair's knight errant, her honourable Captain, his arm protectively around her as she leaned back against him, sleeping babe in her arms. Save for the breeze ruffling their hair and Catherine's wrap, they looked like marble statues, nestled together in a perfect triangle of symmetry, as if they had been placed there under a tree in order to decorate the landscape.

What should she do with this letter? Dare she spoil the happiness that she saw before her?

She hesitated for only a mere moment before she broke the seal. She did not have the scruples that an innocent maiden might —she, Lydia Barrow, natural daughter of the Duke of Rutherford, shunned and despised by the Duchess of Rutherford and her four ugly daughters, as well as all of their connexions—but it made her uncomfortable to open Lady St Clair's private letters nonetheless. She turned her back to the happy couple in the distance, scanned the letter. Fear gripped her heart.

"My dear Lady St C, I hope this missive finds you well and reunited with your Captain. May I congratulate you on the birth of your heir? Rumour has it that your esteemed Captain has left active duty, but with the French, no one can be at ease. He may be called back again soon, as we always have need of brave officers at sea. I promised the Captain that I would deliver a certain item to Wansdyke, but I regret to say that I have not been able to do so discreetly, as I am forced to abandon my plans to travel to the Americas in order to take care of some business matters. I will, however, execute the task at the earliest possible moment. The item is safe in my hands. L."

Lydia crushed the letter in her hands. She turned, giving her lady one last backward glance, before walking slowly back whence she came.

He was not destroying the portrait or giving it up—because he wanted to keep it. She knew it as well as she knew her own name. He wanted to keep this power he had over Catherine, this dream of owning her. He did not care whose happiness he destroyed. He did not care about the new, blameless life that had arrived to grace Catherine's own. He simply did not care for anyone but himself.

Men! She hated all men with a passion.

She would not allow Sir Lyle to destroy this fleeting happiness that had taken so long for her mistress to acquire. She would not have it. She would take care of that irksome portrait herself. She would do it if she had to murder Sir Lyle.

She had done it before. She could do it again.

SPECIAL OFFER

TO READERS OF THE PORTRAIT

If you enjoyed *The Portrait*, I have a gift for you!

Sign up for my weekly email missives, and I will send you some of my work-in-progress! My current project is called *Twelfth Night*, featuring (of course) a strong woman, a complicated family situation (of course), and a man who comes to love her for her strength and reckless courage (of course!). I am having so much fun writing it, and I would love to share it with you, the people who are supporting me on this literary journey. (Fun fact: I started the book under a pseudonym, so the cover still has my pseudonym on it! Collector's item, perhaps?)

I send updates, bits of new fiction, and reflections on life in another time and place. Feel free to reach out to me by responding to any of my newsletters! I love hearing from you, and in fact, the sequel to *The Portrait* was a reader request...so you may end up inspiring a book!

Visit me at www.mayarushingwalker.net and click on the link at the top or the bottom of the page or just click here to sign up for my newsletter and download my current project!

ACKNOWLEDGMENTS

Thank you to all who have helped me on this journey. It has been long and arduous, but never dull.

I am deeply grateful to Heather for reading my entire manuscript and helping me to get my Regency era historical details correct, right down to maps, buildings, and where to cross the river to get to Wales! Thank you so much.

Thank you also to Catherine Fitzsimons, copy editor extraordinaire, who went through every word in order to give the manuscript that special "Jane Austen" feel.

Nora K., you have patiently listened to me ramble about my writing dreams for many years. I owe you more than I can express. You are the best friend a girl could have.

To my wonderful husband and children: you kept reminding me that I could do this. And look, I have! Thank you.

ABOUT THE AUTHOR

Maya Rushing Walker writes slow-burn, often romantic, literary fiction set in both historical and modern times, with a strong sense of place. She lives and writes in a 1780s farmhouse in northern New England, where she homeschooled four amazing young adults and was a dedicated swim and row mom. In a previous life, she was a U.S. diplomat and a Wall Street banker, and holds a B.S. in international economics from Georgetown and an A.M. in East Asian Studies from Harvard.

Her two books, *The Portrait* and *Coming Home to Greenleigh*, were previously published under her pen name, Cassandra Austen.

Come visit her virtual home at www.mayarushingwalker.net. Sign up for her newsletter for a free copy of her work-in-progress, Twelfth Night.

facebook.com/mayarushingwalkerbooks

instagram.com/mayarushingwalker

amazon.com/author/mayarushingwalker

bookbub.com/authors/mayarushingwalker

goodreads.com/mayarushingwalker

ALSO BY MAYA RUSHING WALKER

Twelfth Night (a work-in-progress available only to newsletter subscribers)

Coming Home To Greenleigh (January 2020)